In her twenty-five years in the beauty industry, Dana Kline has seen it all. From her first job in a mall working with some of the world's most famous luxury beauty & fragrance brands to writing a book. Her emphasis on learning, from both success and failure, is what makes her journey such a rich fascinating one. A woman straight from the pages of the novel she created.

For Eric, Seat 24, the beginning of everything.
This is my story, this is my song.

Dana Kline

BEAUTYLAND

To: Dsoke

Thnak you - very
Lovely Lady!
xoxo
Dana Kline

AUSTIN MACAULEY PUBLISHERS™
LONDON * CAMBRIDGE * NEW YORK * SHARJAH

A CIP catalogue record for this title is available from the British Library.

ISBN 9781528987783 (Paperback)
ISBN 9781528987790 (ePub e-book)

www.austinmacauley.com

First Published (2021)
Austin Macauley Publishers Ltd
25 Canada Square
Canary Wharf
London
E14 5LQ

Thanks to my publisher who worked so hard to deliver my story. Especially, Vinh Tran and Kevin Smith and production teams always patient and diligent answers.

This billion-dollar business creates brands to give you confidence, enhance your health, keep your features forever youthful. Beautyland salutes advisors, sales people, make-up artists, hair stylists, countless men and women working in retail stores all over the world. Fragrance, playtime with make-up creates illusion. Like the wizard behind the curtain, the troops behind the beauty counter have the magic to transform your day while stoking the engines of this industry. On the other side of the counter, my thanks to the sales teams, counter managers, freelancers, marketers, creative artists, designers, buyers, retail managements, press agents, WWD, Beauty Fashion, and bosses, both good and not so.

Leslie Davis Guccione, novelist, teacher and freelance editor, embraced my story. Over three years she shared skill, advice and a keen eye—what to enhance; what to cut; what to save for another story. I can now spot the gun over the mantel in every movie and book. With generosity and encouragement, my 'Tom Ford of literature' challenged me to be a better writer.

Thanks to my fellow 'Fixer' Cate Johnson, a friendship begun twenty years ago in Scottsdale, Arizona, where we were charged with rehabilitating a failing Givenchy beauty in the southwest territory. * To industry mentors Lauren Anderson and Shawn Doyle who've helped me navigate all things corporate and appreciate the importance of motivation, especially to those in need of inspiration to be fabulous.

To Margaret Todd, who loved me from day one, I appreciate all you've done for me, the influence that helped me know how I wanted to live. * To my sons. Eric Kelsy, light of my life, now accruing accolades in baseball and coaching. * Simeon, assistant, stylist, photographer, merchandiser, party coordinator, publicist and artist who debuted at six as a mini-groom to my bride in a Lazarus, Columbus, Ohio, wedding theme event. We moved a lot of Alfred Sung perfume! Your ear to the cosmetic selling floor—who's stealing, who's quitting, who are the best freelancers to poach—kept me on trend and one step ahead of the pack. To my generous sister Jennifer Harris Vanhoose. Somehow two little girls found a way to survive. Always know you are beautiful.

Miss Neil Harvey & Dale Spear, chronicler of crazy family sagas and mentor extraordinaire, from opera, history, travel and entertaining, to art museum protocol.
My parents Daniel and Diane Harris.

And deep thanks to those that I was fortunate to work with, supporting my career and inspiring BEAUTYLAND!

Diane Von Furstenberg, Susan Posen, Zac Posen, Tatum Getty, Tommy Cyr, Ali Fadakar, Vesa Kalho, Gail Yount, Daniel Smith,Patty & Torrance Kirby, David Tenzer, Rachel Whitmore, Tracy Bregman, Scott Hart, Chantal Roos, Piia Toikka, Susan Cotton, Jim Maki, Justin Welch, Steve Johnson, Sullivan Gimaret, Chad Lavigne, Aisling Connaughton, Leighton Atchison, Neil Clark, Josh Blaylock, Pavllo Zengo, Trish Mendiola, Vittoria Federico, Cristina Brown, Dan Buckle, Jason Haun, Jem Jender, Jennifer McGarrigle, Jenny Pashkov-Pike, Kasi Buttery, Kate Knoop, Kristen Sinclair, Tom Crutchfield, Suzanne Tesche, Laura Eschricht, Mindy Franco, Amy Pratt, Michel Whitehead, Matt Stapleton, Beth Frost, Caroline Smith, Barbra Beller, Marc Runz, Heather Lindgren, Sha Bishop, Denise Stein, Dennis Hays, Esther Chi, Jesse Boatright, Jacklyn Krajewski, Sara Jakiel, Mackenzi Wallace, Roxanne Vaghefi, Peter Born, Eric Michelson, Simia Arslane, Michael Hawley, Susan Robran, Jodi Fries, Bettina O'Neill, Margarita Arriagada, Gary Borofsky, Terry Morrow, Joni Allen, Jessica Hanson, Roslyn Griner, Jonia & Bradley Skaggs, Nick Gilbert, Nicholas Ratut, Pierre Brezillon Yves, Eden Grimaldi, George Ledes, Dabra Davis, Mike Valentino.

To the readers, if anyone tells you, "You'll never do it, you're not good enough," be grateful for the resistance, it will push you to be better, cementing your success.

Synopsis

Beautyland chronicles rise of tenacious Emma O'Farrell Paige, from her traumatic, hardscrabble, '70s Midwest childhood into the glamorous fragrance industry where she plays to win among world-class dealmakers.

The story opens fall Fashion Week, September 2003. Lower Manhattan churns with construction on the second anniversary of 9/11 as Emmen arrives at the federal courthouse to depose her former boss, the mastermind behind counterfeit perfume ring. As her driver maneuvers onto FDR drive, Emma relives her own scams, beginning in St. Louis middle school summers collecting door-to-door for her parents' bogus charities, their scheme to cover school clothes and bar tabs. By thirteen she has honed shoplifting skills; at sixteen she passes for a university co-ed to hook a fraternity hotshot. When her parents force her thirteenth movie, this one to rural Bruckerfield, MO, Ethan Paige enters her life. The high school athlete's dysfunctional background mimics hers and Emma falls hard for the handsome, equally adrift hometown star baseball pitcher. A year later the misfits land in a shotgun, long-distance marriage. Ethan begins a semi-pro career in Australia as Emma uses instinct, salesmanship and lifelong survival skills to enter the beauty business.

Driven by desperation and nothing to lose they set out in the world with big dreams and blind faith can do. Through trenches of the beauty biz, Emma goes from the ground floor up to the corporate boardrooms of New York, London, Paris, and beyond. On her climb on the top Emma forges loyal friends, meets strong, influential mentors who try to bend her to their will. She grapples with business adversaries, no more challenging and breath-taking than mysterious Julian Petrenko, her boss, nemesis, and perfect match. As Emma climbs higher, closing a string of licensing deals with the trendiest designers and celebrities. When Emma lands the highly sought after a three-hundred-million-dollar fragrance deal boy band 'UK CONNECTION', she unveils the secret inner works of the vaulted BEAUTYLAND in all its backstabbing, sexual harassment, litigation, and triumphant glory.

"Character. Intelligence. Strength. Style. That makes beauty"

– Diane Von Furstenberg

Chapter One

I had to look perfect. Felon Carmine F.X. Isgro, late of the late Ciao!Beauty Company, decided to sue me. Thank God for my closet, a woman's version of a war chest. In fact I chose my Fifth Avenue apartment for the en suite bath and dressing room so I could organise my clothing by designer, sub-grouped in colour coded order. My wall of shoes included boxes—part of the art.

"What the hell?" Tommy, my ever-faithful driver, muttered a string of obscenities in Staten Island-ese, and gripped the steering wheel, incongruous in his white gloves.

"Emma, I shoulda cut over to Second Avenue. FDR..."

"Just get me to court in one piece." I rotated my ankle and pressed the tender spot, then slid my foot back into my Yves St. Laurent, a Paris design not yet available in the States. It complemented my fitted navy and black high waisted Zac Posen skirt and a custom silk blouse with proper English bow. TMI, no doubt, but designers eager to give me hot-off-the-runway fashions was one of my job perks, a key to my survival as well as motivation to stay sample size, no larger than a four.

Tommy inched us past the ear-budded multitude, jostling through the Manhattan canyons. Too much time to think. I faced litigation without real basis, a nuisance suit. Angry men resentful of women, waited in the Financial District court room to intimidate me. I had no experience with legal matters but I'd watched *Law and Order* and been prepped within an inch of a bar exam by my attorney. Most of what I had to say would be expected. But I also had leverage, the kind best served cold.

The crisp, clear September day was the kind we still associate with the horrors of 9/11. The city—the whole country—had just marked the third anniversary. While Lower Manhattan churned with physical repair, Midtown churned with the controlled hysteria of Fall Fashion Week. Renewed energy with a hint of autumn helped the city shed its summer lethargy and more of its lingering grief.

During bi-annual Fashion Week, clothes seem new again. Familiar trends fade; new one's launch. Brutal editorial critics make or break designers' careers and drive CEOs to drink. The slightest innuendo is critical. Backstage make-up fads become the latest look at the beauty counter. Marketing strategies are created, edited, then edited again based on the runways.

Hand in hand, Fashion and Beauty provide tools to feel cool, hip, confident and sexy. Nothing beats backstage access to fashion shows, a world many dream about but few know intimately. The beauty aspect alone represents billions in sales. In my branch of the business, Fall Fashion Week signals the start of the fourth quarter. It makes or breaks the financial year.

That 2003 September I weeded through hundreds of men and women to find that needle in a fabric haystack: the up-and-coming designer or celebrity destined for massive success, often an eccentric and colourful narcissist.

My challenge? Getting them to commit to a fragrance license before they reached the top of their game, and keeping their royalty rate low to ensure profitability. The environment's insane but addictive, my drug of choice, my alternate universe. I contemplated that guiding principle and my court case as Tommy finally maneuvered us onto FDR Drive. One final ankle rotation convinced me there'd be no limp. Then again, even if sprained, I'd have toughed out a power walk into the court room.

"Stay, Chloe!" had greeted me on my routine run around the Jacqueline Kennedy Onassis Reservoir as a snarling mid-sized mutt lunged at a walker's loose-leashed lab. I pivoted hard and turned my ankle. Chloe stood her ground, growling low in her throat. The mutt turned tail and ran. I guess he picked the wrong bitch. I would do well to follow her lead.

Nearly thirty years earlier I was just as tense, prepped that time, not by a high-powered attorney for court, but by my high-octane mother for another flimflam. When I was ten, my thirty-four-year-old father retired from real work after a mid-sized sedan rear-ended his industrial size City of St. Louis snowplough. From then on, he milked DPW disability for every dime he could get.

We called a string of pigsties home. Even when my parents cajoled, whined or demanded fumigation from landlords, cockroaches infested all of them. By the time Darby, the youngest of the three of us, could reach the wall switch, he and my sister Genevieve made a perverse game of entering a dark room then snapping on the ceiling light. Hundreds of cockroaches scurried into corners and crevices leaving behind webs of speckled remains. To this day I cannot stand to look at coffee grounds.

The summer after the snowplough incident my mother instructed Genevieve and me to decorate coffee cans. We were two years apart and thrilled with her enthusiastic arts and crafts afternoon. The next day she drove us to through middle-class areas of St. Louis, past single houses, neat lawns, and new cars. This, I felt sure, was where the rich people lived.

"We're gonna collect for charity. The American Lung Association," she told us. "We'll be helping all those poor sick children."

"Mom—"

She made eye contact with us via the rear-view mirror. "Don't sass me, Emma. We'll start at the corner and work our way down the street. You take this side. Genevieve, over there." She flicked her cigarette ash out the window.

"But we don't know—"

"Stop whining. I'll keep tabs on you from the car."

"Thank you! Thank you so much." I swiped my eyes. "And Merry Christmas."

"They're playing Christmas music and giving out free stuff. It was awesome," Genevieve reported as we climbed into the car.

"The saleslady even made Emma cry."

My mother turned from the front seat. "She better not have. Miss La-di-dah Saks Fifth Avenue. Was she a bitch?"

"No! The perfume made my eyes burn, that's all." That wasn't all, of course. A loyal customer was born. And as hard as I tried to smother it, what passed for my conscience immerged.

We drove down to Animal Cracker Park for Christmas at Gram and Grandpa O'Farrell's. Dinner included Dad's cousin, my first encounter with Neil Harvey. His parents were gone now but their mothers had been sisters. The cousins had grown up together and somehow Neil had become a successful antiques and fine arts dealer in San Francisco and Los Angeles. I was awestruck. This polished, funny, stylish man had sprung from our family? When Genevieve and I surprised Mom with the Saks gift bag of designer samples, he sealed the deal with oohs, ahs and trendy, knowledgeable comments.

My parents made it clear higher education was not in my future, but I entered high school on the college-bound track. The courses kept me circulating with friends I meant to keep, including Maria Romano from my biology lab. In tenth grade she Alexandra and I formed an unlikely triumvirate with neglect as the common denominator. We skipped school to hang out at Alexandra's and watch *The Young and The Restless,* two families fighting over a cosmetics company.

Maria and Alexandra took risks; I elevated my behaviour to reckless. I missed sixty-two days of classes but had wits enough to turn in minimal requirements, devote all-nighters to hammering out decent reports, and study for my exams. I passed.

I'd been sharing beers with Dad for years, including sips in his favourite hangouts. By fifteen I could talk myself into local bars, which astonished my new crowd. Most of them had licenses, even cars. Nagging got me underage driving lessons with Dad. More than once after my parents fell asleep, I took the car keys and tooled around just because I could.

As spring segued into summer, week after week Alexandra's house parties started on Thursday night. I essentially lived across the street from my parents, raising myself.

I considered losing my virginity, but not to one of the boring locals. I wanted a rich boyfriend with some style. This wasn't going to happen by waiting for a classmate to ask me to a high school dance, or sharing a joint in the former maids' rooms on the Campbells' third floor. I was hell bent on expanding my social horizons.

Maria's twenty-one-year-old sister, Dina, attended Washington University, not only renowned in our posh suburbs, but Maria assured us, a hotbed of hot guys. "The kind with pedigrees," Alexandra said. I gave her a blank stare. "You know, guys with rich parents and famous ancestors."

"At least totally brag worthy," Maria added. The place to be was a campus bar. Dina Romano agreed to put our names on a guest list to ensure we would have no hassle getting in. This was no smoke-filled escapade with my dad and his construction friends lined up on their stools, talking above blaring Johnny Cash songs. The three of us walked past students stretching down Main Street. The total coolness of the scene engulfed me. I could do this!

One-dollar drafts flowed all night. College kids packed the dance floor, some gyrating with sloshing drinks. Just off the floor a guy ordering beer for his friends made eye contact: 5'10, Ralph Lauren polo shirt, perfect biceps, perfect teeth, collar up. He might as well have had dollar signs in his eyes. Mr *Cosmo*politan ad offered to include me in his order. I accepted.

His friends dispersed and he ushered me to the edge of the dancers. "Liam Weller," he told me. From Forest Park, nineteen, running back, football was his life, oh, and Dad was a heart surgeon at Barnes-Jewish. Even I knew the hospital affiliated with Wash U Medical School.

Crap! It was my turn. Sweaty dancers packed the floor, bumping into each other. Thank God for the blaring music. "Outside Cleveland." Outside any city would have rich neighbourhoods, right?

"I'm majoring in Co-mun-i-cations."

"I like girls who communicate." Little smirk. Little smirk right back.

"Do you have a name?"

Kimberly. It was the perfect time for my favourite name, except Alexandra and Maria would have to remember. And so would I, drunk or sober. "Emily. My friends call me Em." Close enough and the last part was true.

The beers flowed and his hands roamed. I wasn't exactly swatting him away when he asked if I wanted to get some air. Of course we wound up making out in his car. Of course it went from fun, to too fast, and too soon. Plus I wasn't about to lose my virginity in somebody's back seat, not even his Mercedes SL. I made up an excuse and we went back to the bar.

All the way home Alexandra and Maria, as psyched as I, plotted our next move: fake IDs for the following weekend. They had it easy—borrow their older sisters' driver's licenses.

Not so simple for me. I had no older sister, not even my own license to tamper with. My mother couldn't have cared less about my under-age shenanigans, but the search for my birth certificate annoyed her profusely. We've moved so much who knew where it was. She said I didn't have one.

"I must. It's the law! How'll I prove my age for my license? Or a passport? There's gotta be something that says I was born! That's not legal. We need to call the hospital."

"Christ." She took a drag on her cigarette. "Every little thing with you's a federal case. You're a damn mutt with a bone. Look. Emma, the hospital screwed up. All's they gave us was some shitty piece of paper."

Better than nothing. "Then we must have it, right? The shitty piece of paper?"

We did. After searching through beat up cardboard boxes dragged around with every move, I found a stained, dog-eared letter stating the basic details. I managed to iron out some of the wrinkles and clean it up. Thanks to Wite-Out, our ancient typewriter, and the Campbells' copy machine, Voila! a new DOB and identity. I had my own fake ID.

Two weeks later Maria drove us back. We explored the bars and ended up at The Orr Club, the football team hangout. I spotted Liam, then positioned myself so he had to see me and make the first move. Sure enough he sauntered on over. We spent the next few hours drinking and dancing. We closed the bar way past Maria's curfew, and Liam walked me through the parking lot. I pressed him against her car and gave him a goodbye worth remembering. He asked for my phone number.

He called a few days later. He and his communal house of guys were putting a party together. Would the three of us like to stop by?

Yes, indeed…

Their rental, a turn-of-the century manse from St. Louis' heyday, retained its lustre. From original woodwork to decent furniture, it was far more prep school than the *Animal House* frat cave we expected. The guys and their dates were as polished as the mantel trophies.

By this time I'd mimicked Alexandra and Maria enough to be secure in my rebranded self, smug in my transformation from townie to coed. After two beers my intimidation faded as I chatted up pre-med and engineering majors, future attorneys and Wall Street scions. I drew laughs when I made up an incident allegedly talking my sociology professor into letting me research *The Young and the Restless* for an upcoming assignment.

I wanted what those girls at his house had. I even contemplated buying a monogrammed sweater or Bermuda bag.

Liam remained attentive and we drank our way upstairs into buzzed bliss. I ended up in his room, then in his bed. Within a short time he waved a condom packet at me and we were at it. I stayed the night. The perfect place to lose it.

I awoke dry-mouthed and hung over, not sure how I was going to get home. Liam looked at the ceiling and asked me if that had been my first time.

"Yes. Guess you could tell."

He smiled, clearly proud of deflowering his latest preppy co-ed, then changed the subject. He had a football meeting, could he drop me at home on his way? We showered separately. I watched him dress in college-issue athletic gear, happy to see him bask in my frank admiration. Within the hour he drove me to what I told him was my off-campus rental.

19

"There's some woman at the window," he said as pulled up to the curb.

"Downstairs tenant. Total pain-in-the-butt busybody." I kissed him and opened the passenger door before my mother could shoot out of the house to check out the fancy kid in the fancy car. Her welcoming smirk said it all. I spent my childhood listening to her and my Aunt Kelly's graphic sexual innuendos and I was in no mood to hear them now. I went to my room, locked the door against her ignorant remarks, and slept the rest of the day.

I started my high school junior year unexpectedly invested in my Liam fantasy. I replayed that night, and recalled conversation as much as the sex. He had called me. Called and invited me to the house party. This made it a real date, right?

The college girls had laughed at my stories; offered me chips and salsa. I could fit right in, couldn't I?

I heard from Liam a few times—classes and football had started and he was traveling with the team with limited time to party. If these were dropped hints, I ignored them. We caught up a few more times, the last at the bar where we'd met. He seemed all ego and attitude. I ignored that, too.

Deep into fall he asked me to another house party. I gladly accepted on behalf of my friends since I needed a ride, but he offered to pick me up. This felt like progress, dangerous though it was. My parents were out as usual. Genevieve and Darby barely looked up when I said I was going out. I waited for Liam outside in the glow of the streetlights. The party matched the first one. Free-flowing booze on the first floor and clean sheets on the second. I presented myself better than ever. I chatted easily with the hot crowd until Liam suddenly tugged me away—a total ego boost. He hustled me outside and turned romantic while showing me the harvest moon. We kissed at the potted mums on the front steps, under the oak tree by the curb, and along the hedges lining the driveway to the service entrance.

I knew what turned him on. We entered the kitchen. As we passed the fridge, I whispered my idea of soft porn. Or more precisely, suggestions Aunt Kelly'd been slinging around in my presence.

"Oh, baby." He opened what I thought was a pantry door but it was the old back staircase for the help. Up we went. I was still new at this so I managed my drinks and stayed just buzzed enough to laugh as we crossed the hall into his bedroom.

I swear I woke up grinning, all hazy from our wild night but hangover free. I was stone cold sober, clearheaded enough to recognise that the tight rope I was walking threatened to wobble but aching to make my magic act last. I reached for him under the covers.

He put his hand over mine.

I propped myself up on my elbow and arched my eyebrows.

"Don't tell me you want to wait till next weekend?"

He threw off the sheet. "Let's go for a coffee…starving…"

I knew his every expression and voice inflection. This wasn't good. I swung off my side of the bed and into the bathroom. His introspection and need for breakfast raised concern. Had he talked with Wash U communications majors? Did he suspect the woman at the window had been my mother? Shit. He'd probably noticed I never mentioned going to any of his home games, or classes or much of anything. Internal alarms sounded by the time we headed for a campus bistro. He'd caught one of my lies, for sure. I kept quiet, afraid I'd say something wrong and lose my advantage.

He bought us coffee and egg sandwiches. "Look—"

"I'm guessing there's something you want to tell me." He shrugged. He sipped. "Fuck."

"We did."

He didn't laugh. "Look, Emily, I might as well explain. There's this girl. This other girl. Jessica Carpenter." He sipped again. "Jessica."

"You said that."

"Fuck."

"You said that, too." Some ditz named Carpenter and here I'd thought he was on to me.

"I swear it doesn't matter. She and I agreed—" he said to his egg sandwich.

"Go on."

"You and I… You know it was, like, just pick up sex. But then it was your first time and all."

Now I got it full in the face.

"You're amazing, Emily. It's never been like this. You're never in the way. You totally let me get my work done. No demands. You're never hanging around the locker rooms or thinking we need to study together. It's like you're not even on campus. You totally get me. And…" Deep breath. "The sex is pure fireworks. Like you're in my brain and my blood."

"This is a problem?" I looked him in the eye. "Because there's this Jessica. Let me guess. You're totally lying your ass off to her."

He winced. Well, he explained, the thing was, she'd been his high school girlfriend. Very serious. Total commitment. She was at Stephens College, now. All women. So he didn't worry.

I chewed on that one. Didn't worry about *her* activities or didn't worry about getting caught? He was sure as hell worried about something.

"Emily, I swear Jess and I have an understanding," he said a third time. …Dating other people…free to enjoy the college lifestyle. Blah blah blah. Trouble was—

I needed to say it before he did. "Let's review. You have an agreement." I was not speaking to my egg sandwich. "What, exactly is the trouble? You're feeling guilty that you're—I'm guessing here—way more involved in the 'college lifestyle' than she thinks you are? Way more than she is? You're more involved than she knows about. In fact you're lying your ass off?"

"Yeah. That's about right."

"So you and I need to cool things off? Or we need to quit all together."

"Hell, no. We need to be hyper careful, that's all. Like last night. You had no way of knowing, but I realised that girl you were talking to by the couch is in Jess's dorm. I don't know her, but I've seen her in their lobby. That's why I acted like I was taking you home or we were hitting another party. Why I got you outside."

"Outside, Liam, and then upstairs." I ate my sandwich before my grip on it forced the yolk all over my fingers. It gave me time to put my thoughts together. "And here I thought it was the moon."

He laughed, all smug and relieved. "Quick thinking, right? And the thing is, homecoming's next week so she'll be at the house for the weekend. Jess, that is. Jess'll be here but I'll call you Sunday night."

I wished I hadn't finished my coffee so I could throw it in his face. "As I see it, Liam, you and Jess have an agreement. You're lying through your teeth about your end of it, plus it's not exactly the same agreement for her. And being at a girls' school sort of keeps her in your back pocket."

"That's not how I'd put it."

"Liam, I know where you put it."

He looked at the patrons closest to us. "Okay, okay. Let's get out of here. We can talk outside."

I was quiet until we hit the sidewalk. "Is it you're afraid she'll find out how you really feel about me? Or maybe you're afraid she'll find someone who gets in *her* brain and *her* blood three times in one night. Or both."

He grew pale so fast I hated that I knew him better than he knew himself, the two-timing motherfucking slime ball. "Here's the thing," I said. "We do have some great fun together. Yes, the sex is amazing. I love what you teach me."

He stepped closer and grinned at me. Grinned! "Careful. We might have to start all over again."

"We could," I said, "But since this is true confessions day, you should know something."

"What could I not know?"

He took a few paces while I took a few breaths. "For starters, I'm only sixteen."

He froze. "What?"

"Sixteen. In fact I'm never on campus because I'm at Riverview High School. Eleventh grade."

"Are you fucking kidding me?"

"Fucking you, yes. Kidding you, no way. I guess we both have secrets. Jessica's yours; being a sixteen-year-old townie is mine. I'd hate for her to get the real story."

"Don't be an asshole."

"Me, Liam? Me? Real is your football coach, the university, and your parents finding out you've been messing around big time with an under-age high school girl. You even took her virginity."

"You little bitch."

"I know you're all about football and your college lifestyle, so let's make a deal. You and I go to the bank right now; you withdraw three hundred dollars from your account and give it to me."

"Fucking extortion."

Man, the F word was flying. "Yes, but in return you'll never see me again."

He had no choice. We went to his bank; he withdrew the money out of his account and handed me the envelope of cash.

"This isn't what you think, Liam. This is payback for Jessica, the girl who loves you. The one who trusts you." I flagged down a taxi and asked for Plaza Frontenac. "I'll bet you took her virginity, too. You always remember your firsts." I hissed the plural.

Saks Fifth Avenue was as beautiful as I remembered. I made a beeline for the cosmetic department fragrance counter. It smelled amazing. I purchased Oscar de la Renta perfume for myself and my sister. As the saleswoman rang up my purchases I glanced at the next counter. "And that gift assortment on the middle shelf, Confession."

I told her I had a friend in college with a birthday. ...not sure of her campus address. Was it possible... I offered her a gratuity, the first in my life. Fifteen minutes later I had a promise: Confession parfum, eau de Toilette, body mist and bath gel could and would be delivered via USPS to *Jessica Carpenter, freshman* in care of the Stephens College student union post office. I printed only *LW* in block letters on the gift card.

Why should I care about some asshole jock named Liam Weller? For days tears sprang from nowhere. Okay, my wild ride derailed. Why did guilt flood me when I thought about his random, rich girlfriend I'd never meet? I cried and cursed alone, embarrassed by my emotional upheaval. I wallowed in my misery, then dragged myself back into high school mode. Thanks to Alexandra and Maria I had real friends. I paid attention.

The circle widened when classmates discovered my old man would supply beer and pot for a wink and a wad of cash. Among other things, it supported his four-pack-a-day Marlboro habit. Both my parents were slowing down, changing their buzz of choice to prescription meds. My mother's streak of mean went right up her spine but Dad's eccentric personality hovered around humour. When I ran track that spring, he was an overweight, overzealous presence at every meet, egging on other parents to scream our names. My lifelong humiliation softened. Dad genuinely resonated with almost everyone, not just teenagers.

I was a master shoplifter and, as a polished con artist, a damn good judge of character. It was easy to separate airhead schoolmates who brownied up to me when they wanted a buy, from the few who laughed at my sarcastic wit and praised my defiant behaviour. Cream of the crop they were not, but I was finally part of a loyal band who sought me out and made me feel welcome.

Once school let out, Alexandra, Maria and I were inseparable and at it again. The underage word was out on the Wash U campus so we expanded to different colleges and events on the Mississippi. Gambling, drinking, boat parties and St. Louis river life was back in style. My parents loved them and now it was my turn. My part-time mall job selling balloons from a cart put enough cash in my pocket to keep up my weekend festivities. This time I kept it light.

I slept at Alexandra's so often it took four days to realise my mother wasn't schlepping off to her job at the local convenience store. Darby confessed that the manager caught her stuffing his backpack with cigarette cartons. He's been wearing it at the time. And then mid-summer my parents stopped me as I came through the door. I knew the look and braced myself.

"Out in the county. I swear you'll like this one," Dad said.

"My ninth! Yes, I keep track. New town, new rat trap. Now a new high school for my senior year?"

"New school equals new chance, Emma. We're moving to that extra house on Gram and Gramps' property."

Middle-of-nowhere Missouri. "Animal Cracker Park? You're shitting me."

"Eighteen sweet acres." My mother set her shoulders in a

way that was all too familiar. "Your father's back gets worse all the time; you know he can't find work. Without my pissy paycheck, we barely get through the month. Instead of his parents renting out the extra house, we'll move in and be caretakers in exchange for no rent. All's we have to do is maintain their property. Look, Emma, it'll get us by and you'll get a fresh start. You can leave those mean motherfuckers and screw-ups behind."

"They're not!"

"Don't sass me. It's not like we got a choice. Stop acting like it's all about you. Quit your sad ass whining."

"I've worked my sad ass off—"

"Hawking balloons at the mall?" She looked at the ceiling.

"Don't be stupid."

"I'm stupid? I'm not the one got fired for stuffing Darby's backpack—"

She raised her open hand. "Iris!" Dad caught her by the wrist.

I marched across the street. It wasn't about the job, and I was far from stupid. Only my decent grades kept me from expulsion for chronic truancy. It also wasn't a battle I could ever, ever, ever win. "It's practically in Arkansas," I wailed on Alexandra's kitchen stoop.

"Bummer." She passed me her joint.

While I argued and moped and plotted, my parents packed our crappy belongings, rounded up Darby and Genevieve, and left. I moved in where my toothbrushes had been since the ninth grade. Unfortunately Mrs Campbell was no longer spending every breathing moment with her French chiropractor. To say the least, her youngest and I were a handful. Three weeks later she put her foot down. I couldn't stay.

Two weeks before school started, I traded a childhood of roach infested city dwellings for Animal Cracker Park, wrangling my fury and impotence into determination.

Chapter Two

I would be the new 'it' girl, fashionable, just this side of bitchy. I'd find the most popular, successful, decorated athlete and make him mine. This wasn't middle school. I'd fit in or quit, maybe head to Cousin Neil's in or San Francisco.

We lived eight miles outside Brucknerfield. Eight miles along Route 30 rising to Main. No Saks anchored the mall of my dreams. In zigzag order working farms gave way to a chain grocery store, the bank, Motorland Auto Parts, and Quality Bail Bonds, Inc. The movie theatre faced The Beehive Fashions and

Accessories, then Bush's Restaurant, the liquor store, plus Dairy Queen at the last corner. Two steepled churched bookended empty storefronts, the post office, and Rusty's Bar and Grille, along the cross street.

Out the other side, Route 30 divided Gerty's-on-Thirty

Tavern and Motel from Al's Bowling Alley and Pinball Hall (boarded up). The combined fire and police station shared a parking lot with Town Hall. After a few acres lined in cattle corn, Bruckerfield High School perched on a rise next to the town cemetery.

Boys tooled around in pick-up trucks with shotgun racks; girls, out of style by ten years, formed small hovering swarms around town like yellow jackets over spilled Dr Pepper. Hillbilly Heaven.

I had my learner's permit by then and a few nights before school started Dad loaned me his '78 red Nova for a run to the DQ. I primped and arrived, all Princess Di hair, padded shoulders and ruffled rah-rah skirt. I sat in the parking lot scoping out those who looked old enough to be my schoolmates. A few cars packed with girls or couples parked long enough to get orders. I finally dodged a red, stuttering pickup on its second run through the parking lot, and headed for the counter.

As I turned from the order window with my Blizzard, a girl with Aqua Net hair gestured with her chocolate cone. "I've seen you before. You must be from the big city. You look different."

God, I hoped so. "Yep. Just moved down."

"What class?"

I was tempted to reply, "Lower Working," but she didn't look like she'd have a clue what I meant. "I'll be senior."

"Woo. That'll be tough. Brucknerfield's not real accepting of new kids." She licked her ice cream. "Just so you know."

I could feel a hated flush crawl into my jaw. "Fine with me. I'll be outta here in eight months."

"You pregnant?" she whispered.

"Shit no. I meant I'll graduate and get the hell out of this sorry, sad ass town. My dad's cousin's a high-end antiques dealer in San Fran," came right off the top of my head.

She gave me quizzical look.

"San Francisco," I added.

"Oh, duh. Right. I've been thinking about Reno or Houston." Another lick. "I'm Missy. California's rad. I'd go with you but I'm only going to be a junior." That was a relief.

"Plus my parents would have a cow if he's a dealer."

"If who's a dealer?"

"The cousin you're gonna live with."

"Not drugs. Antique dealer. Fancy furniture." I pushed my spoon through my Blizzard to keep from laughing. "I'm Emma. And since I'm not pregnant, who's top of the list around here?"

"You mean like the main guy? Probably Ethan Paige. Hot. He drives that red truck that just cruised through."

It didn't have to be a Mercedes SL but what had possessed me to think anybody within spitting distance of Animal Cracker Park had the money to drive something decent? "The hottest guy in town drives that hunk-a-junk, rusted hulk held together with gum and duct tape?"

"You're funny, you know that?"

"Yeah, life's a laugh fest." A car pulled up with a bunch of dorks shouting "Miss eeeee—"

"See you around." She gave me another once over, climbed into the back seat and left me in rising dust.

Oh, right, I thought, *like I'd ever take you with me.*

California. The idea took shape as I drove home to Animal Cracker Park, the edge of my personal precipice. I finally understood what my teachers hinted at: I would drop like a stone into an abyss of failure if I didn't teach myself to fly. California put some light at the end of my high school tunnel. Reinvention began my last first day of class.

I entered Brucknerfield High School and followed the senior herd to homeroom at the cafeteria lunch tables. Covert buzz about my being the new girl triggered a blush. Since I didn't even have junior Missy to focus on, I labelled my Trapper Keeper folders and raised the latest *Vogue* to my face.

Despite my history of truancy and recalcitrance, I had already passed enough required high school subjects to allow a relaxed senior schedule: four academic classes among a sea of study halls. I started off strong. I finished assignments and turned in immaculate required work. For the first week I ate lunch alone buried in a textbook or fashion magazine. The second week I chose random tables. By this time BHS girls considered me more exotic than dork so I was never rebuffed. Not that anyone called my name and slid over.

Soon enough even I knew I had too much free time. the guidance department assigned me to help a few teachers grade papers. As I'd done all my life, I adjusted to my new environment. By now I knew enough to make the best of my circumstances and fit in.

The next crisp, sunny day, during my late morning study hall, I took my assignment files out to the stadium bleachers, climbed up nearly to the press box and worked through the lunch bell. Clanking on the risers and a sudden shadow across my algebra quizzes made me look up.

A combination James Dean, Rob Lowe, Emilio Estevez studied me. "You're in my seat." Half smile, half smug grin. "Sorry to disturb you but since you're new, I guess you don't know I have my lunch in these bleachers. I sit there. Twenty-four."

Lunch appeared to be four Little Debbie snack cakes and vanilla ice cream overflowing a Styrofoam cup. I smirked at his lame pickup line and glanced at the empty metal rows on either side of me. "Doesn't look reserved to me."

"Common knowledge. I guess no one told you."

"Right. I guess all my new best friends forgot." Cripes. "Always seat, twenty-four?"

"Always."

"Some kind of ritual?"

He sort of cocked his hip and looked me over. "I guess so. It's the number on my football jersey."

"Wait. It's your player number? You're a jock?"

"An athlete," he replied.

I stood up, papers against my chest. The pencil clattered on the metal frame and dropped to the ground. "Well, we can't have you lose the big game because your ritual was interrupted." My intended flirtation came out sarcastic and half-assed. This James Dean-Rob Lowe-Emilio Estevez person looked confused and embarrassed. My spunk drained and wit left me. Instead of sliding into seat twenty-three, I hustled past him to the railing.

"Hey! I didn't mean—"

"Eat your lunch, Mr Athlete." I hustled down to the track and headed for the cafeteria.

"They said your name's Emma," he called. "Ethan. Ethan Paige."

I gave him a thumb's up but kept walking.

After I left Stadium Seat Twenty-Four, I plunked myself into a cafeteria gossip gaggle of familiar faces. They all said hi and got back to badmouthing someone named Jennifer. I pulled out my assigned reading paperback of *Macbeth*. I needed to look uninterruptable while I ate and obsessed over my bleacher meltdown. A year ago it had been football fanatic Liam and now I convinced myself that Ethan James Dean-Rob Lowe-Emilio Estevez Paige was just another conceited jock jerk.

By the time I slid my lunch tray into the kitchen pickup window, truth weighed me down. He was either a really bad pickup artist or he just wanted me to get the hell off his lucky seat. I had been the total asshole. The bell rang again and I hustled down the hall to grab my earth science text. Mr Athlete stood slouched against my locker. A high school miracle.

"Why'd you shoot me the bird when you left the bleachers?"

"Oh my God." I raised another *thumb's up* gesture. "Does this look like my middle finger?"

For the next week we met daily, sometimes in seats twenty-three and twenty-four. Small talk was not his forte. Halting speech caused him to pause, or catch his breath in odd places. I'd reply thinking he was finished. Then we'd tumble over

"Sorry, you go."

"No, you finish."

I asked if playing football beside a cemetery bothered him.

"Hell no." He said the Paige family plot was laid out along the shrubbery and red bud trees separating the properties. "Living Paiges are total buzzkill. I've got ghosts right there to cheer me on."

Like mine, his family was screwed up. He lived nine miles from school now; used to live in town but his mother couldn't cope and dumped (his word) her three kids with his father, stepmother and new family. His brother and sister were now on their own. "It's like the clock's ticking till I have to get out, too." He halted with a flush rising from his collar.

I told him about trying to live with Alexandra when my parents dropped the Animal Cracker Park bomb. I made him pinky swear he'd never tell, and then described Genevieve and Darby's cockroach game. Once he got a drift of my situation he loosened up. He lived beyond us, out on what had been the Paige family farm for three generations. "Just our house and trailers now. My old man rents out lots." I knew enough to keep still. "Plus they own the Methodist church on the parcel across the road."

"You own a church?"

"Yup. Crazy, huh? And the preacher's a woman, Maxine MacElroy…Sees I'm in Sunday School every week. Closest thing I got to a mother looking out for me. I get some odd jobs from Charlie the maintenance guy." It was the most sentences I'd heard him put together.

Football practice was in full swing so I took to sprinting around the cinder track every afternoon. When the coach finally approached me, I explained I'd done well on my St. Louis team and was keeping in shape for spring try-outs. For the lunch room girls who asked, I mentioned training for the Olympics trials.

The next lunch period Ethan mentioned FFA.

"F A?"

"Come on. *Future Farmers of America.*"

I smothered my guffaw into a snort. "Sorry, I'm a city girl. Cows and stuff?"

"Damn straight, 'cows and stuff'. I could tell you about my meat judging team but you'd fall under the bleachers from laughing your ass off."

"No I wouldn't." *Yes, I would.*

"My old man's a butcher at the ACME. There's a shitload to learn like Meat Evaluation and Technology."

"So you want to get your family land back to farming?"

"Hell, no. Even if I did, no way he'd let me."

"A meat judge?"

"Hell no. Pro ball. Baseball. If you're good enough to be drafted out of high school, you'll have an agent. If not, you play for the major league farm teams or the Independent Leagues. I'm pretty fucking good but if I can play for a college team, I have a better chance to make it work. Get an agent; make the major leagues." He grinned. "And I'd even have a degree." And on he always went about baseball. Always.

We made a game of sharing worst family episodes, at least the ones we were willing to reveal. I mentioned Dad bragging with his bar mates over my pharmacy exploits, and a humiliatingly hilarious episode when he cheered me on in blue language as I struggled to finish a regional track meet relay.

"I got nothing funny. My mother's out of the picture. My asshole father's a bitter, dried up son-of-bitch."

His parental figures were the overworked Methodist preacher and church janitor across the lane, and the BHS lunch ladies who snuck him extra food. The real kicker? My life was far closer to the Brady Bunch than his.

A few days later bleacher seat chit chat lead to, "So, do you have a girlfriend?"

Ethan fidgeted. "Nope."

"So I guess I misread that kiss you laid on Brittany from my Driver's Ed class as she got on the bus yesterday."

"Cripes, Emma, you can be intimidating. I figured you wouldn't go out with me if I told you."

"No shit, Sherlock. I'm not a two timer."

"See? You're totally, I don't know, in command, about your life. About everything."

Talk about revelations.

"I swear-to-God, before school started, I planned to break up but I'm no good with confrontation. Especially with girls. Just so you know I ended it this morning." He made eye contact and crossed his heart.

I asked him to hang out at my house. I wasn't as ashamed of this one, especially after Ethan's farm descriptions. His first Sunday arrival after church, he and Dad talked baseball, especially Cardinals trivia. The moment he left Dad hailed me from his ratty orange recliner. "Emma, you see to it that boy knows he's welcome any time."

Football games, shrill whistles, the marching band, concession food aromas—all of it ignited the rest of my fall weekends. I'd traded my screwed-up Liam Weller-Wash U-college Fantasyland for real life with high school hero Ethan Paige. My heart hammered every post-game as he emerged from the locker room, in required khakis and dress shirt, all wet hair and aftershave. We'd heft his duffle bag of equipment and head for his gum-and-duct taped pickup. We shared beers in parked vehicles and weed in his older brother's seedy apartment, complete with Goth wife and baby. Brucknerfield *terra firma.* I lived under a blanket of neglect but Ethan was under a boot heel of abuse. I understood the void in his personality and the caring soul beneath it. He took me to meet Maxine whose concern for both of us was genuine. Even my parents recognised a kindred spirit. They gave him rides home and by the new year Dad's *welcome anytime* included an open-ended dinner invitation. We made a good pair. It felt like love.

Like every other Brucknerfield High School couple, we yearned to consummate our devotion at Gerty's-on-Thirty, known to all as Dirty's-on-Thirty. Eighteen-year-olds sang the motel's Prom Night praises. Porn could be rented on the TVs, weed procured in the parking lot.

Dad got wind of Gerty's, and let me know when he, too, suspected Ethan and I thought it felt like love. "That motel's a drug bust or prostitution raid waiting to happen. And my new passel of bar mates knows my car, Ethan's truck, and every other mode of transport you two might be thinking would fool your mother or me."

Instead we explored the Paige nine acres and settled on cave-like nooks in the rock formations off from the trailers. After some long-forgotten spat, Ethan's erratic, hateful stepmother went from loving me to forbidding me to visit. We'd scampered off to The Nook in warm weather, but the chill forced me to fine-tuned night time excursions. Quicker than you can say *clandestine,* I oozed through his bedroom window then vanish before daylight, leaving my Oscar de la Renta-drenched panties on his bedpost. I mastered the midnight run; Ethan mastered *coitus interruptus.*

In early February I wandered into Beehive Fashions and Accessories, hunkered into my parka. Even inside Genevieve and I made constant fun of the dress shop, clearly named for the hot sixties' hair style. The mod décor screamed

Brucknerfield, The Town that Time Forgot. With the closest mall a hike and a half, the shop stayed in business by covering the gamut from grandmas to teens, with a kids' department tucked in the back.

I was cold and bored. A handmade: *Help Wanted Ask for Ruth Birnbaum* on the jewellery counter had fallen forward obscuring the low display rod. As the nearest saleswoman chatted away, two bracelets practically slid themselves off the hanger and into my pocket. I made a point of perusing the blouses and sweaters on the way back to the door.

"Miss O'Farrell?" The hand on my shoulder shot my pulse into my ears. The woman smiled at me. "A moment in my office?" Cripes. She led me into the storeroom and motioned to the corner desk, chairs, and file cabinet. I sat. "You know my name?"

"My sister works in the high school guidance department, and coordinates the paper grading you help with. She pointed you out in here one afternoon."

Not good. I scrambled for a light bulb moment. "Small world. Are you Mrs Birnbaum?" I stood and shook her hand. "I saw the sign. I'd like to apply for the job you're offering."

She did the raised eyebrow thing. "I'm familiar with your comments about my inventory."

"Oh. Sorry."

"No, You're right. The shop could use a youthful touch, but then, you know that." She moved to the file cabinet. "I have to get back to my customers, but you may fill out the application and leave it on the desk."

I looked at the door half expecting cops summoned by some secret alarm button. When no one appeared I took the paper and got to work. On the way out of the shop, I made a big deal of straightening the sign then slid the bracelets back in place.

Mrs Birnbaum called me back the next afternoon for a real interview. I talked my way into the job with specific suggestions for the teen section, surprised by my itch to bring it into the current decade, but mostly anxious to start saving for my California plan. You'd never have known there'd been anything amiss the day before. If she didn't want to mention it, I sure as hell wasn't going to bring it up.

As the school year progressed, I became the consummate shelf straightener. I rubbed polyester between my fingers, silk against my cheek. Mrs Birnbaum taught me the difference.

Glamour, Elle and *Vogue* fashion layouts swam in my head as we concocted fresh ensembles for the window. I became less of a smart ass as I realised women of all sizes, ages, and incomes wanted to feel satisfied or confident with what they bought. I made suggestions; customers listened.

By spring the addictive risk of my romantic Ethan escapades fed our insecurities, and exacerbated our dysfunctional behaviour. He'd break up with me; I'd beg him not to. I'd insist it was over; he'd want me back. Even when he was legitimately too busy to be with me, I stayed mired in doubt.

When his family flat out refused any financial support, like mine, his dream of college collapsed. "I was a fucking idiot to get my hopes up. Parents who won't pay for my lunch aren't about to cough up tuition." Ethan swallowed his fury and dug in his heels. Not playing on a university team left him one option: try to secure a spot with an independent league. He pitched with decent control and velocity of eighty-nine to ninety-one miles per hour. He was convinced he could work his way up to the major leagues.

The unlikeliest person in my life progressed to role model for goal setting and perseverance. I daydreamed about getting to California, but Ethan Paige practiced to get into baseball. He filled notebooks with everything from coach's advice to sketches to sports magazine articles. That spring while he played and planned, I shopped for my first prom outfit, shoving dresses along the racks as I obsessed over change, maturity, and my empty future.

In April fact replaced rumours. The local paper announced a Hollywood production company planned to use deserted area landmarks to film scenes for *Mischief,* and posted their cattle call for hundreds of teenage extras. My mother presumed my drama queen personality and fashion obsessions would land me a major role, her a way to score some cash. Ethan wasn't thrilled until I insisted, he'd make minimum wage of three forty-five per hour.

The high school granted a half day off and teenage hoards packed our gym. Ethan and I shared the only free chair and desk. *St. Louis Post Dispatch* photographers roamed with local pros, shooting the casting team talking to prospects. As Ethan and I huddled over the paper work trying to stay on the chair, a middle-aged man swooped in, asked questions, and initialled our applications. "Perfect."

A photographer stepped forward. "What's perfect?"

"These two. They have the look we're after."

We learned he was the director Sunday when *The Post-Dispatch* printed it as a cover story, complete with feature photo of Ethan and me working on our applications as he leaned over us. Brucknerfield's football/baseball hero and Miss Pseudo *Vogue* Fancypants had been hand-picked by the director himself. Overnight we became local celebrities. I wondered if Liam had seen it and done a double take.

Celebrities or not, reality returned. I'd spent every Beehive dime on my full-skirted gown, and neither Ethan nor I had money for the pre-prom dinner. Instead, he escorted me in rented tuxedo to Burger King, ridiculous but hilarious. I looked like a teenaged Cinderella-Barbie-bride gliding around the dance floor in my white poofy ensemble with Prince Charming. My plan to bolt for Los Angeles grew dimmer with every slow dance.

The call back from the casting company came a few days later. This time Ethan and I drove the thirty-five miles to Manchester for fittings. Racks and racks of vintage 1950s clothing lined a giant trailer parked behind the empty high school. The team dressed us in outfits appropriate to our assigned scenes, took a series of Polaroids, attached a profile to the paper work, and sent us home. We'd be called with final instructions and paid the promised $3.45 an hour. True Hollywood.

Since the day we'd moved in, serious chores mounted at home. Eighteen acres required attention. Sparks flew between my parents and grandparents. Doors slammed; phones rang; tension hummed. "And I should've known the best you'd do is some dumb ass movie extra," my mother told me.

BHS, class of 1983 May graduation came and went. June arrived with no Hollywood news, but Mrs Birnbaum increased my shop girl hours and responsibilities. Ethan landed a maintenance job with the Brucknerfield Recreation Department while he kept up his baseball training. During a pizza date, as we discussed the mundane and Ethan talked about the intensity of ball practice required to make the pros, I picked off a slice of pepperoni. "It'd be a lot less boring around here if the movie deal had worked out."

"It did," he said. "That casting guy called the house yesterday. They want me in the drive-in scene."

"No way!"

He shrugged. "I have to get time off from work, find a way to the location—total pain in the butt. They're keeping their word about the money or I'd blow it off."

"What the hell! You don't give a rat's ass and I'm the one who wanted it so bad." I was still muttering as we left the pub, and more vocal when I got home and complained to my mother.

She scoffed. "You're aware our phone was disconnected two days ago, right?"

"You mean even if they tried, they couldn't reach me?"

"I told all of you."

"You never did!"

"Well, you can take the blame, Emma. I've warned you before. You run up long distance bills calling all those friends in St. Louis. This month it was either groceries or phone bill. Groceries won."

"You're the one who wanted this so bad. You thought I was good enough for a speaking part."

"I'm sorry." She pinched her nose closed. "The number you are dialling has been temporally disconnected."

"It's not funny! You were hell bent to make money off the deal. You've ruined it! Just like you fucking ruin everything else." She slapped me.

The confrontation went from bad to worse. It always went from bad to worse. Fury with my mother morphed into obsession over Ethan. His ten minutes of fame prompted a fan club. I was smart enough to recognise I was rubbing salt into my wounds, but my insecurity won. I demanded to go with him, unable to admit I ached to be part of it and convinced he'd pick up some random lusting extra.

As a child I developed a recurring nightmare. I found myself inside either a strange house with locked doors or a familiar house suddenly barren. In either case my mother refused to answer my calls. My senior year the dream returned except now I roamed the empty rooms and it was Ethan refusing to reply.

The union professionals refurbished an abandoned drive-in. Ethan finished May filming for ten hours while I laid back like a stalker. He enjoyed interactions with the cast and frivolous gestures with flirtatious schoolmates while I fumed. The oddball kid, out of step, excluded, powerless. Loser. Outsider. We fought, one misfit haranguing the other until we exhausted each other.

Shortly after the filming, I received a financial settlement from a lawsuit based on a St. Louis tanning booth episode the year before. There were no caution signs for eye protection; I was in the booth, eyes open, looking around. I recovered but it nearly blinded me. Alexandra's attorney uncle took the case for no fee. I told my parents I'd lost the case, but was awarded four hundred dollars, a safety cushion I swore not to touch.

Ruth Birnbaum moonlighted as the Brucknerfield Avon Lady and kept a product selection at the shop. By summer I was the full-fledged window dresser and display designer. A strictly teen section with posters, open copies of fan and fashion magazines, plus our newly hip mannequin, brought them in, ready to spend their babysitting money. But our married clientele included a fair amount of tire kickers.

The downtrodden, rural women I'd secretly derided rarely spent money on themselves. That summer I realised they came inside for the air conditioning as much as the browsing, and spent their time in the children's department. The latest polyester blouse or pleat-front slacks might be out of their budget, but Avon's Odyssey Ultra Cologne Spray or New Vitality Conditioning Shampoo were not. I challenged myself to give them something affordable. "Have you thought about a fragrance or beauty product? You're welcome to a spritz at the counter. My go-to response to 'Just looking' became, 'Something just for you.' The positive change in their demeanour over their aromatic wrists and small orders yanked me back to my joy over the free samples at the Saks Christmas counter."

Summer steamed along until Ethan's "You're a fucking useless excuse for a human being," blew the lid off the Paige Farm. After another go-round with his alcoholic father, the last kid from the first marriage was out on his butt. Ethan bounced among random white trash, drug dealer relatives, and gave me some cousin's phone number where he could be reached. In August he landed at his sister's in one of their father's revamped trailers. He held onto his Rec Department job, determined to qualify for an Australian baseball program a scout had mentioned in one of his try-outs.

Predictably, Grandma and Grandpa's failing deal with my parents slid from nagging to threatening eviction. The O'Farrell lid blew at Animal Cracker Park. A year after my parents uprooted me from St. Louis, and a week after turning eighteen, my mother dragged on her cigarette till the tip glowed. "We got bills to pay and mouths to feed. Go on welfare or get out."

No way welfare. Meagre as it was, I had income and Mrs Birnbaum's encouragement. I had my lawsuit nest egg. My gypsy life would be my undoing unless I fixed it. My mother's directives disintegrated to a screaming match. I locked myself in my room; she beat my door with a broom. Dad broke it up with "Em, we got our own issues, it's better this way," nonsense.

I sure as hell couldn't move across the acreage to my grandparents' house or escape to Alexandra Campbell's. My only choice was bunk with Ethan. Dad dropped me off at his sister's trailer with a half-hearted apology.

Door frames sagged; sinks backed up; the septic system drained into the creek. We had to get out. Mrs Birnbaum listened to my fibs about friends' pressure to return to St. Louis and the city's job opportunities. I quit with her best wishes, a fifty-dollar Beehive spree, letter of recommendation, and Avon assortment. And then I finally brought it up. "You knew, didn't you? That day you steered me into this office—"

"Emma, I had every intention of reading you the Riot Act. Something about you made me think twice."

"I've been grateful."

She patted my arm. "Frankly, I also watched you leave. If I hadn't found those stolen bracelets returned without my prompting, I'd never have considered your application. It was important to see you dig yourself out of your hole."

"You could have called the police."

"The police were not what you needed." She swiped her eyes and shooed me to the door. "Now go make yourself a good life."

Chapter Three

Ethan and I found a small duplex behind a glass factory in downtown St. Louis. Two misfits together for every wrong reason was still better than living within proximity to our families. Low self-esteem, zero self-confidence, and our obsessive trust issues magnified the effort but we worked at being happy.

California dreamin' bit the dust. I clung to my nineteen-year-old Superman. Ethan, in turn, considered our relationship temporary. On-off-on-off continued even under one roof, but he agreed to help me establish my independence. "Once you get yourself situated, we can go our separate ways," he repeated.

His separate way? Play for a US farm team in crappy living conditions with poverty wages, or settle for bat, ball, and glove eighteen thousand miles from Missouri. Then I missed my period. I confirmed my pregnancy and braced for the worst.

"We'll figure it out," Ethan said.

Not exactly the marriage proposal I dreamed of but his heart of gold melted mine. He called Maxine. The following week we drove our duct taped 1978 Pacer back down I-55, out Route Thirty and sat with her for the consultation. Attendants were required but the last thing we wanted was family present. I corralled Genevieve, thrilled to be my maid of honour, and swore her to secrecy. Charlie the church sexton told Ethan he'd be proud to stand up for him.

We returned for the ceremony, me in my Beehive ensemble, Ethan decked out in the blazer Maxine provided for graduation. She performed the ceremony at the altar, blessed our union and hugged all four of us. Ethan and I headed back to St. Louis but on a whim checked into Dirty's-on-Thirty. We spent our wedding night laughing and far more creative than the fakers in the infamous X-rated TV rentals.

Two weeks later the scout who'd set the Australian possibility in motion came through. Ethan was drafted into the Melbourne Aces. From October through April season they'd provide housing and living expenses. He'd never flown, could barely navigate his path to *someday*. Now he had a baby coming. Since we'd met, we'd barely spent a day apart. I'd never lived alone but I could not be the reason he gave up his dream.

I made lists for him, hauled his clothes to the Laundromat, showed him how to fold, roll and pack to fit his duffle bags.

"Jesus, let me breathe! I can do it," he demanded.

"Ethan! How many times have I jammed my crap into duffels and moved?" I demanded he take his blazer. "Dressing well builds confidence."

"Thank you, Mrs Birnbaum but ball players don't give a damn about clothes."

"You're not just any ball player. You might have a newspaper interview or a sports dinner," I threw back, determined he feel cared for, an emotion he barely knew.

We drove to the airport in our crappy car, no air conditioning or heat, the ground visible from the floor boards. The engine stuttered all the way to Lambert Field – St. Louis International drop off. We joked about our late spring due dates: mine for our baby within days of his return. "Stay strong, Emma. Have faith." His voice broke as he whispered thanks into his hug.

This would get me through, I thought, as he disappeared into the sea of travellers. Loving another person terrified me.

Per usual I was on a mission, this time determined to find a job before my pregnancy was obvious. I threw out our Halloween pumpkin and answered a classified ad in the local paper for an advertising sales position at start-up magazine *Fairfield Monthly*. I fabricated credentials, elaborated on my Beehive sales history, and submitted my resume with Mrs Birnbaum's letter. They asked for an interview. I purchased a briefcase, black high heels, and arrived at the office praying they wouldn't fact check. My life was a shell game I'd been playing since middle school. I could do this.

Turns out they were under the gun to get the first edition out and woefully behind schedule. They offered me the job on the spot at a flat monthly rate of one-hundred-and-sixty dollars plus ten percent commission once I made the audited goal.

Vickie Spaulding, older than me with twenty years' experience, served as the senior rep. All accounts were split between us. Hers included anything political and high profile, banks and car dealerships to schools and municipal offices. No surprise I was assigned gas stations, bars, smoke shops, and every other establishment most likely to never advertise in anything let alone a new cool magazine. The deck was stacked against me but I worked relentlessly. My life depended on it.

I dressed for success but more important, I had the smarts to recognise my customers as variations of folks who sat at the bars with Dad, or spritzed their wrists at The Beehive. My accent, grammar and mannerisms were theirs. Managers and owners listened, considered my points. I morphed into the Cold Call Queen, amazed the publishers and raised a bit of healthy jealously in Vickie. In no time sales increased. I exceeded their expectations and mine.

I was not, however, as successful with written work and business protocol. "All this carelessness will kill you with clients," Vickie pointed out incessantly. "I'm bringing in a shitload of new accounts."

"Swearing like a sailor won't get you promoted beyond the class of clients you're so successful with."

"They're important!"

"Emma, of course they are, but that's not the point. I've got twenty years' experience on you. Frankly, most employers wouldn't bother to tell you what your issues are. Don't get your hackles up. Listen."

I had no clue what hackles were and my blue linguage had always raised reprimands, but the rest wasn't carelessness. I shrugged, too embarrassed to explain ignorance had me around the ankles. I needed her skills and polish to save Ethan and me. From then on, I covertly studied Vickie's reports and office memos, not for content but the way information was presented. Soon enough sales provided a steady cash flow, more than paid the rent, and allowed me to afford a newer, safer car.

My life-long street smarts and bravado kept me comfortable as I adjusted to the neighbourhood, and solitude. Our very own chaos-free apartment! I exchanged letters faithfully, and every two weeks Ethan called from the baseball club office line to report on playing, pitching and all things Australian, mate. Together we were making it work. The holidays came and went. I focused on my job and spent enough free time with my sister so she wouldn't feel I'd abandoned her. *Mischief* came out and we attended together. Gen clapped and cheered when Ethan appeared at the drive-in larger than life. True to my personality, I sank lower in my theatre seat re-wallowing in my location day angst.

One damp, miserably chilly morning during my typical last-minute race-around, I tripped down the front steps. I swore a blue streak, wiped the mud off my coat and pulled on a fresh pair of pantyhose. I kept my morning sales calls, but by noon I felt lightheaded and frightened. Dreaded abdominal pain began then deepened. I finally drove myself to the hospital and miscarried in the Emergency Room.

Ethan could not know. Emotional upheaval would destroy his concentration, perhaps sink him into I-should-have-been-there or worse, Emma needs me. I dealt with it alone. *Fairfield Monthly* gave me a week with pay to recover.

I returned to sympathetic co-workers and job security which helped. During the day I focused on my ambition and drive. But at night I shredded my list of baby names, sobbed for the child who would have loved me, and the fantasy family I'd imagined. Loneliness and anxiety smothered me in grief. The miscarriage deepened my angst. Could Ethan and I survive as a couple without the baby? We had explosive chemistry. We needed each other. Could that be enough?

I embraced retail therapy and transformed our apartment into cosy digs neither of us had ever had. It oozed style, right down to pots of daffodils on the front porch. I was back to steady on my feet. In April, just before he concluded his Down Under season, I wrote him about my ordeal so he'd to absorb the news without hitting him cold when he saw me.

A few weeks later, heart in my throat, I watched Ethan emerge through the airport doors. Sex, our primary mode of communication, was the safest place to start and surest way to connect. Despite his jet lag we stayed in bed till dinnertime and even managed to talk about the miscarriage.

Beyond sex, he made me happy and bolstered my confidence. I couldn't put it into words then, but he gave me a sense of self. I provided the resourcefulness he lacked. We needed each other whether he knew it or not.

We mulled over our situation for the next few days. We should stay married, Ethan concluded. His career showed enough promise that in three weeks he was scheduled to leave for spring training in Phoenix for the first of many teams within Independent Leagues. He'd be bussed along the circuit through September. We planned out the next six months beginning with serious birth control. He'd keep working on his pro ball dream; I'd work on my career and support us financially.

He put his arms around me. "Emma, we'll help each other get out from under our shitty backgrounds. I swear we can make a future—baseball world for me, Beautyland for you." I loved him even more.

Shortly after he left for Arizona, I spotted a newspaper ad for models. As a blonde with enough height and a decent figure, I hoped local side gigs could supplement our income. I was naïve and clueless but managed an interview scheduled at a private house. A woman answered the door, introduced herself as Beth Komanski, and ushered me in. She could have been a brothel madam for all I knew.

In fact Beth was under contract to most established beauty and fragrance companies to find people to execute special events or sell to customers during high traffic times at high-end department stores. That May she was looking for a few young women to promote the seasonal Clinique products at Saks. After an hour of discussing job requirements and my qualifications, she offered me a trial assignment. I left her house with a white lab coat uniform and a manual of regulations. After a week of nightly study, I was an expert on all things Clinique. The next time I entered Saks I held a tray of products and wore a grin from Plaza Frontenac to Brucknerfield.

"Excuse me. Allow me to show you the skincare product that will change your life."

"Welcome to Clinique. Today only, with any purchase of twenty-eight dollars, you'll receive a bonus gift worth sixty-five…"

I talked to everyone. When I'd sold enough to kick my confidence into high gear, I veered from the usual model station and strolled around the department creating a bit more excitement and more sales.

The following week Beth called me to inquire about my experience.

"I'm thrilled," I told her. "Loved the work. It was fun. I'd love more assignments."

"I hoped so. You're what I'm looking for. If you're willing to make a career change, I can guarantee ten dollars an hour. Thirty hours a week, more during holidays."

"No shit?"

She laughed. "No shit."

The next day I gave *Fairfield Monthly* my two weeks' notice.

Vickie presented me with Strunk and White's *Elements of Style,* Letitia Baldridge's *The Complete Guide to Executive Manners*, and a business writing guide. Fifteen days later I started my first official assignment at the very same Christmas Eve Saks Fifth Avenue. It felt like full circle.

I didn't know a rough from a fairway but golf season and *OPEN* men's cologne kick-started my persuasive style. I sold it as though Oakmont and Winged Foot were on my bucket list. My sales soared. Big names from Ralph Lauren and Giorgio Beverly Hills to Halston soon called Beth to book me at their counters. I worked to prove I was capable, unwittingly breaking sales records for my assigned brands. With my extra money I booked a surprise visit to Phoenix.

We barely got beyond, "Babe! Geeze, I wish you'd called first. …Of course I'm glad to see you. With having to concentrate and all, it's not a great time…"

We found a diner and went back to Ethan's low budget motel room. *Not a great time; not a great time.* Why wouldn't he have a thing going on the side with some baseball groupie slut? Great sex and decent conversation did little to convince me otherwise. I went to a few games and sure enough several trashy types waited for him near the locker rooms.

I nagged for details. Ethan bristled. I demanded honesty. He accused me of spying and harassing. Discussion dissolved as if we were back on the movie set. F bombs flew. I shouted about sluts and white trash, convinced he hung onto me because I was his meal ticket. I left the next morning while he slept. Back in St. Louis I threw myself into making my work a career. I heard from him two weeks later. Then one June evening I returned from Saks to Ethan sitting on our porch. We agreed to go on, two dreamers barely out of high school, tripping over the baggage we dragged with us. Our damaged souls needed each other, but to make it as a couple we had to figure out who we were as individuals.

Ethan flew back to Arizona, the best location for a promising professional pitcher. I threw myself into analysing the politics of the beauty world. We pounced on our career possibilities with nothing to lose.

As a rough-edged outsider I needed store people to support me and the fragrance brands employing me. I connected the industry dots and devised a strategy to be my own interpretation of beauty queen. Raw talent, street smarts and innate perception kept me employed, but even I realised my professional and character flaws drew the wrong kind of attention.

My department memos, the bedrock of business communication, rambled in strings of run-on sentences and phonetic spelling. Vickie's parting gifts founded my business library. I studied her gifts and added frequently. My jump from print ads to the fragrance industry paid off. I was a natural at selling and delivering results.

I also knew my brash, sandpaper nature isolated me.

Fragrance counter cohorts were as standoffish as my high school classmates. It kept me an outsider but I'd be damned if I'd let my flaws keep me from my goal of New York City executive. I revved up my competitive instincts.

Estee Lauder and Giorgio Beverly Hills jolted the industry. Their now-standard concept of GWP, *Gift With Purchase,* created buzz like I'd never seen. In prestige stores throughout the U.S. *RED – Giorgio Beverly Hills* took over the entire entrance of the cosmetic department. Suddenly customers from coast to coast entered on a red carpet running along five to ten glass display cases jam packed with the cleverly staged single brand *Red. Red* banners hung from the ceiling, *Red* posters displayed the related items. It became impossible to wander through the store without some sort of brand encounter. The goal? Spritz, spray or sample, *et voila*! Purchase.

To alert the press and engage the consumer, New York and Los Angeles, plus smaller regional markets, held launch parties and spared no expense to ensure camaraderie. Every sales person was to feel like a key part of the movement. Suddenly fragrance companies scrambled, hell bent to climb on the band wagon. As much as scent, brand recognition depended on one perfect package of colour, logo, font style, even musical theme. Fragrances launched with massive budgets soon produced fifty percent higher sales. In a pre-GWP year thirty to fifty new products might be introduced. By the time I was fully involved, over two hundred were launched.

National and international brands loaded the local sales force with bonuses, incentives, product, and most importantly, reassurance. Our one-on-one customer efforts were the key to success. Like a beauty industry version of Studio 54, buyers, and top executives mingled with local store managers and sales personnel. Daytime work segued into after-hours play; discretion segued into rumours that became the stuff of legends. My street smarts and outsider status served me well as I plunged into Public Relations 101: Look, Listen, partake, and stay above the fray.

I had dozens of glory days soap opera antics to share with Alexandra and Maria but only university post office boxes for their addresses. Over Chinese take-out in my empty apartment, I penned a detailed letter to Alexandra at Vanderbilt, and a short note to Maria at Duke. Alexandra replied with a postcard. I never heard from Maria.

I also wrote to Ethan:

I swear, I'm panning nuggets in this beauty and fragrance gold rush. From what I can tell everyone who wants in makes it. I love you! This band wagon could be my ride to success, and <u>our</u> chance for a good life <u>together</u>.

Below my signature I drew *a sketch* of a naked couple *in flagrante delicto* nestled against what he knew to be 'The Cave', our Brucknerfield rocks. He called me.

Meanwhile my elbows-on-the-counter co-workers dissected our competition daily. I listened, often half inside an open display case, sliding my artfully stacked cologne bottles closer to the glass front. "He's bland and boring, the last person I'd pick for success."

"You haven't seen him in action. He knows who counts and studies every player's *modus operandi*. He's a political machine."

What was it to be political? How could I get that skill? What the hell was *modus operandi?* I was a diamond in the rough, according to the few colleagues willing to look past my 'very abrasive traits'. No news there, but I didn't know what I didn't know. Thanks to my teen comportment classes with Alexandra I could make eye contact and shake hands with the best of them, probably even walk a runway with a book on my head. Table manners, vocabulary, business communication? Not so much.

My blunt, frank style was my biggest flaw. *Coarse, crass, crude* and *uncouth* were whispered in my presence. My standoffish routine kept me from seeking mentors when I needed them the most. Selling and self-promotion were my strong suits. I claimed I could do it all to anyone who'd listen and then set out to prove it. Genevieve and I had routinely fixed up our mother for her 'evenings out' so I added makeovers, facials, even hair styling to my portfolio. Like a good mimic I picked up tricks of the trade fast. Per usual my resume/sell sheet included fifty percent fabrication. I sensed what I learned to be true. If I could sell and execute with big results, no one gave a damn what was on it.

Freelancing for small, unknown brands honed my aggressive style: No breaks. Remain in front of the counter, circle the floor to spot a potential customer before anyone else. I was often the first point of contact at the entrance to the fragrance department. I dominated consumer traffic. My ignorance proved to be an advantage. Every brand I represented was an equal opportunity to make a sale.

No surprise. Within six months my results-oriented approach widened the gulf. Sales people were known to exaggerate their numbers yet I delivered high sales with no real experience. I'd have told them I didn't spend my day leaning against a Dillard's glass counter full of merchandise. I didn't bitch about slow sales. I didn't kill time in the Galleria Mall stock room whining about the person (that would be me) selling too much. No one asked how I did it. Instead saleswomen working for other brands petitioned the store manager to kick me out. "Emma Paige grabs all the customers," they said. "We don't have a chance to make our goals."

"All I know about perfume is your panties on my bedpost," Ethan said when I ranted about them.

"I'm serious!"

"Common sense, Emma. Whiny ass co-workers ganging up on you means you've got more power than you think. Power's like influence. If they're jealous and complaining, sure as hell the big shots are watching you and liking what they see."

"You're a genius."

"I'm a rookie in a locker room always watching the scouts and coaches for who they're watching. If you get hauled up in front of your boss, give him all you've got. Show him your stats. Make it your job to show him why they're jealous."

I did. I had the support of the brands employing me. My first attempt at business politics involved discussing the complaint with the manager, showing him three months of my documented sales results and proving my contribution of recent retail volume. "The thing is, I love what I do and I'm damn good at my job," I concluded, remembering steady eye contact. "I'm proof anyone and everyone can get results like mine. Why, shit… Sorry. Why, heck, they just need to use their time properly. Use it for customer contact. For selling."

My manager dismissed the complaint, asked for consideration of others and reminded us top priority was positive customer service. Word about the resolution spread. Jealous sales people black balled me resulting in loss of some of my brands. I had not been reprimanded but false accusations left that out.

I zigged, then zagged around obstacles and found freelance opportunities with luxury European brands barely known to American customers. They'd done their demographic homework and sought aggressive promotion to place their fragrance in American hands. I was a perfect fit. On a good day I introduced a thousand samples to wandering Midwestern shoppers, producing more than five hundred 1980s dollars. Not bad for unpronounceable fragrances.

I, who often slaughtered the English language, was now required to translate French and Italian to women (and men shopping with them in mind), clueless about the romantic message printed on the packaging. To demonstrate my action-oriented approach to the naysayers, I hustled on the floor. I offered free gift wrapping and kept a log of every customer, from personal contact information to birthdates. I memorised their names and complimented a new hairstyle or outfit to build customer relationships. They sought me out.

My reputation improved. Intuition knocked me on the head. In any anchor store, from Saks to Famous Barr, my freelance success partially depended on the employees behind the fragrance counters. They worked forty hours a week, day in and day out. I thought of Saks, that kind Christmas employee, and the one so willing to figure out the campus delivery. Counter (primarily) women made lower hourly rates than I, but could easily boost their salaries as much as forty-five percent with commissions. It was in my best interest to win them over.

I applied my clientele approach to employees and tried to penetrate their unwritten code. Many kept me at arm's length, reluctant to become entangled with me. So be it! I picked the underestimated, marginalised underdogs new to the beauty world. Common sense told me to empower those who supported my ideas. The sales force advocating my dismissal remained but those who dubbed me *the people's salesperson,* had my back. I was one of them. I learned the definition of *egalitarian,* my management style, born from selling Mrs Birnbaum's Avon products in The Beehive.

My international employers paid no taxes and could afford additional cash bonuses to independent contractors like me for exceeding the daily goals. My hourly rate increased and they sent me to the best malls throughout the Midwest. I discovered the more I travelled the less I obsessed over whether Ethan was ignoring or enjoying temptation. When he returned, we holed up and lived like the married couple we tried to be.

He had a pitch to perfect; I concentrated on mastering the progression of advancement in the fragrance industry.

Chapter Four

From St. Louis anchor stores up to the Indianapolis, Cincinnati, Columbus triangle plus north to Chicago, I honed my Midwest reputation. As green as I was, I knew selling required more than moving products. Staff at every level were my most important marketing tool. When I wanted to know what was wrong with my brand, my answer lay in the stores.

I practiced my air of confidence on sales people as though I'd been born into a different family, as though I fit, as though everything came easily. Within months I had a small army.

Fine tuning my image took as much effort as my business skills. By the mid-eighties Donna Karan and her DKNY label had burst on the scene and I wanted to be a part of all product categories: purses, shoes, hosiery, jewellery. Her designer clothes were above my budget but her work kick started my obsession with expensive designer ready-to-wear. I checked her price tags with flashbacks to my pre-barcode childhood when I stood in dressing rooms watching my mother switch garment price tags to make her choices suddenly affordable.

I asked to travel to Chicago where newcomer *Moschino* planned to launch its fragrance. Their progressive national ad featured a masculine woman in a gold push-up bra. She held a decorated bottle of the perfume, straw inserted as if she were about to sip. Franco Moschino cut his design teeth as a sketcher for Versace, but his critical take on design and the fashion industry created the kind of innovative, edgy work I loved.

I left my hotel and entered Marshall Field's decked out in blazer, blouse and pencil skirt. The Moschino-scented beauty department hummed with stylish reps spritzing in mid-calf skirts. Big-hair, padded shoulder beauty advisors hovered at their edgy display.

As I chatted with the employees and complimented their displays, my total unhipness hit me full force. An attractive guy sizing up my outfit didn't help. I needed the women's department pronto.

` "I love Moschino. It just screams, 'You need me,'" he said as he sauntered beside me toward the escalator.

"I thought it screamed, 'We don't need you till you do something about your pitiful outfit,'" I replied. "I hope I can find something upstairs to help. I feel totally frumpy."

"Oh, I wouldn't say that, Sweetie." He gestured and we stepped on side by side. "Those pumps are terrific. Anne Klein?"

"They are!" I made sure he realised I was checking out his impeccable attire. "And you know damn well they're the only thing going for me."

"You have plenty going for you. But I have to admit, your banker-on-a-spring-afternoon ensemble does not exactly scream *Moschino brand.*"

"At least I'm not representing them. No affiliation except admiration."

"Oh, heartbreak! I've been trying to pick you up so I can get my foot in the fragrance door."

We stepped off the escalator laughing. "I'm not a rep but I am a fragrance freelancer. Does that count?"

"You bet. I'm up here in women's fashion and just the man for you. Of course, by coincidence—" He fanned his nose. "—I'd love, love to make the jump to fragrance."

I shook his hand. "I'm Emma Paige. Do you have time for coffee after I, um, nose around?"

"Andrew Case and sweetie, if you've got connections in fragrance and you'll let me spin you through some accessory displays up here, I've got time for coffee, or dinner, or our honeymoon."

We met after work at my hotel bar and swapped war stories, from insane customers to incompetent department managers. I explained that my Chicago assignment covered the Michigan Avenue store plus three in area malls. After a little wine and a lot of brain storming, I left my newfound friend with newfound determination. Back in my room I crunched the numbers, thrilled I was able to carve out enough of my freelance funds for a lucrative weekly sum to entice Andrew. In less than twenty-four hours we sealed the deal. He'd work exclusively for the handful of luxury fragrance brands I was representing.

Customers loved Andrew and he loved them back. His flamboyance and humour lay on a solid foundation of drive and dedication to all customers. "Fragrance has no size," became his mantra and he meant it. He sang my praises to the department and meant that, too.

Andrew rotated among the major retailers where he'd sell, run training sessions, and put on special events for sales growth. When I joined him every two or three weeks, we'd put on a *blitz event* where we'd double the fun, double the exposure, and more than triple the sales.

I arrived one week to discover he'd designed custom referral handouts that looked like lottery cards. We bribed sales people in Jewellery and Hosiery at opposite ends of the store to pass them out. This pushed customers to us and created massive foot traffic.

"We got 'em. Now what to do with them," he replied to my compliment.

Next thing I knew he'd designed a catwalk style visual, complete with bright colours, music, and refreshments.

"Genius," I exclaimed.

He spun me around. "You're my muse, Emma Paige. I feel sure we're twins separated at birth."

Curious customers wandering in from other departments lingered. We offered them fragrance layering on their hands, a bowl to dip into scented shower gel, a finger massage with the body cream. Andrew spritzed the air and taught them how to properly wave an arm in order to catch and wear the ultimate well layered fragrance.

No matter they didn't know the Moschino brand. We created a fantasy they wanted to be part of. When shoppers asked for scent advice, the Marshall Field's clerks who made three percent on our sales, gestured to us or walked them over, happy to recommend our collection. Soon store employees followed me all over the floor, eager to take credit when I closed a sale before another clerk could seal it.

My 24/7 fevered determination paid off. I stunned my family by moving into a new luxury building in Forest Park. I loved the modern, cutting edge design, amenities Ethan and I'd never had, a few we didn't know existed, and state of the art security covering my late and erratic hours during the long periods he was gone. Cockroach days were history. Ethan could travel to and from a real home. My proudest achievement.

In the midst of applying Andrew's techniques to my St. Louis territory, My pitcher returned with the cold from hell. Mornings I left Ethan propped on pillows with tea and toast. As my work days wound down, I handed pleased customers off to the closest sales woman so I could drag myself home and heat up Grandma O'Farrell's chicken soup recipe.

I schlepped meds from the pharmacy and kept him in clean sheets. Once he'd buried himself back under the covers at night, I slept on the couch and barked more orders than usual at my local mall anchor stores.

Ethan's gratitude and stuffy, "Babe, you're the best," stoked my fury at his horrendous childhood neglect. Even my poor excuse for a mother was ever-ready with a cold washcloth and her never-fail whiskey-honey-lemon sore throat concoction.

Six days later I dropped my sneeze-free husband at the airport and headed to Dillard's. My local Moschino display of bath products, already displayed on the least prominent glass case, had been relegated to the shelves behind the counter.

"Someone's moved my samples," I muttered to the middle-aged woman leaning on the glass.

"That's not allowed. I'm sure you're mistaken," she said.

"I know the rotation." I returned a handful of shower gels to the glass top. "You really think I'd do this to my client?"

"What I really think is you bust in here with your no-name merchandise and think you can do whatever you like."

"Hey!"

"We're tired of your la-di-dah 'Look at me' attitude."

"It's not 'Look at me,' it's 'Look at my product.'" Vickie Spaulding's warning voice filled my head. I took a breath. "Okay, I'm aggressive. I admit I don't always follow protocol."

"But you win, too, Shannon. I'm not the one writing up sales."

"It's Sharon and neither the hell am I. We all know you favour Carol and Tina."

Two weeks later I was back in Chicago giving Andrew an earful as we entered our favourite pub. "—and I swear I don't favour anybody. I don't even know Carol from Tina. In every retail store I visit, my priority's connecting to people. Okay, I admit I want to be known for delivering results, but Sharon's got the whole department fucking hating me."

He minced around me as we took a table. "Now, now, we don't use obscenities, Mrs Paige."

"It's not a joke."

"Neither is learning diplomacy. Some rules you don't break. I've been at this retail game a long time."

"And they love you."

He leaned in. "Some do. And some call me *The Fag of Fragrance*."

"Oh, Andrew."

He brushed it off. "The Mean Girls of Beauty can be the clique from hell. Learn to play their game. Your brand lives in a launch case, then it moves to the backdrop, then the drawer, then, voila, the product's out the door."

"Profit or my ass is on the line."

"Exactly. Your goal is to schmooze, but not just the customers. When they're soaking in their tubs with the purchase, your salespeople are still working their asses off at the counters. I don't care if it's Dillard's or Saks or Macy's, never, ever forget whoever rings up the sale for you gets the three percent commission. That makes them competitive as hell with each other. The bottom line? You're the engine but they're the engineers who keep the fragrance train oiled and running."

I opened my hand. "Pinky swear you'll keep me on track?" He linked my little finger with his.

Thanks to Andrew Case I learned the politics of the profession at this ground level and took it to heart. As a freelancer rotating among stores and territory, I had to keep my clerks supportive and that meant neutrality. From then on, when infighting occurred, I'd say, "Switzerland," with hands in the air. Practice made perfect.

By the end of the eighties, fresh, controversial advertising hinted at conflicting sexual orientation. The portal widened for bisexuals, drag queens, and gay men who grew up idolising their mothers' fashion and make-up regimen. The face of customer service broadened. Andrew and his cohorts openly added a theatrical perspective of passion and drama. They taught women how to *work it*. Most important, they could be themselves.

As long as I could remember, I'd ached for a lifestyle beyond my reality and I recognised that same tug in customers pining for the top of the line. Brucknerfield's Beehive never left me. Brand prices run the gamut as do customers, from no-purchasing grazers only spritzing or handling every brand, to compulsive shoppers whipping out charge cards. I engaged them all: upper and upper-middle class to the all-important lower middle-class customer who bought the most. I even offered samples or designer shopping bags to the window shoppers.

The beauty industry ends each season still flush with products so I gathered what I could from trash earmarked for the Dumpster. For those with no money,

I handed out samples. For those making a purchase, I created a custom GWP program.

During those two years it seemed every hot designer suddenly licensed their own fragrance. Competition crowded the counters. My clientele file bulged. I purchased an electric typewriter, one more way I practiced Vickie's etiquette advice. I typed bounce-back messages on brand-embossed postcards from their corporate offices. Although those New York headquarters didn't sanction it, my customers received a weekly newsletter. I was in the Midwest; apparently no one was watching.

Ethan remained a bottom-line guy regarding my career details. One miserably rainy week of big news and forty-eight hours of leaving messages in sun-drenched Arizona, I gave up and dialled my one-man cheering squad. Andrew picked up on the second ring. I gave him an earful. "…Plus Gaultier could be the next big thing. He's totally out there from what I heard."

"St. Louis, a better rumour mill than Chicago? Name your sources."

I laughed. "Carol told Tina, who told me. I learned my lesson; I now know them apart. These are the older forever counter women, the base of Sharon's gossip corps."

"With too much time on their hands," he replied.

"Not if they really wanted to kick some butt, which they don't. That's my point. I've got the hang of protocol and politics. I'm ready for the next step. You know I am. Say you'll support me. This is the perfect brand to make my move."

"A jump like takes time, work and sweat. You're an unknown, sweetie."

"Not for long."

"How did I know you'd say that?"

Per usual I jumped, and feet first. I networked and pestered my St. Louis and Chicago stores until I got a lead. A New York City field sales director licensing Jean Paul Gaultier, Boucheron and Issey Miyake, the hottest new fragrances, had just made a presentation to store management.

Gaultier! Landing a piece of that account would put me front and centre and showcase my talent. New York City executives would know my name. I finagled the corporate office phone number and left a message. No reply. I called again, then daily. At long last Field Sales returned my call.

"You know I'm persistent," I said.

"That, I do," the director replied.

I gave him my pitch. "And if you hire me, I agree to drop my other brands and manage the same territory I currently cover." I added statistics for my current work. Two days later he offered me the position with a two dollar-per-hour raise.

Holy, crap. Suddenly I faced the audition I'd worked for on an even bigger stage than I'd imagined. I called the three fragrance brands I freelanced for and let them know I had an opportunity too good to pass up.

In September New York City's Gaultier marketing team chose the Chicago Marshall Field's for its Midwest launch. They sent me reams of training materials to study, as well as retailer merchandising guidelines and advertising schedules. Someone included a pack of Gaultier's current season fashion slides originally used for anchor store employee training. I applied every ass-saving, cram-and-concentrate high school skill I had as I filled my head with requirements and possibilities.

Rather than waste the slides, I found a local electronics store willing to put together a video loop combining the Gaultier catwalk presentations with stills of the Paris season highlights. I had all of it synced with Madonna's best songs and made enough VHS duplicates to ensure my biggest stores would have them playing on top of their fragrance counters. I flew to Chicago and put together a dream team of two sales people plus several freelancers. After I met with them and the department manager, I took Andrew to dinner.

"Get ready," I told him. "This group will sell in a retailer cosmetic department like no one's seen before. I've looked at the mock-ups. Think Madonna. Gaultier's bottles are tiny bustiers! Can you stand it? Bustiers complete with his signature cone bras just like his designs for her."

"Oh, outrageous!"

"And we're gonna make it even more so."

"Ship it in, Sweetie. We'll set Chi-Town on its ear!"

"Prepare for an all-nighter. I've got more ideas than I can count."

As was my style, before I left, I wandered the Field's storerooms. I chatted about the scheduled Gaultier shipments with everyone, floor manager to forklift operators. I even thanked the janitors ahead of time. I returned with twenty-four hours to spare and everything in place. Field's closed at nine p.m. On set-up night I arrived at eight-thirty in jeans and a jersey, ready to work. This event was as much about me as the world-famous designer.

Even my detractors never accused me of prima donna behaviour. Within thirty minutes of closing, I was slicing the stacked cartons open, placing contents on counters, and stuffing packaging back inside as warehouse employees wheeled in more. We sorted GWP giveaways, posters, tissue, banners and organza, all in a sea of red, metallic mauve, and silver.

And did we ogle the factice bottles. "Genius," I exclaimed as I unloaded the large perfume replicas.

"Madonna, eat your heart out," Andrew sang as he inspected the bustier style container.

By midnight the store techie had my loop running on the television propped on the main counter. Even bleary-eyed and up to our shins in empty boxes, my crew recognised a guaranteed draw to my fragrance counter, as clever as I had envisioned. We celebrated over beers at a nearby pub, and agreed 'Three Per Centres' retail associates could easily make sales even when team members or I were elsewhere.

The next morning customers entered Marshall Field's through the fragrance department's swaying banners emblazoned with the Gaultier national logo. Red organza draped the banners and enlarged fatices in windows. Pyramids of perfume-related items filled the glass counters. A poster I'd had laminated lay on the floor like a welcome mat. Madonna wafted from the loop on the TV, and the new scent permeated the entire department thanks to my 'accidental' spill. The display filled every available space in the entire cosmetic department.

Toward the end of our allotted week, I raced off the second-floor annex escalator smack into a heavyset woman in fuchsia.

"Whoa not so fast, missy!"

"Sorry! I'm rushing these Gaultier testers to my team." She arched a heavily pencilled brow. "You're the one responsible for all that Madonna business down there?"

"I am."

"Then I can blame you for losing my own outpost these past two weeks to some no name newcomer?" Her voice held scorn but pancake makeup, overlaid with rouge, eyeliner and mascara, made it hard to read her expression.

"Gaultier is the fragrance to watch."

She looked over the rail at the display and back at me. "That I grant you. A niche fragrance company competes with the likes of Estee Launder and L'Oréal. I'm annoyed but impressed."

"I'll take that as a compliment." She smiled and I hustled on. A tribute from the competition!

Within days of the closing our Chicago sales were on par with the top five U.S. markets. The vice-president wondered what had spiked the statistics. "We pulled out all the stops," I told him. Under the radar preparation, over the top results.

Of course I told Andrew over the top results called for over the top thanks. His eyes sparkled. "I've been thinking the same thing since our opening. The entire cosmetic department got behind us. They need to know how grateful we are."

I grinned. "Your thoughts?"

The Garage. Hottest bar in town, gay or straight, plus, my tranny pal Nell-E's just who we need to pull off this celebration of all celebrations. She'll call in the troops."

It took costume designs from his New York theatre connection, rehearsals, and as much coordination as the fragrance launch. Nell-E designed a catwalk to fit the space. The night arrived. Marshall Field's cosmetic department employees, from senior managers to the cliques, to part time college kids, gathered round, drinks-in-hand.

Madonna tunes filled the room and transgender models emerged through the curtains, lip syncing as they Vogued their way past the guests to cheers, catcalls and applause. I stood in the wings with Andrew, heart racing until bam, Our cue.

Express Yourself began. Out we went, identically dressed in Madonna-inspired black suits, iconic Russian Red Mac lipstick and beauty marks. We morphed into precise imitations of the one and only, mastered her dance moves, and managed to stay synchronised.

At the end of the catwalk, at precisely the right musical cue, Andrew and I ripped off our jackets revealing gold and pink Cone Bras.

Chapter Five

Now that I no longer sought emotional or financial support from my parents, our relationships eased and I shared work highlights. My mother regaled her eccentric friends with my catwalk escapades. Dad shared the racy and ridiculous at Rusty's Bar and Grille. Cousin Neil got an earful on a rare visit and dropped me a congratulatory note. I kept his monogrammed Cranes card on my dressing table for inspiration.

Genevieve married her high school love. Her heart of gold lead her to certified work for children and the disabled in a downtrodden area worse than Brucknerfield. By the time I pranced down *The Garage* runway, she was pregnant for the second time.

By the mid-nineties Ethan's routine defined our marriage. Baseball teams traded, cut, and re-signed him. In March he left for Spring training then pitched April into September on mounds dictated by the current season's league. After a two-week break, Fall Ball kicked in, then home from December until March. We survived via those rambling phone messages or callbacks, now from my first-class hotels and Ethan's motel rooms too often on par with Gerty's. The major leagues remained his dream as New York City became mine.

On my professional front, Olympia Beauty, a cool indie makeup artist brand, nipped at Gaultier's heels with its combination of colour make-up, skincare, and decent fragrance. The start-up had gained enough traction in the Midwest to require an account executive. I imagined a global trend, tracked down the Olympia contact information, landed an HR phone interview, submitted the usual paperwork, and was told to call Field Vice President Linda Clarkson in New York.

I wiped my sweaty palms on my pants, dialled and unleashed my short, sweet sales pitch. "No one will work harder for Olympia than me." I cursed my grammar skills. "Than I will. I'd welcome the chance to talk about the position or my career. Honestly, I am your perfect candidate."

"Ms Paige, that will be my decision." I closed my eyes.

"Which requires an interview in person. I'll be back in your territory the first of the week. Let's put something together at the airport Thursday before I leave for JFK."

I tried not to sound like a thrilled and grateful teenager. Thursday afternoon, still tamping down nerves, I entered the VIP lounge. A middle-aged woman, bemused, smug, and as heavily made up as when she'd confronted me at the top of the escalator during my Gaultier launch, stood and motioned to me.

"Ms Clarkson! My gosh, I'm sure you don't remember—"

"We've met. I've seen your work, Emma." Gaudy Lucite bracelets jangled over her minty linen sleeve as she opened her file and what passed for my resume. "Frankly, your Robinson May store managers and buyers tell me you're worth this interview. They had lots to say about your enthusiastic intensity."

"You won't regret it!"

"Some of it cautionary."

I kept my mouth shut as she launched into responsibilities, outlining expectations in bulleted sentences. When she finished, I shook her hand. "Ms Clarkson, I know a lot of people want this job. I admit up front I have no college degree; I'm rough around the edges. I know I'm the most unqualified on paper." I held her eye-shadowed gaze.

"I also know I'm the most skilled at getting results. That's the qualifier that counts."

She flat out grinned. "Enthusiastic intensity noted."

All the way home I recalled and obsessed, recalled and obsessed over every interview detail. Linda Clarkson knew damn right well who I was, how we met, how I performed. Even before she made the phone call, manipulation and savvy business skill kept her ahead of me, a fact worth emulating.

I heard from Olympia within days, this time for an interview at O'Hare with the vice president of sales. I timed it with a routine Chicago district trip and tried not to let anyone know how distracted and edgy I felt. The VP might as well have been a banker, all business and projected sales figures with none of the Clarkson panache or frank opinions. I raised my lack of credentials, countered with my own sales stats, and how I could apply techniques to Olympia. He was impossible to read. Weeks passed. I worked from Indiana through Ohio. By the time I returned to St. Louis, I'd made peace with my lack of education and the brashness so hard to shake off. On my second morning home I pulled on pantyhose as the phone rang.

"Emma? Linda Clarkson from Olympia Beauty, How's it going?"

I hopped to the edge of the bed. "It's going great. I'm just on my way out to make some sales."

"Just what I like to hear, Kiddo. Ready to join my team?"

Kiddo! "Really? That is, yes. Yes, of course."

"You're in. I'm keeping you in your familiar Midwest territory. You'll start for us in two weeks."

"Two weeks!" Mental math and my memorised calendar filled my head. "Thank you so much. I'll give my notice tomorrow."

"No, you'll need to give your notice today."

Protocol. "Sure. Certainly, Yes, I will, Ms Clarkson."

"Please, call me Linda."

"I'm very excited. Thank you, Linda, I won't let you down."

"No you won't. If you do, I'll fire you."

"Right." I prayed my reply sounded hearty.

"Kiddo, My assistant will contact you with the details, including a jam-packed training session. I'll see you out here in New York in two weeks. You're a natural." *I wish*, I thought to myself. Always to myself.

A beauty industry position with a New York City home office, strong salary, company car, and corporate credit card thrilled Ethan in Arizona. Less than twelve hours after handing in my resignation, my own thrill drained. Feverish flushes and palpitations in nightmare proportions startled me awake.

My grammar was faulty; my spelling atrocious. Too often I spoke before I thought or took offense where none was meant. I looked at the ceiling short of breath. Could I rescind my resignation? Ethan and I could do well and live comfortably on my current situation, couldn't we?

Coulda, woulda, shoulda. I'd be lucky if Linda kept me for a month. And then what? Sweat turned my skin and pajamas clammy. I closed my eyes but blurry gold circles swam in and out of black tunnels behind my lids.

I didn't know anyone in my building well enough to call, no one who'd sit and talk me through the anxiety fuelling my panic.

Instead panic rekindled my anxiety in a cycle that continued till dawn. Flushes finally trickled away as grey daylight seeped through the blinds.

When I trusted my rubbery legs, I used the bathroom, crawled back into bed and called Andrew. "I've worked like a maniac for this but I'm a clammy assed, walking panic attack. Linda Clarkson'll see right through me. Olympia will eat me alive."

"Emma, you're New York's idea of perfection. you've got street smarts, massive innate ability, and a spine of steel. Who wouldn't be nervous? Play it smart. This Fag in Fragrance knows panic. When you find you're in hostile territory or being judged? When you know you're out of your league? Mouth shut; eyes open. Look attentive and they'll think you're taking it in. Ask your own questions and they'll think you're brilliant."

"I guess I can do that."

"Of course you can do that. Have I mentioned you're perfection in a cone bra?"

Our laughter soothed my nerves. I dressed, went to work and prescribed myself retail therapy.

"Anything I can help you find?" came over my shoulder as I slid blouses along the rack after work at my St. Louis Saks.

"Confidence," I blurted, before I'd thought about it.

The sales woman smiled. "Like you were born with it?"

"Exactly."

"What's the occasion?"

"I've been hired by Olympia Beauty. I have an orientation and training program in New York City. Work sessions all day plus dinners and some evening events."

"We can do this." She pulled out a silk, padded shoulder blouse. I found a hip length charcoal blazer. She gathered a box pleated skirt and a second blouse.

The 747 touched down at LaGuardia with the sun setting. I exited into hoards running, napping, eating, talking, and dodging me with the occasional glare. I found the baggage claim; I found an airport worker directing us to the taxi area as he sang *New York, New York*. The interminable line inched its way forward until I reached a hulking driver, cigar between his teeth. He cocked his chin. "Var to, Meese?"

"New York, please."

"You're there." He poked the air with his cigar. "Here eez Queens. Brooklyn, there. Bronx up, Manhattan down." He grinned at himself. "Staten Island also down."

"Manhattan but I'm not exactly sure where. Let me find the address of my hotel." I rooted through my briefcase. "The Essex Hotel on Fifty-ninth Street."

"Stop searching. Is Midtown."

"No, I was told it's in Manhattan."

This immigrant with a limited command of the language, knit his brow and shook his head at the total rube he's gotten for a passenger. He also grinned. "I show you."

I survived the road rage, near misses, raised third fingers and blaring horns. Andrew had been right. The energy and directness in the atmosphere matched my own. By the time we crossed the Queensboro Bridge, Mikhail and I were on a first name basis. My anxiety dissipated as he had me memorise the five boroughs and boundaries of Midtown. By the time we hit East Fifty-Ninth Street I was laughing at his accent-laden advice.

He pulled my luggage from the trunk as I figured the tip and I marvelled at the grandeur. He gestured with his cigar again. "Here is Essex House." He swivelled. "There is Central Park. You call family and tell them you made it safe and sound." I left a message for Ethan.

The next morning I walked down Fifth Avenue to Olympia corporate headquarters, buoyed by blending into the sea of black-suits. After signing in at security, I rode the glass elevator to the forty-fourth floor. I stood against the brass handrail imagining I was the representative for the entire Midwestern branch not the gawking combo of Mary Tyler Moore tossing her beret in Minneapolis, and Annie dancing backwards up Daddy Warbucks' grand staircase.

The receptionist provided me with folders filled with agendas, general information about Olympia, and social activities from dinners to a coveted Broadway ticket to *Sunset Boulevard*. The sessions stayed professional, procedural and on time, exactly how I like them. I listened; I commented. Andrew's advice was exactly what I needed.

To complete my orientation a driver as personable as Mikhail transported me to the Long Island manufacturing facility. We traded Manhattan polish and for an industrial park cheek-by-jowl with logistics companies and distribution centres. Their operations manager played tour guide beginning with the sector's *piece de resistance*. We tucked our hair into net caps, pulled on lab coats and gloves, slipped covers on our shoes and entered a large glass room gleaming with stainless steel equipment. In front of me nearly fifty women, wrapped as we were, sat on barstools and pulled single tubes of freshly made lipsticks off a conveyor belt. The Flaming Room.

With a flash of wrist, each one waved her lipstick over the constant blue glow shooting from apparatus in front of her. I walked through six identical sections as the women produced perfect sheens on six shades then fit each tube into an egg carton style container, ready for final assembly. Visually intoxicating. *Charlie and the Chocolate Factory*'s candy production meets *I Love Lucy* at the conveyor belt.

From there my guide led me into the Customer and Client Services building. Middle aged women of every stripe filled wall-to-wall cubicles. They pecked on new-fangled computers while taking and placing customers' orders. Women in the second, nearly identical room helped sales field and retailers process large orders and trouble shoot issues.

No sterile, stainless equipment here. As far as the eye could see, posters of puppies and kittens, family photos, and memorabilia competed for space with troll dolls, mini-fans and giant containers of coffee, water and sports drinks. The spaces buzzed with Long Island accents and boisterous enthusiasm; one customer service rep more eager than the next to explain procedures I'd soon use be for my St. Louis sales.

Next my guide and I crossed to the high-tech building. Stacked cardboard boxes lined walls and conveyor belts, overseen by uniformed workers in bobs or hairnets processing retail requests. They had me track a Macy's purchase order from inception at the phone out to the loading docks where the guys gave me the once-over.

All-to-familiar covert female scrutiny followed me too. The nape of my neck tingled as they sized me up for future reference in case this green, twenty-something evolved into a bossy know it-all from the St. Louis office. They'd never know had I held onto the cards I was dealt, I would have barely qualified for any of their jobs. Emma Paige's *Most Likely*? Pole dancer more likely than fragrance industry field executive.

I met everyone at the corporate office, participated in product training, sales administration re-caps, marketing overviews, and the seasonal advertising plans for the retailers. Linda capped my final day with lunch and a tour of her office.

After thanking her profusely I rose from my chair.

"Emma, I have a few directives. Marching orders, style guides—call them whatever you like. They'll keep you professional, not to mention in my good graces." She handed me pad and pen. "Before you go, you'll want to take a few notes." I sat back down.

"You're to wear suits or dresses, navy or black, knee length; not an inch shorter. Black opaque hosiery, low black pumps. Three-inch heels, max. No jewellery except your wedding band, and studs in your ears. Pearls if you must, but no longer than sixteen inches."

This from a woman who sounded like a walking wind chime and looked like she dressed from the Ringling Brothers gift catalogue?

"If you adhere to my system for store visits, you'll never be caught off guard. Binders. Keep one for every store and within it, a section for each visit. You'll have a bio page for each Olympia employee we're to see. Includes name, title, how long he or she's been with us and with the store. Attach a Polaroid. Your notes section will include any gossip good or bad, motivations, and shortcomings."

"Got it." I stared at my pad. "Under the name, a small box labelled *Should we Fire Them*." I looked up; she remained passive.

"I hate the feel of paper; plastic sleeve for each sheet."

"I'm sure this keeps them from smudging."

"Precisely. And I'll need a chronological recap faxed within twelve hours of my St. Louis departure."

"Please be explicit here, too. Time is money," I said before she could begin.

"Very good, Emma."

Hot damn. I knew how to play her game.

"Write the particular visit at the top followed by each meeting, store checks, and people involved. List by time of day. Fax it to me here at headquarters with proper cover."

"You'll have it within the next business day."

"I'll have it within the next day, period."

"Of course."

"Lastly, my visits. Never waste my time with a stop for gas. You meet me at the airport with tank full. Have the printed agenda and local paper with you. I read while you drive. No chit chat until I've checked my voicemail and looked over the paper. I hate useless chatter. It's all business." That much I'd already perceived.

"Commit this to memory, Emma-the-Rookie. You're in a trial situation for the first year. Make no mistake. If you can't follow these guidelines, you're gone."

I returned to St. Louis in low-heeled pumps from Barneys, my particulars in a black suede Prada tote, and a black knee-length dress from *the* Saks *on the* Fifth Avenue. Emma Paige as polished as an Olympia lipstick. I hit the ground running.

It took no time to learn Linda Clarkson had elbowed her way up Olympia's Midwest ranks to top seller. From there her brusque style and no-nonsense work ethic garnered a promotion and transfer to the New York office. I joined her monochromatic fleet while she worked her magic in caked mascara, rouge, gleaming lip gloss, staggeringly bright clothes, and jangly jewellery. Iris Apfel with twice the heft and determination.

The terror of Olympia Beauty was old enough to be my mother and shared her narcissistic bent. But while Hair-trigger temperament and anti-social defiance consumed Mom, my boss used the traits to her advantage and advancement. Professional results countered her sandpaper persona but she was often reported to HR. Linda Clarkson could talk her way out of a harassment complaint like my mother got my father out of a bar tab, and all of us out of apartment evictions.

Linda flew into St. Louis from JFK like clockwork, overdressed, overweight and overzealous. Memorising her techniques and strategy reduced my stress to a simmering adrenaline rush level. After two months of shadowing her routine store manager meetings, and filling binders to her approval, she assigned the paperwork preparation to me. The night before our conference at the Eastland Mall I swigged cold coffee and reviewed my document, from sequential page numbering and chart layouts, to margins. From there I double checked the topic agenda handout for my notorious spelling.

The next morning, six minutes into the meeting, Linda's flush crawled from her neck into her scalp. The store manager's eyebrows appeared permanently arched. I'd forgotten his retail MTD, STD and YTD totals (month, season and year to-date statistics). Nor had I tabulated the DBR/daily business reports – counter employee records filed at the end of every shift—all of it critical tracking of business transacted from storeroom to counter to register.

"Since our statistics are missing, let's move on to our focus products." The manager's charitable suggestion ignited my pulse. I had no clue which products generated his largest percentage of counter sales, nor could I name his top selling beauty advisor. My ears rang; my heart thundered.

"She's new. We're clearly wasting your time. You'll have the information by this afternoon," was all I absorbed of Linda's apology as she closed the meeting.

"I'll quit," I managed as I trotted after her across the parking lot.

She waited until we were in the rental car. "I took a monumental chance on you for this position. I hired you with my eyes wide open. No college; no polish. But this? I had your assurance you are up to the task. No statistics? No DBR? How is it possible you don't know the salesperson doing the most for a store manager's fragrance counter? Have I totally misjudged you? You represent Olympia Beauty. You also represent my sound business judgment. I convinced management you were the one."

She leaned back in her seat. Somewhere a horn honked. A woman hefted designer bags into her trunk. "I want you to know your business. Cold. I want you prepared with the required information as if staff meetings are final exams. You wasted his time. You wasted mine. You wasted yours."

"I'll hand in my resignation this afternoon."

"I will not have management think I've made a judgment error. Your resignation would reflect directly on me. Quitting will only prove the naysayers right. Don't you dare resign." I started the car.

"And do not fuck up again."

That night I put Magic Marker to Post-it Notes. and stuck **DNFUA** on my bedroom mirror, refrigerator, and desk chair.

Ten months into my job Olympia Beauty selected St. Louis as one of twenty-five cities for its 'On Location' launch. Linda flew in, assembled our group and played with her turquoise necklace. "I don't need to tell you this event is major, major. Olympia's goal is seventy-five thousand dollars of retail sales in five days. We'll exceed it, of course. I hope that's understood."

Her clanking bracelets made it hard to decipher her directives, and I asked for a repeat.

She turned her cold steel gaze on me. "What can you possibly not understand? Take a class in lip reading if you can't decipher the king's English. Every one of you knows how to push sales over the top or you wouldn't be part of my team."

Her plane hadn't left the runway before my fellow employees threatened to report her (again) to HR, as much for her condescension as her implied, unrealistic number of counter appointments. My declining to sign the petition chilled the atmosphere. I busied myself at our local stores, pressuring, firing up, then enlisting the cosmetic department sellers' help.

The clock ticked. Having to report exaggerated booking numbers to meet Linda's expectations chewed at me as I freshened a counter and picked up a discarded section of the St. Louis *Post Dispatch*. The lead article highlighted a breezy, upbeat report on local beauty trends. I reread it standing at the counter. Bingo! Within the hour I contacted the *Dispatch* fashion editor and pitched the idea of an exclusive story: Olympia Beauty as the key to the latest make-up artistry.

I had no idea what I was doing, but I piqued the editor's interest. *DNFUA, DNFUA*. I presented logical details on how and why *On Location* would be like nothing anyone had experienced in the St. Louis area. She loved it. I had my miracle.

Three days later the *Post-Dispatch* coverage ran as the fashion section cover story. The editor included photos of me with Olympia and store staff, plus the all-important counter phone number for prospective clients to book *On Location* appointments. My booking totals were lies no more. We added additional make-up artists, took over the entire first floor, and expanded all the way to the escalators. Final sales reached ninety-seven thousand dollars.

Linda returned to St. Louis. "So, Emma-the-Rookie, you've shown a real burst of creativity based on you own initiative. You've been listening after all."

It was impossible to keep a step ahead of her but I managed to stay abreast by steeping myself in all things cosmetic, including company newsletters and trade publications. I confessed ignorance only to Andrew who implored me to dig deeper into *Women's Wear Daily for* hard news on the high-end brands. Sheer determination and midnight oil paid off. I detangled finance-speak within managerial information. The gist of inner workings, from Chanel and other powerhouses to unfamiliar companies like 'sleepy', 'strapped' Platinum Beauty made sense.

All of it educated me and helped connect the dots within regional buying offices and familiar faces at executive levels. My co-worker support system fell away as the Olympia fast track propelled me at breakneck speed.

I ran on Linda's hamster wheel while she lectured in fuchsia silk, and plastic bangles. "I'm untouchable. I can wear, do, say, even act any way I want which is what happens when you hold the record for highest sales in the history of a Fortune Five Hundred company. I'll grant you this, you finally get it." I must have looked perplexed because she rolled her eyes. "Achieving your goals. You've done a damn good job of integrating your personal drive with Olympia's bottom line."

"As if I'd dare do otherwise."

"Smart girl. If you have a prayer of any sort of career in this beauty business, you go through me. I own you, Emma."

My success was her success. She could not have spelled it out more clearly. When she deemed me qualified, I accompanied her to seasonal corporate office summits. We joined senior managers and staff at their big round tables for tailored, thoughtful business discussion. Professionals in suits. More than once I kept a poker face as introductions produced names, I recognised from employee gossip floating after a launch party.

The first time it happened, I hissed, "Good lord, remember the August launch at Dillard's?" to Linda over drinks; she pressed my arm. "Commit this to memory: bad behaviour and dirty little secrets stop with you. I don't care if a co-worker whines about condescension toward employees, or you witness a VP trading hotel keys. Unless it's criminal behaviour, listen all you can; record all you want. Then keep it to yourself. The beauty industry is a very, very small world." Words to live by. With the exception of Andrew and a few others, my long-distance marriage, prickly personality, and headstrong dedication to work already kept me at arm's length from industry social connections. For once I felt good about it.

Although there was never a lull in the Olympia pace, I convinced Linda to send me to a three-day industry conference at the Manhattan Midtown Hilton. She may have thought she owned me, but I needed the seminars on unfamiliar topics and a chance to fine-tune my business small talk.

I wore Donna Karan, knew Midtown, and enough to keep quiet during gossip sessions as juicy as elevator speculation over Kearny, New Jersey, warehouse raids for packaging fraud. I chatted up anyone who'd listen regarding market potential within the Chicago-Indianapolis-Kansas City triangle. The final evening, dressed in my charcoal cashmere Olympia representative finest, I headed for the dinner and a panel discussion by fragrance legends seated at the head banquet table.

I exited the elevator as the woman in front of me glanced at her companion. "Remember, time is money. Don't waste either on those at the castaway tables. The place is crawling with Estee Lauder and Liz Claiborne wannabes."

Good to know, I thought, until I found my place tag on the table closest to the hallway, farthest from the glitz. "Ah, join us, *ómorfi gynaíka*." An impeccably dressed gentleman with thick greying hair stood and pulled back my chair. "Tonight I have the pleasure of joining... How did you call us?"

"The nobodies," a woman seated on my right replied.

"Ah, but I am all the time thinking soon to be somebody." He offered his hand. "Nikos Christopoulos."

"Emma Paige, from Olympia Beauty."

By the time we'd finished our salads, we'd all exchanged names and business positions. Two Harvard MBAs tracked sales and trends in the burgeoning pre-teen market. The Naomi Campbell look alike directly across from me was a new executive assistant at Bath and Body Works. Mr Christopoulos started his distribution company in Athens with a single fragrance and fifteen fragrances later, moved production to Milan. He happily explained although now established in New York, he attended the seminars to further understand the "*Trelós*. This crazy American capitalism." Castaways we may have been, but well before the pros started up front, I'd learned a workshop's worth of industry minutia.

Gradually my gut-eating anxiety and restlessness no longer blindsided me. My life with Ethan was predictable in its oddness. Communication boiled down to great sex when he was home and catch-up phones calls when he wasn't. I managed the insecurity always nipping at my heels and marvelled at our St. Louis life. Bone deep drive kept our careers on the rails.

I owed Linda plenty, but she could turn on me as surely as another screw up would fan her fury. Scarlett O'Hara and I shared the *As-God-is-my-witness-I'll-never-go-hungry-again* syndrome. Instinct kept me tuned to job shuffles and regional openings. I obsessively updated my curriculum vitae and covertly threw out feelers. Weeks might pass, sometimes months. I went to a few interviews to stay fresh, all the while working an insane schedule to carve out the niche required to rise in St. Louis.

Within two years and my twenty-seventh birthday, I had the first Midwest five hundred thousand dollars sales total. I resuscitated a failing counter from the exit list to money-maker, pulled over one hundred-and-fifty thousand dollars in sales and 'overachieved' territory sales by thirty-five percent.

On occasional family weekends Dad offered his brand of affectionate advice. He was a creature of daily habits: four Cokes, four cigarette packs a day, *The Price is Right* from his orange recliner, then beers from the local bar stool. His lifestyle was taking its toll. Darby made it through technical school and put his automotive skills to use at the Main Street gas station when he wasn't smoking weed behind it.

Genevieve stopped tolerating her husband's abuse, divorced and stayed in the boondocks. Fast food raised her weight, sporadic child support and low wages barely covered her expenses in the emotional and nutritional desert. I sent hundred-dollar bills tucked into upbeat cards.

I earned every penny. I barely had a life outside work but my boss apparently had none. When the double edge sword of voicemail and faxing burst into full swing, she had Olympia issue me the revolutionary car phone. Linda Clarkson knew no boundaries.

In the independent leagues, putting players on medical leave was cheaper for the team than decent treatment from sports specialists so Ethan stayed home that fall to rest his arm from overuse. I loved having him home. Husband and wife time forced me to juggle Linda's 24/7 expectations and improve my time management skills. One chilly Friday evening after an exhausting week and flight from Chicago, "Call me ASAP," waited on my car phone in long-term parking. I put off the DNFUA moment until I got home and shared a beer with Ethan.

Linda answered on the second ring. "It's Emma. I got your call. I can have the Field's personnel stats by Sunday—"

"I'm calling about you, not Chicago." I glanced at Ethan and steeled myself.

"You've had one hell of a year. You know it, I know it, and now the industry's hearing it officially. Congratulations, you're Olympia's Account Executive of the Year. You're making me and your district look damn good, kiddo."

"Wait. That's what your call is about?"

"That and the five thousand dollars that goes with it. I can fire you if it'll make you feel better." Her laugh; my relief.

"Oh my God, Linda! I won? Me!"

"You. And your report can wait till Monday."

I hung up and threw myself at Ethan. "Big award. Five thousand dollars! This calls for great sex and superb shopping."

"Whoa, Babe!"

Saturday, I dragged him to Nordstrom's. He agreed to decent khakis and a few polo shirts, then parked his baseball-cap-and Levis self in the TV rest area for a college football break.

"Knock yourself out," he said, "I'll stand guard on the loot."

I went back to cruising. We'd come so far and worked so hard. Did we look like any other twenty-something upscale couple fussing over linens and gourmet kitchen gadgets? How I hoped so. Ethan had nearly ten gruelling years with the independents, Florida to Maine, Minnesota and California with two weeks off March till December. His pro career wasn't progressing as fast as we'd hoped, but he arrived at his March bullpens with my salary making it possible to concentrate and travel the West Coast with the team.

Occasionally one of us brought up the subject of children. We agreed. Our dysfunctional backgrounds, minimal parenting skills, and career schedules made it incredibly complicated, and unfair to the child. Even my parents didn't bring it up.

Shortly after our award mania, Linda took me out for drinks and dinner to celebrate my third anniversary with Olympia Beauty. She could—and did—turn on a dime, which made complete contentment impossible. Nevertheless, I was grateful and made sure she knew it.

The chaos of spring in the fragrance industry kept me clear headed. Employees dealt with their kids' spring breaks, seasonal rains, up-coming Easter and Passover, delayed shipments, and order SNAFUs. Whatever could create havoc did. My office phone rang non-stop.

I was on a second cup of coffee during a second chaotic day of listening to my voicemail backlog when I hit a recording from an assistant to Marsha Johnson at Platinum Beauty. Ms. Johnson had reviewed my query of November (November!). She was due in town for Robinsons-May CEO's annual steering committee meeting with select vendors. Could I make time for a drink or dinner?

It didn't sound like a question. I reviewed my applications file. I'd sent my November query to Platinum HR unsolicited. There'd been no reply. Fifty-year-old Marsha Johnson had joined the firm about the same time, charged with rebuilding the sleepy company. (Thank you, *Women's Wear Daily.*)

I knew her name from glossy publications to managerial gossips. She was often nose-to-nose over issues with the cosmetic industry's notoriously chauvinistic, egotistical men on her rise through their ranks. Now this female CEO and Platinum Beauty had captured the cosmetic and fragrance license for the house of Italian designer Salvatore Rosa. I admired his luxury handbags and owned shoes from his ready-to-wear collection. Yes, indeed, I'd find the time for a drink or dinner.

We met at The Green Door, upscale with a discreet ambiance quiet enough for serious conversation. In the mid-nineties, like a million other tall blondes, The Princess of Wales served as my style maven right down to her iconic royal haircut. I arrived in pearls, kitten heels, dark stockings and a classic charcoal suit, banded with a thin, leather belt.

Marsha—the antithesis of Linda—appeared in impeccable black with her red hair in a demure French twist. Small talk segued right into her strategic five-year plan to vault Platinum into the U.S. market's top ten.

We ordered, and handed back our menus. "My agenda's aggressive. I'm after new talent to help implement my aggressive agenda, specifically field sales director, the highest profile sales job in the company."

I touched on a few of my successes.

"You're here tonight, Emma, based on that track record. I've gone far afield for talent since the best sales people are usually not found in New York. I've been assured you'd be a good fit. I want to bring you into the fold. This means extensive travel, as I'm sure you know. Home base will be New York City."

After lengthy details, she offered me the position on the spot. A five-thousand-dollar clothing allowance, company car, cell phone, and company paid health plan augmented the ninety-five-thousand-dollar annual salary. Relocation expenses would be reimbursed after ninety days of employment. Marsha expected my answer in twenty-four hours.

Linda Clarkson barely caused a ripple in my over-heated brain. I would have accepted at the table, but explained the need to discuss it with Ethan, hanging his major league hopes on yet another league's spring training. "Holy shit," I sang, whispered and shouted all the way home.

Ethan took forever to make decisions and I bristled as I tapped out his phone number. He now had a Nokia; it routinely went to voicemail. No answer; no surprise. "It's New York, Babe. Field Sales Director, the highest profile sales job in the company. I have to move this at the speed of sound. Please get back to me. I love you."

I left a second message at three a.m. his time, a third the next morning. Marsha Johnson was not the type to accept wussy behaviour. Despite no word from my husband, as promised I called her, used my best professional voice, left out the Ethan details, and accepted her offer.

The rest of the day consisted of in-store counter reviews with two reps, both of whom commented on my upbeat mood and enthusiasm. Ethan returned my calls at six-thirty with the usual tedious recital…just getting back to his hotel. Rain caused a twenty-four-hour travel delay. Elbow pain giving him fits meant lousy nights on the mound. "And now half-assed phone messages about us moving across the country."

"There's nothing half-assed about this major, major offer!"

"Well, it's half-assed to think I'd want anything to do with New York. I can barely stand using an elevator where we are now. How I'm going to live with some high-rise one?"

"This is about sales not fucking elevators!"

"What the fuck happened to St. Louis being perfect for sales? We're doing great right where we are. You know St. Louis's is the perfect Midwest solution for both of us."

The excrement hit the fan. I threw *abrupt, rude, closeminded*, and *cold* back at him. "Let me get this straight. You've spent years traveling all over creation. You chase a dream you're not sure will ever actually pay for anything while I work my ass off to support it. If it weren't for my career, you'd have been forced to stop playing years ago."

"Thanks for laying it out for me again, in case I didn't get it the last sixty times you've reminded me. It's a pain in the ass getting home as it is. New York's on the other coast, another planet in one more fucking time zone."

"Why can't you understand how important this is for our future? I was clear three years ago. My goal's always been New York. This is my major league, Ethan. And it lets you keep trying for yours. I don't want to fight with you."

"Then don't. It's not going to work."

"It will if you make it work."

"Don't take the job."

"I already have."

He hung up. I swore, changed into sweats, paced around the apartment, and called him back.

He picked up on the second ring, "I can't believe you'd make such a totally life-changing decision without me."

"I didn't call you back to keep fighting."

"Damn it, Emma, then accept I can't move to New York. I'm staying in St. Louis."

I should have taken a deep breath but raw emotion raised my voice. "Ethan, no way can we afford two households. It's New York with me or return to your happy Paige homestead in Brucknerfield. I'm sure your father can rehab that trailer next to your sister's."

Dead air. "We're done, Emma." Second hang up. This time mine.

Chapter Six

Agonising over Linda kept me from a meltdown over Ethan. She still railed at me when I questioned her tactics or strayed from her directives, and yet I was one of her favourite sales people. Surely, she'd expect me to grab such a golden opportunity. Hadn't she done the same? Didn't everyone?

My resignation had to be face-to-face. I owed her that much. And far more, but it was easier not to think about it. Her executive assistant in Manhattan confirmed she'd left for three days in our southeast territory, working from the Selwyn Regency in Charlotte. I booked a flight, a room, and left a message that coincidently, I was due in town on family business, and hoped we might get together, even briefly to catch up. She agreed to meet me in the hotel coffee bar.

I arrived in classic Clarkson-mandated attire. "You're looking positively funereal. I'd presume you're dressed for a family memorial service if I didn't know it's throw-Linda-under the-bus attire."

Oh shit. "Linda—"

"Don't play me for a fool. It's in my best interest to stay one step ahead of anyone I've put so much faith, trust and training into."

"And I appreciate every minute of it. I've done everything your way, team building with each year more successful than the last. It's just time for my next step."

"Your next step? We're just getting to where you're worth my effort, Rookie Emma."

"I have an offer to relocate in New York."

"New York? Don't be ridiculous. A Missouri red neck, rough as sandpaper? I own you. I'm untouchable. I can do, say, wear, act, however I want. That's the reward when you deliver the profit and break the record for highest sales in the history of a Fortune Five Hundred company for twenty plus years."

"I know. And I'm grateful for every minute with you."

"You were a nothing when I picked you up on the selling floor peddling your low budget fragrance. You think you can just jump over to my competition with no consequences? I can destroy your reputation before you hit the tarmac at JFK." Her bracelets jangled like a room full of rattles. I remained still.

"If you have a prayer of a career in the beauty biz, you have to go through me. You'll never make it east of the Susquehanna, let alone the Hudson. New York's way out of your league. I can make sure your welcome comes with a wakeup call that'll have you running right back to St. Louis." I looked her in the eye, heart banging against my ribs.

"I'm taking the next opportunity. You've done this too, in your own career. I give you total credit, Linda. You've taught me fairness to all employees, the importance of listening to their suggestions and concerns, and recognising work done well." Her employees complained to HR so often, we both knew the last part was a complete crock. "I've flown here to explain face-to-face." She sipped her coffee, no doubt as stone cold as she was.

"I'll give you twenty-four hours to reconsider."

"Darling Emma, Linda's savvy and sensed this was coming," Neil said when I called from my hotel room. "If not this offer, you'd take the next one. You're quick, smart, and not the type to be stagnant in your career. Of course you want to behave professionally—fair warning, proper exit and all that—but you must watch out for yourself over everything and everyone else. It's the lesson every O'Farrell learns in the crib. Now buck up. I'll see you in New York."

Sweaty fist-to-queasy gut I called Linda's voicemail within the twenty-four hours, couched my message in gratitude, and added I'd accepted the New York offer. She did not reply.

The stand-off with Ethan continued. He left our business matters to me, and the lease was in my name. Our landlord agreed to break it. (He could raise the rent for new tenants.) I left Ethan the details in voicemail.

Mid-month, in decent weather, I returned to Brucknerfield for Easter weekend. I attended Maxine's church service by myself, hugged her during the greeting, and assured her Ethan was well. My parents were speaking to Dad's parents again so we crossed the field. Darby arranged an egg hunt for Genevieve's kids, and while my nephews searched the sorry landscaping for plastic containers, Dad ground yet another cigarette butt into the dirt and slung his arm around me.

We lingered over what passed as family dinner as my sister's well-being, Dad's health, and my disintegrating marriage chewed at me. The distance to New York, and my doubt chewed at me as I assured my ragged family I'd stay in touch. I needed the separation as much as the job. Ethan did too, whether he knew it or not. New York would keep us from life in a doublewide off an unpaved Missouri road.

My Olympia team surprised me with a farewell party full of my key regional directors and loyal store managers. No Ms. Clarkson, of course, but even Andrew caught a turnaround flight from Chicago to laugh and reminisce. I returned to my half-packed apartment and a phone message that Ethan had rented an apartment with a teammate. He didn't name the place or the person; I didn't call him back.

The morning the van arrived, Dad surprised me in his latest beat-up car, insisting on helping me pack. Never mind there was little left to do. I burst into tears and buried my face into his familiar, tobacco-scented shirt.

He held me at arm's length. "O'Farrell's got another success coming. No tears. I already brag on you like I do Cousin Neil. In fact I brag to Neil. You'll make us proud, up there with them corporate big shots."

"It's not working out the way I planned," I whispered.

"Look here, Ems, you know Ethan's got a dream he can't shake, stubborn as me and your mother. He'll come around."

I hugged him hard, terrified of the hole I'd dug myself into, but there was no backing down. Movers packed the truck for the cheapest corporate relocation ever. I'd gotten rid of our hand-me-downs, cast-offs and thrift store items. They loaded Ethan's motley treasures, our out-of-season clothes, and the few decent household items we'd bought together, all of it destined for storage. I'd been allotted six weeks in a residential hotel while we—now I—found permanent housing.

The sterile apartment looked as though we'd never occupied it. The truck drove off. Dad hugged me as my airport car service idled at the curb. "It was a good run," I managed, not sure if I meant my professional St. Louis days or my marriage.

My flight to New York was as bumpy as the trail I'd blazed to get there. My burgeoning luggage and I were delivered to the Upper East Side boutique hotel the company provided for eight weeks. *Welcome to Platinum & New York! See you Monday morning, All best, Marsha,* peeked from a spring arrangement.

I unpacked and settled into the eight hundred and fifty square foot suite. The wet bar included a microwave, fully stocked mini-fridge plus tea/coffee station, and pantry shelf. Comfy couch and club chairs separated the almost-kitchenette from a pine desk and work space. Ethan would love it all.

When I was sure I could trust my voice, I called him. "I made it. I'm here," I said to the recording. "You'd like this hotel. It's right over from Central Park. Practically an apartment. We have French doors into the separate bedroom. It's all English country style, the sort of sofa you'd plop right into—" I stared at the dark TV screen.

"Never mind. I'm tired of rambling into an empty phone every time I try to talk things out. You're out there chasing your own dream. I get that. You know I do. You make me crazy, Ethan. Okay, Maybe I hate you for refusing to come with me, but that's not the worst part. The worst part's I love you. I need you here." I hung up and filled the cast iron, claw foot tub with scalding water and complimentary bath salts, then soaked till my fingers pruned. Navigating life alone in New York City had never been the plan.

We'd been given the weekend to settle in and explore so Saturday I crossed two blocks to Fifth Avenue, thinking of the Missouri bumpkin five years earlier here to train for Linda Clarkson. She lived here, too. I wandered up to the Metropolitan Museum of Art over to Madison, half expecting her to spring from behind a bush or a bus.

I paused for men loading a Range Rover and followed them into Lobel's Meat Market. Charts on the wall and the sound of cleavers and hacksaws. I ached for the son of the butcher who had to convince me Brucknerfield had a meat judge team.

Monday morning, the last week in April, 1995, I left my hotel at 8:30 a.m. sharp, for the brisk walk to my new office. Corporate headquarters filled two floors within a midtown high rise and Marsha had spared no expense. I had just enough time to admire the frosted glass, gleaming chrome, high tech ambiance of the executive area before I realised the executive hall crackled with tension and awkward whispers.

Marsha called me into her office and gestured at the chairs facing her desk. "Welcome. I am not a fan of gossip and you're not to be, either. I know things appear unsettled."

"No more than I am." I sat down. "I'm looking forward to unpacking and digging into orientation information."

"You should know I've let the director of sales go."

"Was there a problem?"

Brief as it was, she studied me. "Emma, I've been brought on board to fulfil an agenda. *Entre nous* You're not to tell a soul but this termination's been in the works for weeks." *Entre nous*?

"Things are going smoothly. I timed pulling the plug to your arrival." She studied me again. "There's another issue, however. One that's less clear. I've been led to believe I might have misjudged you."

I shifted in my seat.

"An old nemesis who disguises herself as a colleague seems to think she's done me a favour by forewarning me. 'Not ready for The Big Apple' is how she put it. '…a reputation for brash behaviour. Disloyal.' Frankly, she's never exactly had my back."

Her phone call was decidedly out of character. I could feel the heat in my face.

Marsha's feet barely touched the floor but she managed to spin in her chair, French twist pivoting in front of me. "Have I hired an incompetent, scheming, Missouri red neck?"

Oh my God. "You're referring to Linda Clarkson. You ask so I'll answer. Linda put time and effort into my training and it paid off. You've seen my resume, the awards for my results. She and Olympia Beauty have profited a lot from my expertise. She's furious, vindictive – I'm appreciative. I was loyal. I gave her everything for five years." We made eye contact. "She's lost the best account executive she's ever had, but it's time I move on from my Midwest territory."

Marsha spun again. "And I can count on that loyalty?"

"Of course."

"Thank you. You're being quite diplomatic, considering." She had no idea how long it had taken me to understand vindictive, snippy, truth telling could haunt me worse than any business foul-up. "I'm aware of her anger, but I'm also aware of what she's losing."

Marsha raised an eyebrow. "I shall remain cautiously optimistic."

The office manager handed me HR folders on relocation services and orientation, then whisked along a two-floor tour covering corporate team introductions to coffee making kitchen rules (four scoops per full a pot).

Veronica Williams, Director of Marketing, took me to lunch. I returned from comfortable chat sprinkled with industry politics to find a third woman waiting.

"Welcome to Platinum. Shelia Bianco, Marsha's assistant." She gestured. "Second best office on the executive floor." Second best and clearly recently vacated. It even smelled faintly antiseptic. Manhattan filled the windows. Cartons and files marked *Emma Paige* sat on the sleek desk in the otherwise sterile space. She smiled. "When you're ready to start house or apartment hunting, let me know and I'll connect you with Platinum's relocation team." She handed me a thin folder.

"You'll need to review and sign this revised employment letter." I skimmed until I hit $105,000 on the annual salary line.

"There's a mistake in my salary."

"No mistake. Marsha increased it this afternoon." She patted my shoulder as I signed, whisked the contract into the folder, and disappeared, closing the door behind her. I sat down and put my head between my knees.

On Tuesday a flower arrangement with "*All best in the city that never sleeps, Love Neil,*" arrived as I hunkered into remaining set-up tasks. Sheila gave me keys to the executive bathroom, a black car service account, details pertaining to my extensive travel budgets, and a fistful of lipstick samples. "*Everlasting Shine,*" she said, "Meant to stay glossy all day, I'm told."

Hall buzz confirmed Marsha was now firing sales people. Jangling, clinking Linda Carlton, had been a belled cat of a boss. By comparison Marsha Johnson glided within the Platinum department like a phantom.

"Emma?"

I spun in my new ergonomic chair and slammed my knee into the file drawer. I rubbed my leg as she asked about the silver framed, eight by ten of Ethan on a pitching mound in wind up position. I fibbed about his career success level and omitted details on the current condition of our long-distance marriage.

"He has my sympathy. I travel about sixty per cent of the time. Of course I don't sit in dugouts all day."

Neither did he by a long shot but I had no idea how to interpret her remark. I offered a chair. "Anything else?"

"You know I hate rumours, yet the gossip mill is churning."

"I might have heard of more firings."

"It's true I've let a number of sales employees go. Dead wood. Unprofessional conduct, negative attitudes, low performance ratings…" She glanced out my bank of windows. "Frankly no style, either. If Platinum is to reign, we can no longer afford mediocrity."

"That sounds like something I should memorise."

"Well, damn right!" She laughed and turned. "That's why they hired me, and that's why I hired you. It can be thankless, but Platinum'll be stronger for it. I come by my grit naturally. I'm a Houston girl, both parents United Oil executives. Their professional success and work ethic set me on this track."

"Like a tick on a hound."

"Well, sugar, you got that right! Let's get lunch."

I chalked up my first forty-eight hours to a dynamic woman moving fast to execute change. Marsha found fault with an alarming number of employees but compared to Linda's hard-edged demeanour, she was downright cosy with me. Her sterile office gave few hints of a personal life but by the end of lunch I knew her parents met at petroleum conference in their late thirties and had their only child at forty-one. She'd never set foot in public school, went east to Wharton for her MBA, and favoured black set off with beige or neutral Manolo Blahniks.

I offered personal tidbits but revealed nothing of substance, a routine I'd started in middle school.

She'd divorced twice, no children by choice. She raised her iced tea. "So here I am: pre-menopausal and at the top of my game. Don't get me wrong, I love men generally. Specifically? Pfft. Occasionally in the bedroom. Rarely in the boardroom."

I settled in, soon forced to navigate Marsha's erratic reasoning that could blur minor afternoon decisions. Having no one to share my suspicion of two martini lunches fuelled my anxiety. I ignored Linda Clarkson's admonitions running in my head. I would not turn tail and bolt. I would not.

I concentrated on my upcoming assignment, getting to know Saks, Bergdorf Goodman, Bloomingdale's, Macy's Herald Square, and Barneys, the city's flagship stores.

"Walking onto the selling floor in Manhattan is like being the lead actress on Broadway," Marsha told me my second week. "Curtain up; out you go. You're there to impress them. You know it; they know it. Quicker than they blink, they size you up. Commit this to memory, Emma: before you can inspire them with your products, they expect to be inspired by you."

I'd come a long way since Andrew Case curated my wardrobe, but Manhattan and Marsha's directives required an upgrade. Retail soothed a host of issues. I enhanced my charcoal grey and black basics, bought the season's freshest blouses, couture handbags, and shoes that looked like works of art.

Marsha prepped me with tidbits and financial back-stories, then extended the mentoring session over drinks Thursday evening in The Oak Room of The Plaza Hotel. "These flagships represent thirty-forty percent of each store's chain business," she added. "I count on you to concentrate on their salespeople with the biggest client books. Shake hands, exchange pleasantries, and get down to business."

I returned to my boutique hotel digging through my purse for my key and came up with Sheila's lipstick samples. "Fuck, fuck," I muttered gin-weepy with nerves as I found the key. What good was any of this without Ethan? Who would keep me grounded? Who'd offer clear-eyed opinions and observations? I wasn't a Marsha Johnson, all class and education. I wasn't even a blustery, self-confident Linda Clarkson, as next week's store visits could prove to everyone. I scrawled DNFUA on the bathroom mirror in *Everlasting Shine's Moonglow Coral.*

I needed a fresh perspective from someone with a soul-deep connection. Andrew Case answered my call on the third ring.

"Emma, my Big Apple heroine!" He mellowed as I filled him in. After exactly the pep talk, I needed on my sales ability angst, he changed course. "So Ethan won't move. What's he hate about relocating? The concept? Getting from Point A to Point B? Leaving the known for the unknown? Scary life in the big city?"

"Probably all of it."

"You can't fight fire with fire. Who can shout louder or come up with the most ultimatums never works. Start with empathy, my Sweet. We know he's not Mr Cosmopolitan. You have me for that." He chuckled. "Figure out what he needs to be comfortable. Get him into his comfort zone with small solutions. This business can eat both of you alive. You must not let it."

"That's why I called you."

"Sweetie, I'll always be your sounding board. But I'm telling you, get that man of yours to see the light. Better still, make him think he saw it on his own."

"He's nursing an injury and sweating the Disabled List which makes his mood even worse, but I'll work on it, I swear."

We hung up. Before I lost my nerve, I memorised an upbeat message and tapped out Ethan's Nokia number. He answered. "Ethan! Well, hi. I didn't think you'd pick up. I've been thinking about your arm. You know, hope it's improving; hope it won't side-line you."

I tried not to fall into our destructive routine. From that first afternoon stomping out of our high school bleachers, it had been a constant go-round of Drama, Accusation, Stand Off, Explanation, Reconciliation; Drama, Accusation, Stand Off…

"It's not much better. How's this week been for you?"

"Pretty good. Monday, I visited our mid-town flag—" Someone shouted his name.

"Damn. Emma, bad timing. I'm late. We'll talk later." Same old, same old.

As much as I doubted my abilities, my first big time visit – Bergdorf Goodman – proved as successful as any during my St. Louis days. I loved the rush of prepping then making an entrance. The grand dame flagships of retail merchandise would fill my week.

On the other hand, the business of business swamped me. Math and chicken scratch notes buried me. As I corrected an order error, Sheila arrived with files I'd requested, I barely acknowledged her. "Thank you, I guess."

"Accountability's never fun." She looked at my photo. "If your baseball player ever needs sports medicine when he moves here, there's an excellent group right over on Columbus Circle."

"Mmmm." I studied the paperwork.

"Seriously," she added from the door. "My son plays NCAA soccer for Fordham. Knees, ankles, elbows, shoulders, they do it all. PTs, orthopaedists, injury specialists. X-rays to MRIs under one roof. For you, too, if you trip in Central Park."

"Shelia!"

"Sorry; I know you're busy."

"No, no, thank you! Ethan… Seriously, thanks a million. I'd love the office address and details. You're a genius."

"That's a first. Make sure to mention it to Marsha." She returned with names and contact info and left me to my plan. Wahoo. I had a carrot to dangle in front of my mule-stubborn husband, the carrot that might get him to Manhattan. After work I grabbed deli takeout. Ethan's recent, almost pleasant tone of voice buoyed my spirits. I transferred my Bergdorf—here's-why-you-stand-to-profit—with—Platinum voice into Ethan—here's—why—you—stand—to—improve—with—New York Orthopaedics. I filled his voicemail. "…an appointment within twenty-four hours… MRI and physical therapists on site…covered by our insurance…professional level sports medicine. Your rinky-dink trainers will be thrilled; no cash outlay for them. Book a flight to LaGuardia. I'll meet you or send a car. Pretend you're Mariano Rivera. You've worked so hard. You deserve the best." I regretted *rinky-dink*, but the rest went well. "Call me ASAP."

He did! His trainer agreed as long as consultation and treatment could be arranged immediately and he was back by Saturday. Ethan would make his own orthopaedic appointment so he could explain his injury. I hung up, joyfully teary-eyed and laughing as I wiped DNFUA off my bathroom mirror.

The next day Marsha called me into her office after lunch.

"I'm sorry," I blurted at her door. "I'm taking care of personal issues. I know you've heard I confused the stats for—"

"—Good lord, sit down. First, never burst into apologies when you haven't been accused of anything. Second, if issues have to do with your move, the sooner resolved, the better."

"They do." True enough in the broader sense.

"And yes, I know about your stats screw up. You need an assistant. I hired you for your potential. I want you out front. We'll bury someone else under paperwork."

Before you could say, "New York minute," I had resumes to consider, and back-to-back interviews scheduled for Thursday. Ethan grabbed a seventy-two-hour turnaround from Tampa, arriving the next morning during my appointment with the big guns at Macy's. I hired a car service and had the driver hold up a contact sign reading: ETHAN PAIGE/MARIANO RIVERA.

My successful store presentations and his orthopaedic workups filled the day. We started the evening chatting as we walked over to Central Park and around Azalea Pond. Ethan's MRI showed minimal damage and he'd booked a therapeutic massage and physical therapy session for the next morning. I landed a significant Macy's order. Ethan paused at a rocky outcropping.

"Will you look at that?"

It looked like our Brucknerfield nook. A bunch of rocks in the middle of Manhattan evoked identical responses in us. Couldn't it be a powerful omen?

We celebrated in bed. whether I pranced around in Victoria's Secret, or bundled up in flannel, sex remained our universal language, even when we were unable to communicate on any other level. Or maybe because of it. For now it served as a reprieve from our stalemate. Before we grabbed dinner, I convinced him to try the claw foot tub. I slid in with him but let him soak in silence.

"My apartment's not working out," he finally said over a beer and lasagna at a corner hot spot. "Brad's a slob and he snores. It's worse than living out of motels."

Progress! "My offer still stands," I replied over the din.

He looked past me. "You know I can't do this."

"I know you'd be away more than here. I'm sorry I made the crack about the living in a family trailer. I love you."

"Whatever."

"Not 'whatever'. Ethan, you know better than I do, you need a home you want to return to."

"Do you mean that?"

"I do."

He fooled around with his pasta. "I have a teammate from Morristown and our rookie outfielder's from Mendham. They swear we can find something more like we're used to than a Manhattan high rise. And close enough so you could commute."

"You've been talking this over?" He shrugged.

"Well, hot damn."

We called a truce. I agreed to consider a rental in an area similar to what he knew and loved. "Similar, Ethan. That doesn't mean double-wides. And no Animal Cracker Park."

Suburban New Jersey wasn't rural Missouri, but his teammates swore it was possible to find something. At two minutes after nine the next morning I threw myself at the mercy of our Human Resources professionals. They assured me their relocation specialists worked with frantic agendas like ours and New Jersey had its share of rolling countryside and small towns.

I gave them Ethan's contact number, told them we wanted a rental with a view of the high school football field, and left for Saks Fifth Avenue. Ethan had two days to pull this off.

I got back to our hotel at seven. "We started in Hoboken and worked our way west," he reported. "The next think I know they're telling me it's Jackie Onassis horse country. The day's one big blur. Brad's right, though, there's some nice stuff out there." His massage and therapy sessions had worked wonders, and he had a full house hunting schedule for the next day.

Thursday as he looked at houses, I looked at potential assistants. My mental light bulb illuminated about 11:30. Fresh out-of-Stanford Dustin Walsh looked like he'd just left a Ralph Lauren photo shoot: prepster with an afro, confidence rather than attitude, top of his class in business and communication. He served a two-year internship at Apple before heading east.

"Apple to the Big Apple," I quipped. "This is impressive, but why your interest in us and the fragrance industry?"

He opened his arms. "I'm black, gay, and pragmatic. I'm interested in business management. There's less discrimination in this branch of trade, commerce and merchandising."

He convinced me but I gave him another ten minutes so we could chat about my responsibilities and how he thought he could enhance productivity. "Before you hear it from someone else," I told him, "I'm a hell of a saleswoman but you'll find me rough around the edges. My grammar's not great and when I'm right, I'm prone to arguing."

"Thanks for that. I should mention I was captain of the debate team, plus Stanford's debate champion two years running."

He grinned. "Fair warning, I win arguments."

I grinned right back. "You've met your match. I've talked my way out of more situations than you'll ever know." We shook hands and I hired him on the spot. He could start on Monday.

Ethan called in about two pm. He'd found a house. Four square antique colonial in need of repair, but, he swore, it had the country charm we loved. A pantry, a fireplace in the kitchen, two and a half bathrooms. Maintained by the owner.

Great landscaping.

"You swear it's not Animal Cracker Park?"

"I swear. It's in Ludlow, out here between Bernardsville and Bedminster. Classy towns, Emma."

"Can you see the football field?"

"Practically. And the baseball field, too."

I wasn't at all sure it was the right place for us, but if it got Ethan with me, I wouldn't raise a bunch of red flags.

"It's right on the train line. Lots of charm, Babe. Hilly and green. Brucknerfield with money and in-ground sprinkler systems."

In yet another New York minute we signed the lease with occupancy July 1. We spent our final night together hashing out details we could control (I'd handle the move), and ignoring those we couldn't (Ethan's team commitment put him on the road until September). And then he was gone. Back to baseball, as determined to make his passion his career as I was to make my career my passion.

By the weekend, between my three successful store visits, Ethan's turnaround behaviour, and Dustin signing on as my assistant, I was nearly terminally exhausted but the happiest twenty-nine-year-old in Manhattan.

Within the industry lack of funding, shortage of raw materials, and any number of other issues often complicate new project manufacturing schedules. During Dustin's first week Marsha called a meeting. Our Milan office announced newly acquired *Salvatore Rosa* fragrance was behind on its development plan, which meant a delay of up to twelve months for the North America launch.

Nevertheless, they requested we meet with the global marketing team. Marsha decided 'we' included Sales Manager, Veronica Williams and me. Dustin helped schedule a ten-day jaunt to Milan with return by way of Paris and London to give us a feel for competitive marketing tactics.

I assigned him my responsibilities and scrambled aboard Veronica and Marsha's International Trek 101, my first exposure to the global scope of the fragrance business and how the Americas stacked up against comparable markets. I'd been at the fragrance industry management level long enough to know the grousing and concern when return on investment comes in lower than projected. Ten days in Europe opened my eyes to the system for senior executives, my crash course in executive perks. As a dedicated, top-level executive with skills equal or greater than most of her male counterparts, Marsha spared no expense. We flew first class in and out of three of the world's most fashionable cities. After the brass tacks business in Milan, we arranged board room conferences with luxury retailers in Paris and London. We stayed in five-star hotels, and ate dinners with A-list wine selections.

We finished with suites at Claridge's. I would have loved to sample their renowned Afternoon Tea but I discovered it was Marsha's domain. Her *Me Moments* Veronica explained, when Marsha met with A-list men. When needed I delivered files and remained standing (un-introduced) at her table only long enough to refresh her memory on random points.

When not in the boardrooms or at tea, we spent more time shopping than even I had imagined. Veronica met my wide-eyed, expressions with a subtle nod or affirmative smile. I splurged on linens for the Ludlow house.

Marsha left JFK airport with two large suitcases. As we prepared for home, she had our Claridge's concierge deliver four additional carryalls to hold the luxury shopping bags we'd gathered. From Via Montenapoleone, to Avenue Montaigne, to Mayfair, she spent thousands of dollars for personal reasons and reported them as business expenses. Marsha Johnson in action as single woman executive was a seminar in itself.

Chapter Seven

As always, I returned to New York anxious over looming responsibilities. Hard as I tried not to look back, I felt like ninth grade Emma O'Farrell holding her breath as she crossed the street to Alexandra's, always half expecting to be turned away. My nearly fatal lack of preparation incident with Linda taught me to be meticulous and swallow my fear of asking for guidance. When I confessed to Marsha about my DNFUA Post-it Notes, she laughed and created a game. She'd name an appointment and goal; I'd have to tell her what facts and references she'd need. "Saks Wednesday to discuss inventory," she'd say. "I scout this week. I provide names of top sellers across the floor, a list of their best-selling products, plus labels."

"Why?"

I grimaced. "Give me a minute."

"Never forget the logic. Knowing the *why* of any task gives you an automatic to do list. It makes the prep much easier."

"Got it. My info gives you the confidential intel to pump your *ask,* your request for more wholesale orders."

"And why do I need more wholesale orders?"

"To make our sales budget." I got a high five.

On the home, and away-from-home fronts, Ethan attributed his improved pitching to proper physical therapy, thrilled it kept him on the roster full time as they travelled all over the Midwest for the season. Meanwhile I arranged Lehigh Valley and New Jersey store appointments via I-78 that let me shoehorn side excursions into Ludlow and get my bearings.

Fieldstone houses, clapboard churches, and brick sidewalks peppered *Brucknerfield with money* in a wide grid of shaded streets bordering an active commercial district. Our c.1860 rental sat down a pea gravel lane, behind a cluster of newer, handsome houses on acre lots. We'd call the rental location 'the back forty' in Missouri; Ludlow called the whole shebang Webster Farms. Twice over lunch in a Victorian inn on the main street, I listened to the whistle as the train arrived on its way into Penn Station. I could make this work.

Next, I squeezed out two personal days to expand the Tuesday Fourth of July holiday, and supervised the move into our Ludlow colonial. Air conditioning consisted of two ancient units in more ancient double hung windows, one in the living room, the other upstairs in the master bedroom. I set them on refrigerator mode and placed fans in the hallways. I survived the heat and set to surviving my new ninety-minute commute.

On Thursday morning Marsha called me into her office. My petite boss, flaming hair and size zero couture, always appeared like a child in oversized furniture. Her physical presence fooled many which I soon realised put her in the perfect position as a powerhouse negotiator.

Without a snippet of small talk the legend offered me a chair. "Our wholesale shipments are behind by over a hundred and fifty thousand dollars. I need you to fix it."

"How can I help?" seemed the correct reply.

"I'm sure you know *Galeries Lafayette,*" the French retailer, took over the Bonwit Teller space on West Fifty-Seventh. "Thank God I did."

"Next to Trump Tower. I've been in. When Bonwit bailed, Mr Trump bought out their lease through the bankruptcy trustee," I added in case this was one of her tests.

"And why?" she asked like the mentor she was.

"He fills the empty space with a lease-paying tenant and raises cash against it."

"Very good."

"I read the *Wall Street Journal* on my morning drive in." She gave me a thumb's up. "Trump's cash poor but his financial problems don't concern us beyond his leasing to tenants we do business with."

"*Galeries Lafayette?*"

"Yes. We're losing the high-end fashion anchors on that chunk of Fifth Avenue to mass merchandise heaven. No complaints; the tourists love them. And this one owes us sales. The boss, Pierre Meysselle, has relocated from Paris."

I could practically see her wheels turning.

"I was in Sag Harbor for the Fourth. As I handed out little flags for the hostess, I was thinking 'Emma, has to get out here'. With or without your ball player, it's an excellent environment for making contacts."

"Thanks for keeping me in mind."

"I offered a darling man a flag. He launched into 'Merci, Mam'selle, but I await my own flag, *le tricolore pour La Fête Nationale, notre jour de Bastille.*' Quintessential Frenchman. He oozes charm like warm butter on a hot biscuit. You're the one to find a way to work with him and solve our problem."

"Not you?"

"I'm too old for him, and I'm due back in Milan without a free hour before I go. It's a feather in your cap, Emma." As long as I didn't become a feather in his. "I'll have Dustin set up a dinner."

"A personal call from you is in order here. It's July; everyone's on vacation but our newcomer Pierre. He has time on his hands, at least before Bastille Day, the fourteenth. Your personal touch and attention could make all the difference." Her smile was not altogether reassuring.

From my earliest fragrance related gigs I'd fended off drunk and sober passes, flirtatious to seriously suggestive. For the unknown Pierre Meysselle, I wanted familiar surroundings. Dustin found me staring at my desk phone. I described my assignment and he handed me the receiver. "Get on it, Boss." I handed it right back. "I swear I'll call. Give me some privacy." It took another twenty-four hours, but M. Meysselle accepted my invitation for Wednesday the twelfth in English laced with *zee accent française.*

Dustin booked a room for me at the St. Regis, a six-minute walk around the corner and just south of *Galeries Lafayette* and dinner at the Plaza's Oak Room. I knew it well by then, just a few blocks north and around the corner.

Even in July a little black dress served the purpose with my Gucci jacket in case the air conditioning was cranked up. As I had anticipated, Pierre, probably ten years my senior, arrived impeccably dressed with a practiced *je ne sais quoi* that drew glances as we were seated.

"A pleasure," he murmured, shaking my right hand a tad too long, despite my wedding band on my left. He glanced from me to the curtained windows facing Central Park. "No view, tonight. From my suite I see the lake and all the splendour."

"Ah, you're living here at the Plaza. Excellent choice."

"*Mais oui, j'accord.* I think so, yes. And you?"

"No. We're in the suburbs." Our waiter appeared and I left it at that.

Dinner was an amiable, delicious three courses with excellent wines. We relaxed into pleasant chat, from Steffi Graff's win at the French Open, to his vinyl record collection.

"I have a bit of everything. Maria Callas, *Madama Butterfly,* to Michael Jackson, *Thriller.*"

"*Thriller.* My sister and I played that LP till I was surprised there were any grooves left."

"And you collect?"

"Hardly. During our moves my mother threw out all my albums and CDs."

"*Quel dommage.*"

I regretted my comment, had no clue what his reply meant, and moved on to the business at hand. I dropped scuttlebutt on The Trump Organization's lease agreement and by the time we finished the main course, he realised I knew *Galeries Lafayette's* international reputation, thought it worthy of our products, and considered it in an excellent Manhattan location. "*Mais oui.* Excellent landlord. I have been his guest at *Mar-a-Lago.*" Pierre feigned intrigue. "*Le Donald* made sure I knew *Mademoiselle Presley et Monsieur Jackson* chose it for their honeymoon." We'd finished dessert and the last of the Merlot.

"Quite the marriage," I motioned for the check.

Pierre leaned in. "Emma, may I suggest some brandy or espresso upstairs? The night is early. Perhaps I play for you some Michael Jackson…"

My smile was genuine. "I appreciate your offer. Forgive the cliché, but mixing business with pleasure is never a good idea."

"But here we sit doing that very thing, *n'est-ce pas?*"

I signed off on the tab comfortable—or buzzed—enough to admit we were. On the ride up in the elevator, just to prove I could be a sophisticate, I added that rather than Thriller, I'd prefer to hear a bit of Madama Butterfly.

His Plaza suite was impeccable, if impersonal. I put my jacket and purse on a club chair and glanced at a grouping of photos on the mantel. Maria Callas broke into *Un Bel Di Vedremo* as he approached from behind and turned me around. Heart breaking music; heart thumping kissing in an embrace so tight it left nothing to his imagination or mine. I pulled away and pressed two fingers against his lips. Melodrama at its best.

"I think you call this French kissing, *oui?*" he murmured in the vicinity of my collarbone.

"Yes, we do."

European superiority oozed as he explained how an affair naturally enhanced business relations. Was I not a savvy New Yorker? Was I not a modern woman who understood these things, even if I had not admitted it at dinner?

"Pierre, you are a very persuasive man."

"Emma?"

"Which is why I'll say goodnight." I offered my hand, determined not to sour the mood. "Indeed, I have business to accomplish and a goal to achieve. It may require more than a dinner, but I'm not offering myself as dessert." I kissed him again, mouth closed this time. "You have been a perfect gentleman. I should not have encouraged you. I'm to blame."

"There is no blame. Emma…"

"I'll see myself out. Stay here, I insist. The concierge will call my car. Thank you for this lovely evening."

"The pleasure remains mine. Now that you see how the French culture works, perhaps I can make you a Francophile."

"I'm not going to have an affair with you."

"All women say that." He opened the door. "At first."

I smiled my most endearing smile. "You're temptation itself, Pierre, but we've begun a business relationship I very much intend to maintain. And, I have a marriage to consider."

He took my hand again. "Ah, *imbécile!*" I yanked it away.

"No, no, I am the fool. *Une promenade dans le parc*—I should have suggested only a walk in the park. I have wasted the pleasure of a beautiful woman's company. We should be under the glow of a full moon *ce soir. Peut-être* over my holiday weekend, together in the Hamptons, as well. *Jour de Bastille.*"

"You, Pierre Meysselle, are the French-est Francophile in Manhattan." I started down the hall only to have him catch up, *Thriller* album-in-hand. "To replace the one you loved."

"Pierre—"

"I leave for my holiday tomorrow evening. If you do not intend to join me and combine business with pleasure, be at my office before noon. We shall see about a substantial order."

The night was balmy; I needed the six-minute stroll to my room at the St. Regis for head-clearing. I didn't look for the moon. I glimpsed waiting carriages along Fifty-Ninth Street, and stared at the album as I waited for the light at Fifth Avenue.

Looking out
Across the night-time
The city winks a sleepless eye…

Michael Jackson's wispy, haunting *Human Nature* banged around in my head as I passed Trump Tower and *Galeries Lafayette.* I was a damn good business woman; Pierre Meysselle's behaviour confirmed it. Would Ethan, so fond of his countless groupies, ever appreciate or even acknowledge my faithfulness? Was his current contentment due to career improvements and a marriage based on telephone calls? Was mine? I entered the St. Regis and headed for my room feeling foolish. And cheated.

I did indeed visit Pierre in his office the next morning. Marsha added Mykonos to her Milan turnaround and after a week away, congratulated me on the sizable *Galeries Lafayette* Pierre placed. Then she dropped into her frazzled, manic mode. We needed four account executives for the northeast, the hardest territory to fill. "Consider it your Priority Number One." Throughout the endless process, Dustin and I bitched about vacationing support staff, swore at the heat, and hired three. As August melted Fifth Avenue, I barked orders for another round of classified ads and inclusion of *Beauty Insider Executive.*

"Yes 'm, Miz Emma."

"Dustin Walsh, that's a racist slur."

"Only when you say it." He dropped into my extra chair.

"I'm broiling and cranky. What the hell is *Beauty Insider Executive?* "

"BIE is a waste-of-money cosmetic industry club. For three hundred smackers a year it promotes beauty products and supposedly helps women secure careers. In my opinion, the most annoying industry executives make up the board so they can hold events and boost each other's egos. Join or find yourself blacklisted." I made us iced coffee. "You need to know BIE promotes extreme political business agendas that make little sense and accomplish less."

A week later he was back at my desk. "Bingo. You may hate B I E, but we've got a live one from the ad." He handed me two sheets. Jennifer Rocket, an account executive for a five-billion-dollar company, included a cover letter with her impressive resume, noting she'd resigned suddenly after seven years. I

95

arranged an interview for the end of the following day. She arrived wilted by the weather, without flash or pizzazz, but well-spoken and enthusiastic. Despite sterling achievements, she'd left due to an abusive boss and was looking for a stable environment. She was a few years younger, with a more conservative management style. She struck me as the complete package. I needed someone to balance my too-often frenetic tempo. I ran her recommendations, and hired her. A few days later I overheard Sheila Bianco compliment my new hires and refer to me as *Mini Marsha.* Marsha replied, "Thank God."

My effort and Marsha's *cautious optimism* paid off. I was an asset, and I intended to remain one. She paid me handsomely in salary and amenities, and had my time and attention 24/7. I sent a healthy check to Genevieve. In the middle of August I turned thirty, successful and self-sufficient. Ethan and I celebrated between his summer and fall line-ups.

By then I'd given up New Jersey Transit. Upon arrival at Penn Station, it required tangling with taxis or the subway system where car service let me adjust my hours to avoid the height of rush hour, waited at my door if I were still scrambling. During my hour of productive back seat time, I now studied financial pages as well as *Page Six* and *The Times.* I added *Fortune* and *Wired* to *Forbes,* plus *Elle to Vogue* and *WWD.* During Ethan's two-week break, Dustin proved a genius at scheduling my on-site appointments west of the Hudson. I was home in time for dinner and Ethan's chatter. He'd introduced himself to the local football coaches and often jogged over to watch afternoon practice.

We explored rural New Jersey on the weekends in a used pickup truck Ethan bought. We hauled rustic chairs and Warren County peaches from a Belvidere flea market, then a Welsh sideboard and blanket chest from two Schooley's Mountain antique shops. My first six months in the big, bad apple passed with Linda's bluster having no effect. She neither popped from the bushes, nor followed up on her threats. I had much to celebrate, a bit to lament, and even more to ponder.

Jennifer Rocket's calm demeanour balanced with solid business perception more than lived up to my expectations. She found her niche in field sales. Dustin Walsh had full permission to correct my grammar but his genius lay in transforming my hand written notes and business knowledge into the impeccable Power Point presentations I was routinely required to give. His two-year Apple internship made him the go-to guy for all of us struggling with technology. He leant his prep skills to anyone in the department needing technical glitch checks, or more important, pre-meeting prep and set-up to insure a smooth presentation to employees and high-end clients. Pierre remained an excellent client, but *all-things Française* in Manhattan failed to ignite the tourists. His company abandoned Trump Tower. *Niketown* moved into the space while I pursued other accounts. Linda Carlton's work ethic and Marsha Johnson's aggressive determination served me well. I still tamped down my prickly side, always mindful of creating an environment of fairness, respect, consistency and security. I made sure everyone, from my Platinum associates to the regional reps, flagship retailers, and those representing us behind their counters, knew how valued they were to the process.

Right after Halloween, Marsha called me into her office. The Energiser Bunny buzzed from bookcase to couch to coffee table. She'd hired a new Vice President of Sales. I would be reporting to him. "He's just terrific. Brian Cox. Terrific talent. Badly needed." She moved a ceramic pumpkin from her desk to coffee table and cocked her head. "I'm trying to read your expression. Annoyance? Shock?"

"This hire's out of the blue, that's for sure." She finally sat down. "You've taken on a much bigger role than I brought you on for, Emma. Let's lighten the load some." I pulled up a chair. "I thought that's why I hired Dustin. We're handling everything."

"No need to get defensive. In the seven months you've been here, *Salvator Rosa* still hasn't had its global launch. Their glitches are to your benefit."

"I haven't had anything to do with the glitches!"

"Relax. I meant the delays have given me time to think. You're too green for the massive responsibilities we were charged with. Brian's in his early thirties. Jumps right in. Already a seasoned pro with experience to oversee global sales." She stood, my signal to retreat. "Terrific talent. You'll thank me, I swear. Brian's coming in so you don't get burned out." The following Monday I hustled through our wide glass doors and down the hall to my office. I froze in my doorframe.

What the fuck?

"Emma! It's nothing—" Sheila Bianco appeared at my side. "Nothing? My shelves are bare. My desk's naked. And you're beet red."

"Don't have a cow. I wanted to get to you before you just plunged in. Marsha asked me to work this weekend to rearrange the deck chairs."

"Deck chairs?"

"Marsha's term for relocating everyone."

"You've been at this all weekend without letting me know?"

"Please relax. You're in the smaller office but it's just to the right of Marsha's. It's closer. Better view, too."

"And here? Let me guess. Brian Cox." Of course, new hire gets it the same way I did when she canned the Director of Sales. Shelia's loyalty to Marsha trumped my anger. "Sorry for the tantrum. This took me by surprise. I'm one hundred per cent behind the decision. Bad commute. Lincoln Tunnel nightmare."

Friday over a bistro lunch, Jennifer asked how I liked my new office. "The bigger issue's the person soon to be in mine. Marsha's convinced we need a Vice President of Sales. She's damned proud of poaching Brian Cox from a competitor."

Jennifer remained thoughtfully quiet.

"Am I boring you?"

"No, no." She skewered a cucumber slice. "To be honest, since I heard the buzz, I've wanted to ask how you know him."

"I don't. Not at all. Do you?"

"Not. A close friend worked for him at Windsor Limited."

"Jen, I'm relatively new to New York. If there's something Platinum or I should know, I'd consider it a personal favour. I always protect my team."

"Nothing scandalous or illegal but Brian Cox has zero people skills and bizarre behaviour. Evil. Scary manipulative."

"Jen? *Evil and Scary manipulative* are strong terms. You can keep this anonymous."

"Thank you. My friend's team reported to him. When a group member laid out a projected sales slump, Brian yelled 'Total fabrication. Just shut up. I can't stand to look at your face. You're useless.' Stomped out of the room, slammed the door... 'My god.'"

"New York's an at-will state and two weeks later she was fired. My friend saw him behave like this more than once. She was so rattled she came to my apartment to talk about it. A group of us used to keep a file of horrendous management types—*I'm So Special; Sixty Hours a Week to Start; Just Let Me Get This Call.* Emma, this guy's in a category by himself. I don't want you in a dicey situation."

"And he starts with us on Monday," I replied.

We hunkered into our coats. I lightened the mood on the walk back to the office with tales of my green-as-they-come Big Apple orientation and the lipstick flaming rooms. Nevertheless, I returned to my desk confused and fearing Marsha had poached from a firm secretly thrilled to get rid of him. Why else would she hire this personality type?

Perhaps Jennifer's friend was difficult; perhaps Windsor was a hostile environment. Should the story surface, no doubt Brian would have his own explanation. What did Marsha know? Worse, what didn't she know? Brian Cox, Vice President of Sales, would inhabit my office. Was my head on the chopping block?

It worried me all the way to our empty, drafty, antique rental. Enthusiasm for the Ludlow commute and living out there alone was fading, exacerbated by Ethan's ever-tenuous career issues. He'd returned to baseball tense and distracted. Even if I could get him to answer the phone, I knew enough not to season this stew with Brian Cox news.

Monday morning car service returned me early. I dressed in vintage black and white Chanel, ready for anything despite my churning stomach and sweaty palms. Gossip and conclusion jumping ran rampant in the fragrance business. I could at least draw my own Brian conclusions.

I arrived to an empty floor with the exception of low voices spilling from the conference room. Marsha's recognizable chat was punctuated by lilting, theatrical directives. "Mark my words, Marsha, oh my very goodness, such, such potential. Absolutely imperative… Marsha, you will be so glad." Our new VP of Sales had arrived.

Chapter Eight

It wasn't in my interest to wait. I needed an immediate face-to face with Marsha. Her facial expressions and body language could clue me into the tete-a-tete. Shelia arrived with Brian still pontificating and I gave her my Marsha request before she'd changed out of her sneakers.

She stepped into her heels. "Why the rush and intrigue?"

"No intrigue. Crushing agenda."

"Anything for Emma," she quipped. "Seriously. Marsha left her morning open for Brian's indoctrination. She has the time; I'll get you in as soon as they finish."

I barricaded myself in my office with a fake conference call to make sure he didn't pop in when he left the conference room. True to her word, about ten o'clock Sheila signalled for me to head next door. Marsha came around and sat in her guest chair beside mine, body language at its most readable: concern. Our small talk and pleasantries slid into industry gossip: Friday's WWD coverage of *Galeries Lafayette's* departure; an upset at Saks' corporate buying office. I treaded carefully. "Marsha, you're the perfect mentor. Thank you for all you're doing for me and my career. You inspire women throughout the industry. I can't wait for our *Salvator Rosa* launch."

"It's my pleasure to help a fellow saleswoman. They tend to be driven, get the numbers. The best CEO's are from sales. You, my friend, will be a president or CEO someday."

"Thank you!"

"Trust me. You're the genuine article with the guts to make it to the highest executive level. No doubt all that talent jumping to my side's what stuck in Linda Clarkson's craw."

Her train of thought and spin on Linda caught me off guard. I slid forward. "That means a lot coming from you. I hope you're right. My goal's to be a vice president."

"You'll get there, trust me. I'll make sure."

"Thank you. I hope your morning conference went well."

"Brian's full of fresh ideas."

Eavesdropping had told me that much. Her enthusiastic, energised expression knotted my stomach. "I also wanted to discuss my career path," I heard myself say. "It's not easy to tell you. I've received a sales vice president offer. Unexpected timing… It's been a wonderful, strong few years but I'm sure you can imagine my concern now that you've brought in Brian Cox. There may be not enough room for both of us."

"You can't resign!" She narrowed her gaze. "You're not going back to Linda? She cannot have you back."

"Linda? Of course not."

"Emma, you mustn't think I've put you in any position that warrants worry. I swear I'm protecting you. Frankly, there're a few things going on with the Italians I can't discuss. I've gone to great lengths to set this up so that if numbers aren't achieved, your lack of experience can't be blamed. You're still a little green, but I see big potential."

I stayed at the edge of my seat. "But you can appreciate that I don't want to become a third wheel."

Marsha paced to the coffee table and back. "I get it. How about I increase your salary to one hundred and fifty thousand dollars, and elevate your title to National Sales Manager?"

"Goodness. I'm honoured you feel this strongly about me." I meant it and I damn sure wanted to believe she did, too.

"I've informed Brian you're a dotted line directly to me. He'll be concentrating on other aspects of the VP position. You're not his focus. We laid it out this morning. Call me selfish but we'll be a good team."

I sat back. "We do make a good team. Will you make sure Brian's aligned with my new role?"

"Consider it done."

"Then consider me staying."

Marsha put her hands on her hips. "Now go tell whoever's trying to steal you away from me, you're not for sale." Shelia appeared as if she'd had her ear to the door. "Okay ladies, time to get back to work."

Marsha told her to set up a meeting with Brian at five thirty. I returned to my office turning internal cartwheels, still awestruck at my gumption and the deal I'd brokered for myself. I updated my team and still avoided him.

Sales and marketing reps are often at each other's throats. Marketing people, Type Bs, give little attention to numbers. I exemplify the high expectation, aggressive Type A sales representative. Nevertheless I asked Veronica Williams, our marketing director, to lunch for much needed team camaraderie.

Marsha pushed her daily for more analytics and I'd recently received comparable business information from a friend at a competitive company. Over lunch I passed Veronica detailed info she could use to impress Marsha and shared enough on our new colleague to make her wary.

Brian's most daunting aspects was second-hand info and he deserved a chance to make a good impression. Late afternoon I sent him a welcome email suggesting a morning meeting to go over the exciting business we'd be working on together. Any new employee fares best in a private, welcoming atmosphere and I could assess for myself.

He confirmed. Dustin and I collated reports, field staff names, wholesale and retail numbers, and a Strength, Weakness, Opportunity, Threats-SWOT-report. As the well-trained prodigy of Linda Clarkson and Marsha Johnson, I left nothing to chance. While Linda epitomised the adage: *know the rules before you break them*, whether gay, straight, male or female, de rigueur wardrobe panache defines the fragrance industry. From eavesdropping I expected Brian to exemplify industry cliché, a spiffy Andrew-Dustin combo of impeccable style and industry enthusiasm.

The following day I waited in the conference room wearing Donna Karan and my best neutral expression. He shuffled into the room, five feet, eight inches of heft wedged into a Sears-issue suit, polyester tie, black shoes and brown belt. Sweat beaded his upper lip and a full set of orthodontic braces wired his smile making him look even younger than early thirties. The shock brought me up so fast I knocked my flip phone off the table. After making a production of checking it for damage, I closed the door and rambled about his experience and how lucky we were to have such a pro joining our team.

I passed him copies of the files and dug into reviewing key points and team details. "Please let me know if any of this is repetition," I said as his expression shifted from bored to inattentive. "Veronica Williams can be a great help with analytics." I rattled papers. "Brian? I'm concerned. No notes, no questions. Has

Marsha already given you these stats?" He shook his head but my reviews appeared to be torturing him. Body odour wafted through the room and he gleamed with perspiration. Maybe he was having a heart attack. I opened the door. "Are you Okay, let me get you some water."

"Water would be nice. I'm okay; anxiety makes me to sweat."

An anxiety attack! I softened. He excused himself to use the restroom which gave me time to turn down the heat and grab a pitcher of water from the kitchen. When he returned, I handed him a filled glass. "I struggle with anxiety, too. I've had some awful attacks. They can be terrifying."

"For god's sake. Do I look terrified?"

"No. Of course not. I just thought—"

"It's none of your business! I'm absolutely fine."

All right then. We sat down. I broke the silence by returning to the net sales plans and my team hierarchy. "Of course Shelia's the go-to person for Marsha, especially if you have schedule questions."

I reached the innocuous when Mr Hyde turned into Dr Jekyll. "Why would I have questions? Why wouldn't I know her schedule?"

"Excuse me?"

Suddenly Brian didn't like our chain of command. Did I not understand he would deal directly with Marsha, not Shelia? He shook a file at me. He wanted everything printed in colour. "My last visit to Saks was a total, total disappointment. Terrible counter team. Inefficient, condescending snobs. This cannot possibly be news to you."

"One at a time, Brian. Your Saks information is, indeed, news. I'd like specifics so we can address this."

"Condescending snobs!" He digressed into flamboyant monologue, mincing, ranting but never making solid points.

I thanked him, gathered and offered the papers for him to keep. "My assistant Dustin keeps abreast of my schedule."

"Dustin! And what, what, is the situation with that man?"

"Situation? He's a quick study, bringing fresh perspective."

"Well, he doesn't bring coffee. We're to share him. I made that very clear, asked him to get a simple cup of coffee and he turned aloof and uppity."

Sharing Dustin? If true, Brian had wormed the agreement out of Marsha. I mentioned his credentials. "He's likely to be promoted quickly. Dustin's fast tracking to the next level."

"That's jumping the gun, plain and simple. And no doubt he'll expect an increase in pay. I am not fond of awarding additional salary to someone new to the beauty business. He's curt, condescending, and certainly not accommodating. When I asked that simple favour, he sat and stared at me," I chuckled.

"You find this funny?"

"He's a hard worker with specific thoughts on what's appropriate. I've been known to get him a cup of coffee."

"That sets dangerous precedent. He doesn't know his place."

"Many of today's topics and these printouts were his idea. Personal tasks for us are not in his job description. There's no need for alarm."

"I don't appreciate taking sides against me or your condescending attitude."

He'd used *condescending* four times in five minutes. I held my tongue, and hid my alarm. "We're all adjusting to each other and the demands of this company, but we're on the same team. We've gone over enough for now."

"That will be my decision."

"I should continue?"

He downed his water. "No. I must get back to my office. This has been informative but I don't have all day to chat." I shook his damp hand. "I look forward to our teamwork."

"I certainly hope so. We have work to do." Over lunch I filled Dustin in and reassured him that neither his work ethic, nor attitude needed changing. Under no circumstances did I support bullying in the work place. "I'm not rattled by tantrums and hissy fits," he said.

Ethan's winter break began in time for Thanksgiving. I was gone all day and he hobnobbed with the Ludlow high school football coaches. Our steam radiators clanked and the windows rattled but the chimney needed re-pointing which rendered our four fireplaces deficient and useless.

I feared the same about Brian. His approach to the team Marsha and I had in place plagued me. Merchandising to marketing, he talked a good line, but his aloof demeanour, rude behaviour, and barked orders smothered flashes of competence. Bloomingdale's to Macy's, I steeled myself for our store visits. He did everything but drape himself over the counters. An oversized cashmere dress coat, complete with white silk scarf, covered his considerable bulk.

Amid the Christmas shopping mania in Nordstrom's, he put his hand right over the salesman's, pointed to our latest cellulite cream and asked for a sample hand massage. "Make me a believer, as if I appear attentive but you sense there'll be no sale." At Saks it was our beauty serum. His wink-and-a-nod routine ended with a little smirk. "If I may be of any help, my door's always open." I might as well have been invisible. Meanwhile, amidst the wafting Christmas carols, store reps he wasn't trying to seduce took me aside. While reluctant to admit they needed verification or explanation, did I know Brian's directives seemed incomprehensible, or flat out wrong? Marsha and others at high levels appeared convinced his experience and solid work ethic would show results by the end of the fiscal year. I'd have called his routines fragrance industry as Fantasyland but second-guessing Marsha was neither smart nor practical. From the back seat of my town car, pivoting in my desk chair, or running errands in Ludlow, I stewed. Would I be *persona non grata* for expressing my concern, or *persona non grata* for keeping it to myself?

Ethan and I flew home to the usual dysfunctional Christmas. Dad schlepped in loose slippers, no longer hiding his wheezing. I made Darby swear he'd keep his eye on the family and slipped a generous check to Genevieve. Half a day in the house reminded me how critical my employment was, Cox conundrum or not.

I bit the bullet the second week of 1996. Thursday Brian and I had retail visits across the Hudson at The Mall at Short Hills. I asked him for a drink Tuesday afternoon. We chose Happy Hour at *Rue Fifty-Seven Brasserie,* and over the din I chatted about our career paths, keeping my own information brief and upbeat. I touched on my St. Louis days, mostly Linda's successful approaches at Olympia.

He downed his first apple martini while bemoaning his middle-class Cincinnati upbringing, and the high school gay bashing. "Of course I persevered." He snapped his fingers. "Shoe buyer. High, high-end. Gucci, Ferragamo, Cole Haan... Downtown Gidding-Jenny. Of course you know their history."

"No, sorry I don't."

"Well, my, my goodness. Emma Paige in her Stuart Weitzman and Louboutins doesn't know Cincinnati's iconic emporium?" He knew my shoe brands? He'd been stalking my feet? "...next door competitors back in the day. They merged. Fabulous, fabulous historic building right down town. Rockwood Pottery on the exterior... They loved me. Loved me. But I met Mr Right and we were off on a grand adventure."

By then he was off on his second martini while I'd sipped about a third of my one and only.

"Kansas City. Hall's housewares buyer. Hello gold rimmed latte bowls, everything Cuisinart. I revitalised the entire department. I stocked the best and you've never seen such staging. Cooking classes, table setting demos. Queen City's snootiest knocked down our doors to buy, buy, buy. Very tough industry. What I did for *Mauviel* fish poachers… You cannot imagine the vagaries of housewares." Yes, I could but I let him ramble.

"The antithesis of fragrance, I can tell you. Slam, bam. No subtleties. Work. Work. work. Then Mr Right turned out to be so, so wrong, a cheating, two timing slime ball. Did that stop me? You bet your sweet ass it did not."

Brian was fond of his own voice, yet somehow, he'd eaten the entire contents of the pretzel bowl. He sipped and explained he'd ditched the two-timing slime ball and found the right partner in New York. ("My 'Daddy Steve'. Older and wiser. Solid, solid"). He interviewed for luxury, luxury, Windsor Limited, and made the leap. (Perhaps out of a fish poacher).

"So here I am, based in our Big Big Apple for five years."

Long enough for his meltdown and destruction of Jennifer's friend, I thought.

"Representing Windsor sent me all over the map overseeing our foreign markets. On the fly constantly. Major Italian launch. *Tutta Italia, Venezia a Napoli*. Once you get some experience under your belt, I'll have to take you over there. We'll set up some Amalfi gigs. To die for!"

I had no idea how much truth supported his information, but he rambled and I studied him. With nearly every personal triumph he listed, Brian threw a personal dig or dagger about my knowledge, talent, or expertise.

"Then bingo," he added. "Marsha had to have me at Platinum, A S A P. (ah shish ape ee). Such a wide range of experience. Emma, I am so ready to take the pressure off your shoulders and bring Platinum the glory it deserves. Professionally I am at the top, top of my game."

Top of his game, bottom of his third martini. I called for the check. He oozed himself into a cab; I took the town car home to Ludlow under the glow of my light bulb moment. Brian Cox had convinced Marsha Johnson to bring him in as a Vice President with the sociopathic, *Here's what I know – You know nothing* behaviour that shaped my childhood.

Thursday Marsha and Jennifer departed to bounce around snowy New England on routine first-of-the-year inventory visits.

I got into work early, ran routine business past Dustin, then left with Brian for Short Hills, New Jersey.

The mall, renowned for its Fifth Avenue stores, had just completed another major expansion and Platinum had substantial accounts with all four anchors: Bloomingdale's, Macy's, Nordstrom, and Neiman Marcus. Classical music filled the sound system while Tiffany's to Crate and Barrel, Armani to Polo Ralph Lauren, Kenneth Cole, DKNY, Betsy Johnson, and Max Mara beckoned. Ethan and I lived just thirty minutes farther west, knew it well, and used it often.

A white dress shirt with properly knotted rep tie peeked from Brian's overcoat. The braces were off his teeth which allowed him to chew Tootsie Rolls and Kraft Caramels obsessively. As we passed Foot Locker, I pointed out Reeboks Ethan had purchased.

"Jesus, enough with your idle chit chat." He shoved his first candy wrapper into his pocket. "We do not care about Ethan and his Reeboks. Yes, we know you're familiar with every little nook and cranny in here. On point, Emma. Stay focused."

"You're right." Kowtowing worked every time.

"Thank you. I've been here without you even before I was your boss. Windsor's huge at Neiman's. Huge. As for Platinum, I've worked my ass off for three weeks to establish rapport with our Short Hills managers."

I knew that to be entirely false.

We'd been drinking coffee so we found the restrooms which gave me time to pee and count to one-hundred. Ten minutes later on he went with his plan for the day. If I were needed, he'd let me know. We were not to get off point by discussing topics unrelated to fragrance, sales or markets. As we reached the Nordstrom wing, he instructed me to check on the counter displays while he met with the purchasing rep.

"That's not protocol."

"You're contradicting? I am vice president for a reason." His glare startled me into silence. If I weren't included in these scheduled strategy sessions, why was I here? At Nordstrom's I followed orders and stayed on the floor. A handsome twenty-something salesman popped up from stocking Platinum counter shelves and reported that our body wash practically sold itself.

He leaned in. "Brian Cox saved my ass. I was brand new, doing things old school, standing out front of the counter where you are. Thank god he explained I was to stay here, behind the glass, not out blocking the view. 'It's all about

product. Draw them in, drawn them in.' You know what? He saved my job."
Brian just now meeting the reps had apparently already checked out the counter
boys. I tried not to think about the hand massages.

"The next thing I knew, he invited me to dinner."

"Dinner?"

"At his apartment? Pre-War Delancey. Totally cutting-edge decor. Seriously,
he does high-end design if fragrance doesn't work out. I had fabulous salmon
with them. Daddy Steve, as he's called, is an amazing cook. Great guys, both of
them. Brian gave me so many hints and tips. Platinum is so lucky."

"Thank you," I managed. Brian wanted the sales crew behind the counter?
Sales people were to be on the outside greeting customers, glass cases seen as a
barrier. Brian's directive ignored protocol and placed unproductive distance
between seller and consumer. Marsha would have a hissy fit.

And so it went. By the time we hit Macy's, he either felt more confident in
me or less confident in himself. Now I was to attend the session.

Ten minutes in, Brian's commentary subtly dissolved into smoke and
mirrors. He discussed any topic—new hires, projected sales, our manufacturing
centres—superficially then defer to the buyers. He let the employee digress so
he/she led the conversation in another direction. Next, he opened subjects, and
ask me a question. He repeated my replies and encouraged me to continue.
Psychiatry *Modus Operaendi* 101. Brian had obviously been in therapy. Not
successfully.

And then he got hungry. Since our arrival, he'd consumed more sugary,
gooey junk than a ten-year-old on Halloween, but our last conference dragged
into early afternoon. The mall restaurants bustled but he seemed edgy, anxious
to grab something elsewhere. I had the car deliver us to neighbouring Summit
Diner Ethan and I discovered. The funky landmark provided a safe topic for chat
and booths for privacy.

"Back in a minute," he muttered and headed for the rest rooms. Dr. Jekyll
returned as lunch arrived. Brian bit into his Taylor ham and cheese sandwich and
licked yoke off his fingers.

"Do not ever do that to me again. Ever."

I looked into the stare from hell. "Do what?"

"Jesus, Emma, don't pretend you don't know. You made me look like an
idiot in front of Jerry Kovac."

I wracked my brain. "Bloomingdale's buyer?"

"Bloomingdale's buyer?" He chirped with his mouth full.

"Don't play stupid and don't ever correct my stats in public."

"Correct you? I asked which products lead counter sales."

"And made me look ill prepared."

I tried to change the subject. Brian stayed on point, careening into behaviour I'd endured at our office intro. I apologised, back peddled, and flattered. Thanks to everything holy, he ranted at low volume through gritted teeth. "Make me look bad and your inexperience reflects on Marsha and Platinum." He finished his lecture and sandwich. I left my BLT untouched and suggested we find our town car. Our driver's cheerful greeting at the curb was lost as Brian yanked open the back door and wedged himself in, another Tootsie Roll already stuffed into his mouth. I tapped the front passenger window. "Brian's going to head back. I've got a splitting headache. I'll finish up at my home office."

Over "Sure thing," from the front and, "What the fuck," from the rear, I stepped through the snowy mush, hunkered into my down coat, and disappeared around the corner toward the Summit train station. In twenty-degree wind I rewound my pashmina, but my head was bare and my kitten heeled boots pinched. My phone nearly froze to my ear as I trotted the long block. I dialled and redialled Ethan. No answer; left a message. My bone chilling fury erupted as sobs. I stood at the crossing light, stared at the coffee drinkers in the Starbucks window, and turned for the station. It should have been Brian on New Jersey Transit to Penn Station and me driven home in the Lincoln. I caught the Gladstone Branch two-fourteen to Ludlow. Ethan got my message and met me on the platform.

Routines help. The next morning, coffee-in-hand, I stared out my office window prepared to address office minutia, and two emails from Nordstrom questioning Brian's directives.

"Hair of the dog?"

I jumped. "From yesterday? Dustin, I wish. Cold sober is no way to spend time with that heinous, stupid, overbearing, narcissist."

"You may want grammar corrections from me but there's nothing wrong with your vocabulary."

I expected a laugh but he stayed thoughtful. "Emma, you know Brian's digs are disguised as offhand comments. When he got back here yesterday, he implied your two-martini lunch got the better of you and he had to send you home early."

"Oh my God, oh my God. I had coffee in the morning and Sprite at the Summit Diner while that bald-faced sociopath devoured his lunch. Now I discover he's confused our Nordstrom floor manager. I swear he snorts coke in the restrooms."

Chapter Nine

The powers that be finally named the *Salvador Rosa* fragrance *Charade* as we settled into massive planning mode with prestige retailers in North and South America. We scheduled the global press event launch at the Guggenheim Museum during New York Fall Fashion Week. Advertising and creative backstory would emphasise 1940's vintage fashion and Henry Mancini's music.

Marsha did indeed travel nearly sixty percent of the time. She and Brian maintained separate out-of-the-office schedules. For all I knew, by design. With the *Charade* launch looming, she spared no expense taking me as National Sales Manager to meetings with Platinum's largest retailers, prestige department stores, and highest profile designers and CEOs.

Our Midwest turnaround jaunts were familiar, of course. But LA, San Francisco (and Rodeo Drive side trips to upgrade my wardrobe) kept me breathless. I gained invaluable exposure, watched this pro at work, mastered the business lunch and deals over dinner. Marsha was the reason I rose so high so fast.

Pleasing Marsha remained Priority One, despite anxious moments when her padded expense accounts or aggressive behaviour ignited flashes of my rules-bending childhood. Platinum employed me at her behest; I was wary but not unwilling. Although none of my winter-into-spring Manhattan appointments had the pizzazz of my Pierre Meysselle evening, Dustin continued to arrange hotel rooms when events kept me in the city. Ludlow was losing its appeal and until Ethan left again for spring training, he often joined me.

Months of Brian in this mix strained everything from decorum to deception. He grandstanded endlessly, inflating sales and fabricating personnel contacts. If his advice resulted in mistakes, he routinely inferred I held some responsibility. When Jennifer Rocket discovered a counter rep in her New England district masterminding fragrance fraud, she orchestrated a risky sting in the high-end

Connecticut store, and quietly removed the culprit. She never alerted Brian. He would be held accountable and use it against me.

Less than a month later she insisted on lunch outside the office. "You know how Brian raves about Daddy Steve and their domestic bliss. Saturday, I went gallery hopping with old roommates in our old Chelsea neighbourhood. What are the frigging chances I'd be standing at the light on Tenth and he's leaving the 'spa' behind me?"

She made air quotation marks and looked at the ceiling.

"It's a cover for a notorious gay brothel. We locked glances and Mr Pillsbury Doughboy fell into full Smokescreen Mode, red as a sweaty beet." She grew serious. "He babbled his head off. Steve had asked him to check on a painting for their living room… He couldn't find the gallery… He'd thought someone at the spa desk could give him directions. Did I love watercolours as much as he did? Was that me at MoMA Thursday night?"

"Emma, I wanted to be anywhere but there. Now I know his creepy little secret. You can bet our *Charade* launch he assumes I've told you. Don't be surprised if he's even more paranoid."

"Or vindictive," I replied. "This stays between us. Period. No Dustin, no Sheila or Veronica. It's a private matter and knowledge could blow up in their faces if he decides to scream harassment or a million other things, he's capable of." She crossed her heart.

Brian's solution seemed to be increased travel with Sheila as our go-between. All fine with me. In early March he interrupted my desk-side conference with Marsha. "Can you believe it?" he chirped as he entered without knocking. "Just back from LA. Our retailers are coming to blows over who's to have *Charade* first. Had to share! One even hinted they'd attempt to block, block competitors from selling it at the same time." Marsha swivelled in his direction. "Very flattering but of course Platinum has major sales targets to achieve. You know it's impossible to exclude any large luxury accounts."

"Well, of course I do." Did he?

"Just thought I'd share the excitement." He left as abruptly as he'd arrived. Marsha returned to our business so I kept doubts to myself. One more situation to keep tabs on. We did give Saks New York a two-week lead. For all other accounts we scheduled shipping dates to ensure by fourth quarter the fragrance would be located front and centre in case-line, étagères, shop-in-shops and installations. At a cost of nearly one hundred and twenty-five thousand dollars per store, *Charade* would launch in fifteen full installations throughout North America.

The morning Brian noted his sixth month Platinum anniversary by distributing cupcakes embellished with *BC-6*, Dustin entered my office and closed the door. "There's too much of a pattern not to share this with you."

He opened his customary file of expense reports. "Yours, Emma, cut and dry, per usual. Our esteemed Vice President Cox? He expects Platinum to cover Rodeo Drive men's beauty products, South Beach spa treatments, six bottles of Sonoma Cabernet Sauvignon, dry cleaning on Boston's Newbury Street, airline kennels, and canine tranquilisers."

"Apparently Daddy, Steve pays his own way, but the dog does not," I said.

"And this is just his American Express company card."

Dustin studied me. "Since he enjoys treating me as he's an errand boy, you should know twice I've stumbled over loaded flasks, one in a coat he had me take to the dry cleaner. A different one's in his desk drawer next to the calculator he sent me to get."

"You are not to handle his dry cleaning!"

He waved it off. "I don't need a Stanford business degree to know he's a risk in every way imaginable. Dicey as hell emotionally and professionally. This affects us."

"No more errands, Dustin! For now, complete the expense reports. Include mine, then leave both in the CFO's in-box." Brian was not the only one padding expense reports. For all

I knew, Marsha turned a blind eye to this MO. Despite the Chelsea spa episode and six months of his smoke and mirrors, I needed visits with him to flagship stores in the New York City market. It grew imperative to see first-hand how much he honestly knew about driving retail.

We worked the day-to-day business. Our major launch requirements gelled. Visuals were set. Store teams scrambled to involve all departments within every retailer. When I discovered Brian adding costly events without Marsha's approval, I recorded details and backed up my notes, and practice learned from my ever-vigilant and covert boss. Did our CEO realise how much she needed to know about her hire?

A week later as I reviewed my punch list for setting up one of Brian's presentations, Sheila appeared at my door. "Marsha's concerned we're understaffed in a number of markets. Brian's on the floor today, too, so she wants to discuss it in the conference room."

"When?"

"Ten minutes."

My startled expression got only a shrug and, "Good luck." I arrived to find Brian in mid-sentence with Marsha. He motioned to a chair. "Marsha confirms we're losing store people she's known for years. Her confidential field checks confirm – sorely understaffed on the heels of this big event."

"I can speak for myself," Marsha said. "You know as well as I do, we're approaching the monumental undertaking for which I was hired." She glared at both of us.

I slid her my file. "The right staffing has always been my number one concern."

"Then why should I suddenly discover low numbers? I expect seasoned professionals at every level, perhaps the most critical right smack at the fragrance counter." She flattened her palms on the table. "This ship floats or we drown."

Brian excused himself. Marsha stared at our paperwork; I watched the sheeting rain distort the view. He trotted back smelling of mouthwash, and unwrapped a Kraft caramel. Marsha swatted it out of his hand. "We are so close to launch; this situation stands to jeopardise our projections."

"Then let's look closer," Brian said. "It's all about alliance and camaraderie. Frankly, I have serious doubts about Jennifer's handling of her territory. And it's no news our entire New York team's weak, weak, weak."

"You've met the new hires. They're working well," I said.

"Shipping's down but retail sales are up twenty-five percent. I've also improved brand exposure with the store managers."

"'People, Presence. Product, Promotion.' I know the drill." Brian knew the slogan. But if shipping's down and retail's up, someone's not getting their due from the buying office. He was the first line of communication for buyers. Couldn't Marsha see our clients were dealing with an ass?

Another nugget from my days with Linda: Buyers who commit to programs that don't deliver will cut the orders just because they can. As Vice President Brian outranked me and could hide this situation even from Marsha.

"Yes, you restructured less than a year ago." He glanced at me. "But much of the numbers blame lies right here within certain departments on this floor. I can only accomplish so much when I'm thwarted at every turn."

Marsha scowled. "It's impossible to replace key players this close to the launch. For now you work with them. Whatever it takes. Tomorrow Filene's buyers will be down from Boston specifically for your review and presentation, Brian. They're expecting good news, high anticipation."

He face glistened. "And they'll get it. I have the visuals all designed and ready, plus handouts with specifics right down to *Gift With Purchase* ideas. Filene's gets excited, writes a booster order for stores ASAP, and the GWP boosts our Q Four. We add a promotion to hike up shipments and push retail sales trends even higher."

He was quoting the manual but it beat his previous Jekyll and Hyde behaviour.

Marsha gathered her paperwork. "Whatever it takes from both of you, sales goals are to be over-achieved at every venue. Now stop wasting my time and yours." She stormed toward the door. Brian huffed his way behind her but stepped on the caramel, hopped and yanked his shoe. "I'm sure you find this hilarious."

"No, not at all." I did, but I replaced my contempt with ego polishing. "Look, we both need Marsha happy and satisfied. I assure you my team and I'll have this room set up perfectly for your presentation, from handouts and their goodie bags, to your bottled water." I leaned in, the complete conspirator. "You can see how much pressure Marsha's under."

"We all are. Pressure, pressure, pressure," he muttered.

"Have Dustin double check your Power Point."

"No Dustin necessary. Thank god I'm a perfectionist. I've put together an excellent presentation. You know all things technical are my specialty. Of course you'll have the screen set up, connector cable, projector…"

"Of course."

"I do appreciate your little group preparing the room."

"Thank you. Let me know by the end of the day if there's anything else." Little group, hell. He went back to caramel removal and I went back to my office, teeth gritted.

The next afternoon I met Jennifer and our Filene's buyers for lunch. I enjoyed and respected these savvy women, major players who set the pace in her New England region. While we settled into the conference room, One-man-band Cox moved from goodie bags to his laptop. "Lights, Emma," Brian sang, the moment Marsha made her perfectly timed entrance.

The room went dark and a beige out of focus image filled the entire screen. Out of focus *Charade* promo? Brian shrieked. My FFA husband would have identified it as the squeal of a stuck pig. The rest of us gasped. The image sharpened into a close up – an extreme close up – of an erect penis. Possibly two. "Oh my God. Oh my God. Oh my God. I am so terribly sorry. I—This—" He slammed his laptop shut. "Sabotage! This is someone's terrible, terrible idea of a prank to ruin me." I turned on the lights.

"Us, to ruin us. All of Platinum. And *Charade*. Someone's—"

"My office. Now." Marsha, impeccably cool in her fury, pointed from Brian to the door. She turned to the speechless Filene's group.

"I am terribly, horribly sorry. Please disregard what you've seen, if that's at all possible." To Jennifer and me she hissed,

"Pick up the pieces."

The room remained silent as she herded Brian out the door. "Never in my entire career…anything so unprofessional…no words…" and, "Gone! …out of here for the rest of the day," trailed behind them.

I looked back to the table of women. "We work to keep Platinum the talk of the town, but that opening was not what I had in mind."

The head buyer shook her head. "I thought I'd seen it all with Brian Cox."

Her assistant nudged her. "You mean all of Brian's cocks."

"Betsy!"

"Well, he's always seemed an odd duck."

"Odd dick. Odd dicks," a third said.

The room erupted. I finally blinked the lights, choking back my own laughter. "Let's take a breather to get this under control." Truth be told, I could have come up with a million more hilariously derogatory one liners.

Five minutes later our whirlwind in high heels returned to the head of the table. "Ladies, what do you think of our new advertising campaign?" shifted into a deep, professional apology, then right back to the business at hand. As the meeting concluded an hour later, Sheila appeared with replacement goodie bags double the size of those on the table.

Marsha thanked them a final time. She finished as the consummate pro, doling out tidbits of *Charade* chatter, insider launch scoop, and a promise to underwrite a Ladies Night during her next Boston visit. Before the elevator of Filene's reps hit the lobby, Marsha'd instructed Sheila to set up a meeting with HR and ushered me to her office.

"What do I really need to know about Brian and sabotage?" I remained standing. "Marsha, the closest anyone could come to sabotage would be unplugging him or messing with externals. He considers himself a technical expert. Dustin, anyone in IT, even Jennifer and Veronica will tell you *no one* is allowed to touch his computer. He sets up every presentation himself. The porn downloaded into it is his and his alone."

I ached to add that the sociopath was drinking at his desk and possibly snorting coke in the men's room. He fabricated reports and padded expense accounts. He remained aloof to disguise his incompetence. He'd had it in for me since I'd first suspected, and doubled down since he'd run into Jennifer outside the brothel. I kept it all to myself. Marsha had hired him, given him key responsibilities he was clearly unqualified for, turned a blind eye, and kept him on despite the obvious. At that moment I realised she had enough to answer for.

As expected, by Rush Hour the following morning Platinum was electric in its silent SNAFU. "The old *In and Out*," Sheila reported. "Marsha and reps from the CFO office met with Legal and HR last night. They terminated Brian at eight this morning. Gonzo by eight-thirty to keep the gossip down." She grinned.

"Fat chance. By the way, you can have your old office back."

"No way in hell," I replied.

After a year's delay and countless organizational shifts, the *Charade* launch left zero time to dwell on anything but final details of the global press event. The flood of Brian gossip dried to a trickle.

In October Fashion Week transformed Bryant Park into its famed tent shows. A-List fashion VIPs, from luxury retailer CEOs and editors Anna Wintour and Muriel Beausoleil, to Andre Leon Talley and celebrities filled our Guggenheim guest list. The foreign and domestic fashion press would happily follow the herd from the park to the famed Upper East Side museum. Industry buzz told us our *Charade* was the most anticipated fragrance event in past thirty years. As frosting on the cake, three Salvador Rosa originals arrived at our office, made to our dimensions. His couture guaranteed Marsha, Veronica, and I would be as *au courant* as the fragrance.

And then it was Launch Day. Marsha spent most of her time in the conference room with our CFO preparing for the board meeting scheduled for the next day. When we'd dressed for the event, Marsha asked Veronica and me to join her, the public relations team, finance department reps, and our Chief

Operating Officer. Sheila worked her magic with flowers, light canapés, and glasses of bubbling Tattinger. Toasts, sips, and we were off to the Guggenheim.

We mingled, networked, and accepted compliments from suppliers, colleagues, as well as celebrities in every fashion, fragrance, design, and client category. Air kissing and glad handing took place to pose and snap as hundreds of international photographers clicked away.

As luck would have it, Marsha finished murmuring one of her directives to Jennifer and me at the moment Carolina Hererra approached with Muriel Beausoleil. Marsha introduced us during more pose and snap. As they wandered away, one of the photographers, all pony tail, designer Chelsea boots, and state of-the-art cameras, lingered. "Thomas Schuman. Yours for the evening, ladies," he said. "I'm shooting your gig for M. Beausoleil, in fact several global clients, agencies, the trades—WWD…" He and Jennifer exchanged cards after intriguing conversation left the impression, he recognised Platinum as future potential.

The Schuman shot of our fragrance visual merchandising made the cover of *Women's Wear Daily.* Within the week Jennifer received two five by seven candids from him, one of Marsha and Anna Wintour, the other Muriel Beausoleil and me. I framed and propped it on my desk within the month. Gut instinct? Valuable resource.

Bergdorf Goodman and Saks New York presales came in above our projected goals, breaking records for the biggest launch at all Manhattan retailers. Marsha was thrilled—and thrilled with our team effort. It wasn't until I'd settled in the back seat of my town car and kicked off my shoes that I realised how relaxed and confident I'd been without Brian Cox at my elbow. For the first time in my career, I'd had a situation that resolved itself. He would not be missed.

I arrived at Ludlow close to midnight to find Ethan waiting up. He kissed me. "Babe! I made it work! …new Southwest Indie league starting up…based in El Paso…very decent offer…" I fired up a sincere smile and kissed him back. Ethan's elation said it all. I didn't share his enthusiasm but he needed to play and this was likely his last chance. He had a week to prepare and I pledged my complete support. Marsha revealed her human side, thanked me for all things *Charade* and Guggenheim, then granted me time off with Ethan before the long, lonely autumn ball season kicked in.

Ludlow was an issue. We'd made the best of the charming, isolated house but the winter of record-breaking snow topped the troubles list. I wanted no more living alone out there, either. While the El Paso departure clock ticked, we found our solution close to my boutique hotel and Lobel's Meat Market I knew he'd adore. The eighteen hundred square foot, two-bedroom Pre-War apartment sat at Seventy-second Street and Fifth Avenue. Former help's quarters had been reconfigured into a small home office, plus dressing room and bath for the master bedroom. High-end kitchen, bright spaciousness, view of Central Park and proximity to Lobel's sealed the deal.

"We're not in Brucknerfield anymore," Ethan whispered.

"And never will be again," I replied.

Two weeks into Ethan's new job, with Marsha off to London and Milan again, I wrangled legitimate Neiman Marcus appointments on her behalf at their Phoenix and Albuquerque stores. I sandwiched El Paso in between. As with most of his baseball gigs, Ethan and his teammates made do in low rent areas, this one near the border. We spent the afternoon in Mexico, much of it handing out hundreds of dollar bills to the impish but needy children. Close to the bone for both of us. We'd fought misery living together but now we fought misery being apart. He asked me to stay on. Couldn't I fib to Marsha? Pretend to sprain my ankle? I couldn't. My arduous next-day Phoenix schedule was set in stone so he drove me to the tiny airport, more like a private airfield for drug cartels. "No stoned, roaming around after dark, playing El Paso cowboy," I said.

"Babe, I know the drill. Besides, we're on the road more than we're here."

We fought waves of separation anxiety knowing our careers would keep us busy, but I couldn't wait until this baseball dream was over. Still, I played along to ensure Ethan would transition to a more stable life with me. Once it ended, we could be a normal couple. Couldn't we?

Marsha and I spent the rest of October crisscrossing the country, planning the next phase of Platinum's growth agenda. My antidote was always work. I may have been 'Mini-Marsha' but by now our symbiotic relationship gave me pause. Her risk taking alarmed me. In Chicago with buyers, and Dallas after a day with divisional executives, I suspected she'd offered kickbacks for over-writing inventory sales. 'Pump and Dump' could ruin her.

And ruin me by association.

We finished on the west coast and I stayed on alone in LA to interview candidates for open sales field positions. By then I was a regular at The Sunset Tower Hotel in West Hollywood, a step back to 1940s glamour. Yet in all my five-star accommodations, a table for one, or more often room service, served as constant reminders of my social, and sometimes professional, isolation. Now my restless nights second-guessing Marsha's agenda matched my sleepless stretch over Brian Cox. I spent the following day in endless interviews. My final candidate was legitimately running late, I was starving, in no mood for room service, so we agreed to meet for dinner. He suggested The Abbey but I arrived to find the hip West Hollywood bar/restaurant closed. I was now starving and furious as a quintessential LA-handsome guy waved me closer.

"Atticus Baron?"

"Yes indeed."

We shook hands. "Your choice is closed."

"Yes, but only to the public. We have a private room, available to friends of the owner."

"That would be you?"

"That would be me." He ushered me in.

I thawed over excellent food, wine, and panache as he fell into professional yet easy conversation laced with Québécois English. This guy, a former champion French Canadian figure skater, had found his niche as an A-list California celebrity make-up artist, currently exploring opportunities within the fragrance industry. We had mutual friends in the business. Atticus had Andrew Case's wit, plus business savvy akin to Jennifer and Dustin. He explained a recent breakup with his long-term partner as the impetus for his search in new directions. Once again, I'd found someone whose qualities and potential made up for inexperience, a pattern that served me well. I hired him that night. We agreed he'd continue building his reputation within his celebrity world while working as my LA resource.

That entire fall Ethan and I spoke infrequently as he made the most of his last-ditch effort with the El Paso league. I feigned enthusiasm as often as he hid frustration. We'd decided on the Manhattan move to the upscale apartment, with Ethan leaving the rest to me. It didn't help that Platinum's pressure to succeed in sales and new venues erased the *Charade* afterglow.

Work and apartment issues filled nearly every waking hour. By now I trusted my taste and hired a gaggle of professionals to implement what they referred to as my aesthetic. I'd fully adjusted to financial comfort and my earning potential. From Texas my I'm-not-afraid-to-live-in-a-tent husband adjusted to it as well. It let him play ball even after more than ten years of semi-pro and every gum-and-duct tape combination that kept him pitching.

We managed Christmas with my parents, a repeat of Easter but with a gaudy tree next to the orange recliner. Dad's frustration with his declining health and my mother's ever erratic temperament set us more on edge. Maxine's Christmas Eve service in the church on Paige property was as close as we got to Ethan's family.

Platinum's Energiser Bunny CEO went into 1997 New Year's overdrive as the board of directors leaned on her, and she leaned on us. For starters she increased our return on investment (ROI) to three million dollars, projecting our profitability at a staggering twenty-five percent over the previous year.

As we oozed into summer, the 1997 Asian economic crash exacerbated Platinum nail biting. By Labour Day when the board wanted more frequent meetings—more overhead accountability from CFO to CEO, I'd been with Marsha long enough to recognise a troubling pattern.

When the business trades, or *The Wall Street Journal* highlighted Platinum's successes she was upbeat and professional. When *Page Six ran* her Anna Wintour *Charade* shot months later, I knew for a fact she'd put someone in our PR department on retainer to keep her own name in print. Stressful financial or personnel issues made her contradictory or worse, seemingly erratic and unstable. Our competition, her own vice-presidents, and anyone else in the business could perceive this as weakness.

To moderate my stress, Dustin surreptitiously coordinated my travel schedule. When Marsha was in, I often hit the road or worked from my home office. When she flew off, I tackled responsibilities from headquarters. We weren't getting along as swimmingly as the early years, but it let me maintain chumminess. Her congratulations on my strong west and southwest market sales felt genuine. However, she stayed frazzled as the calendar year wound down.

At our holiday party I grabbed a Santa hat and raised my glass. "To Marsha!"

"To Marsha!" rang out. She needed to hear it.

Chapter Ten

That Brucknerfield Christmas my mother's ever-erratic temperament included sarcastic comments about my success and throwing it at Darby and Genevieve. On departure day Dad uncharacteristically let Mom speed us to the Terminal A curb. When he remained in the passenger seat as Ethan and I pulled our luggage from the trunk, I kept my alarm to myself.

"You two take care of yourselves." His eyes shone. "And each other. I love you, Emma. Great to see you." I hugged him through the rolled down window.

Ethan had finished his fall pitching season with the news that his El Paso outfit could use him 'midwinter' in their Laredo camp for off-season coaching. Midwinter meant mid-week, mid-January. He stayed faithful to his New York sports medicine regimen and flew back on the eleventh. He'd continue to limp along; we'd spend more time apart.

Marsha and I overlapped in the office all week but her office door remained closed a lot. If restructuring rumours were true, it would buy her time to fix the problems, or even find a new gig if need be. Rumours floated that she planned to reduce marketing coordinators and sales field people.

I steeled myself for closing January with her inevitable requests—regional appraisals, employee evaluations to estimated sales. I suggested we grab dinner at The Four Seasons. Even on short notice and Early Bird seating, it was the place to be seen. Heads turned as we approached our table in the pool room. "I'm flattered," she said over the top of her menu. "With Martin Luther King Day on Monday, I thought you'd have holiday weekend plans with your All-Star."

"My All-Star's flown back in Texas. Coaching new draft picks, helping plan Spring training." I embellished to keep conversation going, grateful when our orders arrived.

The gurgling pool made her silences comfortable but I hoped she'd raise Platinum issues herself. Instead she commented on the Four Seasons' art collection and their Picasso curtain.

I raised my glass. "You're a Renaissance woman, as up to date from the arts to our business. Another toast."

"Emma, don't—"

"Here's to your superb leadership. I suggested dinner tonight to assure you I understand the pressure as you overhaul our overhead. Flow charts, number crunching – Any assistance you need in the next few months, you can count on me."

She blanched. "You've done some excellent work, a real evolution since our first dinner in St. Louis. Linda Clarkson was nothing but jealous. I see big things for your future."

"I'm happy to hear it."

"Someday you'll be the CEO facing hard decisions. Right now it's on my shoulders."

I nearly patted her hand. "Let's get Sheila and Dustin to schedule some time to put our heads together."

"Emma," she said, "the cutbacks start at the top."

"They've let you go!"

"Oh my God. No."

"That's a relief."

"No, unfortunately I have to eliminate your position." I put down my glass.

"…cutting corners to make the board happy… More important, to make sure they don't fire me." She gave me a brittle smile. "Don't fire me so I can make sure you're taken care of. I've assured your security for the immediate future…a stunning reference letter."

"What the hell. You agreed to dinner to terminate me?"

"To explain that streamlining and financial belt tightening is in the best interest…"

Could I have been more naïve? My ears burned. "So much for being Platinum's Mini-Marsha. You've been my role model."

"This is never easy."

The gurgling reflecting pool kept our conversation private as I fought the urge to toss her into it. "I've supported you even through the Brian Cox fiasco."

"I'll help you find your next big thing. You're young, talented, smart, and beautiful. Quite a package."

"You made that clear when you poached me from Linda and Olympia. My god, I invited you here to offer my assistance."

"And I accepted so we'd have a pleasant atmosphere for me to explain." She morphed from embarrassed to steely-eyed and dismissive. "In these five years you've learned how the industry works. You're a cat; you'll land on your feet. It's nothing personal."

Like hell. "When would you have told me?"

"Tuesday afternoon when you return from the Tri-State Mall appointment." Without pause she produced the folder she would have given me then and slid it across the table.

My throat closed as I fought a mental image of Sheila Bianco and Marsha conspiring over the appointment calendar, choosing the most opportune time to lower the boom on me.

I stood. "You'll understand if I don't stay for coffee." I paid for our meals on the way out, and left the Seagrams building overheated by the embarrassment of shoving Marsha's exit folder into my satchel. Humiliation propelled me out to Fifty-second Street and over to Park Avenue Rush Hour-dinner-theatre-holiday weekend pandemonium. For once I'd worn my flat heeled Louboutin boots. I leaned into the crusty cold and headed blindly up the twenty blocks toward home.

Fragrance industry waters roil with sharks, most of them female. We were nearly at the millennium. Weren't we supposed to support each other? Show the bastards in suits a better, civilised, cooperative way to succeed? Hadn't I been loyal? Okay, I'd bailed on Linda Carlson and Olympia to take the Platinum job. But from Day One with Marsha I'd swallowed concern over her tactics, turned a blind eye to her spending sprees and protocol stretching. And so much for keeping my mouth mostly shut through the Brian Cox fiasco.

At Fifty-fourth I elbowed my satchel against my ribs and pulled on my gloves. I hadn't been this cold and furious since I'd abandoned Brian at the Summit Diner. The subway ran under

Lexington; buses crawled up Madison. I knew diddlysquat about either. At Fifty-sixth Street I swiped my tears. This time no train to catch. No Ethan waiting at the station.

Oh god, what about Ethan? What about my ability to support him and our half-assed, long distance excuse for a marriage? I snivelled my way north, swamped in melodrama, my feet as cold as my cheeks were hot.

I had sixteen more frozen Park Avenue blocks plus two along Seventy-second Street, when a cab pulled to the curb. A mink wrapped woman decamped.

Before her doorman could bow and usher her into the high rise, I pressed into the vacated backseat, suddenly the ten years old pressed into Dad's recliner. I spent fourth grade bearing the brunt of my 'mean and hateful old witchy witch' teacher's sarcasm, demeaning comments, and snide insinuations. By that afternoon my obscenity-laced kick to our threadbare couch was one too many for my father.

Dad stubbed out his cigarette and slung his arm around me. "Emma, now and forever you got to remember two things." He tapped my forehead. "First: when troubles come atcha, it's not always about you. Mrs Peterson might be worrying she can't pay her rent. Maybe her husband doesn't love her anymore. Maybe—"

"—she swallowed too many mean and ugly pills."

"Could be!" He tapped my forehead again. "Second thing: Even if it's you giving her fits, you need what that old witchy witch has. Knowledge! Soak it up. Be a sponge. Get knowledge from her and use it for you. That's how you get ahead in this world. Know what them's in charge know. That's how you lead people." He widened his fingers. "This makes **V** for Victory."

I looked at his nicotine stains and separated my fingers.

"Someday you'll look back and laugh at that old witch and know you won the battle. Now give me a high five!"

I did.

I reached my apartment and tossed my keys next to the fabric swatches and invoice for three rooms of custom window treatments. Home! Upper East Side, beyond expensive home. Was it shock or my constant companions Anxiety and Low Self-esteem that had me in a tailspin? Fifteen years in the fragrance game. Who was I kidding? Employees were expendable at every tier. I was no different. The wasn't DNFUA, it was SOP.

I changed into my sweats and called Atticus, Jennifer, and Dustin. With each voicemail I left my news and discreetly implied I'd be coming after them once I found my new position. On the home front my unconventional marriage worked in my favour.

Per usual Ethan did not need to know, or worry, or criticise. But for his sake, too, my new position had damn well better materialise ASAP.

Saturday morning I studied Marsha's severance package: six months' salary and health care, plus my unused but booked airline tickets. A perk to keep me at least satisfied, if not happy? I had no experience with legalese so I emailed my

125

attorney, Darlene Duke, the news, and hoped we could discuss it Tuesday. She called within the hour and asked for the full package, read it and call again. "Take the offer and run!"

"Wouldn't Marsha expect me to negotiate?"

"Nope. Platinum's giving you more than a standard exit package. New York's an 'At Will' state. They don't have to offer you anything but a *So Long, Farewell* walk to the door. Negotiation's not in their vocabulary. Plus, you've got nothing big to counter with, no sexual harassment, no discrimination. Plus you're not a Bobbi Brown or an Estee Lauder."

"Not yet."

She laughed. "Soon, no doubt. All the more reason to leave Platinum with a clean break and firm handshake. I'll contact HR first thing Tuesday and make it clear you'll be in with the original document and a copy, both signed. The sooner you accept and close, the sooner you get paid and get on with your career." Darlene's advice eased my anxiety and set my weekend path. By Saturday afternoon my credenza top was cleared of Ethan's scouting files. I laid down Marsha's folder of now-signed documents. Next to it I created *PEOPLE,* a file of regional reps to notify with stars for those I could network with. I added a spiral notebook for agenda notes, and a 1998 bank freebie wall calendar, the perfect day planner. I shaded February eighth. The annual fragrance industry suddenly loomed as the perfect venue to schmooze and explain my new employment position. I finished Day One on our home office carpet, studying, highlighting, and tearing out classifieds from the week's *Women's Wear Daily* and *Beauty Universal*. Sunday, I reviewed my resume, regularly tweaked to match interviews and job openings. Mini-Marsha on a mission. From my window Central Park looked like a monochromatic photo: bare sepia-to-charcoal trees, blacktop, iron railings, against oyster skies and remnants of snow. Scarf-wrapped tourists and locals hunkered into parkas and down coats. I buttoned up, yanked my Louboutins over my jeans. Thirty-degree wind propelled me two blocks down Fifth Avenue to the Frick.

When Ethan was away my solitary, tunnel vision life often caught up with me on empty Sundays. No best girlfriend to commiserate with, not even a pack of friends to meet for lunch. I rattled through the museum galleries, past old masters, and French porcelain, lost in thoughts of what would have been my packed upcoming work week.

Oh, to be a fly on the Platinum wall Tuesday morning as Marsha dealt with the schedule, she'd yanked me away from. Oh, to have another job by Tuesday afternoon.

Snow started early Monday morning as I frumped around in my terrycloth bathrobe. The robe stayed on and the snow fell through the endless grey holiday. Ethan was pinning his hopes on his new coaching gig, extra work and easier on his pitching arm. Part of me wanted him to succeed, part of me wanted him home getting on with whatever came next. All of me was our financial support. By mid-afternoon Atticus and Jennifer returned my calls and commiserated. When Dustin checked in, I asked him double check everything when assigned to pack and arrange delivery of my office contents.

"No worries. I packed and shipped Brian's crap, even the damned Tootsie Rolls stuffed in his desk drawers. I'll do a clean sweep for you, right down to bubble wrapping your photos of Ethan and Muriel Beausoleil."

"I'm so sorry packing for departed employees is required of a Stanford graduate sales manager," I said.

"Emma, I'm sorry pounding the pavement is required of a savvy, self-made woman who took a chance on a business major who didn't know *Eau de Cologne* from *Eau de Toilette*, or Aldehyde from Bergamot. You've given me constant opportunities."

I held that thought for the rest of the day, that and the reality that within twenty-four hours there'd be no physical evidence of my having occupied the executive wing.

As planned, Darlene called with instructions Tuesday morning. Fresh snow, bright sun, designer clothes, and good concealer helped me survive the exit process. I wore Versace to deliver my signed agreements and cool my heels in Platinum's Human Resources waiting area. Ten minutes later I left with my document co-signed by the CFO. No tears till I hit the sidewalk. My four-day out-of-body experience had me on automatic pilot, running Dad's advice through my head. "Get knowledge from her and use it for you."

My work was my life. By the end of Tuesday, my life was finding work.

By Wednesday that picturesque Monday snow had morphed into grainy, gritty, curb residue the consistency of an ugly *grattachecca*. I schlepped as my pavement pounding weather fluctuated from snowy to frozen drizzle, to clear and freezing, and back to spitting rain. One Bad Hair Day after another. I dressed for success as though Georgio had called me to Beverly Hills, or Calvin Klein waited at his desk. What could be more presentable than Manolo Blahnik spike heeled boots or flat heeled Louboutins; Gucci maxi-skirts; Chanel or Givenchy mohair jackets as I pulled the resume from my Prada satchel.

I interviewed for positions clipped from WWD and other trade publications, overqualified for some, others only vaguely related to my experience or skills. I networked with my top Manhattan retailers. There was little available at my level. Dustin's packed and delivered boxes of all things Platinum now sat in the middle of my home office. I propped my silver framed Ethan and Muriel framed on top.

Week Two, Jennifer suggested a head hunter exclusive to the industry. That round of interviews turned out to be temporary jobs or positions I'd want to leave within a year. I kept Ethan clueless, happy to listen to his elbow news, his raves about *Titanic* he'd seen with his Laredo rookies and anything else unrelated to my turmoil.

Five years of car service and fancy-schmancy Manhattan based clients left me clueless about the outer boroughs. Suddenly I had to hail cabs and negotiate the subway. I knew more about navigating Los Angeles than crossing the East River. In January my heel caught in a grate at the Fifty-ninth Street subway station. Unlike the movies it did not snap off. In defence of my blood-curdling scream, I thought someone had grabbed my ankle from below.

Five days later I stumbled on DUMBO's icy brick sidewalks while searching *Down Under the Manhattan Bridge Overpass* for the Brooklyn loft housing a start-up packaging design group. The twenty-something creative director interviewed me as I dabbed my skinned hand with his graffiti inspired paper napkins. On Groundhog Day I left a Chinatown interview and skidded into a Canal Street sidewalk cart of counterfeit Louis Vuitton luggage.

I faithfully filled my agenda notebook with possibilities, appointments, follow-up reminders. Jennifer Rocket's tale of her friends giving titles to horrendous interview styles, had nothing on mine:

Daddy's Helper. The nervous HR director for her father's fragrance industry consultation firm, sat in her Madison Avenue office and read my resume back to me. She paused after each line for my comment and seemed clueless as to what Vice President of Sales entailed beyond my listed accomplishments. I heard about her Dartmouth degree, her internships in LA, Paris and, "right here for the family business. Quite the dance card," she said. "So tell me about your education."

Our ninety-minute session mutated into my beauty industry tutorial. She masked her ignorance with sarcasm and covert study of my Prada *vs.* her Banana Republic attire. I recognised the look. There wasn't a prayer of a job offer from someone who knew I knew she was inept, over her head, and under dressed.

Odd Man Out. I arranged an interview for a sales person for an import/export brokerage business back down in Chinatown. I maneuvered Canal Street again, still at its iciest, for an interview with owner Jack Smith. His office sat above The Jade Garden, via a staircase lined with black and white photos of mid-century greats. Judy Garland, Bette Davis, Dean Martin, even Sammy Davis, Jr. and Frank Sinatra posed in separate shots with a middle-aged man sporting various disco era ensembles and a full head of dark curly hair. I knocked on the door.

He answered and offered me a chair. *Odd Man Out* wasn't Asian but he didn't look like a *Jack* or a *Smith* either. Regardless, in person the man in the photos, now in his mi seventies, was a combination of Alfred Einstein, Gene Wilder and Christopher Lloyd. The aroma of hoisin sauce from downstairs, and marijuana from Mr Smith masked whatever odours lay in the stained, rust colour carpet. He complimented my resume and rambled about his need for someone in the business to get him more clients. This segued into the vagaries of importing and the joys of exporting.

I expected he'd reference the glory days depicted in his staircase gallery, but a cockroach appeared on the wall behind him. My train of thought vanished as the insect worked its way toward the ceiling. I gripped my chair, fighting flashbacks to my infested childhood apartments. When I could finally concentrate on his expectations, I brought the interview to a close, shook hands, and closed the door behind me.

My past pressing against my future stopped me on the stairs. I took a deep, cockroach cleansing breath and a closer look at the photos. Everyone was of Mr Smith glad-handing Madam Tussauds Wax Museum figures.

Touchy Feely. The owner and CEO of a well-known event rentals company needed a sales and marketing director/ supervisor. The position was a lateral move at best, but I knew their high-end work. I'd reached Week Three with no job. This midtown address was two blocks from Platinum. Familiar territory. So far, so good.

Or not.

He introduced himself to my breasts as he shook my hand and held it a moment too long. He offered me a chair. The cockroach free wall behind his walnut desk showcased celebrity-infused photos of living people: Giants, Yankees, and Knicks players, a rock band, and two mayors. The framed women were recognizable by their NFL cheerleader uniforms, beer labelled bras, or pasties and feather headdresses.

He expressed genuine interest in my experience and was familiar with my resume and many of my successful events enhanced by his rental products. After sincere compliments, he leaned in conspiratorially. Hadn't I left some information off my resume? We both knew big wigs could get out of control at those events. (He chuckled.) He'd heard stories that had the industry buzzing. So had I.

I refused the bait. Instead I asked proper and pertinent questions about the company. Somehow this got him extolling the virtues of his Mercedes Benz. Cross my heart, he put his hands behind his head, leaned back, rested his Gucci-loafered feet on his desk, and suggested dinner in his Fifth Avenue penthouse.

I can coat anything with sarcastic humour, but three weeks of crappy weather, unfamiliar transportation, sketchy neighbourhoods and few opportunities set my teeth on edge. The perfume event loomed the following Wednesday and weekend three of unemployment mired me in anxiety. I paced my apartment in conference with myself. Had my years with Marsha been a fluke, success never again achievable? Worse, did I exemplify the Peter Principal? Had I reached my personal level of incompetence?

I called Andrew. He offered to ship me a Madonna bustier, a cone-shaped bra, and a major dose of confidence. "But, Sweetie," he added, "you already have what you need: preparation. Folks like us get nothing handed on a platter. When you're in the right place at the right time, you'll recognise serendipity and your opportunity to make the magic happen."

I filled my free time with hair and nail appointments, chose an impeccably appropriate ensemble, and awoke Wednesday to brilliant, thirteen-degree sunshine. I took it as a good omen – the perfect evening to stay warm at the familiar St. Regis. As with many industry events, for their *Winners Table* Hall of Fame night, The Perfume Society of America sat a mix of companies, titles, and ages together to enhance cross industry camaraderie. Neither Marsha nor any other Platinum employee would be at my table. I neither saw neon clothing flashes, nor heard clanking bangle bracelets. Linda Clarkson was either absent or avoiding me. I could do this.

I mingled among senior executives, directors, marketing and sales managers as though I were running for mayor. Had they heard I was in a career change… Time to broaden my experience…intend to bring my skills in driving sales teams to new venues. Dustin waved from a few tables over as I found mine. Coty's field sales rep Ken Lopez sat my right, deep in conversation with the fellow on his right. He stopped long enough to greet me and introduce Nikos Christopoulos. We shook hands and they went back to business. I sat down. Thick white hair, impeccable suit, broad accent. Hadn't we met? Years ago.

Chicago? St. Louis?

Wait staff served dinner but he continued to lean toward

Ken. It hit me! The Hilton seminars during my early Olympia Beauty days! The gentleman at the Nobodies Table. Over clinking glass and silverware that accent continued to hold my attention as I recalled his kindness.

Twenty-four years and fifteen global brands, he explained to Ken. I remembered. Distribution for one company. Greek, he had told me, but made his career in Milan before his New York move. Ken nodded. "It sounds as though you're mostly under the radar of the big retailers, even with this new account."

"Under the radar. Yes, the right expression. Especially this new one. Ciao!Beauty needs the right kind of awareness for our global reputation."

I nibbled as the self-made multi-millionaire explained he was investing in a new project. I leaned in, as attentive as if wired for surveillance.

"It's time for my family to be major players. It's time for me to connect to prestige retailers. We say *Efaga porta*. I tried before. It didn't work out. You understand?" Mr Christopoulos raised his goblet.

"So I try again."

When he finally put food in his mouth, Ken turned to me. "'Didn't mean to ignore you, Emma. Quite the tale. Nordstrom's corporate buying team's expressed interest in a new French fragrance he's bringing over in six months." I pounced.

Chapter Eleven

Ken flinched as I shot my outstretched arm across his chest. "Mr Christopoulos?" I tapped his sleeve. "We've met. Six or seven years ago at a conference at The Hilton."

He smiled indulgently, his mouth full, then turned as the host called us to attention. A waitress removed my plate. "We sat together back then, too," I explained to Ken as the ceremonies began.

The rest of the evening Hall of Fame induction and speeches blurred. Nordstrom's corporate buying team would be Seattle.

When? The *how* jelled. *It's only serendipity when you recognise your opportunity and make the magic happen.* Thank you, Andrew. Amidst applause, brightening lights, and attendees leaving their tables, I said goodbye to Ken then reiterated details of the long-ago Hilton conference to Mr Christopoulos.

He broke into a grin. "Of course, of course, our table in the back corner. *I am Nobody.* Well, look at me. Grey hair from making all my success. And Emma Paige, still so fresh. No longer green. I think you must now be a very big shot at Olympia, no?" 'A very big shot' made me grin. "We have a lot to catch up on. Do you have time for the King Cole Bar? It's right here." He shook his head but fished out his business card. "When we met my headquarters were in my Long Island warehouse. No longer! The Empire State Building. How about that?" He studied me. "I have a second thought. Perhaps a quick cappuccino?" Something made him change his mind. Second pounce. We chatted over the din of attendees. I offered sales stories from my earliest Brucknerfield counter days (ah, she's self-made), to the *Charade* launch for Platinum (what a skilled professional), tidbits I hoped would stay with him.

"Such press! And the Guggenheim. Extraordinary Launch. I confess, I studied it."

I mentioned my experience in terms of what I knew his

Nordstrom agenda required. "Fifteen years in the business, Mr Christopoulos, display counters to product presentations." He smiled at my broad hints and regretfully explained he was not hiring.

"But still, you must come and see my Ciao!Beauty office," closed our *kaffeeklatch.*

I called his personal assistant the next morning. Perhaps not the right time to make the magic happen, but hiring or not,

I needed my foot in any door except the one on Canal Street.

Nikos Christopoulos' twenty-seventh floor Empire State Building address made it clear he intended to run with the big dogs. However, rather than steel and chrome, the Ciao!Beauty! lobby screamed, "I made it to the big-time mid-century." Oversized, classic, black and white photos of Las Vegas entertainers hung on a panelled side wall. Despite his Greek and Italian roots, vintage French travel posters lined the hall. We talked fragrance. I hoped to see Provence's lavender fields one day; Paris was magical…

We reached the oversized conference room, the first I'd seen with a piano. My host bemoaned the demise of good Manhattan piano bars for entertaining clients. He mentioned hosting Nordstrom in the room after they struck the deal. *Voila*, I had my opening into his Seattle presentation plans. Like a lawyer in court, I dribbled and drabbed my way, asking only questions for which I knew what his answer should be.

- Who would hold influence among the corporate buyers at the table? He blinked.
- Would he share his strategy for the six months leading to his launch with them? He blinked.
- Would he hint at having chosen them over their largest competitor? He flushed.

The pause grew awkward. I'd gone too far. I opened the piano fallboard and asked if he played.

"I pay others to play." Okay then. Deep breath.

"I fly over Neiman Marcus headquarters to reach Seattle."

"Pardon me?"

"You ask if I hint at their largest competitor. No hinting. I say to Nordstrom outright, 'Nordstrom, I fly right over your Dallas competition to make sure I get to you first.'"

"Yes! Yes, great idea, Mr Christopoulos. That's the perfect idea." This time the pause was comfortable.

"Such flattery, Emma Paige."

On return to the lobby I commented on the posters again, the *je ne sais quoi* of Paris's fabled shopping. Did he know *Galeries Lafayette* had tried to make a go of it in Trump Tower? "Indeed. Pierre Meysselle. Eighty-five thousand square feet they rented. A risk for the French, but all guts, I think."

"He was my client," I replied. "Bad timing for them. High fashion lost its stronghold in that location."

"New tourists in Nikeland, I think they don't buy fragrance."

My childhood of second guessing taught me to interpret body language and nuance before I knew there was a name for it. My host was back in his comfort zone. Amidst sincere thanks for his time and tour, I thought: *consulting.*

"Mr Christopoulos," I blurted, "I've done so many presentations myself, I'd be honoured to review your Nordstrom pitch. While I figure out my next professional move, I'm freelancing. I'd been happy to help."

Nikos Christopoulos was Old School, Old Country, old enough to be my father, if not grandfather. I was too young, too female, too bold.

"*A poco, a poco,*" he said. "Little by little and hard work. I am a stubborn old man, eh? But now, I'm thinking *efharisto*. Thank you, Emma. Nordstrom is—" He shrugged.

"Your brass ring."

"Yes, but maybe the ring falls through my fingers. All my years in Milan...my Italian strangles my Greek. My Greek accents my Italian. And oh! English."

"You're trilingual. It adds to your charm."

"You are too kind."

"I'm not. Fragrance is international. Your gift is being multilingual and your success no accident. Even if you're thinking, 'This from a woman,' and 'too young," Nordstrom's is interested in what you have to say and present."

"No, I am thinking, 'Nikos, you want to win this luxury account. Here is the professional, standing right in your office. Stop being stubborn."

I grinned of course, and swallowed the urge to hug and high five him. "I know how to put you and your products in the best light possible, for the results you want." To be more precise, I knew who to call. We struck a deal and the minute I left The Empire State Building, I dialled Dustin's number.

Over a freezing weekend of collaboration in my home office, he designed a template for the presentation. After work Monday evening he returned so I could provide specifics from an additional meeting at Ciao! I opened the door to find him holding an arrangement of roses.

"Be my valentine a day early." He handed them to me. "I confess, they delivered as I arrived. Your phantom husband?" I nodded and showed him the typed card:

Happy Valentine's Day, Love, Ethan

I explained Ethan's current baseball gig and confessed to keeping him in the dark about my situation. "That kind of stress affects his game and, frankly, what good would it do?"

"Secrets aren't healthy, either, Emma."

"We've walked this tightrope our whole marriage."

Dustin could read me as well as I'd read Mr Christopoulos. He knew to abandon Ethan analysis and we got to work. As he'd done for me at Platinum, he turned my notes on the arrival of *Clos-Vougeot* into an impeccable business-cantered presentation for the Italian-by-way-of-Greece lover of all things French. "I'm a realist," I said as I wrote him a check three hours later. "Ciao!Beauty isn't hiring beyond this project, you and I are a damn good team, Dustin Walsh. This could change his mind."

"Damn right. My thoughts exactly. Get yourself to Seattle. Make sure this sets Nordstrom, Ciao!Beauty, and Mr C on fire, then make me an offer."

Ethan and I managed a Valentine's Day call and I thanked him for the flowers. I let his enthusiasm for scouting reports and managing rookies keep our conversation weighed heavily in his favour. I'm guilty of the sin of omission, but I didn't mention the trip to Seattle or Nordstrom presentation. Mr Christopoulos and I shared a car to the airport and settled into the plane's Business Class section. As with my early days shadowing Marsha, nothing breeds familiarity like seven hours seated together. Somewhere over the Midwest he reiterated his language frustration and I asked for some Greek lessons. We moved into Italian phrasing, and then French. All things French was his passion, his idea of class, and "The epitome of the good life," he added, expounding on his new fragrance, and his belief in the venture. After all his years making, losing, investing fortunes, He was still nervous over this first presentation to a legitimate, American luxury department store.

As we checked into the four-star hotel, I mentioned Nordstrom's reputation for the best shoe salons in North America. "I should arrive at the conference in a new pair."

"As well for me," he replied. Sure enough, he met me the next morning in a pristine pair of Ferragamo lace up oxfords, Burberry Clinton Check tie, and a designer's dress shirt whose name escaped him. With his head of thick grey hair, he looked like a well-aged John Stamos. As agreed, I'd taken responsibility and already prepared the materials, dressed the conference room, and double-checked equipment with their sound engineer. Ready, set, go. Mr Christopoulos held the buyers' captive. Nordstrom was the place to shop. He lifted his pant leg and then his foot to display his purchases. "Dallas is closer to my Empire State Building office, yes? Still, I fly right over your competition to be sure I see you first."

Appreciative laughter set the tone and he was off and running, pitching *Clos-Vougeot* to attentive buyers with a polished visuals from charts of projected sales, to a teaser preview of the campaign's mildly erotic print campaign. He took me to dinner that evening, confident grin still in place. "I walk on air, Emma. Such a moment for us."

We touched on specifics and business strategy. Rather than push, however, I summoned patience. Our return morning flight would be the ideal time to revisit my input into the project. He thanked me again at breakfast. But "A change in itinerary," he said. "I have unexpected family business in Las Vegas. I'll fly in this evening. So?" He grinned. "I will see you off to the airport shuttle. Then I take the Nordstrom head buyer to lunch. How about that? On a Saturday."

"If I may be so bold, we make a good team," I said.

"You may be so bold. Perhaps I need your services again." He agreed getting together in New York would be a good idea, but no job offer as he handed my carry-on to the driver. Treading lightly was worse than second guessing.

I flew home and killed the weekend fighting jet-lag. Vickie Spaulding's departing gifts from my early *Fairfield Monthly* days still sat in my home office. I consulted *The Complete Guide to Executive Manners* Sunday afternoon, and composed a thank-you to Mr Christopoulos on my monogrammed stationery. Vickie's grammar and comportment corrections stayed with me. No doubt she'd marvel at how far I'd progressed. My jangling office phone startled me out of the reverie.

"The old man finally kicked it," my brother said without a greeting. "I guess five White Castle double cheeseburgers at one meal and his four-packs-a-day habit weren't good for him."

"Darby!"

His voice broke. "Mom said he just fucking keeled over, pouring a fucking cup of coffee. Emma? Emma, can you come home?"

I knew Ethan wouldn't go with me even before I dialled his Laredo number. Early spring training meant tournaments. Managers wouldn't let players go, especially pitchers. Injuries were common and affected the bull pen. Maybe more to the point my husband's feelings for his own family generated more PTSD than loyalty, obligation or affection.

I tried anyway, barely avoiding a shouting match. I closed with, "Don't make me do this alone."

"Let your mother handle everything. Listen to me, Emma. Let her bully, let her help your grandparents. Pass what's left to Darby and Genevieve. For once in your life stand back."

"I still have to go!"

"Okay, I get that, and yes, this sucks big time. For me, too, Babe, but you know I can't get away. I'm at the top of my game and I can't leave the team in a weak place."

"You mean you still have to prove loyalty above all else. I don't know why I called. I knew you'd have an excuse."

"It's no excuse. I'll send flowers. Even if you're pissed at me, listen to one more thing. Emma, do not show up like the goddamn family hero. You know damn well they'll be wanting you to take over their lives. Handle this, settle that. Helping Genevieve is one thing, but blink twice and you'll have your mother on an allowance and living in our guest room."

There was too much truth to it to laugh. As dysfunctional as we all were, Daniel O'Farrell was the glue that had held us together. As much as anyone could, he kept a lid on my mother, and held court from his ratty orange recliner in every godforsaken dwelling we occupied.

Dad never knew a stranger; he'd talk to everyone without judgment, probably learned from his earliest days defending Neil Harvey. He professed atheism but read the Bible multiple times. He pounded his red state bar mates with Democrat rhetoric but remained tight-lipped at the ballot box. Despite legendry alcohol intake and his own dabbling in the prescription world, he used my sister's video camera to conduct surveillance on suspected neighbourhood drug dealers.

Grief kept my anxiety at bay, and anxiety held back the grief. Ethan was right. I let family know I'd be there as soon as Dad's service arrangements had been scheduled. Scheduled by them. "We know what he wanted essentially nothing," I told Genevieve. "Let Mom hash it out with Gram and Grandpa."

She reported back that my lapsed-Methodist mother and Dad's Irish Catholic parents compromised on a secular memorial service at the local funeral home, and cremation. His ashes would be scattered at his favourite fishing spot. I promised to be in Brucknerfield in time to stand in the receiving line during visitation hours the evening before the service. I thought Neil might want to know and tracked him down through his Nob Hill shop, *Neil Harvey Antiquities*. He surprised me on two fronts: Gram O'Farrell, his Aunt Claire, had already called him. He'd booked a reservation at an airport hotel, and insisted on getting me a room and meeting my plane. I barely remembered what he looked like, but as I hustled with other passengers from the jetway into the terminal wheeling my carry-on, "Emma, darling!" sailed over us.

"Neil!"

He threw his arms wide, all cashmere coat, silk ascot and kid gloves, and pulled me into a hug. "I'm so, so sorry this is how we reconnect. Sorry for both of us. Honestly, I owe every drop of self-confidence to Cousin Danny." He slung his arm around my shoulder and steered me toward the familiar exit. "Oh we had our spats, lord knows, but when the chips were down, and they were very often down, Daniel O'Farrell was in my corner."

"That means a lot. You two seem so different."

"Skin deep, darling girl. Single sons of close sisters. He had his own quirks. And that cigarette habit! He let me try my first one behind our shed. I couldn't have been more than ten. Danny was probably twelve."

Down the escalator and out past the luggage carrousels, Neil kept up his monologue. I tried to reimburse him for the hotel but he brushed me off.

"My treat. You need a place to decompress and steel yourself before we tiptoe through the family minefields." I took comfort in the *we,* and his insistence the two of us drive to Brucknerfield together. He also insisted he'd stay long enough to drive me back to the airport. Solid guidance in my personal life was so rare it was hard to accept, but a two-day headache, frayed nerves, and the usual anxiety convinced me. He also cajoled, sympathised and listened, listened, listened. Over dinner in the hotel restaurant, Neil heard the details of my six weeks of hellish job hunts in hellish New York weather, and the irony of my successful gig for Ciao!Beauty, only to come home to Darby's phone call.

"I'm still unemployed and I've lost my father." I swiped my eyes with my napkin.

"Darling girl, it's time you kept me in the loop. You have reached your saturation point. You're due a good cathartic weep. And I may weep along with you. We're a generation apart, but cut from the same cloth. I am so sorry I've stayed away so long when I have this big shoulder you can cry on."

I suspect he shifted conversation to himself to put us on equal footing. Gratitude eased the sweats.

"Nineteen fifty-nine, fresh out of my god-awful high school career, I worked retail at Famous-Barr. I loved it. Emma, there was a time I could style a store window, a bed, or any of their furniture arrangements. I was King of the Soft Goods Vignettes." It felt wonderful to smile.

"In no time I discovered F, F, and A: Furniture, Fixtures and Accessories. From there, antiques. Barely a year later I bought a one-way ticket to the City by the Bay and opened my first little Nob Hill shop. This gay, blue collar, St. Louis boy got out of the closet and out of town. I've never looked back. Rarely came back, either, as you well know."

"I wish you had, Neil. I so wish you had."

We arrived at the former Animal Cracker Park late morning the following day. Neil drove down the rutted lane still chatting as he steered clear of frozen dirt puddling in the February thaw. "In his own way, Danny was as much a misfit as I am. In his case, too much weight, too many vices. A bit of a con man with too little confidence and even less guidance. But damned if he didn't try to cover it up with a good heart and that enormous gift of gab." He parked and insisted on getting my luggage to the house before driving over to my grandparents.

"Glad you could pull yourself away from that fancy job, Emma," my mother said by way of greeting as she opened the door.

"Well, I'm here, Mom."

"And safely delivered, Iris."

She gave Neil the once over. "I heard you were coming."

"Danny was the closest thing I had to a brother. And you're family, too."

"Thank you for that."

He hugged her right off her feet.

The surprise was not my hard scrabble family. Turns out Dad's drinking, fishing, schmoozing buddies (more likely their wives) stocked the freezer; someone had draped a hand-knit throw on his recliner. Apparently, Mom's ragtag friends took up a collection and hired a cleaning crew. What passed for our living-dining room had flower arrangements on the gleaming table and bookcase, with Ethan's card still poking from his. The entire place smelled like Pledge and Murphy's Oil Soap. My heart hurt.

By the time I arrived, O'Farrells had planned the routine for the next few days (Thank you, Ethan). I fell in line, literally, as we regrouped to receive visitors at the funeral home. Darby arrived after work from his apartment in town; Genevieve drove with her boys from her own godforsaken boondocks.

Gram and Grandpa insisted Neil join in any way he felt comfortable. For two days he held us together, Brooks Brothers to the bone. He changed subjects when tempers flared, broke up the wrestling in the funeral home lobby between his little first-cousins-twice-removed, and served as the perfect usher for the service. His 'Danny and Neil' BB gun reminiscences had Grandpa slapping his knee.

Dad's cronies took it from there. Except for the secular service and no casket, it might as well have been a two-day Irish wake. Day Three we formed a caravan to the fishing spot. Mom and the biting February wind dispersed Dad's ashes along the edge of the lake. My head ached.

Meanwhile back at the Animal Cracker ranch, the stuffing of Genevieve, her boys, and me into our childhood bedrooms, was wearing thin. Friends hovered too long and my grandparents nagged too often. My mother's week-long consumption of lemon bars, brownies, and cold casseroles, washed down with diet soda and booze, punched up with pharmaceuticals, spun her into Mrs

Junk Yard Dog (Darby's teenaged term for her tantrums). "Jesus. You'd think he was a fucking saint," and, "he left me with a shit pile of nothing," she said as often as she crumbled into tears. We were either in the way or not attentive enough. "And that damned cousin. Neil drops from his fancy schmancy sky. Always too good for us, and all of sudden he's queen of the hop and acting like a long-lost son."

"He's Gram's only family left," Genevieve said.

"And I'm yesterday's garbage? Jesus, you're all clueless."

"Mom!" came from all of us. Darby added his two cents, and we were at it like old times.

"Emma, you're worse than the other two put together." She turned to my siblings. "Was I right about her? Was I? Too good for us. Ethan can't bother to give up a ball game and show up, after all we did for him. And both of them, more money than God – Not a worry on God's green earth."

"Damn it!" I stepped forward as Genevieve sent me a warning glance. "I've been out of work for six fucking weeks. Does that help?"

Chapter Twelve

"Six weeks? When, exactly were you going to tell me you got fired?"

"Well, hello to you to, Ethan."

"I call Darby to get carburettor advice and that's how I find out you've been out of work since I flew down here?"

"And what? You would have hopped a plane right back from pre-season to help me find a job? You can't even find the time for your father-in-law's memorial service. I've been back for forty-eight hours. How about asking how I'm doing?" Off we went and it wasn't pretty.

"Look, Ethan, this isn't getting us anywhere. I didn't tell you because I knew you didn't need the stress. Besides, it's worked out. Nickolas Christopoulos of Ciao!Beauty hired me full time this morning." Half-hearted apologies on both ends put us back on neutral ground. "I join as Executive Vice President, General Manager, with an annual salary of well over two-hundred and fifty thousand dollars. In essence I've been hired to show Mr Christopoulos the ropes."

We calmed down before we hung up, but I fell into another crying jag. Whether for my marriage, my father, or the six miserable weeks, I couldn't say. Maybe they were tears of relief and joy.

1998 spun on an unexpected axis. "Seriously, women are expected to make coffee and deliver it to their bosses. Male, of course. Mr Christopoulos calls us Doll Face and Sweetie Pie," I explained as I shared my employment news with Neil. "He sounds like a total anachronism. No mutiny?"

"To be honest, he's a gentlemen to his toes, kind and generous. Impeccable, old school wardrobe. He's the first to compliment a job well done. Most important, Neil, something in my drive or determination has created chemistry. He's got a hard-scrabble background, too. He treats me like a daughter, or at least the way I think a daughter should be treated."

"Darling girl, this is marvellous. Promise to keep me up to speed on all things career."

I hung up smiling. My boss had the Greek and Italian aura of a man brimming with a loving family. He often mentioned his late wife, his Greek sister who'd married into an Italian-American clan, their son, the beloved nephew Carmine, and a gaggle of Long Island in-laws-by-marriage.

I offered polite responses. After my tightrope walk with Linda Carlton, and cosy-to-collapse relationship with her, then Marsha, I worked to keep this relationship professional. In addition to my boss, I had a CFO and a board of directors to consider, all male, each old enough to be my father, if not grandfather. A raised eyebrow, a doubtful expression could flood me with doubt or self-consciousness.

At Ciao!Beauty I was more independent, more responsible, which in turn meant more visible. I focused on enhancing existing procedure that would bring results as quickly as possible. I had to up my A game with the board, our clients and the competition. From what I said to how I said it, *Proceed with Caution* became my mantra. Trust is not my strong suit.

By late spring I'd restructured the sales field, and added positions in our major markets drawn from people I'd worked with during the past ten years. Jennifer Rocket joined as Vice President of Sales for North America. Dustin came on as marketing manager, with an eye toward Marketing/Public Relations Director.

Atticus Baron remained in LA as my consultant on sales and events. Andrew Case left Marshall Fields to work for me in his Midwest territory. I had an inner circle; they had my back. Mr Christopoulos was so happy with our progress he added marketing department to my job description. Sales, Marketing, and Sales Administration/Analytics, Education, and Public Relations all reported to me. Together we created an inspiring environment with a waiting list of job applicants. It took working for this supportive, low-key gentleman to realise how tense I'd been with Linda and Marsha. Nothing in his temperament set me on edge which showed in my productivity. The constant hum of paper shredders, ringing phones, and buzzing employees became my symphony. I was back to driving a well-oiled machine with the largest team I'd ever managed.

There was no managing my mother, of course. "… As for your grandparents, I still do their laundry, keep up the place. I might as well be dead as your father. Not a bit of thanks, not a dime for the work. Tupperware's saving my ass." Representative O'Farrell sold her product line out of the station wagon, and Tupperware had gotten her to Manhattan for some sort of regional get together.

"I got time for a lunch but don't drag me into one of those stuck up, rich people places you and Ethan go to," put us in a hamburger joint on West Thirty-third, two blocks from my office. "Look at you, all decked out in that thousand-dollar ensemble," opened her bitch-fest, and concluded with Darby being arrested for fencing motel televisions, and Genevieve in an emergency room for leg sutures after her ex threw an ashtray.

When I'd settled the check and we were back on the street, I slung my arm around her shoulder and had her look up. "Can you believe I work in The Empire State Building? Wait till you see the view from our offices. You'll love Mr Christopoulos' taste. Ciao!Beauty's decorated right out of the Big Band era. Plus, you can meet the team I've put together. Dustin, my assistant, is the one who packs the boxes I send you."

"Seems like that out-of-work stretch you fussed over didn't make a dent. Must be nice when money and a classy life come so easy. Anyways, I killed my free time over lunch. I'm meeting the West Virginia reps for some girl time, brain storming, drinks—the whole package." She scanned the street with her arm raised.

"Maybe your next visit."

"Sure thing." She hugged me as a cab pulled over. I jammed on sunglasses, swore, steamed, and stewed the entire fifteen-minute walk to my office. I shut my door, and cried my eyes out. My toxic excuse for a mother, who'd brag about me to every Tupperware seller in West Virginia, remained incapable of anything resembling emotional support.

Central Park jogging had become my stress buster. Five and a half hours later I hit my routine trail and approached 'the nook,' as I thought of the Brucknerfield-like stone outcropping I'd discovered with Ethan. Hated tears, closed throat tightened my chest all over again. In our own eccentric way, Ethan and I adjusted to his year-in, year-out scramble from team to team, franchise to franchise, but the schedule made sharing in-the moment despair like mine impossible.

By 1998 even that schedule was in flux. His January call back to coach and develop rookies didn't guarantee more than current season play. Falling short of accomplishing his goals forced his insecurity and anxiety demons to the surface. I put mother issues on the back burner, doused my despair, and concentrated on Ethan.

I insisted the baseball cup was half full, not half empty. We both knew the day would come when he'd have to make major transitions. He might not play as much but his talent was needed, coaching would always be an option. My pep talks were most effective when delivered between the bed sheets.

Cousin Neil wrote us letters in impeccable script often including magazine articles from sports to the arts. A day with Neil was like a week inside an encyclopaedia. He dissolved my gloom by coming east on spring business, full of questions about Ethan's games, as well as the fragrance industry. His success, he told me depended as much on public relations, people skills, and international networking as the antiques and collectables he sold, talents Ethan and I were to apply to our careers.

I welcomed his tutorials, from paintings as we strolled The Frick, to libretto lessons for *Tosca,* my first opera. He arranged my furniture 'to lead the eye' to the framed prints he'd helped me hang. When we finally tiptoed through family minefields, Neil play therapist, grew teary over my dad, and made sense of our shared dysfunctional dynamic. He genuinely cared about Ethan and his goals, and left me with, "Life is too damn short. Make every day divine."

At work I met weekly with Mr Christopoulos and the CFO to review financial and wholesale reports, staffing, and brand acquisitions. Within months I regularly attended the first thirty to forty minutes of the board meetings to assure the directors and our investors allocated funds were being used as planned, and sales projections were achieved. This gave me face to-face chances to answer profit and loss— 'P&L' —questions for their retailers.

The Greek and Italian board members weren't involved in daily operations so supporting Mr Christopoulos with negotiations became my priority. My team's input improved my efficiency. By summer I regularly looked over proposals and investment requirements to assure they were the right brands for the Christopoulos portfolio, and updated progress on newly launched fragrances. The *je ne sais quoi* of board members' body language and tone of voice made it clear they trusted my judgment, or at least Mr Christopoulos' faith in it. Once we had multiple brands, we created strong structural plans for domestic and Canadian markets. Ciao!Beauty showed a profit for the first time in years. Next, we homed in on international sales, from France and Germany, to the biggest opportunity: expansion into merging markets in Middle East, China, and Dubai.

Ethan's coaching and scouting kept him hopeful but his 1998 season was over. There would be no October/November fall ball. Ciao!Beauty was a regular attendee at the TFWA, the October Tax Free World Association luxury trade show in Cannes, France. Ciao!Beauty reserved a ballroom to showcase its brands. Appointments were set by mid-September. "Make this your plan for October, Emma. Like Seattle, we will be a team. We climb up this time. We leave the 'dump and pump,' the crappy brands, behind. I'm thinking it's imperative we expose quality, all that's new to the world." He stretched out his arms. "So this year we meet with new distributors. We get our brands to retailers and editors at the top of the ladder rungs. *Nos meilleurs produits! Ç'est si bon.*"

"My Greek boss is now all things French," I told Neil as I updated him on the Cannes trade show, the dates, and Ethan's declining career.

"Emma! Not only have Dale and I rented a place in Monaco for our October shopping, we've chartered a boat for a small party in Cannes the day you're due back in New York. Stay on a bit. Fly Ethan over and we'll treat you to some fun."

An extra week meant more networking. Mr Christopoulos was all for it. Despite diplomacy, "Stay as long as you like with Neil. You know I hate to travel," was all I got from Ethan.

"For once you have the time. Don't turn down a week together in romantic France. Our American Express Card's in the dressing room safe. You know the combination."

Mr Christopoulos and I flew Business Class to Cannes. He told stories of his poor Athenian childhood, the Italian and German occupations during World War Two and how small reachable goals got him to Italy once he started his business. His Milan years exposed him to the driving force of French style, appreciation for the Parisians, 'and this playground of theirs.' We arrived and he gestured at the roof of our Cannes Carlton Intercontinental. "What other hotel can boast of exterior domes based on the breasts of the French Riviera's most famous World War One courtesan? Or your Grace Kelly's fateful photo shoot while filming." *Et voila*, she meets her prince.

The magnificent hotel hummed with deal makers, icons of international finance, fashion, and business, plus examples of superb plastic surgery. I felt as though I were back on an international spree with Marsha, minus the extra luggage for god knows how many purchases.

We'd registered for the full agenda and discovered our newly licensed brands had even interested those who had no knowledge of who we were. Ciao!Beauty's

Italian board members with Milan residences and manufacturing interests would hold concurrent meetings in a suite down the hall.

I unpacked and arranged my clothes to fit my gruelling schedule, then threw open the antique balcony doors and raised my face to the Mediterranean air. Distant swaying palms, sultry breezes, a bed fit for *The Princess and the Pea*. No Ethan. My room phone jangled. Mr Christopoulos wanted me to sit in on an impromptu meeting. "*Gentiluomini*, Emma Paige, my vice president and miracle worker," brought them to their feet. They greeted me cordially, then returned to our manufacturing company issues, arguing and cajoling in Italian laced English, English-laced Italian, with more than a few international gestures. I said little but concluded mid-afternoon insisting I join them at the evening black tie gala.

My honest insistence I'd brought nothing appropriate for a formal evening prompted Mr Christopoulos to use his Greek. His assistant then insisted we visit the store of my choice with his Platinum American Express card.

Given the Milanese board members, I needed an Italian designer, preferably my favourite. Off we went to the Prada boutique. Within the hour I'd found a stunning understated high style design, perfect except for the three thousand euros price tag.

Lou shrugged. "If Nikos tells you to get a dress, you must choose what looks good on you. The cost does not concern him." The saleswoman boxed it, assigned a staff member to deliver it immediately it to my Carlton suite, and coordinated with the hotel for a stylist who fussed over final details and left me transformed. Ready, Set, Go, required one last twirl in front of the mirror. I left the suite imagining Ethan in a tailor-made suit, impeccable white shirt open at the throat, standing at the French doors with his back to the sea.

Thanks to Mr Christopoulos, I looked like a million bucks, clearly a prop with a purpose, but without a clue as to what that might be. No one hinted at my role as we made the rounds of the ballroom. "Is time you call me Nikos," he said, but when I insisted it felt too familiar considering our age difference, we settled on *Mr C*.

I chatted with his Milan contingent, empowered by their freewheeling conversation. A small orchestra played Big Band era tunes as their conversation oh-so-subtly turned personal. Had I been to Cannes for previous employers? Never to Milan? I must promise a visit. So much to see beyond the Duomo, and daVinci. "And your baseball player," one of them said, "such an all-American career." Was he on the road seasonally? Did I travel to watch him play? By the time they asked about spouse and family, I recognised the chat as employee scrutiny.

"*Eh, bien! Bonjour, Nikos,*" interrupted us. I turned. "Emma Paige? Can this be you? *Quelle chance!*" Of all people, Pierre Meysselle pulled me into full blown air kisses.

Mr C reminded me of their previous contracts and explained my position. "*Tres, tres bien*, Nikos. you know how they say in New York. This woman is the real deal."

No doubt I glowed like a street lamp as I turned to the Christopoulos gentlemen playing *consiglieri.* Oh how the Meysselle encounter raised my rank!

"*Abasstanza, signori*! Enough of the sixth degree of Emma," Mr C said when Pierre moved on.

I laughed. "I think you mean third degree. Although your associates are using their sixth sense, for sure." He offered his hand. The soloist began a Sinatra medley as he led me through *The Way you Look Tonight.*

"I celebrate my instinct. You will be an excellent right hand, man," he said as we moved into *Fly Me to the Moon.*

From that opening reception, nightly customer dinners followed back-to-back hardnosed meetings, gruelling for my boss. The convention showcased every luxury product imaginable, and the chance to witness living like royalty. Heady stuff.

"And now a well-deserved week for you," Mr Christopoulos said as we parted.

"I hope you'll get some rest," I replied.

"For an old man, I kept up! You Emma, put up your feet before your baseball player arrives. Then you have a wonderful time."

It was easier to agree than correct his misunderstanding.

Ethan would miss some of the best life has to offer.

After lunch the next day I walked the length of the hotel dock to meet Neil and Dale. Boat? They'd rented a mega-yacht. I clamped my mouth shut as Dale waved from the stern rail and Neil disembarked in a linen suit, bright blue ascot, Cayman sun hat, and orange Hermes satchel. Mr Flamboyantly Fabulous walked the walk as hotel guests on the beach clearly pondered. I yammered, lunched, and shopped with my one-man-band cousin. Per usual I picked his brain, from family history to the provenance of the antiques he was acquiring for clients, to the evening's agenda. Twenty business contacts and friends were to board at seven for cocktails, dinner, and a recital from an operatic soprano friend.

We parted at four. After a beach run and tub soak, a rap on the door startled me. "Yes?"

The muffled response sounded like English. I opened the chained door a hair. *"Excusez moi?* Say again, *s'il vous plait*?"

"I said the Yankees beat Cleveland seven to two in their play-off opener last night."

"Ethan!" I swung open the door and swung open my bathrobe.

"Whoa, Babe!"

Yes indeed, my speechlessly adorable husband was happy to see me. "Get some sleep there's more where that came from," I whispered when I slid out of bed to dress. I would have loved Ethan at the yacht fandango, but he'd already crossed the Atlantic for me. I took happiness where I found it.

I was at the younger end of the guest list but Dale's exotic spin on my Cannes business kick started conversations. Guests raved about Neil's financial wizardry matching buyer to artifact. After dinner the guest soloist hushed us all with Puccini's *Un Bel Di* and Broadway toe tappers. Hours later I crawled back under my covers, one happy person.

The next day Neil played South of France tour guide for Ethan and me and before departing for Monaco, suggested places the two of us could discover together. "Life is too damn short."

"Make every day divine," we replied.

I bragged too much, and Ethan stewed too long over his elbow issues. The honeymoon aura lingered though we exhausted ourselves and each other. I laid out my gazillion dollar Prada ensemble and Ethan lifted the sleeve. "This is some dress for a business evening. You really expect me to believe you'd spend that kind of money to impress a boss old enough to be your grandfather?"

"Sorry. The men I've been chasing have gone home. Otherwise you'd see them lined up in the hall waiting for you to leave. It was his money; stop acting like I'm trying to match the notches in your baseball glove."

"Well, lucky for you my glove and career'll probably go into mothballs soon."

I shut the door. "You make me crazy. Listen to us. It was an asinine response to an asinine accusation. I'm sorry but I need an apology, too."

Two damaged people with the inability to trust anyone can ruin anything. We came close but flew home to routines including both of us in one place more of the time. Ethan expanded his meagre friend network to include Adam Donavan, our building super. At the end of October they trekked to the local sports bar to watch the Yankees sweep the Padres in the World Series. "Can you believe it," I quipped, "their second title in three years, and their twenty-fourth overall."

"A closet fan! I'll take you to the ticker tape parade."

When loving repartee replaced our rants I could concentrate On the Ciao!Beauty front. The shredder ran high speed, I was back to scrambling, staff meetings, and follow ups with Cannes clients. The holiday crunch kicked into high gear as I balanced gift shopping and gift selling.

Ethan patched together 1999 pitching gigs, but sat out more than he played. Cannes boosted visibility which boosted sales. I convinced Mr C to visit perspective clients for the extra touch. Dustin perfected his pitch and I often travelled with him.

Impending Y2K computer disasters loomed over business world. Might ascending numbering assumptions be short-circuited? Programmers had misunderstood the Gregorian calendar rule which would surely throw it off and us into chaos. Maybe.

Meanwhile Macy's sales failed to meet projections for the first half of the year. I worked with our Macy's West buyer Abdul Maliki, a mathematical genius with a photographic memory. "Tick tock, tick tock. Time is money. Call me back when you have the numbers," was his mantra. I used his stats at the next weekly staff meeting and developed an invaluable relationship. Per usual, the executive team went over P&Ls, revenues, marketing, and sales status. As we closed our folders Mr Christopoulos stood. "So the year is ending and I get no younger. I have an announcement I am feeling proud to make." The entire group exchanged glances.

"My nephew Carmine Isgro will join my family business. My sister's son; like my own. He must jump on board to learn all aspects of how we do things and someday take over the company. This Y Two K worries me. I want him to be not so new if we are in for the big problems when the Millennium arrives, so I choose now." He glanced at each of us. "Before this magic year two thousand, Carmine starts as manager of operations." The team assured him Carmine would be welcomed and well trained to ensure Ciao!Beauty's upward path. We also left the room still glancing at one another, eyebrows raised.

Chapter Thirteen

Three weeks later we welcomed Carmine and designed sessions that laid out years of knowledge he'd never get from college courses. He appeared attentive and sincere, asked about the unfamiliar and dressed the part in well-cut suits, stylish ties and shoes. He arrived on time, contributed to staff meetings and fired up our expectations. Although I guessed him to be in his early thirties,

I considered him young and green rather than a contemporary of Jennifer, Dustin or me.

Mr Christopoulos took me aside at our annual holiday party, well into the eggnog. "You are deserving full credit. I put my faith in you as the one Carmine will turn for such employee situations when I'm gone."

I'd had a few eggnogs, as well. "Gone! Mr C!"

"Ah, no one lives forever but I'm meaning gone from the company. I must pace myself. My heart affects my stamina. Our dance in Cannes? My knee still complains."

"You'd looked just as handsome with a cane."

"You flatter an old man." We clinked glasses.

New Year's Eve 1999 included Millennial celebrations in all five boroughs. Ethan and I avoided the frigid frenzy, stayed in, playing in the kitchen and bedroom. "Here's to the two losers who ended up on Fifth Avenue. Who's Laughing now?" he asked as we waited for the Y2K meltdown that never materialised. Self-doubt and low self-esteem still flared like a match stuck against sandpaper but we worked at recognising the triggers. Ethan started the new year networking and landed a job coaching Iron Hills High School baseball in Clay, New Jersey, between South Orange and Newark, a school district most professionals avoided. Unlike baseball hopefuls with skills to shove them forward, few of his kids could counteract their abuse, poverty and dysfunctional home lives.

"I get it," Ethan said the day he signed on. "Maybe more than any other adult in their lives, I totally get it." Within weeks he was elected to the community task force developing positive examples through athletic programs. This therapeutic chance to make a difference through baseball lifted his anxiety. As he gave one hundred percent to the kids, I knew he'd set a positive example in sports, loyalty and sportsmanship. I didn't know women's calls would fill our landline.

"That'll be Rosalie or Nicole," I muttered over a rare dinner together. "Single mothers working full time only get the athletic department voicemail after work. Some have told me it's the first they've been able to get through to anyone in charge."

"Rosalie gets through a lot."

"Don't go there, Emma. Using our landline number puts everything in the open. For school and for you." He took the call in our home office.

Nikos Christopoulos kept his word and loosened his grip. He showed off his snazzy gold-tipped cane and paced himself in the office. His complex corporate structure included several Long Island interests outside the beauty business, but only on a need to-know basis for my team and me. In September he put his Carmine in charge of them, somehow convinced he'd acquired the expertise to make changes. The more adept and comfortable Carmine became, the more he shed his *I'm here to learn* persona and reminded us he would carry on his uncle's legacy.

Mr C now scheduled an annual October conference following the Cannes Luxury show. Our nation-wide sales field, office staff, and executive team attended morning and afternoon training and job-related sessions. A gala dinner highlighted employee awards and Ciao! Beauty creations. I suggested our 2000 event further integrate Carmine into the mix and let it be known *Putting On the Ritz* style celebrations were my specialty. For visuals to exemplify Carmine's internship and input, I hired Thomas Schuman. I hadn't seen him since the Guggenheim launch, but he was the freelancer to wander our headquarters and provide paparazzi style collage shots. Privately my team called the project NNBT, *Nephew as The Next Big Thing*, but we stopped short of over-the-top shenanigans. Our sophisticated evening, Schuman glossies included, went off without a hitch, thrilling uncle and nephew.

One late afternoon November Sunday, Ethan and I strolled home from the Oak Room through Central Park. He put his arm around me. "Why so distracted?"

"Carmine, Carmine, Carmine. I've set up round table discussions for him tomorrow morning. Half the time he barely makes eye contact. The other half he's tossing out-of-line comments. The more time the uncle spends out of the office, the crasser and more self-serving the nephew becomes. He's morphing into an egomaniac. The rest of the company needs to know."

"Babe, forget *needs to know,*" my street-smart husband said. *"The old man's* brought in young blood and for sure Carmine's got his own agenda. Watch your back. Arm's length for this asshole."

Carmine wasn't snorting coke or stuffing his pockets with Tootsie Rolls, but Jennifer, Dustin, and I recognised the Brian Cox aura as the narcissistic manipulator stacked the deck in his favour. Thank the fragrance gods my team could focus on cosmetics without his interference but by the holidays some of our prestige stores retailers worried Ciao!Beauty was moving backwards in terms of brand-building strategy. Dustin suspected the goal was control of the bank accounts as Carmine used the last quarter to show his uncle what a hot shot manager he was. The scourge of 2000 was not Y2K, it was Carmine F. X. Isgro.

In early 2001, Carmine installed giant televisions in several locations. Fox News ran all day unless Uncle Nikos was in. Then Carmine switched to *Stock Watch* on the Business Day channel and stared. One afternoon when I asked a staff member where my boss was, she cupped her eyes. "Mr C is watching his nephew pretend to comprehend intelligent financial television." Mr C, cane in one hand and occasionally on my arm as well, still whistled down the hall, but "That Carmine! Such a fast learner," squeezed my heart. In February he approved several of Carmine's cronies for unnecessary positions with high salaries and no explanation as to responsibilities, or company value. Worse still, our CFO and COO politely resigned citing better opportunities; other talented executives followed. "Where is the loyalty? Once you are in this company, you don't leave." Mr C's concern over their departures outweighed any apparent doubt over the replacement. Sooner than I thought possible I reported to Mr C with his nephew as CFO and COO.

Carmine called his team The Cabinet and often referenced the President and Executive Branch of our government, but barely understood economic policies, foreign or domestic. Their newly licensed brands required large investments that eroded the bottom line. Beauty business growth slowed. We were neither as successful as predicted, nor as profitable as pre-Carmine days. Nevertheless, he insisted our other companies showed massive profit under his direction and convinced his uncle to put all divisions in one place. Voila! The Isgro Agenda became reality. He renamed the merged units Kinetic Inc. and took control of the operation in early May.

From three-piece suits, to hoodies with backpacks, men (always men) of all stripes crossed our threshold. Family members or Carmine's cohorts replaced most senior executives. Department heads now reported directly to him. He created 'Governor at Large' for his uncle. Mr C, not naïve enough to hand over his life's work to someone barely beyond apprentice, remained in the passenger seat, but president and CEO Carmine F.X. Isgro was at the wheel.

Despite his chummy gaggle of confidants, our inexperienced pilot still needed a seasoned professional on board. Given my profitability-improving track record and Mr Christopoulos' insistence, I was the only one with approved control of the company's healthy assets. Suddenly the pragmatic nephew emulated his uncle's admiration of me. My employment felt secure but it was Marsha Johnson-Brian Cox déjà vu all over again.

Paranoia runs rampant in the fragrance industry and Carmine's matched mine. He included me in monthly meetings, furtive monthly meetings held on a different floor of the Empire State Building. The Cabinet grew to eleven older, wiser men who ultimately controlled the money. I sat at the table, rarely spoke, always smiled. I realised they were diverting our brands to the Middle East, and South America, mainly Colombia and memorised as much as possible. Like our competitors with larger resources, Kinetic, Inc. needed my legitimate company face as someone trusted to impress domestic and global markets.

After a March meeting, Carmine entered my office with a Rolex box and asked for my help. I reopened my briefcase.

"No, no. You're doing a great job and all, but it's the girlfriend. You've seen her around the office. Tall, blonde, Romanian? Looks like a Sports Illustrated swim suit model." Who hadn't? They stared at the TV together.

He opened the box. "Her birthday's tomorrow. A beauty, am I right? Over ten grand."

"I'm sure she'll love it," I replied.

"It's engraved *To my sweetie*. See, if it don't work out I use it on someone better. Genius, right? She needs to know I spent a shitload so let's add – Prada purse, LVMH luggage? Maybe Gucci boots? Whatever just no Canal Street knock-offs. She needs to know it's legit goods."

"You could run over to Madison—"

"Nah. Doll, it's gotta be you. You wear the real deal. You got that look; you know the goods." He picked up my photo of Muriel Beausoleil and me. "Buy her something classy like this babe makes. I need it in the office first thing tomorrow so yous better get going. Thanks," he said to the Rolex. "And pick up a birthday card. I'll sign it myself."

Bimbo shopping? *Put Emma in her place* oozed from him. I closed my briefcase furious with his arrogance and unnerved by his familiarity with my desk.

Friday, he assured me the Prada purse had been a hit. "So glad," I said. "Time for lunch? I'm meeting your uncle to discuss our employee celebration. We could use your input."

"Sure thing," he said.

I'd wangled a table in the It Row at Brasserie 8½. The West Fifty-seventh industry hot spot shared the same building as Chanel headquarters. As I'd hoped, industry bigwigs nodded, waved hello, even paused at our table for small talk. I (gleefully) introduced Carmine then nudged his foot to indicate indispensable power brokers, a power play as delicious as lunch.

Mr C leaned to Carmine. "What I tell you? Until Emma never could we receive this service or respect." He patted my hand. "Thank you for all you've done. For me and such a trooper teaching Carmine and ensuring he leads well once I retire."

"It's a pleasure working for someone who cares so for his employees." We returned to party details and Carmine insisted guests include his outlying reps and officers.

On the home front, Neil and Dale flew in on Spring business and treated Ethan and me to the Met's *Samson et Delilah* with Placido Domingo. Ethan formed a cohesive baseball team from his gaggle of players and finished with twice the wins to losses. Coach Paige signed on for another year. An insistent Ashley, he swore was the parent organising the sports banquet, outpaced Rosalie and Nicole in voicemails.

All Spring my team and I juggled Ciao!Beauty/Kinetic demands with organizational sessions for the fall company celebration. Our decision to salute Nikolas Christopoulos and his fifty years in business revved up the meetings to weekly. Thomas Schuman, now on retainer as house photographer, would capture the event on BRoll video. We booked The Plaza for Friday, October Twelfth, including conference areas, the Ellington Park Suite for Mr C, and blocks of rooms for overnight attendees. Atticus, heading in from LA, and Andrew from Chicago were the ones I looked forward to the most.

And then the second Tuesday in September arrived. The horror of 9/11 solidified us as nothing else could. "We are family," Mr Christopoulos said. We employees united in our loss of neighbours, friends and family and he returned to the office for the next two weeks.

Closest to home, Neil called to check on Ethan and me. His beloved Beverly Hills associate had been on the plane to LAX, returning from a Boston buying spree. New York phone lines were so jammed it took Maxine two days to reach us. She'd held a packed vigil Tuesday night (even my mother attended), and was to conduct the service for a Brucknerfield Marine killed at the Pentagon. Adam Donavan, our building super and Ethan's closest friend, lost his Port Authority police officer brother. Should we cancel the employee event just four-and-a-half weeks away? Reps called, reluctant to fly to New York, let alone spend time in the city. With The Empire State Building suddenly the tallest in New York again, were our offices now a target? Fear emptied Manhattan streets. Tourists cancelled in droves.

With the Yankees again in the pennant race, even the World Series was pushed back to the end of October.

Was it disrespectful to hold a celebration? Surely morale would be at an all-time low. Mr C called us together the following Monday. "It is a go," he said.

"All weekend, 'Nikos,' I tell myself, 'You were a Greek teenager when Athens fell in nineteen-forty. You and your family did not give in to treachery then. You and your business family do not give in to it now." We needed something to rally around and this was it. We quoted him and reservations held. We greeted attendees at our welcome station. and I opened the events at the podium. "Thank you all," I said. "There's much to keep us sombre. Comfort each other while you're here. Everyone in the room had been affected. Support for each other will be part of the agenda."

I smiled. "You're here to celebrate, too. The Plaza Hotel and its employees are thrilled you're here. New York City – Broadway, the museums, every sidewalk vendor—are thrilled you're here. Every cab driver's cheering." I let the laughter die down. "And on behalf of Mr Nikolas Christopoulos, *we* are thrilled you'll be part of our seminars and celebrations."

He delivered a professionally written motivational speech (practiced for weeks) and our event began. Employees attended morning workshops and training sessions, then afternoon marketing programs Dustin created. Isgro Cabinet appointees appeared at some but primarily stayed sequestered with board members and unfamiliar entourages in a private room.

When we reconvened for the evening, Carmine mimicked his uncle's satisfied expression. We'd met our top-quality goals. Big Band classics wafted through cocktail hour. VIP tables placed our top European clients, Middle East retailers, and surprise Milanese relatives to best advantage. When our competitive sales force's appreciation awards prompted entertaining but long-winded acceptance speeches, Carmine's bored expression landed on me. "Hang in there," I whispered. "Sales people love to brag. Brand perks and company celebrations build envy. We need a good year end. This motivates them to hit projected sales targets."

"And I asked for your advice?" he hissed.

Mr Christopoulos announced his retirement, we joined the applause, lights dimmed. The screen glowed with my surprise fifty-year timeline video tribute, and our teary-eyed guests' standing ovation closed the evening.

At midnight I finally excused myself from the impromptu gathering in Jennifer's suite. Jet-lagged Atticus dozed in the club chair; but Dustin and Andrew still held court with reps as I left. Walking the hallway reminded me of my Plaza evening with Pierre Meysselle, so French, seductive, yet the ultimate gentleman. I turned the corner.

Carmine leaned against the elevator wall, thumb on the *up* button. "Well, well, the fucking force to be reckoned with." He whiskey-laced slur stopped me as he stepped forward. "My cabinet calls you the that but I don't buy your brand of Miss Cheerleader bullshit. Pretending you need to guide me; making fucking nice. I don't give a damn what promises my uncle's fed you. Thiza family company; you are not family." He pressed me against the wall. "*Non siete famigilia. Capire?*"

"Listen to your cabinet. I am trying to keep us solvent."

"There is no *us*." Carmine slid his free hand down my back to my butt. I flattened against the wall crushing his fingers.

The elevator dinged, he stepped back and two couples exited. I entered and glared. "Don't even think about getting in, you degenerate asshole."

Carmine Isgro was hardly the first degenerate asshole in my life. My childhood prepared me for the resulting nothing-happened atmosphere. I gritted my teeth, played pleasant and tried not to obsess over Mr C's absence, a hole neither Carmine nor his recruits filled. I focused on holiday sales and pushed the team hard to make year's end planned P&L. Fraternity house replaced Big Band era. Carmine added a bar in the kitchen, and basketball net in the conference room. January staff meetings barely addressed 2002 strategies, yet his team outvoted my every suggestion over structure.

When a colleague contacted me about a high-profile celebrity fragrance license deal coming in the new year, Carmine or no, I met with Cam Hampton, the Brit heading the project. I added this international contact to my own network over drinks at The Jockey Club. Cam laid out projections and stats from players gathering intel on the North American market. He quoted twenty to thirty million dollars as the upfront requirement. Pointless to consider without the Christopoulos influence, but I asked to be kept in the loop.

"Carmine's half-assed directives for Kinetic distort everything his uncle dreamed of for Ciao!Beauty," I whined to Ethan. "I swear Mr C's completely in the dark. His goal to leave it in solid management hands is going down the tubes."

During the chaotic days of 9//11 and its aftermath I occasionally saw a backpack delivery arrive at the front desk. By December I realised the messenger handed the satchel to assistant Bernie every Tuesday and Thursday. Contraband? Gambling? Maybe nothing but trusting my gut had never failed me. Ethan's devotion to team stats rivalled Las Vegas sports bookies. He was now home 24/7 so I developed a wifely interest in running numbers. I didn't dare tell him what I suspected, so I played Twenty Questions.

"I'm analytical," he told me, "You've watched me for years, Babe. No emotional aspect. Some weeks I do trials, say five bucks on the games to see how my formula works with their stats and odds makers' predictions. Depending on how my picks come in, I up the ante the next week. It's important to watch your back. Due diligence, of course. Now money goes right into the bank."

"Or out to someone else's."

"True, but electronics makes bookkeeping clean and uncomplicated, except for the old guys who need the feel of cold hard cash." That gut of mine tightened.

On a January Tuesday, I crossed paths with Mr Backpack and Bernie as I returned from lunch. Due diligence and *what if, what if, what if,* destroyed my concentration. I stewed all afternoon. By the time I finished the day's requirements, the office had emptied. Now, I told myself, before the cleaning crew arrives. I shut my computer down and hot-footed down the hall.

Carmine's locked (Clue Number 1) office required my self-taught lock-picking skills. I got in, stood stock still, and perused every inch of the room without disturbing anything. To be honest, I didn't know what to disturb. Should I search for the backpack itself? For its unknown contents? For related skull duggery?

The interior wall bookcase featured five by sevens of Carmine—grinning from a golf cart, teeing off with a foursome, posing for Thomas at Mr C's annual October event. All were interspersed among gold-plated tchotchkes, and rows of leather-bound law books. Nothing to be smuggled in a backpack.

I swivelled in Carmine's executive chair and stared at a Coney Island souvenir ashtray of paperclips, red rubber bands, a few screws, and pieces of candy cane. Rifle the file drawer for something nefarious? Skim the paperwork on his desk? Fire up his computer? The heating units under each window rumbled and hissed, startling me into reality. Skulking around like Nancy Drew was nuts, not to mention grounds for immediate dismissal sans severance package.

I leaned on the register for a final look at the last of Midtown's holiday lights. Lo and behold, the cold metal cover shifted under my sweaty palms. Only the unit to my right was on. The loose cover of this one lifted without prying. I looked over my shoulder at the screws in the astray, (Clue Number 2), and back at the now-exposed radiator, complete with wedged backpack. (Clue Number 3)

"Bloody hell." I knelt and unzipped it as carefully as if it were packed with explosives. Maybe it was packed with explosives. Nope. Bundled cash. Wads of bills secured in red rubber bands, mixed among a few hand-sized *Soir de Provence,* one hundred millilitres/3.4-ounce fragrance packages. I pulled two out.

The signature lavender packaging seemed slightly off, closer to blue. I rotated it under Carmine's desk lamp but needn't have bothered. Folded paper turned out to be Excel ledger listings, proof of shipping totals to various countries. Bloody hell. Bloody hell. Carmine wasn't gambling; Carmine was counterfeiting our products.

Chapter Fourteen

My heart knocked against my ribs. As I snooped, the bastard could be pressing *27* in the skyscraper elevator; an accomplice could be disguised as cleaning help; The Cabinet Guys could be organised god-only-knew what. Ethan Paige would go ballistic.

A hot, clammy wave of impending anxiety attack roiled. Before I lost my nerve I slid the perfume back in the bundled cash, but removed one of several ledger sheets. I needed collateral. The terrifying Carmine-as-crook scenarios already slammed around in my head. I replaced the screw-less register cover, remembered to lock the door behind me, got the hell out of the Empire State Building, then hightailed it home.

Without the daily presence of Mr Christopoulos, Carmine's casual M.O. grew careless. He left copied documents by the communal printer for hours, so I made additional sets of his private papers. This went on through January until it was all there in black and white. Carmine was not only diverting several fragrances to South America and the Middle East, and flooding the North American market. He'd created the covert company that manufactured the counterfeit brands. I no longer suspected gambling. Backpacks jammed with cash and knock-offs looked more like money laundering or fraud.

I sat at my desk, head-in-hands. This accounted for the profitability of 'other business models.' I thought about our North American stores' loss of market share for the brands we represented. Carmine was slowing down my sales, causing the P&L to look like we were losing money. At the same time he reported manipulated income or revenue to the IRS. Tax evasion.

My Determination to keep my team ignorant and safe kept me silent even when Dustin or Jennifer raised eyebrows on their own. I ached thinking Mr Christopoulos knew about this illegal activity but piecing together earlier events, conversations, and back story forced reality on me. Had he brought me in for legitimacy? Put me under contract while concealing the fine print? Alarm shredded my concentration but fuelled my determination to stay on task and make sense of the situation.

A few weeks later on the way home I got caught in a frozen February storm and ducked into the nearly-empty Surrey Hotel bar at Seventy-seventh and Madison. A man in a dripping trench coat slid onto the next stool and I dug into my purse to avoid chat.

"Emma Paige, don't react just listen." A Tommy Lee Jones drawl came at my ear. "I'm federal agent Munz. We've been tracking you for weeks and have some questions. I need you to calmly get up, retrieve your coat. Exit through the back door to the SUV parked just outside. We can talk in the back seat."

Right. No way would I swallow a trite, B movie spiel from some Texas who-hah Isgro henchman. "I am not getting off this stool, let alone waltzing through a back exit with you."

He slid a folder under my nose. "Open it."

"Look—"

"Open it, Mrs Paige."

I skimmed authentic, illegal Ciao!Beauty and Kinetic information only a federal investigative agency would have. Next came his ID. Agent Munz represented the FBI. I did as directed.

Rainy rush hour and round-the-clock World Trade Centre demolition slowed our excursion to Lower Manhattan. The crawl and his impassive silence exacerbated total terror all the way to twenty-six Federal Plaza. When we finally reached a generic office on the twenty-third floor (wired for sure), I asked to call my husband. I was a workaholic, I babbled. He probably suspected nothing. Still, I was two hours overdue.

In case our apartment phones were bugged, I had to say I was still at the office. Bugged phones? I called, apologised, told Ethan I loved him, and hung up. The men in black offered me coffee as Agent Munz explained the case began two years earlier.

Hells bells.

They had to determine my involvement in illegal activities.

Bloody hells bells. I was in no way involved, but recently noted abnormal, possibly illegal activities, I said. "In fact I've started my own file. Do I need an attorney?"

"Not at this time," Agent Munz replied. "Though you have the right to counsel if you think you need it."

I said not at the moment and wiped my palms on my skirt.

There was not a shred of doubt I'd have to prove my innocence.

The agents expected to close the case within weeks. "Still," Agent Munz said, "To insure you're not implicated, we need you to put eyes and ears in the office. You'll wear a wire to gather the final evidence that will shut them down."

Oh my God. Oh my God. I fought terror and tears this time. "May I think about it? Can we meet tomorrow night with my attorney?"

They agreed, took me out through the rear of the Federal Building to an SUV, and sped me home where I was also to keep this from Ethan somehow. I embellished my earlier lie with traffic and headache complaints and went directly to bed, convinced the FBI had the apartment under surveillance. The minute Ethan left on morning commute I called Darlene Duke's private line and begged to meet with her. I then emailed Carmine of my delay due to a doctor's appointment.

My attorney was her usual snippy self. "Lucky for you I'm experienced in dealing with government agencies. Good lord, Emma, how the hell did you get involved with these idiot gangsters?"

"I swear I had no idea until a few weeks ago and I won't sleep until the FBI puts this plan together. The FBI! They practically kidnapped me. Tell me you can be there tonight."

She agreed. From there I went to work and smothered anxiety in the routine. Of all days Carmine burst into my office falling over himself to tell me he'd brought a new brand into the company. I was to think about ideas for merchandising it.

We'd fine-tuned avoidance since the elevator incident. Asking for advice? Appearing to enjoy my company? This had to be a setup. Caution kept be vigilant but an hour of stupid questions and ignorance convinced me the man was clueless. I finished the day checking my watch every thirty minutes, closed my door at five and promptly ran into Cabinet Guys in the hall.

"You're leaving early tonight. Big date?"

"Dinner with Ethan."

I fled for the town car and onward to negotiations. Darlene and the FBI made it clear it was in my best interest to cooperate for two weeks. Agents, posing as utility workers for Kinetic office repairs, would provide surveillance to the team sequestered in the corporate space across from our interior entrance. Once they had sufficient evidence, I would be excluded from legal proceedings to protect my career, my identity and my life. To further remove me from suspicion, the FBI would pounce on my routinely scheduled quarterly getaway.

Two training sessions kick started my out-of-body experience. I learned to bugs phones, attach tiny cameras on TV screens, and conceal surveillance items in small objects. A female agent came to my apartment, fit me with apparatus and chose attire to hide it. I spent all conversations with board members wired. Freaking mission accomplished.

Complete relief nearly normalised my behaviour when Ethan and I left Thursday night for our 1770 House, East Hampton long getaway. Dustin and Jennifer called Friday morning from breakfast to our bundled beach walk when I finally picked up.

"I have no clue what's going on but until the dust settles, don't talk to anyone. I'd go home and stay home." I hung up and slung my arm through Ethan's. "Major office shake up."

"How shook up?" He pulled me against his down jacket. "You know you want nothing to do with any half-assed gambling operation like the numbers system you pretended to be interested in, right?"

"Right."

"And that means nothing to do with that Carmine guy."

"I'll probably know more when I go back Tuesday." Snow dusted the sand as I hugged his arm. Except for my level of anxiety, the long weekend remained uneventful.

Tuesday morning I returned to work and exited the elevator. Thick silver chains shackled our door handles. A professionally printed notice plastered our entrance:

THIS COMPANY IS CLOSED
INDEFINITELY PENDING INVESTIGATION

Like a cheesy movie scene, I leaned against the wall, slid into a crouch and cried myself hoarse. When composure finally returned, I went home and called Mr Christopoulos.

"Emma! We are in a terrible emergency. Such chaos and confusion. Oh, my dear dear Emma, I am so very sorry. You have no work. So many worries. You must make a promise to stay away from all this mess. You don't deserve to be dragged into it."

"Mr Christopoulos—"

"I have a very extensive legal team. So experienced. They will take care of me. And, dear Emma, make sure your name is never brought up. Never." His strained speech broke my heart. "Two hundred thousand dollars wired to your payroll account. It is done so no argument. I want for you, time away." He voice broke. "You understand, dear Emma? I want for you, out of town."

I understood. Darlene Duke understood. She wanted me out of the country. Ethan had to be told. Since sex was the one thing we never struggled with, it preceded my full confession. That night he hit the roof and it has nothing to do with our talent in bed.

Cash in backpacks? Wired? FBI sting? I hadn't trusted him to keep quiet? Why didn't I walk the minute I suspected? He paced to from the bed to the dressing room, to bed. "This could ruin you! Ruin me by association. As in never being able to work in schools. Emma, what the fuck were you thinking?"

"We'll make sense of it in Cannes. The FBI and Mr C want us out of town. Darlene says out of the country."

"Holy crap."

Only Ethan Paige would agree to a month on the French Riviera because it didn't interfere with his baseball coaching. We told no one and my attorney remained our go-between. We took refuge in The Carlton International like distinguished off-season exiles. The moment the FBI shackled the doors on the twenty seventh floor of the Empire State Building, Ciao!Beauty was over.

We settled in. Darlene reported that Jennifer and Dustin received two months' severance pay and were in no jeopardy. They agreed to sit tight until my return. She next emailed that the FBI kept their agreement. Enough evidence existed to act on multiple charges. I had nothing to worry about. No doubt the case would languish in the justice system for years.

Carmine counterfeited products through shell companies, then mingled his China knockoffs with legitimate perfume. The FBI confiscated sixty thousand bogus bottles at Port Newark with Street value over three million dollars. They scored the largest seizure of counterfeit fragrance in North America.

Updates confirmed my snoop session only nicked the surface. Cash-stuffed duffels insulated space behind Carmine's new sheetrock walls in his company offices, warehouses and distribution locations. The Feds found four million Ciao!Beauty dollars due to be laundered through New York, New Jersey, Boston, Chicago, and Los Angeles banks. It left Ethan and me breathless.

It also seems Carmine had priors. He and his original six Cabinet Guys faced the brunt of charges which meant massive legal costs, hefty fines, and federal prison terms. As I feared, Mr Christopoulos was also held accountable. It was his company, his name on bank accounts and checks. Considering his health, leniency was expected. I hoped so even though I'd probably never know how complicit he'd been.

Disappearing for the first volatile weeks ensured avoiding industry chatter as the press laid it wide open. *Women's Wear Daily*'s legal reporter scooped *The Wall Street Journal*. From *Page Six* to *The Times*' for weeks financial pages rattled the beauty industry. Darlene upped her game. *Emma Paige* was never mentioned. Ethan and I avoided our cell phones. Darlene intercepted our apartment landline voicemails and, in an emergency, the few colleagues who knew where we were could reach us through the hotel concierge. Gradually emotional and physical distance replaced shock and fear with something close to enchantment. We never forgot why we were there, but walking the chilly beach, romantic dinners, and the casinos had no more sense of reality than the chaos at home. As equilibrium returned, Ethan and I rediscovered ourselves and who we were as a couple. Of course the earth kept turning. Mr Christopoulos's deposit cushioned my unemployment but Ethan's New Jersey programs needed scheduling. And then Major League Baseball bigwigs wanted to meet with him at their Manhattan headquarters to discuss coaching California rookie teams.

"California," I whined the next day, bundled beneath a beach cabana. Travel, major time away. Same old, same old. Ethan put down his week-old *New York Times*. "I'm happy with my kids but you know Major league ball's my brass ring. I need to hear them out. It's my career, Emma. Yours always comes first. It's always been about you."

"It's about me because it supports us. No one else me like you do. You're my lifeline. I can endure beauty industry insanity when you're with me. My career's never more important than you. Year after year I pray baseball won't chew you up and spit you out. I'm tired of watching it break your heart."

"Don't go there."

He was right. We'd been down the baseball path so often it was nothing but dirt and gravel.

We returned to mail, messages, New York and reality in late March. Our first morning back, while Adam Donavan showed Ethan his kitchen faucet repair, my cell phone rang, country code forty-one, a repeat of a handful I'd had in France. For the first time, I answered.

"Emma Paige? Julian Petrenko. You are one hard women to reach."

"I'm sorry. I don't take unsolicited—"

"—You may regret ringing off."

"Do I know you?"

"I'm in international business with several companies."

I listened, thumbing my mail, trying to decide if his broad Oxford English was authentic.

"…Including majority owner of The Texas Bulls, NBA Basketball and some minor league baseball dabbling."

A Brit owner of an NBA team? "I'm sorry, I know very little about sports. Maybe you're looking for my husband?"

"Most certainly not. I mention them for the American connection. I've been calling for weeks as I've tracked you down for good reason. I've an opportunity. It's true we've not met but I'm told you're the best of the best in the beauty industry. My bit of a dilemma requires someone fearless."

"I'm flattered but I'm not looking for a new position."

Now the pause was his. "Ms Paige, due to the unsettling circumstances with Kinetic and Ciao!Beauty, I thought you'd certainly consider the offer."

Here we go, I thought as memories of El Paso, multiple Motel Sixes, and pot-on-the-bus flashed. "Mr Petrenko, I don't see myself in a position with anything sports related."

"Certainly not. My inquiry is for something far more suited to your skills. I suggest we meet in person. I'll explain in detail, and how we can help one another. If you'll give me a fax number, you'll have pertinent details within the hour. Peruse them and I'll ring you tomorrow at four p.m. your time."

I looked at my phone. "Mr Petrenko—"

"Ms. Paige, Were it not worth your time, I would not have placed these calls."

"All right. I'll take a look." I gave him my fax number. "I'll expect to hear from you tomorrow."

"Indeed."

"Cripes," I muttered twenty-five minutes later as fifteen emails flooded my computer while my fax machine spit out press reports, articles, even biographical information within publications from *Bloomberg to The New York Times* and

Forbes. Julian Petrenko, mid-forties, British-born of Russian and German immigrant parents. Based in Zurich; financial dealings in Switzerland, Germany, the UK, and the United States. From what I gleaned, his net worth hovered close to three billion Swiss francs, with business interests in specialty medical products, endoscopic surgery systems, even telecommunications.

Why me? Okay, why not me? I wandered back to the living room, reading as I went while Ethan said goodbye to Adam. I explained and held out the sheaf of papers.

"Seriously? Julian Petrenko?"

"Wait. You know who this guy is?"

"Emma, Petrenko is huge fucking deal in NBA circles. I had no idea about baseball. Holy shit. Say yes!"

"To be honest I was annoyed with his approach."

"Don't tell me you countered with your usual *Why should I care* attitude. Oh God, you probably pissed him off."

"I doubt it. He's pretty persistent."

"He'll offer you a massive amount of money. You're damn good, you know."

"Well, thanks for that."

"And maybe we'll get sports game tickets perks." He grinned. "With excellent seats."

"You've never been excited about my interviews."

"You've never been interviewed by NBA royalty."

At four p.m. exactly my phone rang with the *de rigueur,* "Ms. Paige I have Mr Petrenko on the line for you. May I connect the call now?"

"Good afternoon. I hope you received my documents?" opened his conversation.

"Indeed. More intel than I expected. You have a big fan in my husband, Mr Petrenko. To be honest, he's the one urging me to meet with you."

"Smart bloke."

"I don't want to waste your time. Your credentials impress me, of course, but I'm not sure what my next step will be. You seem to know my circumstance so sure you can understand. I don't want to get over my head. Frankly, I have the good fortune of being able to take time to explore my options, perhaps take it easy for a bit."

"Understood, though I know enough to presume you'd not be happy without challenges. Consider this: we meet face to face. I assure you some time in person is the best way to decide if this is what you want to do next."

I let his offer hang for a moment. "All right. How about the day after tomorrow?"

"Yes, fine. Our meeting is confidential; For now I need you to keep this between us."

"Mr Pretenko—"

"Nothing untoward, I assure you. I own some property on the Isle of Wight. My assistant will make the arrangements."

He was doing a lot of assuring. "The UK? You want me to travel four-thousand miles to listen to a job proposal?"

"I fully expect this to be worth your while. Of course I could be wrong about you, or my contacts were misinformed."

"I'm not taking the bait. I deliver results. I assure you your contacts are not mistaken."

His tone softened. "My main offices are in Zurich and London. My schedule demands I remain on this side of the pond, yet it's only common sense we meet in person. And ASAP."

I heard myself say, "I'll make the trip."

"Excellent. I'll see you on the Isle of Wight. And, Ms Paige, relax. It's not but thirty-five hundred miles."

"I hope you're happy. I'm going to the English Channel for this interview," I said to Ethan thirty seconds later. "We're meeting in some country house on The Isle of Wight."

He whistled. "Forget your anxiety. This is an awesome sign, Babe. It shows he's serious about an offer. Sports guys are well trained recruiters, experts at getting top talent."

"He's not recruiting me for hoop skills or running bases. Do I want to get back into that pressure cooker, especially with some high powered international muckety-muck?"

"Emma, I know what I said in Cannes, and I know you think I'm after the perks. I also know in a week you'll be bored out of your skull knocking around this apartment looking for the next big thing. If this is a good package, grab it."

The Petrenko final fax laid out an itinerary as specific as the Cannes trade show. Breakfast meeting, tour of the grounds, overview of Osborne House and the Commodore's Invitational at the Royal London Yacht Club, apparently not in London. His Gulfstream IV delivered me from Teterboro, New Jersey, to Farnborough Airport, ninety minutes southwest of London. I stewed all seven hours, still that St. Louis novice on her Big Apple maiden flight. I'd have understood crossing the Atlantic for Zurich or London to meet company officers. Why the Isle of Wight? Why some yacht club event? This jaunt seemed more about Julian Petrenko than it did my future employment.

An employee met my flight, drove to Portsmouth and escorted me onto a private Hovercraft for the channel crossing. I docked at eight forty-five, a day-long journey to Priory Bay Hotel, Seaview, more intriguing than my Empire State Building caper. I expected James Bond but Petrenko assistant Alistair Downs guided me along the lighted path smelling of sea and wild flora. He concluded seven hundred years of history with a gesture. "Have a look at that bench in daylight. Holofcener's duplicate sculpture of FDR and Churchill. *The Allies*."

I revived in my quintessential country house suite, with a soak. Essential oils, supper and Merlot revived me enough to skim brochures on the island, hotel, and Queen Victoria's *Osborn House*. Alistair had covered it all. I slept and just past dawn, pulled on walking clothes and backtracked down the path. Children already clamoured on the rocks with buckets and twine. Sunlight glinted off the bay; daffodils bobbed. Good opportunity or not, my contentment startled me, deeper than Cannes and far more immediate. If Ethan hadn't insisted, I'd never had known my fairy tale-come-true smelled like an English garden, tidal flats and salt air.

At eight-thirty, in Prada head-to-toe, references, bio and resume packet in-hand, I crossed the second floor and started down the staircase. A man studied the artifacts in the foyer display cabinet below. I studied his caramel-coloured hair, Rudolph Nureyev cheekbones, bespoke business casual linen shirt, wool trousers, soft patina on his shined shoes. I reached the newel post and he turned as if he sensed my presence.

My heel snagged the tread. I tripped and he caught me by the elbow stooped at the base of the stairs. "I move too fast when putting my best foot forward."

He laughed and brought me to my feet. "I do hope you're Emma Paige."

"Yes. Julian Petrenko?"

"Indeed. Now that I've broken the ice by breaking your fall—" He gestured and kept up the banter until we entered the circular dining room. "Take a minute," he added.

A mural of the Isle of Wight wrapped the room, framing the full windows and historically accurate map painted on the chimney breast.

"I understand it was discovered beneath layers of wallpaper during the mansion's restoration," I said.

"Well done."

"Alistair's quite the tour guide, and of course the brochures... It's breath-taking in person."

"I'm a bit fanatical on the historical. Kick me whilst we eat if I ramble on too long."

No kicks. His local lore chat over breakfast gave me valuable time to register first impressions: secure, confident, forthright. Probably meticulous. I suspected Mr Petrenko didn't like to lose at anything, but no evidence of an overblown ego.

He finished a second cup of tea. "Now that we've gotten to know each other a bit, shall we talk business? Do you know about me, my companies, what I do?"

"My husband knew your name immediately through your NBA affiliation. Of course I read the impressive information your assistant sent. Frankly, Mr Petrenko I still wonder why me? Why a beauty industry executive?"

He tented his fingertips. "I've a business that supplies custom oils, the industry's raw materials for candles, air fresheners, all manner of personal products—shower gels, hair care, skin creams. A year ago I increased my shares in a cosmetic company to one hundred per cent to become the owner."

"Would I know names of your brands?"

"Imperial's the supplier. Barely a handful are privy to this. I'd like to keep it that way."

"Of course, there you are! When I was at Platinum Marsha Johnson used Imperial, most recently for *Charade*. I can't say I had direct contact but they're top quality. That includes meeting our production deadlines. If you've read my resume—"

"Yes, Wildly successful *Charade* launch. I've been strictly hands-off on both ventures but I'm to understand the oils do quite well, but the newer, relatively small business is losing money. I don't like to lose money, Ms. Paige."

"Would you share a few details?"

"I purchased the company for forty-five million American dollars. *The Nudes,* an organic skincare line, enhances a woman's natural tones, the illusion she's not wearing make-up or some such. The other's a lifestyle fragrance, *My Elixir.* Our consumer works directly with a perfumer to customise her own fragrance through essential oils. It seemed an excellent match Imperial. We store the recipe, duplicating it in related body products, even home items such as candles. The division also has baseline products based on the top selling olfactory categories."

"I know these brands."

"Spot on. Your impression?"

"I found them last year at Fred Segal in Santa Monica. In fact I loved the customised concept but I stumbled on it, Mr Petrenko. I wondered who was working on it. Why such weak execution reaching the consumer? I'm knee deep in the business but I couldn't recall press buzz. No over-dinner gossip, or word-of-mouth launch hype." I looked at the wall map and back at my host. "To be honest, I forgot about it. I suspect a normal consumer would, too. A shame, a lost opportunity."

"Your point's well taken."

"If I pitched this to you, I'd emphasise exploiting the concept of an astute woman's exclusive scent. There's huge potential."

"Indeed? Then good news. I'm in the throes of evaluation."

"Don't give up. Your concept's outside the box, head and shoulders above the industry junk we see every day. You're onto something. E-commerce, as they call it, will only grow. eBay's bought PayPal; Amazon dot com is making a profit at long last. The elements are key but how you market and sell this concept could easily triple sales in the next two years."

"You have my attention. And the skincare line? *The Nudes*? Viable project as well?"

"Gosh yes! Anti-aging is a trending growth category, a consistent driver with massive development opportunity. You know our term *Baby Boomers*, of course? A huge number of women worldwide are pushing sixty, becoming grandmothers." I raised my finger. "In no way do the identify with their grannies. No sensible-shoes. They're after the Fountain of Youth."

"Bloody hell, aren't we all?" He smiled.

"That's my point. You can repackage and expand this line in a dozen ways for the right people. Yield a large revenue base, even turn a profit. You'll need investment to reformulate. Slick packaging. Maybe add scents that evoke the emotions from this island: botanical, fresh, windswept. Exploit active ingredients *The Nudes* woman would understand. Fewer LA or Riviera plumped lips and tight foreheads, more Cape Cod, Isle of Wight sea breeze. Anti-aging aspects will be key. Perhaps a famous dermatologist contributes to the process. This adds a medical message to the consumer. Buzz foresees this as a big trend over the next ten years. You'd be ahead of the curve."

"A woman's intuition."

"A touch mixed with my years of tracking trends."

"I like how your mind works. Fast, very fast. You've quite the résumé and achievements yet no formal education."

"I don't hide it. My dysfunctional family offered no emotional or financial support. I married my high school sports hero, Ethan Paige, determined to pitch for the major leagues." I breezed through my professional climb. "I recognised my people skills early on selling magazine advertising. Next, I handed out fragrance blotter cards at area malls, and shadowed the amazing professionals around me."

I leaned in. "Observation, mimicking, burning ambition, and a scrappy talent for survival puts me at your table. You've been calling me for weeks and inferred I have time on my hands." I waited. "Clearly you know my history. Things did not end well at Ciao!Beauty for Carmine Isgro or the company he ruined."

He tented his fingers again. "Imperial inadvertently supplied raw materials for his Calvin Klein knockoffs."

"*Obsession*! Do you know Isgro?"

"Only in the most cursory way."

"My connection was far from cursory. I'm fortunate to be rid of him. Bad vibes from Day One. I don't like to lose; I always have a Plan B; I never give up. I'm relentless when it comes to getting what I want in life. But you'll understand my need for a breather before I jump into anything new."

He met my glance. "I'm surrounded by well-educated people, yet in too many cases Harvard or Oxford types lack social intelligence. Connecting to people, instincts, and negotiation cannot easily be taught."

I thought of Brian Cox. "Street smarts. Intuition."

"Spot on!" He glanced at his watch. "I've a meeting in an hour's time. I'd like to regroup by two o'clock." We stood. "If I may, Ms. Paige, Relax, get to know your surroundings. It's brisk but we've a sunny day. Walk the grounds.

Your comments on *The Nudes* and evoking emotion from your Cape Cod, my Priory Bay, struck a chord. Start at the car park. Stroll along the golf course. Let yourself be drawn to sites. Analyse the appeal." "A suggestion I gladly accept." I handed him my essentials. "I'll be brief this afternoon. We've a corker of an evening and I didn't fly you her to exhaust you. I'd like to think we might form an alliance and a plan of execution."

"I'll keep that in mind as I walk. Please call me *Emma*?"

"Then I must be *Julian*. Two o'clock. Again in the foyer."

"I promise to hold onto the banister this time."

He smiled and tapped the wainscoting. A panel opened and he disappeared, as if into thin air.

Chapter Fifteen

I wandered the property, even sat on the bench between *Allies* FDR and Churchill. I meandered to the golf course, trying to focus on ambiance and aromas. Everything smacked of fantasy. I'd been out of touch with reality for twenty-four hours.

Who charters a jet for one person and disappears through a disguised door? Why me in this mansion-hotel hugging the English Channel? I inhaled the salt air, sniffed blossoms as instructed, but kept thinking of this Russian émigré, all Oxford accent and impeccable manners, asking questions, answering few. The man had done his homework but then a power broker in his position would have gathered whatever information he needed about me.

Despite faking it to interest Nikolas Christopoulos, consulting wasn't customary for someone at my level. I could use it as my excuse to retreat If that became his offer. I returned to my suite with an exit strategy, ordered room service lunch and called Ethan. Even at eight a.m. New York time, his phone went to voicemail. A power nap and BBC World News cleared my head. At one fifty I descended the staircase in beige slacks and cashmere sweater, purposely reaching the foyer before Julian. "Sorry you missed it," I quipped as he arrived. "This time I slid down the banister."

His laugh boosted my confidence. Mystery Man escorted me through the public rooms to an archway cordoned off with braided roping. "My private quarters. We'll talk in my office. First let me show you the building's secret."

Fantasyland continued. Back in the Island Room he tapped open the disguised panelling for the second time. Cooking aromas and the familiar clink and shuffle of kitchenware wafted along a passageway lined in built-in, glass-front cabinets. "Back in the day every estate included hallways and separate quarters for the help. God, forbid they used the same staircase." He gestured to the left. "The kitchen's through that door and this hall opens to the lobby." We headed right. "When they brought the building up to commercial code, I had a flat carved out of the butler's pantry and servants' sitting rooms."

In we went past similar cabinets over soapstone counters, sink and stove. Alistair Downs adjusted the flame under a teapot. "Lemon or cream, Mrs Paige?"

"Hello again! Lemon, Lemon would be fine."

"An indispensable man of many talents," Julian added as he guided me by the elbow into a foyer hung with framed artwork. Very good artwork. He nodded at another door. "The roped off main entrance from the public area we saw earlier."

I paused in front of a gorgeously familiar oil. "This can't be Turner's *Angel Standing in the Sun*? I saw this in the Tate."

(Thank you, Neil!)

"Indeed. You saw his final version in the permanent collection. This is a preliminary rendering." He circled the air, inches from the canvas. "A more distinct wing behind the angel's right shoulder. If you work for me, your expertise on good art will be accelerated. It's an asset in my business." He settled against worn throw pillows on his couch. I sat in the club chair. The cluttered desk, sweater on the chair, *Financial Times* stacked on the coffee table put me at ease. Alistair left the tea as I looked out at the bay and described impressions from my walk. I touched on finding the right niche for any target, marketing to older women, and the importance of quality production for enhancement of a fresh, natural look. "You confirm my expectations."

"I'm intrigued on this end, Julian. Your hospitality and the way you've approached this interview says a lot about you."

"Please elaborate."

"You've shared business details. You're refined, hardworking, proud of your achievements. Clearly used to winning, which speaks to ambition. Open to new ideas, critical in the change-on-a-whim beauty industry, by the way." I looked at the sea. "You've told me this destination is key to the interview but we're not in a perfume factory, or even a board room."

He tented his fingers again. "Very perceptive. I own the entire compound. I don't advertise it. It's critical you understand my desire for privacy. No company carries my name. With the exception of the Dallas franchise, I'm as low profile as possible. I'm apt to use a trusted employee in my place. I expect confidentiality and loyalty. I sense you feel the same."

"I do, though my expectations haven't always been met."

"A shame."

"Priory Bay's appeal is obvious, but why purchase?"

"Long story short, Cambridge Five was a spy ring during World War Two based in the university. At fifteen my Russian father was given a new identity and placed in the UK. He recruited several students whose critical information ultimately ending the war. He was apprehended by the Nazis in Berlin but saved by his fluent German. My Jewish mother lost her family to the camps. They met in a German café and during the Cold War became double agents. Reconnaissance for M Sixteen. They were murdered on a London street, presumably by a Russian agent."

"I'm so sorry, but so impressed."

"During The Blitz Priory Bay Hotel had been used as a safe house for children of UK government employees. M Sixteen placed my toddler sister Oksana and me with the caretakers. We were raised here. By the time they passed away it was in disrepair. I had the means to purchase and restore it. Oksana died two years go. Cancer. My family went through so much, it drives my success, keeps me strong. Keeps me keep going."

"I understand." Maybe James Bond really had materialised. "I've laid out what's made me rich. Let's get back to your success. Emma Paige has been recommended to address my floundering efforts. Do I cut my loss by liquidating *Nudes? My Elixir?* Both projects? My other businesses are well run and turning a profit. Is Mayfair Beauty, the cosmetic company purchase, worth keeping? I bought it as a way to test Imperial oil technology and expand that success under my control."

"I don't recognise Mayfair."

"That's the problem, they're too far under the radar."

"And haemorrhaging funds was not part of your plan."

"Never! I've a managing director overseeing the operation but she hasn't what it takes to execute the work. She's to be sacked but now would be counterproductive. I've neither the time nor knowledge to apply directives. I've been told you do." I hoped he was less ruthless than he sounded. "I'm to work with her until she's sacked to pinpoint what's fixable. Suggest a plan of action to turn around the company?"

"Yes. I've gone that route before with great results. Initially I'd place you inside specifically to report to me with intelligence and recommendations. Would this interest you?"

"Not if this director turns out to be a Carmine Isgro."

"Isgro's in a class by himself. My director Wilma Nash, will be cooperative."

Ah, I knew of her and her reputation. A player, strong-willed and political but also known for good concepts and pitches that built enthusiasm. I did a one-eighty. "We'd need to outline terms but, yes, I'm interested."

"A woman who jumps into negotiations! I suggest we draw up an agreement. You consult for me exclusively, One hundred and seventy-five thousand dollars. If we see eye to eye, in six months' time we negotiate a permanent position."

"Fair enough."

"Best you begin next week. I'll explain to the New York office you're to run alongside Ms. Nash. You'll report to me on turning the business into a profitable endeavour."

"And if I doubt that's possible?"

"Honesty's imperative. If it's all to pot, you help me package it or, considering a six-month time constraint, help initiate the liquidation process."

"Fair enough. I believe I can be an asset. Ideally, I'd like to connect with my husband first. I called Ethan at lunch but he's not known to answer his phone. I'll try again."

"And if he doesn't pick up?"

"I'll give you my answer without his input."

"Tell me about your high school hero as we finish tea."

"Ethan's winding down from a professional baseball pitching career. He's athletic. Obsessed with sports, hates to travel, a real homebody even when home was a string of god-forsaken motels on the road. He's generous, honest, great with kids. He's working with struggling, disadvantaged high schoolers now."

"You have none of your own?"

"We don't." I stayed on the surface of my private life.

"Sounds a lovely match. Time to break. You'll need time to prepare for the evening. In addition to the usual members of Parliament, I've been alerted the Prince of Whales will be attending. I expect the island will be in security lock down."

If Julian dropped that nugget for effect, it worked. Ye gods. "Goodness. I may have not have packed enough glamour."

"The English love understatement. I've no doubt whatever you wear will be perfect."

"Thank you." I glanced at the art again as he walked me to his proper entrance. Surreal. All of it. Strong work ethic, clearly presented goals, handsome yet no sleazy sexual innuendo. My guard was up but his offer was too tempting refuse.

My mind raced as I returned to my suite. During my Marsha tenure Wilma Nash was known to combine her considerable business skills and drive with flamboyance. I avoid gossip traps, especially regarding women determined to advance in the corporate world, but even I knew she worked her way up the management ladder juggling a short-term affair with a luxury retailer CEO that ended badly. Either the Nash buzz faded, or I was too preoccupied with my miserable February unemployment situation to know or care where she'd landed. I loathe dysfunctional environments. If her private life remained separate, I'd concentrate on number crunching.

In the midst of getting ready a few hours later, a Petrenko assistant delivered a small blue box with a note tucked under the velvet ribbon. "For this evening," she said with a smile.

Dear Emma,

Thank you for making the long journey to meet with me. My sister, Oksana, was a critical part of tonight's event every year. Seeing her necklace in use again would give me great joy.

Sincerely,
Julian

I lifted the single strand of perfect pearls, divided by a square cut emerald, held and attached by gold strands. Despite my doubts to Julian, I'd packed the perfect Vera Wang satin cocktail sheath, understated and perfect for the necklace. Andrew Case, extolling the importance of wardrobe, taught me to lower others' expectations, then deliver the punch. Impressions were everything. *Prince Charles, The Royal London Yacht Club, ownership of the entire hotel property…* I opened my closet thinking my host was working overtime on his.

I left Ethan another message: job offer, evening activities, and a promise to fill him in. And then for the third time I left for the Priory Bay Hotel staircase. Instead of topping my earlier banister-sliding joke as I descended the stairs to him, Julian greeted me with his voice full of emotion. "Thank you for wearing

Oksana's pearls. You've brought life back into them. You are stunning this evening, Emma."

"It's so kind of you to lend me something so special. I'll cherish the necklace tonight. I feel like Cinderella."

He bowed, brushed the sleeve of his impeccably crafted dinner jacket, and offered his arm. "My driver awaits. No pumpkin worries."

Chemistry sparked but during the forty-five minutes' drive from Seaview to Cowes, Julian was all business. I explained having left a message for Ethan and accepted the offer to consult. We sealed it with another handshake.

At the yacht club he helped me from the car amidst arriving dignitaries of all stripes, royal and otherwise. I glanced across the road at the nautical flagstaff, still flying RLYC colours in the early evening light.

"The club burgee," he whispered. "The royal standard indicates the prince is on the premises. Should we be introduced, you needn't genuflect."

"Good to know," I whispered back. We were and I didn't. I left Fantasyland having met a prince and been treated like a queen.

Chapter Sixteen

My status as a consultant bolstered my jubilation. As perfect as the all things Petrenko appeared, the cynic in me still needed as exit strategy if Julian turned out to be a Brian Cox-Carmine Isgro combo, or I sensed another shove under the dismissal bus. While I was gone Ethan's major league interviews came to nothing, but nearly for the first time he was genuinely interested in my pond hop. I stuck to over-the-top descriptions from Secret passageways, the sea-hugging golf course and museum quality art, to my chartered Gulfstream commute and the Prince of Wales. Two days after my return a Federal Express package arrived for Ethan. He hooted and stuck the note under my nose. *Ethan--*

Much appreciate your urging Emma to meet with me. Like you, I enjoy athletic competition. I hope you can use the enclosed tickets to the next Knicks game at Madison Square Garden.

Best Regards,
Julian

"See? I told you we'd have perks. Amazing seats!" He hugged me, tickets-in-hand. "Babe, I am so frigging glad you accepted his offer!"

I kissed him. "Take Adam, somebody who appreciates them." I spent the evening in workaholic mode on my assignment to decode Wilma Nash's M.O. This was her first CEO general management role but she'd arrived with Big Four experience as head of Marketing and Sales. Due diligence included calling around, reading business publications and trade press. I'd been hired to align, listen, learn, and report, though I vowed to tread lightly.

Julian flew Wilma to Dallas for a Stars play-off game where he explained concerns over the two years of revenue losses. He used the excuse of an audit to justify my presence and made clear her cooperation was critical.

Sacked left a bad taste in my mouth. I preferred to think Wilma Nash would, as the Brits describe it, be made redundant. I arrived at the Rockefeller Plaza office confident she understood the remedy for Mayfair would be Julian's decision.

From fresh spring flowers to Lucite reception desk, Mayfair's décor was as chic and trendy as Ciao!Beauty's had been mid-century Old School. It sent the right message to visitors, but maintaining such a high-end address for a staff of only fifteen was my second concern, and probably easiest to remedy. For six weeks I observed, studied and listened. Wilma and her team focused on creating new products for The Nudes cosmetic line, and signing a celebrity face for both brands. To her credit she'd launched a solid-in-theory polished, catchy quarter-million-dollar PR initiative but the company was haemorrhaging money without proven ability to execute the plans. She made it clear other departments covered the basics but she lacked accountability. The P&L overstated sales vs. results. Her team wasn't tracking cost for new product development. Most retailer accounts barely broke even. Poor execution had cost them close to a million dollars.

Like Linda and Marsha, Wilma built her career in a man's world. We had much in common but I had to keep her at arm's length. My requests annoyed her. No doubt she knew she exemplified The Peter Principle and had risen to her personal level of incompetence. I kept details to myself but incidental chat when Julian checked in always held his interest.

Ethan and I filled late spring and early summer evenings with bistro dinners and walks in Central Park, or take out and Cannes level sex. Midsummer in the midst of putting my report together, Cam Hampton kept his word and updated me on the project we'd discussed at The Jockey Club in December. The celebrity fragrance license venture had sales potential of two hundred and fifty million dollars, yielding over fifty million in profit and bragging rights for executing the biggest fragrance deal in the history of the category. I'd seen the concept as a boost for Ciao!Beauty, but it could be a company saver for floundering Mayfair.

The concept was being pitched to the major cosmetic companies; Cam had three offers pending. My contacts confirmed he was within ten days of awarding a letter of intent. If we were interested, I'd have to move fast. I crunched the numbers. Improved payables and inventory could turn Mayfair Beauty's losses of over five million a year to a profit of seven to ten and solve our problems within two years. I convinced the indie manufacturing company rep who'd made pots of money over the years from Emma Paige orders to pitch Mayfair to the LA team vetting candidates and hear me out. Julian authorised my flight.

"I haven't seen you this fired up in ages," Ethan said the night I returned and got back between our sheets.

I kissed his shoulder. "Total adrenaline rush. I disclosed Julian Petrenko as Mayfair's owner and the atmosphere sizzled. I wrangled a week out of them to pull together a presentation and organise a proper P&L." I propped myself on my elbow. "Me, love, Emma O'Farrell Paige convinced these power brokers to put a hold on competing bids and see what Julian brings to the table."

"Babe, men are impressed with men who own professional sports teams."

"Like you every time FedEx arrives. As for all that LA testosterone, pure gut reaction tells me buzz over Julian can give us a smidgen of leverage over the other contenders."

"You better let him know."

"I emailed in LA and he called me from India. India!" Ethan kissed me where it counts.

Simultaneous work on company restructure plus licensing opportunity required late nights, morning coffee and pacing our apartment before I finally called Zurich. I made it clear a profitable endeavour required restructure and office relocation. I planned to revitalise existing brands, and portfolio expansion estimations 'to provide profitability within twenty-four months with no debt.' I used *our* and *we* a lot.

Julian suggested I draft a full report and we meet in London in forty-eight hours. "Plan on a week in Europe, Milan included. Your input at the board meeting will be valuable for Mayfair as well our raw materials outfit. We'll arrange another charter for you." I smiled at his use of *our*.

Mayfair Beauty had no Chief Financial Officer, so my last day stateside I met with Julian's COO and vice presidents for marketing and sales. Wilma's three top guns reviewed the details but gave the impression the company was running away with itself.

On the home front Ethan flashed FedEx'd tickets to another Madison Square Garden game. "Like clockwork, Babe. Another bribe while your Julian gig requires so much of your time."

"It appears to be working," I said.

He waved them at me. "Damn right."

Despite seven hours' time difference, info analysis and swift decisions lay ahead upon arrival. I slept my way over. Julian booked me a grand suite at Claridge's, flashbacks to Marsha days. I rearranged the furniture into a makeshift office setting. Neither Julian nor anyone else were to expect anything less. I answered the phone to, "Mayfair welcomes you, Emma, our company's namesake and point of origin. Decent flight?"

"Terrific as usual." Twelve minutes he arrived to escort to his penthouse suite.

"You probably know in nineteen forty-five Winston Churchill resided here on the sixth floor," he said as we entered.

"I do. I stayed here on jaunts with Marsha Johnson in my Platinum Beauty days."

"A few months ago I was contacted regarding investing in this property. I made sure negotiations included exclusive access to this apartment. When you see something, you want, move quickly. The only way to be in business."

Julian was all smiles as I glanced at the twenty-foot ceilings. Floor to crown molding windows framed the main room. Muted green, beige and white complemented Diane Von Furstenberg updates. He converted a bedroom into the quintessential English office, looming desk to Chesterfield club chairs.

"It's hard to concentrate on anything but war time London in here. Easy to imagine your parents' war activities, too."

Back in the parlour the butler served tea as I opened my files. "It's critical we move on this. Your business is in distress. Wilma's a product developer with excellent concepts. She lacks expertise to deliver results but there's no financial officer to rein in spending and your COO hasn't partnered with her. We need a director who knows global markets. No company can survive without international as most profitable."

"You've left no stone unturned."

"You're paying me well not to. Frankly, you need complete restructuring. Do away with the COO and Wilma's position. Add a senior CFO as general manager. Put sales and marketing under a combined vice president, plus Director of Operations to oversee product development." I slid the paperwork to him. "The attached Excel file shows five hundred thousand dollars annual savings." I explained overspending, updated systems to cross reference paperwork, then sales field territory restructure. "It's all here but to sum it up, you're bogged down in a very serious situation. Wilma's team seems to advise her to 'Put concealer on it and the problem fades away.'"

"Or splash a bit of fragrance and it'll smell better."

"Good one but Mayfair's not a blemish, or a rotten tomato. In all seriousness, Wilma's doing her job but management's neither guiding, nor calling her to task. You can't thrive on her clever concepts. Two years of this business style is destroying your company. Julian, you're going bankrupt."

"I'm sorry my instincts were correct but elated they're spot on about you. Blinding work, Emma. Now for the kicker. Can you move as fast to get this bloody situation under control?"

"I can. It's not as hard as it seems. We start with key people. Pros. there's not nearly enough time to train anyone."

"Have you the network to pull this together?"

"Experienced men and women who know the ropes."

"Bollocks, this is more serious than I realised. We need to revise our agreement. You're to have a permanent position."

"You might want to think it through."

"I've done little else. I see you as Vice President. Overseeing Mayfair with a seat on the board fills two key elements: an American, and a woman. You're both and brilliant."

"I'm flattered."

"Simply facts. I've taken the liberty of having my attorney draw up a contact. I hope you'll review it this week, with an answer before you return to New York seems reasonable."

I tried to appear casual. "I appreciate your vote of confidence. Are you sure? Should we hold off another month?"

"Absolutely not. As you've said, I need the overhaul now. Come aboard. We align to recoup which assures my goal of every business unit profitable within two years."

I had not yet lit the figurative cigar. "My attorney's in Manhattan. You understand I need her review."

"I wouldn't have it any other way. My friend and associate Harry Steinberg will work with you in person. He's in London for a fortnight. You're to see him at three thirty this afternoon. Standard agreement, mainly confidentiality protection for both of us. Trust me, Emma, this will go smoothly."

"You're a hard man to say no to."

His clear, blue-eyed gaze made it unequivocal. "I take that as a compliment. Now explain this fragrance deal opportunity to make the company profitable."

I poured more tea. "You've heard of the UK Connection, the London based celebrity band?"

"Indeed. They've mesmerised Britain and Europe. Same in the States? Can't say I've paid them much attention."

"Promoter Axel White—Mercury Artists out of Los Angeles – spent three years combining talents of five boys from different British cultures, unknown to one other, each driven to make it in the music world. Uk-C's that rare combination of musical talent, good looks, and charisma, under an umbrella of marketing genius. Indications suggest they're the next big thing." I shuffled papers. "I'm ready to convince you to go after this."

"Fire away."

"For the sportsman in you, stats: forty-five million global fans, six hundred million Wikipedia views. One of the first groups to use breakthrough technology. Digital marketing's referred to as *social media* and they've plugged into it to drive recognition and sales. Do you know Facebook?"

"I know what it is."

"Ten million followers. They post B-roll and documentary style videos. They've have reached over fifty million kids."

"You're speaking a foreign language but point taken."

"Last week they performed in Rockefeller Plaza on our *Today Show*. Girls camped on Fifth Avenue for three days. Their concerts fill stadiums, they're rumoured to be our Super Bowl Half Time Show, and confirmed to perform at the next Olympics."

He tented his fingers. "Fans are fickle. Convince me they're more than a flash in the pan."

"Their world tour starts in six months and already sold out. First UK group to have the number one single here and US simultaneously. Their reality movie similar to Madonna's *Truth or Dare*, launches within the year." I stopped for a breath. "Their debut album hit number one in twelve countries. They'll release a new one annually for the next five. Record sales hit over four hundred and fifty-thousand copies in the first week."

"Impressive, yet if I'm facing bankruptcy. Who's to say this venture won't go all to pot and nail the coffin shut?"

"The biggest fragrance names are your competitors and they've done their own due diligence. I've dug deep and believe you have the advantage. You own the Dallas Bulls; You own Imperial. Your raw materials company can fast track your production and reduce prep costs, a killer combination. The full P and L indicates it's a good property to capture."

"Points well made, Emma. Very well made." He glanced at his watch; a gesture now as familiar as his tented fingers. "I've a Zurich conference call in fifteen minutes' time. While you meet with Harry Steinberg this, I'll give it a go with our finance expert. Shall we reconvene at eight to review over dinner?" Pleasant tone, no inflection. We shook on it. Nothing says *I have the upper hand* like meeting in the former suite of the Prime Minister who brought his country out of World War Two.

I returned to my suite grateful for the break from Julian's exhausting intensity, no doubt the way Ethan felt about me at times. I called the concierge and scheduled a spa massage for the next morning, then dialled Cam Hampton and agreed to see him after I met with Julian's attorney. I ached for a nap but to finalise a letter of intent and term sheet with Julian, I needed as much inside Cam Hampton, UK Connection inside scoop as possible. If Cam expected a kickback, so be it.

An hour later, firm handshake given, I sat down with Harry Steinberg, his contract, and non-disclosure agreement, as straight forward as Julian promised. After a deep breath, I dickered over a few technical points, tacked on a fifty-thousand-dollar annual clothing allowance and twenty thousand dollars to my salary. I asked for a two hundred-and-fifty-thousand-dollar bonus if Julian were awarded the UK-C deal.

We shook again as Harry agreed to revise and email the contract to me ASAP. It arrived in time for me to email it to Darlene before heading to meet Cam. If I'd learned anything to date it was not to trust anyone completely, especially men. I'd never sign anything again without my attorney Darlene Drake's confidential review. We're loved in the beginning but men can be fickle. A woman must negotiate when she's wanted. Cam's renowned Groucho Club hummed with arts and entertainment members who, no doubt, had endless trivia on the country's teen sensation. I gleaned additional tidbits from his helpful UK-C chat, including two of the three bidders' offered royalty rates. I'd hold this intel close to the vest until I had deeper knowledge of Julian in action.

I agreed to a twenty thousand gratuity for Cam if we were awarded the license. U.S. dollars not Pound Sterling made it a very good deal. The night was young. By the time I returned from Groucho's, Darlene had reviewed, redlined, and emailed the contract. I, in turn, emailed it to Attorney Steinberg before I left for Julian's penthouse at seven fifty-five.

"I trust all went well with Harry and we have a deal?" he asked over an aperitif.

"I hope so. I made a few changes and emailed it to him. As long as you can live with my amendments, I'll sign tomorrow."

"I expect acceptable changes. A toast. To our partnership." I raised my glass with pride.

Julian suggested dinner before business and asked if Ethan had received his package and enjoyed the game.

"Oh! I assured him I'd tell you. He was thrilled. I was busy with the restructure proposal. Ethan took our friend Adam Donavan. His firefighter brother died in The World Trade Centre and Adam takes Ethan to Knicks games in his place, a huge honour. This was the perfect way to show appreciation."

"I'm touched."

"And thank you, as well, for the most recent set that arrived just before I left."

"I've put a lot on your plate. We can't have Ethan idle while you're away. How long have you been married?"

"Close to fifteen years."

"And Ethan supports you and your career."

"He does. What about you, Julian. Marriage? Children?"

He frowned. "Divorced. No children. Long, arduous hours building my companies. Ultimately we grew apart."

"I'm sorry. Ethan's sports career and coaching stints give us different schedules. Different agendas mean our share of struggles but he's wonderful at bringing out the best in kids."

"You appear to manage well. What are his hobbies?"

I paused. "On-line sports betting, fantasy football. He and Adam have bonded over it, over sports in general."

"I've mates who dabble as well. I suspect this new on-line gambling will likely make a lot of blokes very rich."

"Ethan thinks so. He studies college football stats like the stock market. Handsome watch." I changed the subject as he made his cursory check

He tapped the rectangular face, banded in black alligator.

"Uncomplicated. Keeps me on schedule. Girard-Perregaux Vintage Nineteen Forty-five. Partial to Swiss manufacture, of course." He grinned. "I've another, I'll show you some time. Multiple time zone chronograph. An ostentatious gift, frankly, but just the thing should I decide to pilot my own Gulfstream, or play tactician for the Volvo Ocean Race."

"You don't have time to take up either sport."

Julian laughed. "Correct on that score." Staff cleared the meal as we returned to business. "I shared your documents with my CFO and four board members. We're in agreement with your findings as well the UK Connection deal. Milan tomorrow gives us a go with the full board. If passed we shift into high gear. I offer whatever's needed as you'll be the face of negotiations."

"I'll be rested, then a morning workout and massage before we leave. I appreciate your confidence. I have a good feeling but could use some insight on them."

"Twelve men, each at the top of his game. Here from Madrid and Milan. Others align with Zurich. Two live locally and invest globally. To a mate, diverse with common threads in the arts, fashion, luxury goods, even five-star hotels and spas."

"Diverse? Arts, fashion, luxury goods, yet not a woman among them."

"Fair enough. We're wheels up at three; plan lobby departure for noon. I'll pitch our proposal. You're to lay out the offer. Discuss whatever's to be considered. They'll be intense but receptive. Three quarters are investors, balanced by key advisors. Be yourself. Your business acumen's as appealing as your—, as the rest of you. Before another reprimand, I suggest we call it a night before we collapse."

I returned to my suite thinking about a watch for Ethan as I punched in his number. He answered with his Julian enthusiasm. We discussed my current adventure for an hour and closed with his reminder of his Madison Square Garden tickets the following night. "Enjoy, hot shot. The red eye puts me in New York by eleven Saturday morning."

At dawn I snatched the London daily from my doorknob and did a double take. A line above the masthead, complete with a shot of Julian, referenced interior coverage of the Royal London Yacht Club dinner. I flipped to the entertainment section. A two by three of Julian and me sat cantered a photo collage of the Commodore, fleet captains, MPs, and The Prince of Wales.

I cheered the coincidental timing of being back in England to find it, and put it aside to show Julian before packing it for Ethan. I was established in the trade press, but this was a new level. Julian was a bigger VIP than I'd realised. Perhaps, with the UK Connection deal in hand, he'd think the same of me.

Milan. I thought of the Christopoulos *consiglieri* enthusiasm for all I must see. How I hoped those kind, cultured gentlemen had nothing to do with Carmine's treachery. Nikos Christopoulos looked to me for guidance but there was no comparison with the powerbroker studying papers across the aisle Nothing like this.

He and I worked separately during the two-and-a-quarter hour trip. This board meeting was the real deal, not Carmine Isgro's fake collection of who-hahs pretending to be business men. Julian Petrenko had me at the top of my game.

We landed and went directly to the dinner board meeting. Despite my fanatical preparation, I hoped Julian's pitch would convince them. His presentation eased my anxiety and bolstered my confidence. I offered additional information on a few points, personal opinions on others.

He looked at me. "Thanks to Emma we joined the action before the deal went to our competition. And my thanks for helping convince my teams of our extraordinary opportunity."

The board passed both proposals: ten for; two against. After the announcement the younger of the London investors glanced around the table. "Ms Paige, I speak for each of us with teenagers at home. If this vote garners so much as an autograph, let alone backstage passes, I'll be father of the year and indebted to you for life." Over laughter and "Hear, hear!" the meeting adjourned.

"Brilliant, just brilliant," Julian added as we headed out.

"If I were Churchill, I'd offer you a cigar." I raised the V for Victory. "If I were FDR, I'd smoke it."

Chapter Seventeen

Just after nine pm Julian led the way to our waiting town car. "Exhausting day, but I've arranged a small stop on the way to the hotel. A bit of a surprise. Is it a go?"

"Sure, Any hints?"

"No but high hopes you'll enjoy it." We wound along city *strada* until our driver paused between quintessential Milanese buildings. Julian ushered me onto a piazza. "Do you know this?"

"For starters, a lot of Renaissance brick and terra cotta."

"Spot on. We're at the refectory of the Covent of Santa Maria delle Grazie. The surprise lies within." I stopped in my tracks and pivoted completely around.

"You know it?" he said.

"Julian! *The Last Supper* 'lies within'. It's been on my list every trip to Milan, but I've never had the time."

"I believe in time for inspiration. I've arranged a private viewing to celebrate tonight's success and your accepting my job offer. I promised art exposure. I am a man of my word."

"And I'm speechless."

"The basilica closes to the public at seven thirty. It was sand bagged during World War Two and even survived that insanity." He led the way past the exterior to a garden. An elderly nun stood in an open doorway, back lighted from within like a Renaissance painting. "*Buona sera, signor Petrenko. Signora Paige. E il mio onore.* My honor."

"A full tour another time," Julian whispered as we followed a hallway smelling of eucalyptus, lavender, and acacia. She gestured to the refectory. "*Pochi momenti da contemplare. Momenti con genio e nostro signore.*"

"*Molto bene, Sorella.*" Julian replied as she left us.

"She's suggested moments with genius and moments with our Lord."

"DaVinci's *Last Supper* in front of me, Giovanni Donato da Montorfano' *The Crucifixion* behind me. Judgment, power, good, evil. Maybe even strength to rise above what life hands out." Julian studied me, not for the first time. Whatever I imagined I saw in his clear blue gaze was left unspoken.

I flew to New York alone, sleeping most of the way, contemplating Julian Petrenko the rest. Ownership of a landmark hotel, Winston Churchill's penthouse, a private viewing of priceless work, sprinkled with royalty and Russian spies, presented in the guise of understated generosity. I was gobsmacked, to quote the Brits. By design, I felt sure. Easy on the eyes, business acumen, multilingual, bespoke wardrobe, finely tuned style—his assets seemed endless. The man also possessed enough charm to mask his intentions. He worked hard to hide it but I felt his scrutiny. Always. Yet even at our most comfortable, he rarely let his guard down. Easy affection, even sexual tension hadn't spilled into flirting or anything overt. Was he working overtime to impress me or reaffirm the Julian Petrenko he presented to the world? Possibly both.

Ethan's enthusiasm bordered on disbelief as I rambled from 'Yes, that's Prince Charles,' to I swear, it's true. A little nun let us in for a private half hour with Leonardo daVinci.

I also returned to Wilma's preoccupation with the upcoming annual Luxury Style Awards. I was using the Mayfair conference room as my main work space, and she hustled into our weekly executive meeting thumbing her Smythson of Bond Street planner. "I am seriously about to burst. I'm on the board, practically running the whole celebration. The night culminates with the Billion Dollar Club winner." She plopped next to me as her fellow executives trickled with a few nods.

The core group addressed the serious business of massive operational and supply chain problems while she surreptitiously wrote Linkedin, hair colour, eyebrow waxing, and nail appointment reminders in her planner. When the meeting adjourned she returned to starring massages and dinner reservations, then crossed her legs in a whisper of silk. "…Already dealing with fragrance icon temperaments, and ego-laced requests from every rising fashion star and industry innovator being recognised." She finally closed her Symthson. "You do know I'll be taking a date. Not just any date. My match maker claims ninety-eight percent compatibility. It's not inexpensive; seriously, over five K, but have I found the perfect guy! The sex is amazing. We've been seeing each other for six weeks."

"And he's your date?"

"You bet. Total arm candy."

I met her gaze. "Business smarts to go with it?"

"Of course, of course." Wilma knew as well as I Mayfair Beauty had to pick up his two-thousand-dollar entry ticket fee, a huge expense when the company was losing millions.

"Wow, after six. I'm off to meet for dinner. And dessert."

"You should join the Luxury Group. I could put in a good word."

I ignored her power play. Wilma liked playing CEO, but didn't take it seriously. I was consulting in a soap opera atmosphere. I waved her off and re-read my notes.

I left for the day by way of the women's room, opened the door and stopped dead in my tracks. Wilma, razor-in-hand, stood at the sink, faucet running, skirt hiked into her belt. She stood on her right foot, left leg propped on the counter, inner thigh wrapped in shaving cream from knee to parts unseen.

"Emma! Oh my God!" She flushed into her scalp but our soon to-be-former operations manager kept her balance and winked. "Just getting ready for my date." I gave an inane reply, backed out, and used the men's room.

During the days I stewed over Wilma, I completed my Mayfair business model. Bringing over most of my long-standing team would allow me to hustle the commitments I'd made to Julian. The executive board governed execution of the turnaround. We had the go for UK-C. Now to get the company on its way to correcting two years of demolition. I assembled key executives and studied Jennifer Rocket's new concept, The Four Ps: People, Product, Present, Promotion. My dream core would be.

Financial Officer: Samuel Garten

VP Global Sales & Marketing: Jennifer Rocket Field Sales Director: LA based Amanda Denton

VP Operations & Product Development: Bill Grose

Director of Analytics and Ecommerce: Abdul Maliki

Director of International Business: Sebastian Ballantine

Creative Director: Dustin Walsh

Two companies remained in the race for UK Connection. In a week Julian and I were scheduled to meet at London record company headquarters to offer management our final pitch. They promised determination within forty-eight hours.

At the same time, Ethan continued to cheer me on as his expansion to private lessons in the city picked up. Word was out. Ethan Paige had the ability to reach troubled kids, improve rag-tag teams, even mentor semi-pro young guns fresh out of high school still trying to reach the next level. His journey, as thorny and meandering as mine, had eased. Hopefully the frustrations of transitioning from pro ball were behind him. I made peace with his disdain for socialising. My introvert husband never willingly went to large events. He seemed confident in his future. For now that was enough. Thanks to Julian he regularly attended NBA games. They had yet to meet, but stayed connected via email and generous amounts of Federal Express packages. Each contained the hardest tickets to score, and the best seats for viewing. Over a quiet dinner at home he showed me the latest package. "I swear I'm trying not to take this for granted. Playoff tickets! Dallas, in his corporate box. Enough to include Adam and a couple of Texas guys I played ball with. Babe! He's even arranged a private jet. Adam'll freak out. Julian's assistant booked The Four Seasons, where you stay in Dallas. We fly down Thursday morning. Game that night, then two more, Friday and Saturday. I'll be back Sunday afternoon. For once we'll be gone at the same time."

"And I'm back Sunday morning. I'm thrilled for you. I'll take off Monday so we can spend some time together. We'll have lots to compare." I kissed him.

"Both of us in Teterboro private planes. Emma, look at us!"

Before I knew it, I was on my flight to London, bolstered by a Xanax to avoid obsessing into an anxiety attack. What if we didn't land the deal? We would; we would; we would. Dustin and I worked on the pitch book for weeks. I was still reminding myself it was flawless as I checked into Claridge's. I met Julian in his apartment/office, thanked him for the play-off tickets and offered Ethan's gratitude for the VIP treatment. I hoped for some chit chat to calm my nerves but Julian stayed on his feet. The board was taking too long. Did they need to inspect every detail under a magnifying glass? Did he seem impatient?

My first glimpse of anxiety in this man of steel raised mine but I hoped it meant he trusted me. I assured him we could kick the process into high gear. We reviewed the letter of intent Dustin and I created. We examined the basics of the deal: large guarantee of minimums, royalty percentages, commitment to a high percentage of sales toward marketing and advertising. Julian agreed it surpassed any licensing contract ever offered a designer or celebrity. We reviewed our strategy to ensure the competition wouldn't go to this extreme.

When I commented on our big company competition not giving up easily, he morphed back into Invincible Petrenko. No matter the outcome, he had gotten us this far, he said. There would always be another deal around the corner.

"Quite the confidence-building session we've given each other," he added with a pat of my shoulder.

"Across the pound we call it a pep talk. Stay positive. As Yogi Berra said, 'It ain't over till it's over.'"

I gave up on sleep before dawn and pulled on workout clothes. *I'd* convinced Julian to take the leap; *I'd* convinced him to persuade the board this venture would to keep Mayfair in the black. Was I being wrong? I ticked the time difference off on my fingers and called Dallas for some Ethan perspective. I could barely hear "Well, how's London, Babe?" over background noise. "Are you in a bar?"

"Great game. I'm getting used to VIP perks. It's the only way to watch. We're back in my suite."

"We? With women. Don't bother to lie I can hear them. Your whole group's in your room? It's midnight out there."

"Yeah, I'm exhausted. Lots to celebrate. These guys think they're twenty-five again. I'm making sure nothing gets broken."

"Broken! You even sound different; you're making a racket. You know I know the manager of The Four Seasons. If your friends get out of line, I'll hear about it. You're on Julian's tab. I don't need this stress! Tell them the guy who pays my salary covers this and it's time quit."

"I'm not stupid. Don't obsess. Nothing's going to happen. God forbid you and your boss aren't happy."

"You're all drunk. Or stoned."

"We're not. I'm not. No nagging. We'll and catch up later."

"My meeting's in a few hours. I wanted your input."

"Shit, Babe. It's hard to talk and you can barely hear me. The guys are celebrating and I'm wiped. You'll be great. You're a pro at this. You know I hope you get the deal."

"Whatever." I hit the top floor health club determined to work off my jealousy, doubt—whatever it was… Whatever it always was. An hour later, dressed for success in a black skirt and Gucci jacket, I met Julian for coffee. "Preoccupied," he said when I didn't pick up on his chat.

"I called Ethan for advice and got a room full of noise."

"Dallas, the playoffs, quick holiday with his mates. The last thing he wants is a phone chat with his wife. From what you say, Ethan's solid, not the type to muck things up."

Julian raised my spirits. Threatening skies, a London downpour, and sketchy directions forced me into the present. Our driver missed the out-of-the-way music company office on the first pass, leaving no time for our pitch review. We were in the office, off with the trench coats, and out of the gate.

Twenty minutes of happy talk and pointless chatter laid a friendly foundation. We pitched and London management team played devil's advocate. *Yes, but; What if* sparring filed another ninety. To his credit, Julian remained brilliant and well spoken (unobtrusively checking his Girard-Perregaux), however he didn't know the beauty business. Discussion dragged on and I sensed he sensed he was losing the upper hand.

"Gentlemen, if I may?" I stood, reiterated, then batted down every *If this should occur* scenario. I smiled. "You're a wise, thoughtful group, but too many men with too many opinions to form consensus. we're all tired. You granted us an hour and we've been here over two, long enough to give our proposition the thoughtful consideration it deserves." I made a point of glancing at the sheeting rain on the window, then back to eye contact with the men. "With your permission, it's time to award Mayfair Beauty the contract or move on."

The room stilled. Stunned expressions replaced slack jaws and glazed eyes. The head of the management company tapped his pencil. "I like your energy."

Julian looked my way. "Emma has every resource necessary to break records in profit and sales. You've seen but a glimpse. She never rests until the job is done. Frankly, you'd be foolish not go with us. Shall we commit to an award-of-contract answer within twenty-four hours' time?" He gathered his papers. Clearly the question was rhetorical.

"Brilliant, brilliant," he said as we got into the car. "Corker of an interruption. I've not seen such an astonishing moment in my entire career. Gobsmacked, to a man. You know it's good news tomorrow."

What I knew was it could go either way. Julian had no clue the power of our competition. I kept that to myself as we grabbed a quick, early dinner in the hotel bar, ending the day anxious, but proud and exhilarated.

"Thank you very much indeed for today," he said as we parted. "You're an amazing woman, Emma."

His compliment had me glowing as I called mid-afternoon Texas. No answer. His Ethan advice nagged and I swore not to tap out his number again. We'd both be back in New York soon enough.

I arrived at Julian's penthouse Saturday morning to a beautiful breakfast set with flowers. "Slam dunk. Emma Paige sinks the deal. You've done it! I'm just off the phone with our UK Connection agent and sending a courier over straightaway with the signed letter of intent and term sheet."

"Fantastic! Oh Julian, I can't believe it. And now, oh my gosh, we have so much to do. My mind's racing. You have to call a board meeting; they'll officially announce the news. I'll prepare press statements."

"I expect the final counter-signed agreement around one today. My assistant's scheduling a board conference call at two. I'm told once our New York attorney receives the final contact, it's to be executed within a fortnight. May I to take you to dinner to celebrate your achievement and my good fortune?"

"Yes indeed. And now I'll admit I've begun backup for product development. Julian, to leverage exposure we should synchronise our fragrance launch with the UK-C tour. I have a creative team and suppliers standing by, plus the perfect photographer to keep on retainer. I'll see the first packaging renditions next week in New York. Then we need to be back here to meet with the talent and finalise. I've briefed Imperial for the actual scent, and will see the London rep tomorrow before I fly home."

"Incredible initiative!"

My turn to grin. "Had it gone all to pot, as you say, I wouldn't mention any of it. No need at all unless we won."

"Which we did!"

"Expect enormous buzz, possibly protest. Pulling a deal from under the Big Four is the biggest upset in Beautyland."

I called my New York team. One by one I woke Bill, Jennifer, Amanda, Dustin, and Abdul, each just as anxious to know the end result. On the east side of the pond, the board of directors' conference call garnered applause and a collective sigh of relief. This investment would yield security for Mayfair Beauty and total corporation stabilization.

Following the call Julian had a car waiting to take us to dinner. It was impossible to second guess this man so I stayed mum even when Piccadilly streets looked familiar. As we turned onto Maiden Lane, I realised Rules was his destination.

I'd been many times with Marsha and business contacts. I adored it. After his Turner and DaVinci episodes, I didn't dare spoil his presentation and played dumb as he disclosed Rules' reputation as the go-to place for upper class men to bring their mistresses. This was going to be interesting and fun.

We toasted our success with first rate Tattinger, at a perfect table surrounded by Rules' famed cartoons, sketches and oils. Over a superb dinner he promised private tours at the National Portrait Gallery and Victoria and Albert Museum. He moved on to books and I confessed to wanting my own library. "Good books that I'd actually read," I added.

"Pop into Sotheran's," he replied. "The oldest antiquarian booksellers in England, if not the world. Life's too short not to have everything you deserve and the correct environment appreciate what's been acquired."

Deserve. Interesting word choice.

We returned to the hotel in easy silence peppered with easy conversation. I explained ways he could combat possible corporate backlash over our amazing UK-C score. As we waited for the elevator, he expounded on de rigueur London experiences.

"Including finally treating myself to Claridge's renowned afternoon tea. Right here under my nose but back in the day strictly Marsha Johnson's domain for her tete a tetes. Off limits unless, of course, she needed me to deliver a file."

"A must!"

"We seem to be mentoring each other."

"Simpatico," he replied, as the doors slid open.

In the morning he'd meet with the big wigs to sign off on the deal documents; I had an early appointment with fragrance developers before my departure to the airport. We congratulated each other for the hundredth time and said goodbye as the 'lift' arrived at my floor.

When I checked out the next day, the desk clerk handed me a small box wrapped in plain paper. "I'm to tell you it's to be opened in flight." Wheels up and I pulled it from my satchel, laid back the paper and opened a worn leather-bound book. Jane Austen's *Pride and Prejudice*. 1813. Julian's handwriting filled his monogrammed card.

Dear Emma,

A memento for your return across the pond. May this first edition start that personal library. Always take time to enjoy the best life has to offer.

Warm Regards,
Julian

I thought of aficionados' love of the feel of the page, the musty smell, the history seeping from the pages. Jane Austen. My perfect place to start. I turned to Chapter One.

It is a truth universally acknowledged that a single man in possession of a good fortune, must be in want of a wife.

It put me off balance long enough to realise I was contemplating innuendo that didn't exist. I arrived at Teterboro well rested, two hours after Ethan's scheduled arrival from Dallas and reached my apartment just after noon. No Ethan, nor any sign he'd arrived. Calling his cell was useless but I did.

No weather delays. Perhaps mechanical trouble in Texas. I rattled around the apartment, unpacked, wrote a checklist for Alyssa, our housekeeper due in the morning, and went for a Central Park run to get my mind off plane accidents. At five I called the airport. The flight had landed at four-thirty, almost six hours late. Ethan walked in at six-ten.

"Thank God! I've been trying not to worry. Six-hour delay! I hope you didn't sit on the tarmac all that time." His all-too familiar expression matched my already frayed nerves.

"What?"

"Look, we won, okay? Two incredible games. Last night was wild and Julian's passes made me eligible for a major VIP celebration today. How could I not offer that to the guys? We joined the players in the locker room, met a ton of people. Your job is fucking fabulous. We're both benefiting."

"It's no benefit to think you're dead on the road or the plane crashed. You never answer the phone; I have no way to know if you even get my messages__"

"You know I get them."

"How do I know? Damn it, that's not the point. It's rude and annoying with so much is going on in my life."

"And you're still in meltdown mode. That's not communicating. It hardly makes me want to answer my phone."

"You were totally preoccupied. You hurt my feelings."

He sighed. "Okay, I get that. I totally get we were both tired and could barely hear each other, but you went ballistic. Why tell you I was staying on in Dallas? To hear more fucking rants?" He picked up his carry-on.

"It's not just Julian's game passes and VIP boxes. You go to his outings and forget our plans. I'm working my ass off for this. We agreed we'd spend this afternoon together. I have a million amazing, incredible things to tell you. The least you can do is communicate with me."

"I agree I should be better, but we need to put this off. Like I said, I'm spent. You're right, I blew our plans, okay? Shelve it till tomorrow so we don't get into a fight."

"Shelve it! Guess what, we're already in a fight. Yes, I'm pissed off. I could hear plenty, including women's voices."

"Well, here's a headline. Believe it or not, plenty of women are sports fans. Some women enjoy hockey, and basketball, and football. Even baseball, Emma. What a fucking concept."

"Sports fans. Get real. This isn't about sports fans."

"Damn it, I don't want to lie. A few strippers showed up at the corporate box each night."

"Julian sent strippers?"

"Part of the package. Relax. Adam loved it and invited them back to the suite. Nothing happened with me. Nothing. Yes, the girls were noisy; yes, Adam cranked it up. I kept the lid on. No damage to the room; no noise complaints. Nothing to embarrass you or your precious reputation with the hotel."

"That sure as hell doesn't cheer me up."

"I told you I didn't do anything. Even tempted I wouldn't go there. You should know that. You do know that."

"Well, congratulations for resisting. Sleep on the couch or in the guestroom. I don't give a damn where except my bed."

"Our bed. Nobody turns on a dime like you, Emma. This is the worst in a long time. Look in the mirror. This isn't all about me." He wheeled his carry-on to the wall and left.

I scratched up dinner and went to bed angry, sad, confused and alone. How did we constantly put ourselves in this state? Most likely Ethan had behaved and he wouldn't care if I had a first edition unless it was Babe Ruth's autobiography.

Without him pacing around the apartment fanning the flames,

I lowered my boiling tantrum to a simmer, which made me clearheaded enough to recognise my real annoyance. He was living like a king with time to hang out with guys he liked, at incredible events. His job entailed twenty percent of what I slogged through daily. I owed Ethan an apology but he needed to consider my point of view. Escorting me to Bergdorf's or Hermes on Madison wouldn't hurt.

I fussed with my pillow. Reacting like he was still Brucknerfield's high profile, low self-esteem football hero to my sorry St. Louis come-from-nothing wouldn't improve a thing. A therapist would have a heyday with us.

I chose not to stay home on Monday as we'd planned. I needed to think. The guestroom door stayed shut while I dressed, propped the note for Alyssa, left her my dry cleaning, and rinsed my coffee cup. Up and out.

Julian made it worth the daily professional stress to maintain this life. The more he believed in me, the more I believed in myself. Ambition drove me as if the next triumph would fix my temper or my confidence or whatever else ailed me. I swallowed a Xanax at the office, forced myself to gain perspective, and muttered about it at lunch to Jennifer Rocket. She put down her chicken salad sandwich. "If you were asking for advice, I might say hissy fits, and retail therapy aren't doing diddly squat for your mood. And probably not for your marriage, either. Memorial Day weekend's coming up. How about you find some getaway for the two of you."

"We do love that inn in the Hamptons."

"No, no. Some place totally Ethan-y. His groove."

"That would be a cabin in the Ozarks."

"Bingo! Seriously, my cousin has a cosy cottage on tiny Lake Allamuchy out near the Delaware Water Gap. Not all that far from Ludlow. I've used it. I'll call them. Ethan'll love it. You will, too." She picked up her sandwich and waved off protest.

I left Rockefeller Centre by way of Stokes Men's Apparel, and headed home with a basic Tag Heuer watch, linen shirt and cashmere sweater. I opened the apartment to dinner scraps on a single plate, Chinese take-out boxes, and Ethan at the computer in the office. Six minutes later, gifts under the bed, he appeared at our office doorway as I sat the table nibbling leftovers in less-than-nothing silky sleepwear.

"Holy shit."

I swallowed my fried rice. "I figured this would get you out of the guestroom tonight so I could apologise."

Saturday morning I drove Jane Austen and my husband through the Lincoln Tunnel, then west along the mesh of New Jersey highways to the Bedminster/Ludlow exit onto the back roads of Hunterdon County, through town and up to our antique farmhouse.

"Look at that, Babe. We were fresh out of St. Louis." Ludlow reminiscing maintained the mood as the crackling woodstove fire warmed the lake cottage. We walked wooded paths around the water and I brought out the gifts over drinks on the porch. He slipped the watch over his wrist. "Fabulous but I can't wear a two-thousand-dollar Tag Heuer around my kids and their parents, let alone struggling teachers."

"Nine fifty. It's as basic as they come. Tell them it's a Casio or Canal Street knockoff." I pressed my fingers to his lips against more protest as he lifted the shirt and ran his hand over the maroon cashmere.

"We're kicking you up a notch. Just a notch."

"You're trying to make me look like Julian."

I gestured at his sweat pants and Yankees cap. "Fat chance, but your Regular Guy choices don't work in the chartered jet or sitting in his sky box."

Even if our fiery temperaments hadn't changed, Ethan and I shared the fascination with all things Julian Petrenko and spent the weekend finally exchanging his Dallas and my London tales.

Chapter Eighteen

We returned from the cottage to Ethan's baseball coaching and my Mayfair restructuring. I'd caught the Beautyland bullet train with only two speeds: Break Neck and Lightning. I spent June hiring, and fine tuning my staff restructuring. Unlike my clueless behaviour at my Four Seasons dinner with Marsha Johnson, Wilma Nash listened over our drinks at the Oak Room. "To be honest, Emma, I sensed house cleaning was in the air. Managing Director requires devoted tunnel vision and a team of advisors. Pretty obvious he provided me with neither. You're handing me a more-than-decent exit package, and it's perfect timing. I suspect mixing business with pleasure's part of the reason I got the gig in the first place. You'd think I'd learn. Promotions not necessarily deserved require too many catch-up tutorials. Ruins one's beauty sleep."

I ignored the innuendo. "Wilma, I knew of your success before Mayfair and before we met. Your first-rate marketing reputation will keep you in the game. If you go back to what you do best, you'll land on your feet. Be thrifty with the severance, and you'll have time to be selective."

"Thank you, Emma, you're probably doing me a favour. I'm sure you know Julian's a blinding, bloody genius, to use his vernacular. He doesn't break a sweat because he prides himself on keeping the best of the best at the top of his business ladders, one rung below him. If your rung climbing is more than just consulting for Mayfair, make sure your eyes are wide open. He can be all smoke and mirrors."

"I appreciated your perspective and I wish you success." It was time she skimmed Match.com in another company's board room, and shaved her bikini line in a different executive washroom sink.

While the Big Apple baked, I continued with *Pride and Prejudice.* Our new accounting and inventory systems allowed us access to financial status for every line in the P&L, and I hunkered down with Sam Garten, my financial wizard. Bill Grose advised dropping slow producing items while renegotiating all supplier contracts projected savings of twenty-five to thirty percent that would ultimately make finished goods more profitable.

As summer kicked in Julian flew stateside for his upstate farm team something or other, I was happy to stay clueless about. He made time for Mayfair so I hosted a solid in-depth afternoon of lunch, glad handing and number crunching with my entire staff. To his credit he stayed engaged, charming and insightful as he put names and faces together. He topped it off—his own last-minute suggestion—by taking Ethan (who didn't have time to stress or decline) to a local sports bar for burgers.

Ethan treated his private session teens to a July Yankees Red Sox double header thanks to Julian who also underwrote bus, stadium food, and top seats for the Iron Hills team, one adult each, plus the school athletic director. In October Julian arranged Yankees play-off tickets for us. They finished the season ten games ahead of the Red Sox with Joe Torres at the helm and me next to my husband in full support mode to soothe my guilt over my hours staying abreast of my own team at Mayfair. Despite Jennifer with Global Sales and Marketing and Amanda

Denton directing field sales, I hovered over implementation of Bill's plan for revising these vendor agreements and territories. Cat naps replaced beauty sleep. I deplored micromanaging but results rested on my shoulders.

Wilma Nash asked me to lunch on a crisp day, complimented me on Mayfair's buzz, and asked if I'd fine tune a recommendation. "Marketing International. Global accounts. Domestic Vice President," she said over Chardonnay and salad. "You were right, Emma. I've hedged my bets, and my brass ring's within reach. They've put me through two rounds but they're dragging their asses. I need dynamite under their butts."

"Julian might have more clout."

"God, no. He hung me out to dry. You're the one who knows my history, plus your press is excellent these days. *Emma Paige* is the name connected to the fragrance industry." She laughed.

"Just stick to my professional history, please."

"Good idea."

"Besides, their CEO, Cynthia Albright, is a very savvy woman. They need to hear from someone with a vagina."

I put time and effort into a strong recommendation. At week's end flowers arrived on my desk with *MISSION ACCOMPLISHED! W.* peaking from the lilies.

Ethan joined Adam's group of Giants' season ticket holders, often tailgating at the Meadowlands by the time I finished my breakfast coffee in our home office. Fall was crazy busy in anticipation of my December return to London to kick all things UK Connection into high gear. To bolster our budget Dustin and Director of Analytics and Ecommerce, Abdul Maliki, patiently explained why drastically reduced print advertising, public relations, and celebrity endorsements made sense. We agreed to reverse everything considered standard in industry procedure. Some thought Mayfair crazy to walk away from the tried-and true model but they convinced me sound financial future practice lay in systems, digital and social media investment. Dustin slashed fifty percent of the traditional public relations budget, hired a niche agency pioneering this new style, and spent less without losing momentum or brand awareness. Depending on the analyst, his outside-the-box approach promised failure or massive success. My teams watched, ready to adapt if it proved solid. We finalised the spreadsheet for marketing, merchandising, and product development well before Thanksgiving. Mayfair Beauty was finally operating like a Fortune 500 company. Trade press followed every step. Their coverage became our name recognition gold mine and we could not have bought better publicity.

Ethan's school gig finished for the season. Over Thanksgiving turkey and Beaujolais Grand Cru I cajoled him into joining me for the final days of my three-week assignment.

Julian stayed busy in Zurich with full faith in my ability to handle the fragrance minutia. I flew to London December First to prove him right. No doubt Julian's promise of VIP everything for the UK-C London concert convinced Ethan to join me.

I settled in at Claridge's and dedicated a Brit's fortnight to The UK-Connection. Basics with Taylor Davies and their other managers was straightforward and efficient. However anything requiring Great Britain's latest heartthrobs themselves needed surveillance and security clearance. Their handlers set up clandestine meeting centres, complete with passwords to keep the boys safe from swarms of Nokia and BlackBerry carrying teenagers, constantly on the lookout.

Taylor met me the morning of my Fragrance 101 presentation. "Mind you," he said as we walked the hall, "You're dealing with five lads, nothing much but music and 'birds' on their brains."

"Lots of props," I replied as we juggled my containers. "They're talented as all get-out, but don't be afraid to play the schoolmarm when needed."

We entered the room and five working class young men stood up. Taylor bowed to me. May I present the UK-Connection. "Gentlemen, have at it." Five hands shot forward.

"I'm George, from Cheshire."

"Cian, Cardiff. In Wales."

"Jasper. Manchester. Not in Wales," Cian elbowed him.

"Tommy. Bibury, Gloucestershire, and proud of it."

"Ennis. Dublin's finest."

I Repeated their well-rehearsed introduction.

"Spot on! Will you listen to that," Tommy said. I displayed my props, explained the fragrance creation process, our plans for their input and distributed storyboards with samples. "The most important will be the name, logo, and package designs. My New York team's offered suggestions but the final decisions will be yours. We like M words for the sound and think it could be called *Moments, Mesmerise* or *Midnight*." They stopped drumming the table and tapping their thighs. "Blimey. Like writing me lyrics," Tommy said.

"Sounds good in the throat. *Midniiiiightt.*"

"Mesmerise." Cian cupped Jasper's chin. "Here's a face, could mesmerise the birds in the balconies."

"And don't he want us all to know," Tommy added.

"Hey now," Taylor said. "We'll vote at the next meeting. Take this seriously."

I passed around iconic bottles. They studied *Chanel Number 5, White Diamonds*, even JLo's recent launch. By then they were hooked. During the break, after finger waving at Tommy and Ennis for smoking, they asked about a husband. When they clamoured for baseball details, I embellished Ethan's farm team career a bit, and took pride in adding that he now coached.

By the next meeting we were old buddies. "We vote today, gentlemen. But first your nose." I brought out 'Smelly Sticks' (Ethan's term). I dipped tongue depressor sized blotters into scents to clear their sinuses. Then they sampled fragrances currently on the market: Vera Wang, Carolina Chic, Britney Spears' 2002 launch.

"Blimey! Petrol and citrus," came from one end of the table, and a healthy sneeze from the other. With an occasional nudge from Taylor and lesser managers, their input grew serious. "Emma, we'll be blinking, bleedin' experts. When our voices give out, we'll just hire out the noses."

"There is such a career," I said. "Perfumers. Seriously. Select men and women with expertise, knowledge of chemistry and an excellent sense of smell. We call them *noses*."

George tweaked Tommy's. "Chemistry? I'm out."

Decision-making closed with the vote and Taylor tallied the slips of paper. "You blokes've agreed on something for once. It's *Mesmerise*. And by god, it's unanimous."

The wet weather stayed mild for head-clearing walks. I shopped and soaked up the English Christmas ambiance, including Henry Sotheran LTD on Sackville Street, half expecting Bob

Cratchitt and Tiny Tim at the entrance. Ethan flew in on December fifteenth. Since our Lake Allamuchy weekend, we'd spent so much time-sharing Julian trivia, I talked him into a visit to Tate Britain. (He wore the cashmere sweater.)

"There," I whispered as we strolled among the Turners. "To the right of *The Shipwreck*. That's Turner's finished version of *The Angel Standing in the Sun.*"

He stepped forward and squinted. "A pot head for sure. 'Painted while stoned.' Says so right there in the small print." We Christmas shopped, compared Harrods' holiday windows to our favourites along Fifth Avenue. We enjoyed dinner at Rules and sex at Claridge's. As promised, my work and Ethan's week concluded with front and centre concert seats amid the screamers. We flew home with photos and CDs covered in personal notes, doodles and autographs from George, Cian, Jasper, Tommy, and Ennis, to my nephews, the ultimate Christmas gift for Genevieve's boys.

Chapter Nineteen

Mayfair Beauty opened 2003 by relocating from Rockefeller Plaza to a slightly smaller space on Madison Ave and Sixty-sixth Street. Our still-fashionable address and smart, creative interior exuded fashion, luxury, and beauty sense. My last piece of the financial revamp upped the aura of best-in-class for beauty industry and saved fifteen thousand dollars a month. In just over a year my New York strategic planning team eliminated excuses. Mayfair ran as a well-oiled machine. Our annual board meeting was months away but Julian required financial blueprints to maintain funding approval and investments to keep the company in the black. It took two weeks but we synchronised schedules. My assistant gussied up the Mayfair conference room. I gathered our VP and director of Marketing; Bill Grose and his Operations team; plus Dustin for all things PR, Special Events, and on-line Social Media Sales. Jennifer corralled New York, New Jersey and Connecticut sales reps. The rest participated via conference call speaker. Our Chief Operating Officer sat at the head of the table with our finance guru. I assigned two executive assistants to take copious notes then distribute them to all present, with CC to Julian, and me.

After anecdotes about the band and screaming teenagers, I leaned forward, flattened palms on the table. "Our *Mesmerise'* launch must break sales records in domestic and international markets. Our small B level beauty company will execute the largest sought-after beauty licensing deal in history."

"No pressure there," Bill said.

"Stay confident," I replied. "According to every focus group, we've produced a winner. It tests *high* to *off-the-charts*. Our pros in Development estimate a ninety percent chance this will be like nothing done in past campaigns."

I made constant eye contact. "We want to shock the beauty industry, outsell the icons. Knock the socks off Chanel, Dior, Prada, Oscar de la Renta—all the big-time houses. And, of course, sweep the fragrance awards from major companies in major countries." My Marsha Johnson imitation revved into high gear. "We industry and consumers UK Connection and Mayfair have created the fastest selling fragrance of all time." Jennifer led the clapping.

"Stay alert for counterfeits. Inside intel's heard back alley, black market operations tidbits already. if any of you hears so much as a whisper pertaining to knock-offs, contact me or our COO to shut it down before they get too far." I handed out the market/region briefs on sales goals and expectations. "We'll review this individually in coming weeks. Consider yourselves neighbours in the village it takes to pull off our launch." I smiled at more applause. "Thank you for the hard work. Consider this a boost to your careers."

Our contract kicked in and clothing designers courted, eager to add exposure, elevate lifestyle awareness. By the end of January I had high expectations for Fashion Week. On a brittle, bright afternoon my housekeeping service reported Alyssa was quitting to care for her aging parents. I had them send her flowers and met Misha Baskin, the eager young replacement for her three-days-a-week routine. Ethan's early commute across the river left introductions to me. We rushed through critical points. I explained Ethan would have more free time to answer her questions, walk her through our schedules, and explain our doorman laundry and dry-cleaning routine.

Nevertheless, clothing to go out or clean pickups in their cleaner bags still hung over the foyer chair on too many nights. Cans sat in the trash instead of the recycle basket. Ethan and I bickered over it and her in the gloom of mid-winter Manhattan. Better than Xanax or Alyssa's' return, February Fashion Week arrived. Sure enough, Mayfair's UK-C contract gave us enough panache and credibility that Diane Von Furstenberg expressed interest. Icy downpours be damned. I left the Bryant Park thrilled her spring collection came with the project. As I huddled in my new neon green rain slicker and dashed for waiting town cars, a man positioned a large umbrella over my head.

"Mrs Emma Paige?"

"Yes, that's me."

He handed me a legal document. "You have been served."

"A deposition," I cried into Julian's answering machine as soon as I reached my home office. "Carmine! The scumbag's demanding I give sworn, expert testimony." I repeated it into Darlene's. My guts were back in knots.

"His infractions and the evidence should have kept Carmine in prison for years," I whined to Darlene over strong coffee. "Hell, no. His deep pockets and flashy-smart attorney found technicalities in the legal process. Bingo, released before the holidays. Most of his Christopoulos inheritance has gone to legal expenses. Emma, he sees himself as broke. You know how the trade pubs covered Mayfair's deal with the UK Connection. Now they're applauding you as running the company. *Voila.* Carmine finds his 'Ah Hah' moment."

"I hate it, but I get it."

"That much you can share with Ethan." She put her hand on my arm. "As for the rest, *entre nous,* Ems. You must understand the rest of this will be confidential."

"Go ahead."

"Apparently our felon hired a forensic expert to retrieve your Ciao!Computer's hard drives, your cell phone records, probably your paperclips and pens, for all we know. With his three-billion-dollar net worth, they're also targeting Julian."

"Oh my God."

"Carmine's accusing you of breach of fiduciary duty."

"Apparently emails indicate you originally met with Cameron Hampton while under Christopoulos employment. Since you didn't disclose to anyone at Ciao! that this deal was in play, Carmine and his legals believe he's entitled to financial reparation."

"How much?"

"Twenty million dollars from you. Plus an additional thirty from Julian and Mayfair Beauty."

"Holy shit. What a bastard."

"They claim your UK Connection agreement should have been Ciao!Beauty's deal to license. Carmine wants a share of the profits for the term of the licensing contract."

Carmine filed the case in New York Federal Court. Despite little merit, publicity cast speculation on Mayfair Beauty, Julian and me. As part of the smear package, Carmine shady west coast publicist's false stories landed in several mainstream venues. Global publications stated outright: *Mayfair Beauty executive Emma Paige secured the high-profile fragrance license as quid pro quo via her affair with the founder/owner of UK Connection, Axel White. In addition, Billionaire Petrenko is being investigated by the Securities Exchange Commission.*

Sworn to secrecy is *de riguere* in the fragrance industry, but this was *deja vous* all over again. Fury that Carmine dragged Mayfair and Julian's name into it, ignited my angst. Worse, Julian blew off my apologies, engaged his FBI sources, and arrived stateside to have himself wired.

He baited Carmine and met to discuss their problem. When Dustin tracked down Carmine's sleazy publicist, I arranged to fly to California to confront him, but Julian took me to lunch and insisted on the task. I argued in our high back booth, spine straight, arms crossed.

He tapped the table in front of me. "Unwind yourself." I played with the salt.

He covered my hands with his. "Emma, Isgro's a mean, insecure son of a bitch with a score to settle. This is not some flimsy kerfuffle meant to throw us off. I do not make light of the libellous slept-your-way-to-the-contract rumours they've already circulated about White and you. I'm horrified I may have precipitated your involvement."

"This isn't your fault."

He waved it off. "Bloody hell. He's trumped-up securities fraud and for all we know a litany of issues they'll use if need be. We've a boiling kettle of libel, slander, defamation of character, and a vendetta drawn on my departure from my brief association with the bastards. To quote my Dallas team, 'This is not my first rodeo.' I'm the one with the PR connection. I'm the one to confront the Los Angeles weasel."

My expression surely gave away my anxiety because he held my hands this time and smiled. "A sex scandal for you and financial scandal for me. The idiots have no imagination."

Seven months later, ironically in the midst of September's Fashion Week, Tommy idled at 217 Centre Street, the historic twenty-eight story building in Lower Manhattan.

"Remember Emma, the lawyers will pretend they're on your side, but they'll try to get you to perjure yourself. Do what the politicians do. 'I don't recall; I don't recall; I don't recall,' any time you don't want to say what they want you to." I patted his shoulder from the back seat. "You'd have loved my dad. That would have been Dan O'Farrell's exact advice." It was Ethan who'd brought up my father as he'd left for school. "Channel Dan." He hugged me. "But listen to Darlene." She met me outside and we entered the colourless sea of black-to-grey suits, skirts, and blazers. After her final pep talk, she cupped my head. "Remember, this is not an interview for *Women's Wear Daily*. You're not on

The Today Show. Say as little as possible. It's not about you or your persona, it's about getting you out of this as expeditiously as possible."

"No one wants out of here faster than I do."

"Good. And no matter the pressure, do not get hostile. It's a dead giveaway you have a weak spot."

We joined the hoards at the elevators, exited directly into the top floor attorney's office and followed the receptionist into a classic conference room. Patina in the cherry table, antique barrister cabinets, burnished leather chairs whispered discretion and money. Carmine F.X. Isgro stood alone in the corner, a beacon of sleaze, suit jacket stretched over a black tee shirt. I offered my hand.

"Don't touch me."

I raised both hands. "As you wish."

His lead attorney, first chair, second and third paraded in. Three assistants rolling banker boxes followed and stacked them behind the lawyers. Meant to intimidate but I'd have matched Ethan's NFL wagers half were empty, nothing more than stupid staging. The intimidation factor was lost on me.

As we settled around the table, Harold Pancake appeared, the attorney Carmine added to his Ciao! Cabinet Guys. Darlene murmured that Pancake got wind of Carmine's move to the big legal guns, insisted he'd started the process and had information for this deposition.

"We need a ringmaster," I whispered back.

Off we went. By the first coffee break they were not only badgering Darlene and me, they were snapping at each other. The court reporter asked them to repeat themselves. I held my own. Each time Darlene objected they'd correct one another or snip demands. The Men at Odds Scramble gave me time to think before I spoke, an excellent stalling tactic. We played them well. After nearly eleven hours of Carmine doodling cartoons on his legal pad and endless questions punctuated by squabbling, Darlene raised her open palm. "Emma's been in this room half the day. Surely there is nothing else to ask. If you insist on continuing, you'll need a motion for an additional deposition." Carmine's lead attorney agreed, and thanked us for our time. "One final question, Emma. Do you remember when you turned over that audio recording to your attorney, we requested a copy and Ms. Drake sent it to us?"

"I do, yes."

"Excellent. On that recording Carmine discusses all sorts of business deals as well as Caio! Beauty legal matters. He mentions being aggravated with how things were going. He says, 'My attorney is more like the fourth string level. When I bring in my first-string team, those guys suing us will wish they'd never started this case.' Emma, you were in that meeting and recorded that conversation, correct?"

"Yes."

"All right. Please identify the attorney Carmine referred to as the 'fourth string'."

"He's sitting right next to you. It was Mr Pancake."

"Thank you. That is all for now."

The final question went, not to my issues, but right back to Harold Pancake as interloper.

"Fiasco," Darlene whispered as we left for the elevator.

Shortly thereafter, the attorney representing Julian and Mayfair moved to have the case dismissed. Once my testimony was presented to the judge, the case was thrown out and a new investigation of all things Carmine opened.

Ethan worked on our communication. His job and time with ever-expanding sports bar mates and my professional preoccupation didn't help the process. Neither did asking me to go easy on Misha who confessed to him she was new at housekeeping, pushing thirty and hoped to make a career of it. I curtailed obsessive scrutiny and bit back jealousy. Another London Christmas getaway would have worked wonders for us but he'd lined up coaching sessions during school vacation, and my UK-C return was locked into mid-January.

I crossed the Atlantic still fine-tuning sessions to keep five twenty-something boys focused on making fragrances for teenaged girls. The more enthusiasm, the better their concentration, the sooner their decisions, the quicker we'd finalise art work. Connecting Mayfair to their personalities ensured our packaging design, perfume, and artistic impressions would depict their personas. It also created the advertising campaign we planned to use throughout the first year. My exhaustive efforts to create workshop camaraderie kicked in and despite their fame, brutal hours, and Mayfair demands, they remained adorable. I rarely glimpsed condescension or spoiled behaviour. Because the boys remained natural under Thomas Schuman's constant presence, his videos and photography captured their spirit. Thomas' excellent behind the scenes content would be edited for micro sites and TV commercials. He edited some of the best for a teaser campaign targeted at UK-C's enormous world-wide fan base, the largest since Elvis, The Beatles, or Michael Jackson.

Out of control 'tween and teenaged girls created so many traffic jams and downright chaos, public appearance required security squads akin to Homeland Security. I received daily email and phone requests from names I barely recognised. Did I have concert tickets? How could they attend an upcoming five guy Meet and Greet?

Based on record purchase tallies, we increased our sales targets by thirty percent. Julian, stateside on sports business before his return to Zurich, needed his Mayfair Beauty presence felt. I convinced him to call a face-to-face first with Long Island then London, to cover filling and product pack-out dates. "And since you'll be in London, you should probably meet with the UK-Connection big wigs, too."

"Bloody hell, Emma. That's a lot of directives. I am due in Zurich, you understand."

"Big Ben's ticking," I replied. "Be glad I'm not suggesting we include your outfit in Sao Paulo."

He managed both and I corralled band management and Thomas Schuman into the Churchill penthouse. Over tea I offered assurances that any further demands on the boys' time would be minimal. Thomas reported he'd secured enough fresh video for a series of mini-movies. The productive session closed with handshakes, optimism, and the usual penthouse historical trivia. I remained to review details of Julian's on-site visits and Asian updates. The inventory to be produced in less than six months required an unprecedented amount of work. "Three continents working on Mayfair should enable us to supply distributors and retailers on time," I said.

He gave me a sly smile. "You know the Chinese Year of the Rat kicks off a month-long holiday? I used my wit, charm, and contacts to convince our container manufacturers to continue cap and spray pump production during the celebration."

"A completion guarantees to box millions of perfume bottles?"

"And delivery. Who'd have guessed my career would include meshing a fragrance, with a boy band, and Madison Square Garden?" He slung his arm around my shoulder. "If it weren't for you, Emma, I'd have sleepless nights over this project. Masterful job, spectacular skills, mate."

I leaned into his hug, then put my weight on both feet.

"That means a lot."

Julian dropped his arm. "Simpatico. Speaking of the Garden, heard from Ethan?"

"Not in a few days."

"Since I was in the city, we took in the Knicks-Bulls game. He's quite the knowledgeable fan."

"Ethan! I'm sure he talked your ear off. He's devoted to all things sports, as you know."

"Quite the game, quite the evening. Excellent company and just the thing before jumping back into boy band hysteria."

We said goodnight and I took the six flights of stairs to the lobby to clear my head.

- Julian would manage the fragrance raw materials well.
- Our spontaneous hug had been nothing more than gratitude.
- Why hadn't Ethan told me about a sports night with Julian?

My pondering continued across the Atlantic. I hit Manhattan exhausted and wrung out, exchanged greetings with our doorman, and let myself into the apartment.

"Emma that you?" Ethan appeared from the kitchen. "You couldn't pick up the phone and tell me Julian took you to a frigging Knicks game? I had to hear it from him?"

"Hang up your coat before you jump into your tirade."

"This is huge, Ethan. I need to know things like that."

"Like he was part of the ticket package this time? I knew you'd be home in forty-eight hours. Plus obviously he told you." I glared as I hung up my jacket.

"Okay, Julian called our land line. 'Blimey, bloke, I've been handed last minute courtside seats to the Kicks game. Seven tonight. Care to join me?'"

"It's no joke."

"I should have turned him down, a frigging team owner?"

"Forget it."

"Right. Your solution to everything. For god's sake. He was generous; I was grateful. He was staying at the New York Athletic Club and suggested their Tap Room for a quick dinner if I didn't mind the dress code. Are you jealous? Worried I embarrassed you? I survived our first meeting fine. Since labels are everything to you, this time I wore the Ralph Lauren blazer with that linen shirt and my Cole Haans. I clean up nice, Emma."

"That's uncalled for."

"So's your insane tantrum. I didn't give away any family secrets. He didn't discuss your work ethic. He sports a Lacroix et Barre watch with multiple time zones. We played with it. Six o'clock in the Tap Room, one in the morning in Cape Town, and ten in Sydney. A gift for underwriting Zurich hotshot sailors in the Volvo round-the-world thing."

He thrust out his banded wrist. "I showed him the Tag Heuer you bought me. He said you'd mentioned replacing my Timex. We had a good laugh."

"That's enough sarcasm."

"Then knock off your hissy fit. It was a great game. We won. I was much more impressed sitting within spitting distance of Jerry Seinfeld and other celebs than by his Swiss chronograph time piece that costs sixty K. Don't correct me, I Googled it when I got home."

I rolled my carry-on into the bedroom.

He followed to the door. "You want the fucking truth, Emma? I drank Guinness with Julian Petrenko, and sat next to Spike Lee. It was such an awesome, fucking, out-of-body experience, I've been counting the hours for you to get home for the full scoop. When this Petrenko gig started you loved me being curious, and supportive. You loved exposing me to all his upper class, finger snapping perks. Now I take advantage of them and you go ballistic. How many hours, weeks, months have I listened to you? How many time have I ignored that even when you're half dead from work, you glow like your radioactive? I knew you'd want every detail. I waited so I could spill it all in person." Oh God. I turned around.

"How was I supposed to know that?"

"Because you know me like nobody else does or ever did. Screw that. You used to. Not anymore. Not in a long fucking time." He left for the computer.

I couldn't reply, couldn't name what fuelled my anger. Frustration with Julian getting too close to home? Shock at their easy camaraderie? Ethan's perks resulting from my blood, sweat and tears? I hauled my suitcase onto the bed and yanked at the zipper. It caught on my favourite pashmina shawl. Freeing the silk from the metal teeth ruined it but I stepped out of my clothes, threw the shawl around my shoulders, and slithered between Ethan and the computer.

Professionally, late nights became the norm, sometimes until midnight. Jennifer was generous with her occasional Xanax. I did the right thing, made time for a tuck-in medical appointment and got an updated prescription I'd let lapse since my Platinum Beauty stint.

Bill Grose, our hand-picked Operations and Product Development vice president, added demand planning staff and an analytics assistant to ensure accurate inventory levels for all brands. With Asian operations on a twelve-hour time difference, the marketing team often worked around the clock. Bill could have used his own multiple time zone chronograph time piece. I condensed the twelve-month process into nine by bringing coordinators and interns to the New York marketing group. We couldn't have shaved the months off without Bill. I planned an off-cycle bonus for all of them.

Conversely, across the pond UK-Connection management nit-picked with Julian over everything from proposed budgets to sales projections. When in London I often sensed they were wary (and maybe weary) of the boys' chumminess with me, as if I were a distracting romance. I understood better than most how jealousy and envy could undermine working relationships.

Ethan stayed flat out with coaching agendas, recurring locker room bullying, and phone tag with grandparent guardians or mostly single, mostly female parents who still gave me pause. When I walked through our apartment door, I never knew what mood awaited me. In all fairness, neither did he. How should couples communicate outside the bedroom? What elements did a healthy marriage require? Neither of us had a clue.

Chapter Twenty

My Mayfair traveling nearly mimicked living with Ethan's baseball schedule. The make-up sex in lieu of conversation made for a pleasant Valentine's Day. I stripped down to my Victoria's Secret tidbits and into Ethan's visual foreplay, but comfort in immediate gratification did nothing for long term solutions. Our marriage continued to drift back to phone messages, scribbled notes and deepening emotional crevices.

Fifth Avenue window dressers had barely removed their heart-themed displays when snow buried the east coast and put Manhattan at a crawl. By the time conditions improved to the inevitable freezing slush and slide, I'd lost my temper with most of my commuting-delayed staff. Bill spent two nights in the sleeping bag on his office couch and I popped my own Xanax as the crucial, final presentation with UK-C loomed.

At the end of the gruelling week, Ethan and I met friends for dinner at Mickey Mantle's on Central Park South, easing our way to a booth through the din of singles letting loose after work and weather. Over the burgers Ethan grew surprisingly chatty. After describing the difficulty of coaching high-risk teens with dysfunctional parents, he mentioned considering pro level coaching jobs in Washington State.

"Really?" I said.

"Really." He glanced at me and back across the table.

We returned to our apartment pleasantly buzzed. "You're seriously considering another coaching openings? Since when?" Annoyance shifted his expression. "It could be good to get back out there on a higher level. You know this high school gig can be a shit storm. It's important to keep my options open if I want to pursue coaching as a real career."

"I understand."

"You don't. You've been pissed since I brought it up at dinner. The MLB meets at Park Avenue headquarters this week. Nothing's set in stone. I'm only going to hear them out."

"Don't commit until we talk about it."

"Right. When you're home long enough to sit and listen."

By then I'd accepted that Misha Baskin lacked Alyssa's drive and attention to detail. Since my Marsha days, leaving domestic issues to someone else had been a godsend but Misha struggled to replicate our three-day-a-week routine. Being closer to our age, more social, and flexible became the trade-off. She shared coffee with Ethan during his school snow days, and we jumped at her offer of semi-regular meal prep. On nights I staggered home at nine or ten, this provided sealed leftovers for me and kept Ethan from junk-laden sports bar meals.

Wednesday, the day of Ethan's MLB meeting, I marched home along Fifth Avenue for some head clearing as I breathed through the Burberry cashmere scarf double wrapped around my face, chin to nose. The gritty, slushy cold reminded me of my post-Marsha job scrambling and ever-evil Carmine. My return to London loomed large and Julian had provided Ethan with tickets to a Las Vegas baseball memorabilia convention at Caesars Place. Before we parted I was determined to sit down and listen, as Ethan had put it. Over Misha's leftover chicken and roasted butternut squash, he brushed off my interview inquiries with one-word answers. They'd talked; he'd listened. Spokane, Paco, Tacoma. Not a good match.

"Just as well," I tried. "On the way home I thought about the amazing things you're doing for Iron Hills High and those kids." His reply was half-hearted so I entertained him with UK Connection boys' anecdotes in my very bad attempt at their accents. "Thank God for Julian and Mayfair Beauty and the shitload of salary that lets you stay here."

He shrugged. "I also have an email from a Paul Jacoby. His outfit fills coaching positions California Triple A teams."

"It must feel good to be able to turn him down," I said.

"I didn't."

"Excuse me?"

"Sure I like what I do and the MLB thing didn't pan out, but Jacoby's outfit suits my credentials. More my speed. If I can make this work—" He stood up. "Are you even listening?"

"Listening? Listening for the zillionth time. Could we please not go through this?"

"'Go through this?' I just listened for the zillionth time how you're to manage the final UK-Connection development meeting before *you* authorise beginning of production."

His perfect quote and vitriol stopped me. "You're right; I'm sorry. I'm totally wrapped up in Mayfair, but this is what you wanted, too. Big time."

"Be careful what you wish for," he muttered.

We carried our plates to the galley kitchen in silence until I opened the clean and still loaded dishwasher. "Damn! How long was Misha here today?" He shrugged. "Nine to whenever she left. Five, probably."

"She didn't even unload the damn thing."

"A meltdown over clean dishes?"

"Her dusting's pitiful; she can't get the dry-cleaning downstairs half the time. Alyssa would never have left—"

"Hell, Emma, she made dinner. Stop being so self-righteous, like you don't know how it feels to work a crap job to survive."

"Crap job? I pay her a ton of money. Maybe if she didn't spend so much time talking to you she'd be able to remember."

"I'm a diversion; she's a talker. Guess what? Her company's nice when I rattle around in this always-empty apartment."

"You suddenly like conversation, Mr Don't-Ask-Me-to-Socialise? You barely talk to me about anything."

"Admit it, Emma. This is so not about Misha. It's about me. It's always about me."

"Or both of you. I come home fired up to listen to you. Instead I get one-word answers and more pipe dreams. You two sit at our table having long discussions all afternoon. And god knows what else," I added under my breath.

"And god knows this is really about the 'what else.' When are you ever here? Never! So what if we talk? How many times have you and Julian been to dinner alone? Am I supposed to believe you're never camped out in his priceless, historic, exclusive, fabulous Winston Churchill Penthouse? That Jane Austen you read every night probably cost thirty thousand dollars. Who in holy hell gives an employee a gift like that? And on top of the hundred other perks. You're fucking him."

"Of course, I'm not."

"Then you will be."

"That's not even worth answering. The same person who gave me the book gives you the best seats for sports events, private jets... Now another trip to Vegas for an entire convention and gambling, hanging around strippers—"

"Well, here's something else I haven't mentioned. I can't fucking turn anything down. Do I really need to attend an entire baseball memorabilia convention? Yes incredible perks. Yes, I thought this would be your best job ever for what I'd get out of it. I admit it. But it manipulates my private life. Julian Petrenko's breathing down my neck from thousands of miles away."

"You never said—"

"And give you another reason to go ballistic? Hell no. But it never leaves me, the what if Julian thinks I'm ungrateful. What if I sit in his exclusive seats and the big wigs hear my grammar's wrong? Or think my clothes are cheap?" He feigned shock. "'That's Emma Paige's husband?'"

"What if something I do makes him annoyed with his genius executive, the perfect Emma Paige? I'm not saying tickets, and dinners, and helping my school kids isn't fucking fantastic, but do you ever think about how many strings might be attached? Does it ever, ever, ever occur to you that he might be keeping me happy so he can run your life?"

I glared at him and yanked water glasses out of the dishwasher, dropped one on the tile floor, and swore a blue streak.

He ripped paper towels off the roll. "You don't give a rat's ass about anything but U K, Churchill, Rules, Prince Charles, Priory Bay, U K, U K, U K. To be honest I was going to tell Paul Jacoby not to bother. Now I think I'll follow through. You're blind, Emma, blind from this workaholic stupor you think is the home run of your life."

He put the pantry dustpan and brush at my feet, and holed up in our office. I finished the evening with Jane Austen, set my alarm to get me to the gym early, and from the locker room to the office. Ethan returned to the guestroom.

The next day included meetings with the marketing department, with input from our PR agency's CEO to ensure a trouble-free initial London press event. Our insurance company's concerns over the venue security required procedural background checks. Details from the mind-numbing chat dissolved my domestic catastrophe looped through my head. I was due in London within forty-eight hours, and while I'd cooled from livid to annoyed, I made a point to be home by six. All that greeted me was a note.

Emma,

No school/teacher in-service day tomorrow so I've left for Vegas directly from Clay this afternoon. I don't want to fight, it's not productive. Probably good we'll both be away with time to think.

Do what you want about the cleaning service, I don't really care. E.

I skimmed it a second time, Ethan's furious voice resonating in my head. *I don't really care.* Who was he kidding? Misha fed his ego, gave him constant attention. Okay, my massive project had me gone too much. And yes Julian was ever-present in our lives. I paced our apartment note-in-hand, but with each reread his furious voice ringing in my head softened until subdued resignation was all the tone I had.

I climbed into bed wrapped in my constant, world class conclusion jumping, and inability to trust. No doubt my exuberance over all things UK-C, secret locations, screaming fans, pumping adrenaline bored Ethan. My misunderstanding and over-the-top reaction to his Knicks game stung. My relentless work schedule was driving him to Misha.

I flew out of Teterboro Airport with his note in my purse, assessing how often Ethan and I were recipients of Julian's generosity. Jealousy was ridiculous, but something in me flared at Ethan's spin on the freewheeling extravagance. He had no clue about generosity at Julian's level of success. Per usual I popped the happy pill. Stay sharp! Business at hand! Jennifer and my Manhattan team would keep the New York gears oiled. Julian, back from two weeks in China, was to meet me in London. How ironic. The more stable Mayfair Beauty, the more unstable my personal life.

For this final, crucial meeting with the band, I had the room transformed into a faux fragrance lab, visuals and props to hold the boys' interest and keep them occupied. Yes, I was back in London; yes, in full throttle mode. So be it.

The band handlers managed to keep our meeting confidential from everyone but screaming fans. The hoards and their paparazzi filled the street, parking lot and shrubbery surrounding the obscure suburban London hotel someone thought perfect for our clandestine work. Even I got a scream or two as bodyguards elbowed my passageway from limousine into the lobby.

I pushed through the doors and from there trotted behind a desk clerk to the conference room. As Thomas fooled with his camera lenses, each tousle-haired heartthrob popped in. George and Ennis rushed me with camera phones and chatter, flattering until I realised Jasper stood behind me pointing to a red fox outside the picture window. I gave into their unruly enthusiasm and nodded to Thomas to shoot some candids. Not all things had to be regimented. They eventually settled down to sign off on the creative press plan and TV commercial storyboards, each chattering in his distinctive regional accent.

Had I ever had their innocence, and uncomplicated happiness? Or the luxury of living without ever more complex problems?

"Blimey, if you haven't kept us toeing the line," George said as we finished. "You're the best of all licensing ladies," came with his handshake.

Sudden hugs closed my throat. "It seemed endless," Cian said, "but you made it fun."

"A right hoot and a half." Jason looked from Taylor to me. "Emma, we want you to come to our premier in New York, 'see it's all done proper in the States."

"See Security keeps the screaming birds from ripping off the doors of Madison Square Garden." Tommy fanned himself.

"You're smashing, of course, but now we're, all of us, keen to meet your baseball player," Cian added. "Say you'll be there. Say you'll bring him to Friends and Family after the show."

"Thank you. Thank you so much," I croaked. "I'm thrilled. Of course I'll be there. We'll be there." I brushed tears with the back of my hand, even as Thomas snapped away.

We snaked through the hotel, out a back exit past linked arms police officers cordoning off fans and photographers and ducked into waiting SUVs, all amidst screams in front and behind with whirring helicopter blades above.

The afternoon chaos settled leaving my brain stuffed with Ethan conversations. I fell into my usual pattern of revision – what I should have said, what points I should have made. He was right, Julian's generosity rankled. The more lavish he became, the more beholden I felt, intrusive emotions I couldn't shake.

I returned to Claridge's mulling over Jane Austen. The first edition I read every night probably did cost thirty thousand dollars. Ethan right again. Who in hell gives an employee a gift like that, and flies her spouse in chartered planes to first class sporting events?

I entered my hotel room to find a desk message on my house phone: I was to enjoy, relax, and recharge my batteries before we met the following day. Mr Petrenko had made me a single reservation for Claridge's Afternoon Tea.

I soaked in a bath, slipped into slacks, pearls and cashmere, and found a message on my cell phone still in the bottom of my purse. "Hey Emma, checking in from Vegas. I sat down with Paul Jacoby yesterday, the guy who reps Triple A California ball. And you need to know I ran into Misha Baskin. No shit, our housekeeper's won tickets for *A New Day*, Celine Dion's show. She brought her sister. Not only were we both in Vegas, the show's downstairs in the Coliseum. Just so you know, yes, she stayed in the hotel."

He cleared his throat. "What are the chances? I know you won't believe this was a coincidence. So you're hearing it from me. Don't bother to call back. I'm about to meet the guys for one of the presentations. It's been amazing so far. Thank Julian. I'll be home Thursday."

"Amazing so far? Yes, Ethan, what exactly are the chances," I muttered on the way to the elevator. If I'd arranged a getaway with my hot-to-trot housekeeper, calling home with 'Can you believe it?' was exactly the smokescreen I'd come up with. I did not let it ruin the bliss of the hotel's famous pastime or my own *Me Moments.*

If Marsha Johnson could see me now. My 5:30 seating justified warm scones, too many finger sandwiches and a Marco Polo gelee with clotted cream as early dinner. While a set of mothers and preteens laughed and sipped from their jade striped cups at the next table, I fought the urge to join them and whisper, "Guess who I've spent the day with?"

Instead I savoured my Darjeeling. Julian and I were due to prep for the board meeting and review international business development. I'd agreed to organise a large presence at the next Cannes Trade Show. Was it wise to disturb our professional-personal balance with a lecture on overabundance of generosity at this delicate time? No, it was not.

The next day keeping to business kept Julian efficient and on target. Mostly. An LA broker had contacted him regarding Windmill Beauty, a brand combined anti-aging ingredients with all natural, organic compounds, products defying the rules of science, for the richest women in America. It was for sale.

"We have a lot on our plate, Julian, I strongly suggest we stay the course and stay focused on our massive commitments to the board and investors. The boys' agents are pushing for more sales commitments to increase their cut of the profits, which are already healthy. Recent financial evaluation show traction from the brand increases assets by forty percent."

"We're on target in terms of sales and timelines. They'll launch on time, in all markets?"

"All set for North America and Europe. Australia and New Zealand will follow in thirty days. We may have slight delays in Asia and South America but not by much."

"My directors suggest we consider merging my fragrance endeavours with most of my interests and go public. Timing is everything. I've alerted a New York firm to be prepared to execute. They tell me two months time's required to work on terms, legalities, filings and such for the IPO. I save millions in overhead whilst increasing revenues."

"My team can balance this but all the more reason to forgo the Windmill. What can we do, stateside?"

"Tell CFO Garten he'll need to know what to prepare. Remind him: no disclosures to anyone. We cannot risk word getting out. We're to stay mindful of hostile takeover threats."

"I understand. Consider it done."

On his second day we had lunch in the Churchill penthouse before he flew on to Zurich. "Excellent effort, superb accomplishments this session. But I sense I'm wearing you out."

"Not at all. Just some stress juggling things at home."

"I trust you took my advice and left Ethan to his own devices during this current jaunt to Las Vegas."

His light tone rankled but my frustration had more to do with Ethan and his devices. "He left me a message, as a matter of fact, asking that I thank you."

Julian smiled. "He's occupied and you're clearly due for some R and R. Every product, every existing and new development shows positive return on investment. Your unstoppable team has New York in excellent hands. Ethan's otherwise occupied. No need for return to an empty apartment just yet. Let me offer you Priory Bay. I admit to an ulterior motive. You'd be doing me a favour by taking an extra day or two for yourself out there. We can have you across the channel by tea time."

"My goodness. I admit, your retreat's my idea of heaven."

"Smashing. My staff will accommodate your change in travel." He covered my hand. "Now full confession. I need to retrieve a watch, the Lacroix et Barre, the gift I mentioned a while back."

"I remember. And Ethan told me you'd showed it to him at the Athletic Club."

"Spot on. I've a Zurich dinner with the committee that presented it to me but I've mistakenly left it out there last trip. Quite bad form to show up without it on my wrist."

"I'm happy to retrieve it."

"Thanks awfully. You know my jammed schedule and this saves Alistair a channel crossing. I was in a bit of a tear emptying pockets. It's in my old chest of drawers, a childhood piece now in my wardrobe. The watch will be in the locked top drawer with clutter—cuff links and such—and Oksana's necklace. You needn't do a thing but bring it off island with you." He paused. "You're welcome to take another look at her necklace."

"Julian, you know I'd be honoured."

"Then by all means. The drawer key's in a cigarette tin, One of the few possessions I have from my father. Centre drawer of my desk." He smiled. "The flat may be open; painters crawling about. Regardless, check in at the desk. We can't have you mistaken for a cat burglar."

"I left my leotard and ski mask in New York."

"Your sense of humour's returning. And I've a corker of an idea. As usual, Alistair meets your Hovercraft at Portsmouth and sees you to the Gulfstream. This time we fly you to Zurich."

"Zurich! No, I don't—"

"Hear me out. Dinner and solid night's rest in Zurich. Have a look round the next day. Perhaps a sit-down with my Swiss contingent, perhaps an onsite visit. As you know, nothing at my headquarters is Mayfair Beauty related, so it's all for fun. A second dinner, then home you go just a day later, rested and rejuvenated on the company clock."

"Julian—"

"I feel sure this will fit your schedule." Neither charm nor determination left his voice.

The following morning I raised my coffee mug to the men in bronze. Churchill and Roosevelt, on their bench outside the hotel entrance, shimmered in the damp March wind that kept me nauseated most of the way across the channel. Portly Sir Winston, smiling and leaning toward the President, gave me a sudden flash of Dad so often in that position in his recliner. I should have laughed, but it deepened my melancholy.

I hunkered into my winter coat and slogged toward the golf course. The longer Dan O'Farrell was gone, the easier it became to recall advice, humour, even his half-assed idea of support and encouragement. The best I'd been able to do in the five years since my mother's New York Tupperware visit was the gift of a decent car, and healthy checks at Christmas.

She'd gone from dating to living with an older man, hanging with like-minded friends, forever emotionally distant. My dysfunctional family no longer kept me at war, but it was an uneasy peace. Ethan's mantra for all things Bruckernerfield became mine. "It was what it was, and is what it is." Ethan. I pushed hanks of hair off my face, and watched the mist on the ferry channel. No sun, no flowers, no children on the beach today. Children. Obsessive devotion to work kept me at the top of my professional game, and my marriage on automatic pilot. Neither lent itself to successful motherhood.

I returned to the hotel, and ate a late breakfast alone in the Island Room while studying the wall map, and glancing at the door nearly invisible in the panelling. *What if I sit in his exclusive seats and the big wigs hear my grammar's wrong? Or think my clothes are cheap?* still looped through my head, and made me ache. Ethan and I were two sides of the same coin, too easily spun by outside forces. I'd been thinking of little else since yesterday's arrival. We could make it to May. Then, with the UK Connection launch behind me, Ethan and my marriage would be my top priority. My mood matched the weather, a far cry from my elation during the magical days of my first visit. Even if it had to be by way of a fancy-schmancy watch handoff of in Zurich, it was time to go home.

Chapter Twenty-One

I updated Alistair, made a two o'clock Hovercraft reservation, and as instructed, met the security agent at the front desk. He gestured to the door across the vestibule. "Flat's open but back entrance'll have to suit. Crew's tackling the proper one." I strolled down the former butlers' passageway feeling smug and privileged as I let myself into Julian's Kitchen and explained myself to the painters transforming his foyer.

The art collection sat in the parlour, propped forward into the safety of the sofa. I glanced at the signatures, stamps and authentications, no doubt even museum loan information on the canvas backs and stretcher boards, then slid the cigarette tin from the packed desk drawer and entered his bedroom. Discomfort from Julian's terry bathrobe on the open *loo* door, bedside table books and the folded duvet on his bed propelled me across the room. His *wardrobe* turned out to be a compact alcove composed of floor-to-ceiling Mahogany cupboards with just enough room for the simple childhood pine dresser. Two silver frames engraved with ***Oksana*** sat on top. A boy and girl holding hands smiled at me from the smaller one. In the eight-by-ten, Julian stood in evening clothes with a female version of himself in black taffeta. The pearls I'd worn to the yacht club encircled her neck, the emerald resting in the hollow of her throat. Could my melancholy get any deeper? I blinked hard and unlocked the top drawer. Just as he'd described, Julian's watch sat with Oksana's jeweller's box among handkerchiefs and silk pocket squares. Cufflinks and the London newspaper clipping of our yacht club evening.

I examined sixty thousand dollars' worth of Lacroix-Barre multiple dials, moon phases, and time zone indicator. It was an hour fast; Zurich time. Oksana's pearls felt cool as they slid through my fingers back into the jeweller's box. Tears from nowhere welled again.

I wrapped the watch in a pocket square and locked the drawer then hustled through the bedroom to the desk, agitated by the intimacy of Julian's private rooms, his father's cigarette tin, his sister's pearls. The desk drawer clutter I'd ignored earlier included two Thomas Sherman photos of my fragrance workshop with the band. Informal golf shots stamped with *ESD Studio, Ryde, Isle of Wight* looked like some sort of business outing. Random business cards included Taylor Davies' stamped with the familiar U-K Connection logo. I had three of his in my file. I picked two others, one printed with red baseball laces, the MLB logo, and Washington State addresses. The second had a silhouette of a baseball pitcher in wind-up position.

Bat & Glove Ltd Paul Jacoby was printed above his address and phone number, the same San Francisco area code as Neil's. *Caesar's Palace RMTWR 313* had been scrawled on the back. Julian was behind the new baseball queries coming to Ethan? I managed cheeriness while passing the painters. Rested and rejuvenated? Bloody hell, I was confused, and suspicious.

I huddled on my hotel bed under a blanket of anxiety, trapped on a frigging island in the frigging English Channel. Xanax and a hot bath returned my sanity but intuition and my lifelong compulsion to find order in chaos had me wired. The minute I drained the tub I left a message for Ethan confirming my return early Friday morning, still clutching my towel as I jumped from conclusion to conclusion.

Why hadn't Julian simply sent Security for the watch and let me pick it up at the desk when I checked in? A watch set on Zurich time. If he'd left it by mistake, why wasn't it on UK time? Surely he knew I'd see the baseball related business cards. It seemed so contrived and sloppy for meticulous Julian Petrenko. A setup? I couldn't fathom why. My devious, petty thief, former self began to sweat.

"Wilkommen in Zurich," Julian said, hustling me from Gulfstream to car as the driver grabbed my luggage. "Chilly, but we've none of the damp English goop, happy to say."

I fished out his watch. "Your handkerchief to protect it."

"Excellent idea." He slid the Lacroix-Barre over his hand and laughed. "One on each wrist."

"I noticed it's on Swiss time." Tick, tick, tick. "Indeed. I never change it. Helps with jet lag, and of course it shows multiple zones." So much for that theory.

Julian switched to running commentary as we entered the highway. "…Zurichberg… Same side of the city as the airport…and the zoo. Twenty minutes…off the motorway, rural…"

"We're headed to your house?"

"Sorry. Indeed we are. Set up for just this sort of thing." What sort of thing? He'd already moved into the next day's agenda, from headquarters on Bahnhofstrasse to lunch with 'mates of every stripe.'

We left the motorway and sped through bucolic farmland peppered with grapevines, livestock, and foursquare stucco houses. I could hear Ethan: *Brucknerfield with money.* Eventually heavily landscaped exclusive neighbourhoods replaced them. "Excellent investment…LeCorbusier…view of the lake…quite the International mix." Behind hedges and ivied walls neoclassic mansions, oversized chalets and stacked glass and steel cubes clung to the hillsides. No A-frames or yodelers on these slopes. *Architectural Digest* on steroids. I would have expected nothing less of him.

Parking pads and garages lined the narrow road but our driver turned up a sloping lane to quintessential wrought iron gates. No name, no number. Of course they glided open. Julian's timber and concrete house faced west, gleaming in the cold March sunset. "Designed for a family of nine," he said. "The second-floor guest rooms and baths were the children's and remain untouched structurally. We tweaked the master suite plus a playroom to serve as a common area, a bit of a lounge, exercise room, office set-up, and kitchenette. I had the first-floor au-pair suite redesigned for myself, my getaway within my getaway. Works quite well."

I'd been throwing out replies since we passed the first Holsteins, but my brain was on Swiss-watch, baseball-business cards overload. Whoever met our car took my luggage and it sank in that I was to be Julian's overnight guest. The driver continued across the paved courtyard to a few sedans in front of what turned out to be the staff house and garages. Dinner would be served as soon I freshened up and we enjoyed an aperitif watching the sun set over Lake Zurich.

We turned out to be three of his medical systems executives. Hannah Bischoff from corporate, her regional directors, Willem DeBeers from Johannesburg and Musa Nkosi from Cape Town, greeted me in the book-lined reading room. I got no further than, "I'm intruding; I should be in a hotel," before Julian insisted this was nothing more than a celebratory dinner after their annual Robo-Technik strategy sessions.

We exchanged pleasantries and moved from the library into the spectacularly spare open floor plan. A houseman served drinks while we warmed our backsides in front of the soaring stone chimney breast and blazing fire. Through the plate glass windows dusk settled over the million-dollar, million Swiss Franc, eight hundred thousand Euro view.

We chatted over dinner in five versions of accented English from Swiss-laced German, to proper Oxford, Dutch-based Afrikaans, Zulu, and my Midwest American twang, each of us insisting only the other four spoke funny (my expression). True to Julian's promise, he limited business discussion to kidding over my glamorous Mayfair fragrance career for customers' exteriors, versus their robotic engineering products for peoples' guts. "I sense this evening was more of a mood lifter than the island stay," Julian murmured as I joined the others climbing the stairs to our rooms.

Five people with five agendas filled Thursday morning. Will and Musa left for the airport insisting they'd see me again in Zurich unless I chose to transfer Mayfair to South Africa. "You must see our continent," Musa added with a heartfelt handshake.

"I'm keen on getting you round headquarters," Julian said thirty minutes later as he propelled Hannah and me toward the car. Of course it's a Bahnhofstrasse address, I thought as she took charge of my stroll through corporate headquarters, and confirmed my assumption that the avenue ranked among the world's top real estate. I'd worked my ass off convincing Julian to cut Mayfair financial corners by moving the office out of Rockefeller Plaza. These unrelated world-wide Petrenko ventures had damn well be deeply, deeply in the black.

By early afternoon I was fighting my automatic pilot comments and replies. Hannah was good company, but I didn't want or need so much management overview, mergers and acquisitions detail, or handshaking. I'd left Priory Bay worrying about too much time with Julian. Now I feared I'd be back on his plane without the chance to present my concerns privately. He joined us for lunch in a bistro among the Paris, Milan, and New York boutiques. Chat cantered on high end shopping and galleries within walking distance. An hour later as Julian settled the check, I offered shook Hannah's hand. "*Auf Wiedersehen* and a sincere *dankeschönn* for everything."

"*Nein!* Let's use *'bis später.'* Only until next time."

"I've a bit of news," Julian said as Hannah returned to her office. "Kirk Hollenbeck, the Windmill Beauty broker, tells me considerable resources—his term—have enabled his client to put Windmill on the map. I'd have had none of it but core executives have left one of the largest cosmetic companies in the world to help build this dream. I confess I still think of folding it into *The Nudes* and *Elixir* and my wider merger. NBA rumblings require my presence in Dallas Monday. Worth my quick jaunt over to LA. I'm hardly the expert in these things. Best you join me at the pitch session."

I swallowed my shock. "At the end of the week I have an appointment with Thomas Schuman to review content he shot over the weekend for the UK-C TV commercial."

"We'll squeeze LA in between your event and mine. We're reserved at the Beverly Wilshire and I'll have you back in New York in time." Again his tone required agreement.

"All right. I'll make it work. Good excuse to touch base with my California contingent. However, I have a standing arrangement with the Sunset Towers, if you don't mind." He frowned.

"Allegiance. I've used Sunset since my earliest fragrance days, meetings and interviews included. I love its Hollywood vibe and they make it home away from home for me."

"I'm so bloody focused on the bottom line, I overlook the importance of business relationships. Loyalty, Emma. I admire that enviable quality in you. As well, you've made quite the impression on this detour. Well worth your stay, you'll agree."

"I can say the same about your network of employees. And your hospitality. Not to mention your house and the view. No English Shabby Chic or country casual on that hill."

"Not here, certainly. I've developed an interest in contemporary design, as you've seen." He laughed and checked his (leather-banded tank) watch. "I'm due—"

"Someplace else."

"You know me too well."

Did I? I asked for uninterrupted time before my flight. "Indeed. Home by five for dinner and chat."

He left me with his driver's number so I could return to his timber and concrete showplace whenever ready. Back at house I managed a cat nap, change of clothes, and quick packing before leaving the guest floor for the crackling fire and fully loaded afternoon tea tray on the Lucite coffee table. Even without

Priory Bay passageways and doors set into the panelling, somehow the Zurich staff remained inconspicuous.

Julian arrived as I studied two black and white prints and an oil pastel over the couch.

"Picasso and Chagall. Modernism's golden age." He launched into an Art 101 oration. We reviewed the pre-selling stage for the UK-C fragrance, and updates on our commitment to Provence based consultants designing a Mayfair and Imperial presence guaranteed to wow the Cannes Luxury Trade Show, still six months away. He concluded with a rehash of Windmill Beauty stats. It seemed prudent to nod. "Julian, I have a few punch list items, too. Mine are closer to home." I took a deep breath. "When you sent me to your desk for your dresser key, you must have known I'd see the baseball business cards." With the exception of a flush along his Slavic jaw, he appeared nonplussed.

"I don't understand. A problem?"

"Julian! You have the cards! You're behind the recruiters contacting Ethan. Paul Jacoby in Las Vegas for one. Ethan has no idea you're involved."

"No idea? He's not mentioned this?"

"The interview, yes. Your involvement, no."

"Emma, my sincerest apologies, but it never occurred to me he wouldn't inform you. Indeed, I did put out some feelers. The major league reps were meeting right in Manhattan. During our Knicks game night he updated me. The interviews hadn't worked out so I sent Jacoby his way—to Las Vegas. Neither effort was any trouble. A bit of networking on his behalf."

Julian thought my concern was that his efforts might have been too much trouble for him?

"We both know…" His pregnant pause tightened my gut. "Ethan's content. He's found his niche with the high school and his local coaching."

"Yes he enjoys his work but It's my understanding your husband's still keen on coaching, committed to professional levels whilst he still has his reputation. Coaching rookies and scouting for the farm league is an excellent use of his talent."

"Jacoby's coaching outfit is on the west coast. We're finished with a long-distance marriage."

"You've an unconventional marital arrangement." He watched the fire for a nanosecond. "Has it occurred to you distance may be the reason your marriage remains intact?"

"My marriage… Julian, this is not appropriate conversation for us." Yet there I sat, on the edge of his living room couch. "This issue isn't courtside game seats, or some Las Vegas gambling or convention trip. Perhaps I'm to blame. You've let Ethan and me take advantage of your incredible generosity." *When in doubt, blame yourself* had diffused many a situation. I moved to the hearth. He joined me.

"I'm so very sorry I've upset you. Since Ethan hasn't mentioned any of this to you, I expect he'd deny I had anything to do with his opportunities. Tread lightly. At the very least, he might insist he had no idea I had a hand in it."

"But he does? I'm the only clueless one with no idea you're so involved in our private lives?"

He laid his hand on the back of my neck. "I'm guilty of sending opportunities his way. Regardless, his decision to sign the contract for San Francisco was his alone."

"He's signed already? With Jacoby? He's taking the job?" Julian's nail in the coffin took my breath. I fought an insane rush to sob in his arms. Instead I started for the staircase. "Bollocks. Though he never said not to mention it, I've surely blown a surprise."

Surprise, hell. "Your interference has given me a lot to think about. You understand I won't stay for dinner. I prefer your driver takes me to the airport, or I'll make my own arrangements. Either way I'll get my luggage to the courtyard; it's best if I leave now."

"Emma, You've hours to wait. Don't be foolish."

I paused midway up. "Do I strike you as foolish?"

Hours later I combined zolpidem and Xanax in flight…*his decision to sign the contract* finally stopped looping through my head somewhere over the North Atlantic.

By the time we landed and the shuttle service delivered me to my apartment it was eight a.m. in Zurich; two in the morning in my lobby. I was wide awake while The City that Never Sleeps slept. Ethan had been due home the day before. I slid the key in our lock. Let him sleep or let all hell break loose? Per usual the Manhattan glow illuminated our apartment interior. Our bedroom door was open and the bed still made. I snapped on the lamp, then backtracked until I spotted another Ethan note on the foyer table.

Emma,

Since my news is big and I DO NO WANT TO FIGHT, I'm being a coward and putting it in writing. I've rented a room from Nicole Messina, from my first season. It's on the South Orange border, close to IHHS. No commute. I've left most of my stuff. Right now I need space to think and de-stress. E.

I thumb dialled his cell phone. "Really, Ethan? De-stress? Yes, you're too much of a coward to face me. You should have thought of not fighting before you and Julian schemed behind my back with those baseball interviews. California! You took the job! You have twenty-four hours to get your files, sweats, grimy baseball caps, and the rest of your crap out of here before I stuff it all down the trash chutes."

I hung up. Oh my God, oh my God, oh my God. I paced from foyer to kitchen, to living room and into the bedroom. Oh my God. Two hours later while shafts of city light illuminated my cold tea and *Pride and Prejudice* on the coffee table, the key turned in the lock. I scrubbed my sleeve over my face as Ethan entered. "How could you do this? Somewhere along the way, you obviously put down a deposit, then moved out while I was gone."

"I meant what I wrote. I need to de-stress. I can't cross the street without you accusing me of having some woman on the other side. My guts are in an uproar. I can't sleep. Even when you're here you're not here."

"You know the pressure I'm under!"

"I know you're totally tuned out. Or tuned in to all things Petrenko for damn sure." He snatched up the Jane Austen.

"Be careful!"

"Right. God forbid something happens to his thirty-thousand-dollar gift. I'm not here to rehash your rant. I couldn't understand half of it except you and your idol sit around dissecting my life. What's to deny? I swore I wasn't going get into this. I'm here to pick up my 'damn crap' and papers before you trash them."

"Ethan, I wouldn't—"

He dropped the book on the couch and entered our office. He returned carrying files. "I have to get to work. So you know, I'll honour my Iron Hills contract, finish my season, and watch my seniors' graduate. My Jacoby job starts next fall."

"I can't believe you'd plan it with Julian behind my back."

"I have no clue what you're talking about. You made this move-to-New York decision; I made the San Francisco one. Yes, it's huge. I knew you'd blow up on a phone call, so I flew home early to explain in person. Only you decide to take two extra days with Julian. I've been waiting until you got back from Zurich-fucking-Switzerland, to explain."

"Hearing you lie about the offer is worse than Julian telling me you would. You know you planned this together. You know he arranged those interviews."

"That's bullshit. Paul Jacoby has nothing to do with Petrenko." He slammed the door as he left.

"Didn't you just get off a plane?" Dustin entered my office late that morning. "You could have stayed home and slept in." I turned from the window. "It's been a damned confusing trip. Loose ends. Weird personal crap. I left Julian's house well before my flight. I insisted. Zurich ended under very strained circumstances. I'm confused and pissed. Really pissed."

"It shows."

"I'm trying not to obsess, but I made him very defensive. Not a good thing. Mayfair's launch success hinges on a zillion elements, including my clear-headed guidance. I absolutely cannot screw up anything for any reason. Now he tells me next week I have to be in LA with him. Hopefully it'll get us on track but I need some control out there. This morning I arranged a meeting for him with Mercury Artist Agency and Axel White. They haven't met directly since we closed the deal."

"Head of the gig. Good thinking."

"I've confirmed it with Julian's assistant."

"Are you and Julian in the midst of some lovers' quarrel?"

"Dustin?"

"It's a logical assumption, especially since you've just referred to his house."

"Don't hang an affair on me because I'm frigging female. It's not sexual. It's a damn watch and baseball business cards."

"Oh, well that explains it."

It felt good to laugh, even as I explained Julian's request and discovery of Paul Jacoby's card. "He loves to impress in his overtly understated British way. You know that. Flies me to his practically private getaway. Interviews me in his suite complete with art tour and tea from a sterling silver service. Been there; done that. So why not this time just have Security hand me his watch at the desk?"

"I'd say because he wanted you in his suite, going through his drawers. Maybe the place is wired and he wanted to see how impeccably honest you are."

"Good God, Dustin."

"Kidding! You're over thinking it."

"Am I? The worst part was the end of my Zurich visit. He had no idea Ethan hadn't told me about his—Julian's—connection to the coaching jobs. I feel manipulated by both of them. And trust me, I've had plenty of experience with that."

"You're turning pale on me, Emma. This is out of character. Don't hyperventilate."

"I'm okay."

"You're not."

He walked me to my desk. "You need to go home. No argument. I'm the Stanford debate champ, remember? We're totally under control here. Don't make me call Ethan."

I closed my eyes against my racing pulse, and sweaty palms.

"Ethan left me. I got home at two a.m. to a fucking note."

Rather than lose it completely, I promised not to keep Dustin in the dark and left. Twenty minutes later I opened my apartment door to Misha Baskin stuffing Ethan's baseball caps into one of his backpacks.

"Emma! I'm just… Ethan said you'd be at work all day."

"Well, I'm not, am I? And you're not due here till Monday."

"Look, I'm sorry but he asked me to pack up some things." I pointed to her purse and jacket, slung on the chair.

"I want you to leave. Permanently."

Her expression wavered between defiance and fear. "Then let me put his clothes back. I've already laid them out."

"Now."

"Okay, I get it, but for what it's worth, he's doing the best he can. You don't make it easy."

"Did you discuss that with him in Vegas?"

She pulled on her jacket. "If it helps, I'm sorry. Sorry about everything."

And we both knew what *everything* was. Shutting the door behind her felt empowering until I found my husband's neatly rolled jeans, t-shirts, underwear laid on the bed next to his balled-up linen shirt and khakis. I shoved them back in the hamper where he'd obviously stuffed them after Vegas and before running off to Nicole's.

I tossed back a Xanax, infuriated by Misha's invasion, by Misha knowing what to pack, by Ethan conferring with her. By my humiliation. By my grief. As

I pulled my LA itinerary from my satchel, Ethan appeared. "I suppose Misha called you," I said without looking up.

"Of course she did. I was on my way here to meet her. She was only going to give me a hand with my stuff. You fired her."

"Yes I fired her. I thought you were working all day, too."

"That's not the point," he said.

I glared. "No, I guess it's not. I can't trust you, never have. In Priory Bay I thought about how much I need your support. And I come home to this. I'm working my ass off for us. Us, Ethan. I fly out again Monday. You couldn't care less about me. I'm exhausted, sick of taking on all the responsibility. You're only interested in the life I provide. Without my career you'd never be considered for a coaching job at that level."

"I get it. I'm not good at anything." He grimaced. "I need time without yelling, time to think. I can't do it here. We can't keep going with this toxic situation. You know we're better apart. We've survived this long because of my baseball routine, not in spite of it."

"That's something Julian would say."

"Not Julian, Emma. I didn't fly home from Vegas; I flew home Thursday from St. Louis. I left the convention and went to Brucknerfield."

"What the hell!"

"I stayed with Darby and talked to Maxine."

"About us? Maxine told you to leave me?"

"No. Maxine listened. She told me to find myself."

"Does she know you suddenly find yourself in another long-distance job, schemed out with Julian?"

"Maybe he sees things clearer than we do. You got your brass ring: status, money, the great apartment, the perfect life. Everything but the perfect man." He pulled his suitcase off the shelf. "You scripted it; you worked for it. Congratulations. I mean that. You've worked your ass off. But you've managed to drive me three thousand miles away. Julian will fill the void."

"That's a half-assed thing to say."

"Half-assed? It's the smartest thing I've said in weeks." He set the suitcase at the foot of our bed. "Look, I'm here because you said you wouldn't be. Go on one of your berserk shopping sprees tomorrow. I'll be here at eleven and gone by noon. I'll pack while you're out." He grabbed his backpack of ball caps and left before I could argue.

I did not leave Saturday morning. Instead, Ethan entered our bedroom and found me reclining on fresh Pretasi sheets, in nothing but a thong he bought me in Cannes.

"Jesus, Emma!"

"You know how good we are together. How good I am for you. For us. You know our sex works magic."

He yanked the sheet over me. "This isn't Fantasyland or the south of France. You're feeling guilty. It won't solve anything. Don't do this to yourself."

"Don't do this to me. I don't care if it's Misha or Nicole or both of them. You know the UK-C Garden performance ends my insane agenda. We can last that long, till my schedules more normal. I'll get my life back; I'll get our life back." He picked up Jane Eyre from the bedside table. "Being on call twenty-four seven to a billionaire who buys majority interest in whatever strikes him will never be normal." He put it down. "Does it ever, ever occur to you that my life matters?"

"One minute you tell me Julian's doing too much for you, and the next you're networking with him." By then I was in the dressing room yanking on my clothes. I hopped into view, one leg in my jeans. "Julian waves his magic handkerchief, Paul Jacoby materialises. *Voila,* you're giving up Iron Hills for California. The least you can do is talk to me about it."

Ethan shot me a glance: *Talk so I get more of this?* "Wake up Emma. What's the word? *Infatuated.* The longer this goes on, the clearer it is that Julian's your answer." He lowered his voice. "I'm not angry. We try and try and try but the two of you are like meshing gears. Same drive, same talents, same goals. I get it. I got it right out of the gate. You know I loved the perks; I loved the hype. But I'm in the way. I'm not being a martyr. It's better for both of us if I'm out on the coast. It's a clean break." He left the bedroom before I finished zipping my pants, and called from the foyer, "I'll get my clothes while you're in LA with Julian."

I swore, cried and swiped tears. I'm not proud of it, but after lunch at the corner bistro, I ricocheted down and across Madison, across and back up Fifth. Between Chanel, Jimmy Choo, Prada, and Gucci, I dropped six thousand dollars, returned to my empty apartment and drank my way through Chinese takeout in front of *The Sopranos.*

Chapter Twenty-Two

Sunday, sadly sober, I paced from our Louis XVI chair to our foyer console, hugging myself against hot flushes and nuggets of truth. Clammy fear and raging impotence roiled, worse than my forced move to Brucknerfield, forced exit from home at eighteen, Marsha's decision, Carmine's deception, and Dad's death combined. Operating on autopilot in Los Angeles wouldn't do squat for me or Mayfair. Neither would be obsessing over every nugget Ethan dropped on me or every gesture Julian made. I had twenty-four hours to shake this off.

Monday afternoon I checked into The Sunset Towers and met Atticus for dinner at The Abbey where we discussed his plans for assisting Amanda Denton with the UK-C's *Mesmerise* personal appearances later in the year. A good drag queen show, and too many martinis with the boys filled the evening. Before my buzz wore off I buoyed my spirits by contemplating relocating Mayfair Beauty to the west coast when Ethan moved.

Late Tuesday morning, fuelled by strong coffee and aspirin, I greeted Amanda at Saks Beverly Hills and brought her up to speed on Atticus. Checking on our market sales specialists blocked thoughts of Ethan while I obsessed over Julian. Even this favourite task took effort.

"By the way," she said on the way to her car, "Any chance that meeting you're out here for is Windy Hill or Wind—"

"Mill. Yes, Windmill Beauty's making a pitch. It's supposed to be on the down low, however."

"Figures. Maureen McDaniel's in my Pilates group. Nice enough with a classic New York City accent that's hard to miss, especially when discussing your boss in a stage whisper. She said her husband was doing business with him. 'so handsome, so British. You know he owns the UK-Connection and one of those NBA teams.' *Julian Petrenko* is not a name you often hear in a Beverly Hills toilet stall."

We chuckled and it got me back on track. Julian's text confirmed his LA arrival as Amanda and I concluded the day in Macy's conference room with her area store managers. My anecdotes brought laughs as I reviewed the band's schedule, but I made sure they understood the level of chaos and extent of required security measures for what was to come.

Within the hour I reached Julian's Beverly Wilshire suite where he and the elephant in the room greeted me. When he pulled back his cuff I found my ice breaker. "Is that a Lacroix-Barre I see on your wrist?"

"Spot on. I made sure to flash it around at the event Saturday. I put you to such trouble to get it to me, it seemed only fitting I wear it here in the States."

"There was no trouble whatever, but I owe you an apology for my behaviour and abrupt departure Thursday." We exchanged glances.

"Emma, no apology necessary."

"I disagree. You know Ethan and I appreciate your extraordinary generosity. I overreacted to the shock that he hasn't been honest with me."

"Whatever I've offered has been with the best of intentions. I should apologise for having any part in your marital dust up."

Dust up. We took our places at the table. "This phenomenal chance for Mayfair to break wide open and come into its own demands my full attention. It's critical I keep my professional and private lives separate."

"I see this is clearly difficult. You needn't say more."

Why? Because I'd successfully blamed myself to make my point? Was he sparing me the humiliation of explaining or elaborating? Did he know Ethan had walked out? It would have been so easy to lay it all at his feet, but if I started who knew where I'd finish. Before I worked myself into a panic attack, I cleared my throat. "Thank you. It's imperative I stay on point today and tomorrow. And you, Julian, your Dallas distraction has been resolved?"

He took the hint. "Bloody hell, not a prayer. Injuries? Trade rumours? Disgruntled coaches and their attorneys? Name your poison. Press and paparazzi exacerbate any and all of them. I'm even registered here under an alias."

"We'll pretend you're a rock star, hiding from fans. Speaking of rock stars, Axel White is connected to the entire industry. A strong relationship is key to his loyalty. And his loyalty to Mayfair could place us above the big-name companies who'll be breathing down our necks to grab our market share. As frazzled as you are, it's worth squeezing in this sit-down at Mercury tomorrow." Prepping Julian right down to suggested conversation boosted my mood and kept the wheels on the rails, but I still declined dinner. I returned to Sunset Towers thankful for room service and the distance between us.

He and I met Kirk Hollenbeck at Windmill Beauty's Melrose Avenue office the next morning. The broker again extolled owner Gregory McDaniel's creative fragrance development 'based on The Hamptons.' When a brand is created without proper research or marketing knowledge it's almost impossible to claim success. His news that winning a New York State lottery provided McDaniel's 'considerable resources' set off my first alarm bell.

One presentation after another filled the morning. I listened, kept my mouth shut but lost count of the red flags. Hollenbeck's attentive poker face gave no hint his ignorance of current industry trends and its lingo made him look like an idiot. We broke for lunch served in the conference area. Julian sat between board members, making it impossible to tell if he was taken in or playing nice. Nevertheless, I felt confident Maureen McDaniel was going to be disappointed.

When we regrouped, I stayed attentive but stopped taking notes as I used the final hour to revise *To Do*, update UK-C, and jot down a staff meeting agenda. Unless they caught my grin as I recalled Wilma Nash's board meeting behaviour, no one had a clue I was brainstorming more important matters. The presentation finally closed with our assurances of an answer within forty-eight hours. We shook hands with Hollenbeck, ever-eager Greg McDaniel, and set off for Mercury headquarters in Burbank.

"Thoughts?" Julian asked as we settled into the car.

"Julian, this morning demonstrated how easy it is for outsiders excited about the beauty business to invest in con artists or creators ignorant of how the industry works."

"Con artists! Bollocks!"

"I'm not saying they're bogus, so much as inept. We need to be careful. Let's hold off on Windmill chat until dinner. It's more important to cram all things Axel White into you."

"Fire away."

I changed gears with a clear head. "Similar personalities, winning is everything. Axel's cultured, right down to an art collection said to be one of the best in North America."

"Most Americans don't know art compared to Europeans."

"Don't contradict him!" I looked at the ceiling. "Forgive me. You know very well how to schmooze with oversized egos."

"That I do but I defer to you better judgment."

"I was out of line."

He covered my hand. "Emma, you are never out of line."

"Well then, save opinions for a chummy chat in your Priory Bay digs or something." I pulled away to open my satchel. "He has several Aston Martins if that's a safer topic."

"Impressive taste in cars, I grant him. The only other hobby that sets a rich man apart from his equals is thoroughbred horse racing. Although I opted to buy an American basketball team, the ultimate status symbol for Russia."

"And American jocks like Axel."

Despite the traffic, we arrived on time and Axel welcomed us into his well-appointed office. His opening repartee did not include art, cars, horses, or basketball. He began by joking about the debunked rumour that I'd had an affair with him to land the UK-Connection deal. I glared at both men. "A rumour hatched to discredit all of us by Carmine Isgro, industry's biggest sleaze ball."

To his credit, Axel dropped the Old Boy innuendos and praised my work with the band. My two days in the L.A. pressure cooker wound down listening to them connect over rich men's champion steeds, sport franchises and savvy business strategies.

"Profitable day." Julian ushered me into our waiting car. "Worth our exhaustion and this detour. No doubt Axel and I can be powerful resources for one another. We make quite the team."

"That you do."

He smiled at me. "I meant us, Emma. We're both of us totally knackered but once again you've worked your magic."

I closed my eyes as we were whisked to the Wiltshire. "Emma?" was barely a murmur.

I opened my eyes. "Sorry!"

Julian studied me. "Never a need to apologise."

With privacy non-existent even in the hotel dining room, we hustled up to his staffed suite. Over martinis and substantial canapés, I opened our files to Windmill's proposal.

"Interesting," I said as gin warmed my engines.

"No need for diplomacy."

"Good. McDaniel's team appears solid in terms of experience but he probably overpays them to compensate for his lack of clout. Too much is murky.

His Kearney, New Jersey, connection has diversion infractions I've known about since my Olympia days. If he has claims proofs, they're likely false. That's dicey enough to warrant our decline. All four of his lead directors hail from *Welch and Griggs.* This implies talent to develop the goods, but the outfit's known for major turnover unless employees fit into their cult-like environment."

"Quite the knowledge."

"It's part and parcel to my work. If you're looking to expand your fragrance dealings, you need to understand how dysfunctional this industry is. The United States is the most difficult market to generate profitability. In Windmill's case, I strongly suspect the owners want to recoup lost money, gone forever unless they find a sucker to buy the damaged brands."

"And their P&L?"

"At first glance, looked okay, but sales figures could be inflated. The distribution doesn't reflect what's in this file. It's bullshit. Mostly, Julian, I don't trust them."

"Bloody hell, you're direct."

My martini had done its job. "We have to be. My team doesn't need this distraction during our UK-C project; you don't need Windmill in your merger plans. Founder or not, Gregory McDaniel's a strutting peacock, green as his money. If you take on Windmill you shouldn't involve him in operations, which he'll take as a slap in the face or a power play. Either creates a toxic work environment just when you need cooperation."

"Bottom line?"

"One positive note: in six months when our confidentiality agreement expires, I can poach his staff, specifically the two smart marketing guys. Bottom line, our UK-Connection tie-in puts Mayfair in the black, but Windmill could drain those finances. Iffy ROI. Return on Investment requires your millions with a chance you'll lose it all."

"Excellent instincts. You've impressed me once again." He emptied his glass. "Full confession—"

"I know that line. I have to fly your watch back."

He laughed. "No indeed. I head to Zurich in the morning with it on my wrist. No, I confess to bigger requests coming. No secret I'm keen on merging my operations. I'm head strong and brash too often. Emma, I'll need you at the top. It's you who has the strongest chance to insure our combined fragrance interests generate profitability and keep us in the black." He cupped my fingers.

"Julian—" The gesture segued into a gin-laced glance and lingering handshake. "I appreciate your confidence in me."

"I'm sure you know the industry's taken notice."

Notice of what? I could feel the flush heating my collarbone as the butler, or whoever he was, reappeared. "Your conference call, sir. Dallas on the line."

Julian thanked him and turned back to me. "I fear this may take a while. Please stay."

Oh God. "I can't. Macy's special events coordinator is pressuring me to commit the band to their Thanksgiving Day Parade. I need to compose a rejection before my appointment with Thomas. Early flight. I have to head back to my hotel." All of it shredded whatever hovered between us. "You'll call Hollenbeck in the morning?"

"Indeed. We'll pass."

"You won't regret it. Best of luck with the Bulls." He crossed his fingers and took the call.

As planned, Dustin arranged for me to meet Thomas at his loft in the Flatiron district to review his UK-C proofs for our national ad campaign. As not planned, the night before, within hours of my return from LA, Ethan called. He'd arranged to rent from Nicole on a month-to-month basis. "So I'll be over here through April. This is what we need, Emma."

"Whatever you have to do." My acerbic reply still made me wince the next morning as I tried to focus on Thomas's project. "I appreciate your coming down here," he said. "Between the two of us and our days with the band, we can cut out plenty before we let the boys have their final say. I admit I hope this saves massive amounts of time. I'm also on the hunt for my *Charade* launch shots of Marsha Johnson schmoozing with the show stoppers. *Fragrance International's* looking for archival photos for a retro piece on her. There's buzz she's retiring."

"Really. I give her credit for holding on at Platinum all this time, but don't count on me at any farewell festivities."

"She's had a good run."

"Right over me."

"Long time ago."

"Whatever."

Thomas shot me a look. "You okay? We've been checking proofs together since my ponytail days. You're not yourself. Distractions? Jet lag?"

Crap. "Maybe both. Tough couple of weeks. For two years I've worked my ass off for Mayfair. It's exhausting."

"In my experience Julian Petrenko's straight up and less erratic than Marsha Johnson ever was, at least with me. I'd also guess his luxury level living on the road makes his beck and call behaviour bearable, no?"

"Amazing perks for sure. Right down to a first edition Jane Austen Ethan says is worth thirty thousand dollars."

Thomas whistled. "Been showing your gratitude?"

"An affair? I'm smarter than that. I've masterminded our UK-C deal to guarantee solvency and reputation, Mayfair's and mine. I'm making him money with plenty for Ethan and me."

"Emma, I didn't mean to hit a nerve."

"I'm too busy to cheat. Forget it if that's what you're hearing." I met his glance. "Is that what you're hearing?"

"You know the drill. Clients, stylists, even party guests forget or don't care I'm at their elbows. On shoots I'm either invisible like the caterer, or treated like their confidant hairdressers. All kinds of crap gets blabbed to me."

"Then you know of Carmine's insane rumours I slept with Axel White to land the UK-Connection account."

"I do."

"Thomas, whoever's blabbing about Julian and me is totally off base. This rat race takes a toll on any marriage. The more success in my professional life, the more turmoil at home. Ethan's a separate issue."

"You don't need to defend yourself, even if you are screwing Petrenko."

"Sure there's appeal but I'm not! You know I have an unconventional marriage but too much of what I thought this job would solve has made it worse. We've separated but you and I have a blistering schedule and I won't let it affect my work."

"I know turmoil at home. Been there, too. I started out as a stringer chasing boy bands. New Kids on the Block, The Blades. Pop culture for *Rolling Stone, Page Six,* My wife left me twice."

"Deserved?"

"Hell yes. It took Rachel walking out the second time with the baby for me to give up stupid. Then nearly a year to prove I had."

"That's a lot to share."

He shrugged and picked up the proof sheets. "The Thomas Schuman you met at your Charade launch was newly, seriously monogamous and freshly sober. Assholes in this business love making up crap to sound important. You're one of my most normal clients, Emma. I've got your back, both sides of the Atlantic."

Julian called an hour later from London to confirm passing on the Windmill Beauty deal. "And bit of an update. Axel White met me for dinner last night. Rules in fact. He's quite the toast of London, here to meet with the band and see his film production's well underway. Big name director, he tells me. He's also keen on investing in professional sports."

"You two can be solid mutual resources. Obviously after Tuesday he thought it'd be worthwhile to meet on your turf."

"We talked about my turf, Churchill's that is. I've invited him join my guests, perhaps Davies as well, for a tour after the Savoy launch. We've Schuman on retainer to be used to best advantage. I think event candids and a formal sitting of the board when we gather for the meeting. My staff will be in touch. You're the one to pull it together."

"Sounds good," I managed. "Our Waldorf reservation is set, Cole Porter Suite booked as you requested. Its dining room sits the board perfectly. Thomas could easily shoot before the meeting's called to order."

"And you'll, of course, be in residence?"

"Absolutely. The Royal Suite's to be my base of operation and Command Central right through Friday's board meeting." I'd already called hotel staff to plan transforming the oversized dining room to replicate one of the last Duke and Duchess of Windsor parties in 42R, their late seventies dinner honouring Estee Lauder and her husband.

"Our event is the perfect place to schmooze. We're including high end buyers—Nordstrom's, Macy's – Wednesday evening I pull out the stops. They've worked night and day for this week." My voice broke. Thursday's Mayfair Beauty celebration dinner would be spiffier but I was most excited about honouring my team. "Julian, you could not have more talented Mayfair professionals. I'm letting them know."

"Excellent all round. Credit is yours. I work for you now."

"I take that as a vote of confidence."

"As well you should. Say, perhaps prime concert seats for the members. Corporate box? Front and centre if you think they'll tolerate screaming and pandemonium?"

Despite the syrup in his questions, there was no 'perhaps' about any of it. "Consider it done," I said.

"Smashing. First thing, of course, when you're over here, we'll run through the board meeting agenda and status update. With this IPO coming up, the meeting's critical. Nothing's to appear precarious. We're to be unequivocal. Proof-in-hand Mayfair's on solid ground, leading the pack."

Leading the pack among *The Nudes, Elixir* and Imperial's other fragrance related interests? Or leading the pack, as in combined fragrance interests versus his medical equipment, sports teams, and God-only-knew whatever else was jumbled in?

Chapter Twenty-Three

My day concluded in Bill Grose's office hovering with Jennifer over his Excel spreadsheet. Macy's opening *Mesmerise* order for over a million dollars added to our fifteen percent over projection, problematic in terms of warehouse inventory. I snapped a pencil in half. "My God, ready-to-ship has to be so bloody complicated?"

Bill took off his reading glasses. "You're not one to micromanage. You okay?"

"Yes I'm okay. And I'm really frigging tired of being asked." I shoved hair out of my eyes. "Sorry. I sound like a total bitch. It's the board meeting up against the *Mesmerise* launch and concert. I should be here till then to cover any SNAFUs, not jetting back over for the London event."

"If it helps, consider the whole shebang a grand finale to one hell of a year. Emma, glitches come with the territory. As your VP for Operations and Product Development, it's my job to worry, not yours. Financials are well in hand."

"You're right, of course and I thank you."

Jennifer and I left him to his charts but as we headed down the hall, she tugged me into her office and closed the door. "It can't be just Macy's inventory or jetting back to London. What's up and how can I help?"

"Nothing needs help."

"Bullshit."

"It shows, I guess."

"To us, yes."

"Two launches; the correct seats for the big guns; retailer point of sale plans—"

"—are flawless. You've said so to Amanda and me."

"Stress, stress, stress."

"With all due respect, Emma, you've scheduled a full staff meeting plus the staff party the week of the launch. You're ready for anything. Stress was Brian

Cox. Stress was inviting Marsha to The Four Seasons to offer your help and getting canned instead. We won't even mention Carmine and his *modus operandi*. Your plans are rock solid. We'll be at your beck and call. You could head to London tonight."

"Thank you." My voice cracked but I cleared my throat. "It's Ethan."

"Again?"

"Dustin hasn't said anything to you?"

"Absolutely not."

"Ethan signed a scouting/coaching contract. No discussion; behind my back. He starts in September. In San Francisco."

"I thought those offers weren't coming anymore."

"It's even worse. In Zurich I discovered Julian arranged it with him. He told me Ethan would deny it. He did but first I flew home from Zurich last Friday to a fucking note. He moved out with only a note. You know we're ships in the night. You know we bury ourselves in our careers, but never this, Jen. Never this." I swore.

"Nicole, mother of a kid from Ethan's first year at Iron Hills, has a boarding house. Rents rooms, my ass. Ethan's moved in with her. Not to mention Vegas with Misha our housekeeper. Former housekeeper. Maybe one or the other. Maybe both. Maybe neither. Who the hell knows when your major issue is trust."

"You and Ethan both suspecting the other's screwing around is old news. There's got to be more."

"There is. I'm so pissed at Julian I have to work at not compromising our relationship and everything professional. You know I'm in critical condition when a six-thousand-dollar shopping spree doesn't help."

She leaned against her desk. "Emma, taking on Mayfair has been the best thing to happen to you since we've been together. And frankly, it's more than the work. You're pumped. Even when our asses are dragging, you're out ahead, trouble shooting, smoothing the waters."

"I admit I'm a workaholic."

"It's more than the work. It's Julian Petrenko. He sought you out to observe and consult and you land him the fragrance deal of the decade. Not only a power broker move out from under far stronger comparable, but you take on the whole package. Two years and you're running Mayfair for him. And flawlessly."

"Oh, please."

"Emma, you've always spent more time with your bosses and career than with Ethan and the marriage. Julian keeps a very low profile but he doesn't make a Mayfair move without you. The industry sees you two as inseparable. Oh, sure there's a husband out there somewhere with his parallel life, moving on a parallel track, but that's, I don't know, incidental."

"I'm completely frustrated by him."

"Are you?"

"What do you mean?" She waved it off.

"Jen, I need truth, damn it."

"You're a walking basket case. You might honestly be unaware that you're falling in love with him."

"What the hell!"

"Damn close then. There he is, all British and Russian; all Savile Row and James Bond-ish. Blue eyes and cheekbones to die for plus, plus, plus the brains to recognise your talents. And here you are: his total package. A babe, couture down to your Louboutins, also with brains."

"This is not what I expected from you."

"It's after five and we're both exhausted, but Ems, you're my boss and a friend I care about. I want to help. Yes, you and Ethan have an unconventional marriage. If I see this change in you, Doesn't he? Maybe Ethan assumes you've found something – Not a groupie, baseball kind of hook up he'd know how to handle. Something else. A soul mate, someone he can't compete with. That's what's new."

"Then stay on my side," I replied from the door.

"Just let me know which side that is." At that point I couldn't be sure I knew.

At nine the next morning the sound of the foyer door brought me face to face with Ethan. "I told you to call first."

He glanced at his watch. "This is your Saturday workout time. I thought you'd be at the gym."

"Well, I'm not."

"I'm meeting Adam for racquetball, I'm only here for my other sneakers." He started for the bedroom.

"Do you want a divorce?"

"Emma, don't."

251

"Ethan don't," I shot back. With my heels dug into this rutted road, we were back to his few words and my wringing every nuance out of them. "It's a fair question. It deserves a fair answer. You've put me in La Land for a week."

"Fair answer? Face it, as long as you've had this career I've been the guy on the side, the phantom husband out there somewhere chasing his half-assed dream. I've been okay with that but we're spinning our wheels. Why call this a marriage? It's anything but. Maxine's right. It's way past time to figure out what the fuck we're doing. And what we're doing to each other."

"And your idea of figuring it out is moving across the river, not seeing each other, not speaking."

"Yes! We do any better talking? I found a place where I can look at what a mess we've made. I want, hell I don't know, two or three weeks away. Away where I can think things through."

His phone rang. "Okay. Lobby in fifteen." He shoved it in his pocket. "Adam's got a quick call on the fifth floor."

"Then give me those fifteen minutes."

He found his sneakers and sank onto the couch. "I'm asking for time, Emma. You keeps saying wait till the launch is over. So okay, by then the launch'll be over. You're practically living in LA and London, anyway."

"Okay. You need time? Take some. No contact till the board meeting's finished. But the concert? The boys asked to meet you, a real baseball player."

"All right. And one more thing. You're accusing me of plotting this job change behind your back with Julian."

"I found it Jacoby's business card in plain sight." I laid out the scenario, from the Isle of Wight to Zurich, including my outrage at Julian and his complacency. "He wasn't embarrassed or scrambling as if I'd caught him at something. Just completely surprised you hadn't told me."

"And you bought it."

"Ethan! You're telling me he's lying? I work with this man twenty-four seven, most of the time from different continents. Trust is our cornerstone." He stood. "As opposed to what we have."

"I didn't mean—"

"You really don't see it, do you? You're in love with him."

Ethan left. For the second Saturday in a row I ricocheted along Madison Avenue. Who wouldn't be fascinated by Julian Petrenko? Who wouldn't be comfortable and grateful? Yes his nonessential perks offset, even speeded up, tasks. His generosity provided comfort and efficiency. Who wouldn't enjoy his company and appreciate his compliments? Who wouldn't be drawn to him emotionally and physically?

At Fifty-eighth I crossed to Fifth and roamed Bergdorf's famed Seventh Floor while rationalising Dustin, Thomas, Jennifer, and Ethan's opinions. The prickly sensation someone was watching me broke my train of thought, but I blew it off.

"Emma Paige?"

I jumped. Wilma Nash, flushed and flashing me the peace sign, hustled from the flatware displays. "Emma! Great to see you. I'm walking off a two Bloody Mary client brunch. Sealed a major deal over smoked salmon and quiche, due in large part to your advice. Thanks again for nudging me in the right direction." She grinned. "Since here we are, I'm just buzzed enough to ask if all's well with you. Feet on the ground?"

"Mayfair's on very solid ground."

"Not Mayfair's feet. Your feet, your solid footing." The grin was a bit lopsided. "Surveillance system in the conference room and all that."

"What surveillance system?"

"Just the usual: Camera, microphones… Jules' gadgets." *Jules.*

"He hasn't mentioned it? He set it up during a major run-in with a New York scumbag."

"Carmine Isgro?"

"Yes indeed. With Jules being so global it helped keep tabs on board members and his executives. But Imperial was Isgro's major supplier till things went south. Jules little system essentially kept him informed when the asshole threw his weight around in my conference room."

I had no clue regarding the current Wilma-Jules dynamic. Engaging in Carmine rumours could blow up in my face. I worked at nonchalance. "Fortunately I moved Mayfair out of Rockefeller Centre and up Madison in January. Surveillance is a non-issue."

She patted my arm. "Let's just say you might want to figure out how to bring up the topic."

"He'd consider installing devices without telling me? That sounds like something out of his parents' espionage background."

"Oh please. Not that Priory Bay, Cambridge Five war spy drama stuff. Priceless art? Emma, Emma. Fabrications."

"I don't think—"

"Maybe you know; maybe you don't. Your boss and I had a torrid affair. I was privy to things that help make sense of who you're beholden to. Whom." She waved the air. "*Beholden.* Now there's a Freudian slip. Bottom line, I can fill in the blanks on the always-Great Gatsby. Julian Petrenko's reinvented himself just like something out of F. Scott Fitzgerald. True enough his German Jewish mother lost her family to the Nazis, and his father was a Russian immigrant. But they weren't spies, they were some sort of housekeepers to the spies, or one of the group. That part's very murky, but bottom line, they weren't double agents bumped off on a London street by some Russian assassin. They were jaywalking in driving rain and hit by a cab. Their double agent government spy guy employer wangled a small education trust fund and the Priory Bay orphan place for Julian and Oksana."

I stifled my shock. "But he does own the hotel?"

"You betcha. Part and parcel to his reinvention. I helped furnish his private quarters. Someone else's monogrammed silver, high end estate sale furniture with just the right old money wear and tear, art from the best copyists."

"Forgeries?"

"Bite your tongue." Wilma laughed. "Perfectly legal. Paperwork included. Want a Picasso? If *Harlequin With Glass* hangs in the Met, you can't very well say that's the original above your mantel. But you sure as hell can hang that dead ringer pastel or black and white sketch of the scene and pawn it off as one of Pablo's priceless preliminary studies for it."

"Very creative," I replied, sounding like Cousin Neil. "God knows he's got the balls to succeed. The Brit's a killer combo of street smarts and business savvy. I was the wrong arm candy for all his role playing and we know my lofty Mayfair position was to soothe his guilt. So be it. He has the financial resources to seek out whomever it takes to put Mayfair on the map. *Whoever.* That would be you, of course."

"Wilma."

"You're right. Say no more. Lovely running into you, Emma."

I wished her well, then ambled home up Fifth Avenue rewinding Priory Bay through my head. Could Wilma be believed The Julian I knew was practically a figment of his own imagination? A surge of empathy for the man driven to manufacture a fictional persona rolled right over my outrage. Hadn't I'd been doing the same since my Wash U fraternity house episodes?

Actually no, I had not. I slowed at the Sixty-fourth Street Central Park Arsenal and zoo entrance. Tourists, dog walkers, and families shuffled around me as empathy evaporated. My all too-familiar gut grabbing angst took over. Passing off Turner and Picasso copies was one thing. Having way more to do with Carmine than he'd admitted, quite another. And god almighty, covert surveillance?

I crossed Fifth wondering if my FBI contacts might recommend an outfit to sweep our new headquarters for listening devices, then dug through my purse to answer my phone. *Thomas Schuman.* "Emma, sorry to bother you on the weekend," he said over background chatter. "You've mentioned living close to the Met. My son's at NYU and we're catching the Struth photo exhibit at four. Any chance I could drop off some photos on my way or after we grab dinner?" He lowered his voice. "I'll explain when I see you. Do you have a magnifying glass?"

"I do, actually, but no need to mess up family time. This can't wait till our flight?"

"*Can* but I'm guessing *shouldn't.*"

"Then I'll meet you at the museum. I have a favour to ask, anyway." At three-forty on the nose I circumvented hot dog trucks, tourist busses, then spotted him among the art lovers under the *THOMAS STRUTH: STREETS* banner at the top of the steps.

"Thanks for coming over," he said opening a manila envelope. "I'll be quick and you can take these home. No clue how relevant it is, but you might want to put a timeline together." He slid a black and white glossy from the envelope.

"Claridge's tea time," I said, glancing at a smiling woman and two girls in the foreground. To their right, a couple in profile leaned in, cups raised. "Holy shit. Marsha and Julian?"

"Yup. This apparently ran in *Fragrance International.* It popped up in their archives under Marsha." Thomas tapped the print. "Look behind them."

"That's me. High Tea was Marsha's domain, but she'd call me to come down with paperwork when she was wheeling and dealing. She rarely introduced me." I looked at Thomas. "During my first Mayfair interview, Julian mentioned having done some work with Platinum. Clearly he didn't remember this any more than I do."

"Doesn't remember or didn't mention tea for two? His free hands on top of hers." He handed me the envelope. "Barely worth mentioning, or having you trek over here except it got me digging. I've included contact proofs from my *Charade* launch, tear sheets, plus a few I've printed on normal paper. Take this home and get them under some magnification." He glanced over my shoulder and waved. "Sorry, Seth's on the sidewalk."

"Thomas, before my brain explodes, this morning I learned Julian had closer dealings with limelight loving Carmine Isgro than he's admitted. I was going to call you about stock photos."

"You want to me get nosy? I've got the company candids I shot for you. Getty Images is an option. Ciao!Beauty right?"

"Ciao!Beauty then Carmine used the Kinetic umbrella when he got his hands on it. Use both."

"This is between us?"

"Julian had Mayfair's Rockefeller Plaza board room wired to cover Carmine's conversations with my predecessors." I looked him straight in the eye. "You're to bill me at home."

"Understood."

I stayed long enough for a round of introductions before hustling home through the Upper East Side canyon to my empty, post war sanctuary.

Early afternoon Sunday, under the glare of my fluorescent kitchen lights, I ate leftover pork fried rice out of the takeout container and studied the Schuman handiwork laid out on my kitchen counters. Julian Petrenko, in one of his bespoke blazers, and Marsha Johnson, *de rigueur* French twist and Armani jacket, shared an intimate glance and gesture. Behind them I'm sporting Prada, my Diana, Princess of Wales, haircut, and a file folder. The Claridge's shot was eight years old.

For the umpteenth time I ran the magnifying glass over the 1996 *Charade* launch contact sheets. Thomas' proofs of Marsha shoulder-to-shoulder with Anna Wintour and Carolina Herrera, segued to her air kissing Muriel Beausoleil and introducing us. Thomas had starred a few, obviously intended for his assignment. Exclamation points sat next to a few more, probably shot within thirty or forty seconds of each other. In every one, including the original that had become my cropped and framed Beausoleil classic, Julian Petrenko stood to the side studying us. Julian and Marsha. A serious precursor to Julian and Wilma Nash? So what? Their relationship was unknown to me then, and none of my business now. Regardless, I expected it to keep me up all night. Instead I dreamed

I left the Guggenheim Museum after the Charade launch and found Ethan in his baseball uniform waiting to drive us home to Ludlow.

After a good cry over my morning coffee, I plunged into Monday as if I were in the midst of Ethan's incommunicado spring training days. No contact, so be it. My UK-C launch fortnight had arrived. He was right. For the next two weeks I'd barely have time to breathe, let alone grieve or try to sort out our marriage. I packed and chose board meeting agenda paperwork. I stared at my framed photo of Muriel Beausoleil and me two dozen times while wrestling anxiety over Julian, and smothering anxiety over Ethan. Teeth gritted, I exuded confidence to my support staff right until I left for the airport.

"As you can imagine, I'm so grateful you're aboard," I said to Thomas while walking the Teterboro taxiway. We kept conversation to small talk until the Gulfstream took off, then inevitably returned to Marsha and Julian. "My guess, business deal with side benefits," I said. "She has a bunch of years on him, but they wanted what each had to offer, business to bedroom. Maybe the affair gave him an insider's look at the business and kicked off this recent hands-on interest in his fragrance investments. It's natural he'd attend the launch, either via her personal invite or the massive industry buzz."

"I hear you. Just don't discount how he's studying you in those shots. Yes, you're a total babe and you looked like a million bucks. Even if that's what caught his eye in the first place, he'd have known who you were for quite a while by Guggenheim Night."

"If that was a compliment, thanks. If Julian was making plans to swoop me away from Marsha, he was late to that party. He could have saved me the unemployed, frozen slush, nightmare pavement pounding, not to mention the Carmine fiasco I fell into. He was probably too busy settling Wilma Nash into her executive position, speaking of combining business and bedroom."

Thomas studied me. "Assignment Two has turned up a Carmine nugget."

"No kidding!"

"I thought about waiting till we've returned, but there's nothing to be done with this info. I trust it won't derail your London demeanour in ways Julian could pick up." He handed me a five by seven, face down and tapped the stamp.

ESD Studios

316 Cranebook Rd. Ryde, Isle of Wight PO33 2EE

"I found it in the *Fragrance International* archives, too, filed under *Kinetic, Inc.*"

I turned it over. Julian Petrenko waved while steering a golf cart bearing the circular *PBH* Priory Bay Hotel logo. His passenger, the popped collar, white gloved, Bermuda shorts clad Carmine F.X. Isgro, looked triumphant. "Holy mother of Chanel Number Five. I know this photo. Carmine had a copy in his office."

"According to the code sheets, it also ran in the *Ryde Daily Register.* May, nineteen ninety-nine."

"Look at the two of them chumming it up," I replied. "Taken in May? The following November Mr Christopoulos announced Carmine's arrival and internship. Bingo, the worm was in the Ciao!Beauty apple. I know it was ninety-nine. Mr C and our CFO were panicking over the looming Y2K computer meltdown."

"Julian would have known all this."

"Thomas, I appreciate your concern. and obviously Julian's lied about a Carmine social connection, but he has mentioned Imperial's accounts with Kinetic. At some point Carmine and his scumbags were important clients, or more likely the reverse. Julian was important to Carmine. His panache and success would make him the total icon, a god to Carmine. So Carmine tries getting personal. Maybe Julian flies him over for a weekend to show off and hammer home that wannabe Isgro would never make the cut. Show him what real class is." I scoffed. "As if."

"As if?"

"Never mind. My point is, I'll bet Carmine placed the PR photo himself. Julian went to the mat over the sleazy smear tactics Carmine's PR firm put out about him." I sighed and leaned back. "This could be no more relevant than the Marsha relationship. Or it could be the tip of a very ragged iceberg. Either way, I've got way bigger fish to fry this week and next. You were right to show me." I opened my satchel and looked at him. "Are you up to speed on London?"

We freshened up on the plane. Alistair delivered us to Claridge's hampered by a classic spring downpour. I'd booked our rooms nearly across from each other, and at ten past three Julian greeted us at his sixth-floor penthouse in his full-on *Hail fellow, well met* routine. He offered Thomas a bourbon and use of his office for equipment or set-up during the party.

Thomas's small talk lead to the Sunday Met exhibit and Julian commented that he'd seen Struth's work in Zurich. For the first time I suspected fabrication.

Thomas departed and midway through Julian's and my review of the upcoming board meeting details, Alistair appeared with our routine martinis and finger food. An hour later Julian raised his glass. "To *Mesmerise,* the band, and Mayfair. You're as prepared as I ever seen you. And here's to tomorrow as well." We toasted to the noon Savoy Hotel press event; early evening Roundhouse mini-concert; and his apartment VIP reception. "I've long suspected you're the asset Imperial's needed," he added.

Suspected for how long? A concierge's call for Julian to meet someone in the lobby was all that kept me from dropping a Marsha reference in hopes he'd divulge something.

As Julian left I returned the tray to Alistair and the chef, busy reviewing their own agendas, and perused the penthouse areas I'd instructed the hotel staff to prepare. My light bulb moment occurred as I used the office bathroom. If Julian had a private file on his dealings with Carmine, it might very well be here in his no-doubt bespoke mahogany desk, rather than Zurich.

I gave myself twenty seconds, slid the drawer open and fingered through the alphabet. One, one thousand, two one thousand, *No Carmine, Ciao!Beauty, Christopoulos;* three one thousand, *Jacoby,* but no *Isgro* or *Kinetic on either side.* Nine seconds in, between *Oksana* and *Priory Bay,* I hit *Paige, Emma.* By the time I counted to twenty, I'd stretched it open and skimmed loose photos: me on my slushy job hunt in Chinatown; me with Mr Christopoulos outside the Empire State Building; me air kissing Pierre Meysselle in Cannes. And then: me sitting at Carmine's desk looking at his Coney Island ashtray. My heart slammed into overdrive. Thirty minutes later the knock on my hotel room door got me off my bed but Thomas' expression confirmed I looked as pale and clammy as I felt.

"Emma? I thought you might want to grab some dinner."

"But I'm just this side of hysteria?" I held back the floodgates with enough cursing to bring him into my suite. "I was looking for a file on Carmine…one with my name on it. Photos of me…before I even knew Julian existed." I sank into a chair and, with my head between my knees, described Carmine's desk shot.

"Panic attack?"

"Not my first."

Thomas knelt and kept his hand on my shoulder. "What the fuck were you doing alone at his desk?"

"Snooping. Rightly so, as it turned out. That's not the issue. About two weeks ago I learned Julian had our Rockefeller Plaza boardroom wired to keep tabs on Carmine when he came to Mayfair meetings." My shallow breathing steadied my pulse. I shook out my hands. "That fact is absolutely between us."

"Okay, fine. But it's one thing to order surveillance in your own offices, quite another for Julian to somehow cover Ciao!Beauty's headquarters, too."

"And accidentally discover me playing detective. Which he has never, ever mentioned." I rubbed goose bumps. "What if he's wired his penthouse and knows I rifled his files an hour ago? I need a Xanax, but I'm too full of gin."

He handed me the empty trash can liner. "Breathe into this and don't cry. You'll get gaspy again and hyperventilate." Anger, my trusted antidote to fear, kept me swearing like a sailor while he ordered room service. My head cleared as I nibbled on smoked salmon on toasted rye. "We agree the photo of me in Carmine's office is accidentally coincidental, but why the hell does he have those others? Why the stalking before I even met him? This creeps me out. What the holy hell is going on?"

"More than we realised."

"If I bring it up, he'll fabricate some believable explanation. I'm beginning to realise how often he does that. 'Bugger all, Emma, at my level one can't be too careful. Kidnapping threats, extortion— ' Oh, Thomas, why couldn't we have stumbled over all this two weeks from now? I don't have time to lie around in a fetal position."

He laughed. Without laying out my life story, I assured him I had the grit to make it through the next sixty hours. We agreed to keep tabs on each other.

Even as we click-clacked across the polished marble Savoy lobby the next morning, celebrity agents jammed my cell phone asking if I could get their clients' daughters into the press extravaganza. It kept me focused.

Hoopla worthy of the UK Connection's global popularity kicked our *Mesmerise* debut into high gear. My fear of raising suspicion in Julian outweighed anxiety over the launch. Unlike New York, I had no responsibility for crowd control or press set-up. Still, it was easy enough to convince Julian I needed to wander the room and study logistics in anticipation of our own press event.

I fluttered around everyone else to keep my distance from him. I hovered with Harrods London executive team as their director announced they'd be the official launch retailer.

Despite knowing the answer, I asked them to explain their exclusive thirty-day fragrance distribution rights on release in North America, Australia and Europe.

After the nuts-and-bolts business, the boys assembled on the mini-stage, with me at the edge. Julian radiated charm as he changed the event's focus from business to band and welcomed Taylor Davies. Taylor primed the boys with humorous introductions, encouraging their kidding and hamming. I smiled at the familiar: *Cian, Jasper, Tommy, Ennis, George; Cardiff, Wales; Manchester-not-Wales, Bibury, Dublin's finest, and Cheshire* routine.

They flirted their way through press questions, including those I invited from stammering fans who'd wormed their way in. My mojo was returning.

The boys posed for Thomas and the European press, then concluded with *a cappella* harmonising to roaring approval. As Axel pulled Julian aside, I shot them a thumbs up from across the room which Julian returned. Done! And back to my suite for some shallow breathing before the early evening concert. By the time I settled into our limousine I had control of both my fear and fury.

We arrived an hour's drive north in London's Chalk Farm neighbourhood to the pandemonium of klieg lights, police escorts and fan frenzy. Conversation was nearly impossible as we took our seats. *Et voila!* Julian had no time for me as he hobnobbed and ushered two dozen VIPs from the Roundhouse concert back to Claridge's.

Under the watchful eye of the hotel's small security force, he enthralled the hand-picked buyers, press reps, Axel, Taylor and production executives with references to Churchill-as previous-inhabitant. Thomas chatted while shooting, based on Julian's subtle cues and I directed staff serving drinks and late supper. I listened as Julian dropped his embellished childhood tidbits into the conversation. His perfect evening progressed and my angst dissipated.

"I'm thrilled to report strong press buzz," I said the following morning when Thomas and I returned to his suite for breakfast.

Julian toasted with his tea cup. "Polished off by a posh night with just the right guests. Thomas, you're quite the pro and perfect fit. Genius idea to snap a few with Axel and me in my office. When he returns to LA, let's post a print to him with a congratulatory note."

"I fly home tonight after I shoot his Mercury Artists reception for the California execs," he replied. "I can pull this together in my studio tomorrow afternoon."

"And I'll have it framed," I added. "Something sophisticated, Julian, like your Priory Bay candid of *Oksana*." I flushed under his sudden scrutiny.

"Spot on, both of you. Exemplary efforts all round. Smashing suggestions." Within the hour he walked us to the door. Thomas shook hands, commented on his New York launch assignments and promised to text me over the weekend.

As he left Julian turned to me. "The board only cares if we make the committed sales numbers. Let's hope results break records to cover more of these fragrance parties. We'll reconcile numbers after the first ninety days' selling results."

"This week's been the perfect trial run." I replied. "You've been absolutely stellar. Will be good to get the second deafening concert and board meeting behind us." He cupped my elbow. "I promise a celebratory dinner, a last hurrah for the launch effort and onward for Mayfair Beauty! I've arranged a well-deserved getaway to Versteckte Hügel in St. Moritz." He gave the distinct impression it would be dinner for two. A getaway to some exclusive Swiss spa? All I wanted was the luxury of time to clear my head, sleep and tackle my neglected, disintegrating marriage.

I arrived stateside in time to close the work week at the office and report on our London success. Just being in the same room with my team kept my blood pressure in check.

"Macy's has placed another million-dollar, order. You can assure the board they're flowing in over projection," Bill Grose said as he handed me a thick envelope. "I confess. Frankly not needed but yesterday I had Sam call Zurich on your behalf. For any sceptical number crunchers at the board meeting, these faxed stats provide comparables. Sports teams to Robo-Technik endoscopic products, to Imperial oils that smell good, you've got the entire Petrenko empire."

"Sam! Bill! You've had enough to do. Thank you so much."

"They just arrived and I've barely skimmed them, but I've kept my own set, in case you need last minute explanations or interpretation over the weekend. Your safety net, Emma." CFO Sam Garten winked. "Consider yourself armed for bear."

Thomas texted me and Saturday I grabbed a cab. I hit the Waldorf Astoria for a check with hotel staff assigned to my Wednesday night team tribute, then on to the Flatiron District.

"You've launched UK Connection right into orbit," Thomas said as we crossed his studio to the work table. "The ultimate grace under pressure."

"It showed?"

"No. Julian's totally taken with you with good reason. My career's built on relationships with behind-the-scenes executives. To his credit he doesn't micromanage. You could finish his sentences. You make it look easy, Emma, especially the effort that required this time around."

We settled on the stools and chose a shot of Axel and

Julian against the backdrop of his leather club chair and Diana Von Furstenberg's upgrades. Thomas drummed his fingers. "I stumbled on some more info. I can hold it until you finish the project, but my gut says now's the time."

"Stumbled?"

He shrugged. "I thought I might find more Carmine details, maybe business dealings between Kinetic and Imperial. It was a no-brainer during the party. I had full use of the office."

"With Julian in the next room? You know I already looked! Your no-brainer could have blown up your entire career."

"Scream at me later." He opened his phone. "Emma, Julian has *Ethan* photos, too. I found them in the *Jacoby* file. All I've done is snap photos of photos."

"Oh, god. Jacoby's the scout who's hired him."

He tapped forward to my husband, me and a cabana. "Our second time in Cannes. We were sent out of the country when the Ciao!Beauty/Kinetic crisis broke. I got unfamiliar calls over there and finally followed up back in New York."

"Let me guess. Julian?"

"Yes."

"So his first contact was as Kinetic went into meltdown?"

"Yes, but his stalking collection goes back to Platinum."

"And from there, he has your job hunt, Christopoulos employment and their company crisis." His comment hung between us as he thumbed his cell phone screen. "I only copied a few. There's a group of kids at Yankee Stadium."

"Ethan's school team. Julian underwrote the trip."

"And Ethan at a strip joint with another guy." He tapped, then turned the screen to me.

"That's Adam Donavan," I said. "Dallas. Julian sent them to the Bulls' playoffs while I was in England with him. Why surveillance? Does Julian think he's got dirt on my husband and this will somehow shock me?"

"There is one with a woman."

"Oh please. Let me guess. Our housekeeper Misha. Courtesy of you-know-who Ethan went out to a Vegas baseball memorabilia convention at Caesar's Palace. That's when he met with Paul Jacoby and got the job. Turns out Misha miraculously had Celine Dion concert tickets. Miraculously overlapping dates, miraculously in the same casino."

I tamped down my sarcasm as he scrolled to Misha peeking from her hotel room into the hall at Ethan. 313, the brass number, was on *her* door. I stood up so fast I knocked his phone to the table. "Careful!"

"*She's* in three thirteen? I found that number written on Jacoby's business card. Obviously I thought it was Ethan's room number. Three Thirteen R M T."

"Calm down, Sherlock. R M T. Roman Tower at the Palace. You already suspect they hooked up. Ethan and Misha meet in Vegas, Ethan writes her room number on the guy's business card."

"I didn't find it in Ethan's belongings. The card was in Julian's apartment on the Isle of Wight." I explained the Priory watch errand and hugged myself against another clammy flush. Thomas pushed the stool against the back of my legs. "Sit down before you keel over on me."

I sat. "Put these pictures on a flash drive or something. Get them out your phone, now. This must absolutely not get back to Julian. He'll ruin you."

"I know and I will. For sure we've discovered a gargantuan mess, but Carmine's role is over. Yes, Julian might be manipulating Ethan. But Emma, he might—"

"—be working with Ethan's full, fucking appreciation."

"Getting him a job's not the end of the world."

"Not your world," I muttered.

"Can you keep it together and plough through next week on autopilot? Put this crap on hold till you can breathe?"

"As if I have a choice."

"Lean on your staff. I'm around on assignment right through the board meeting. Remember how well you did in London."

"New York Launch Week will run without a hitch. *Then* I'll lay the cards on Julian's table." I had no other way to answer.

Two weeks without Misha's housekeeping affected little but meal prep and laundry. Sunday, I dropped my launch trip clothes into our laundry pickup bag and finally emptied the hamper. It still included Ethan's Las Vegas khakis and linen shirt I'd stuffed back in after kicking Misha out. His pants pocket gave up a five-dollar bill and torn piece of paper scrawled with *313 Roman Tower.* The script matched Misha's instructions often taped to her prepared dinners. Anxiety unleashed my demons.

I'd barely been home enough for the kitchen to need a paper towel swipe but I sprayed and scrubbed my counters as if swarming childhood cockroaches lay in wait. Ethan in cahoots with Julian? I vacuumed till my shoulder ached. If Misha was part of the deal why was he living with Nicole? I swiped rubbing alcohol over every chrome fixture. That night Ethan and Misha, Marsha and Wilma, Carmine and Julian stalked my dreams.

Ready or not *Mesmerise* American Launch Week arrived. Atticus, Amanda and Andrew, my Triple A out-of-towners, confirmed their Wednesday LA and Chicago flight ETAs. Our Madison Avenue office buzzed as staff gathered for the final meeting. Most of us had been together long enough each heartily pooh-poohed my opening apology for my stress level. I thanked them and gave the floor to Dustin.

"I'm still fielding hundreds of Thursday concert and afterparty ticket requests," he said. "At Emma's suggestion I've booked the band press interviews on a rotation schedule. The venue's letting me set up partitions and reconfigure the space to avoid a packed room competing journalists in free-for-all. Security assures me they'll keep desperate fans from sneaking in through the air conditioning vents."

"But you're in charge just in case." He saluted me.

Despite Harrods' restricted thirty-day hold, we'd also guaranteed an exclusive distribution perk. "Warehouse shipping is in progress," Sam announced.

"I have it on good authority *Mesmerise* is on its way to the homes of several thousand UK-Connection fans to mesh perfectly with the concert," Bill added.

When we'd reviewed every conceivable item on our launch agenda, I high-fived each of them. "I know Julian's main interest is bottom line cash flow and he's mostly in touch with Sam and Bill, but each of you is a gear in his Mayfair engine. He'll be the first to agree. Take time to socialise with him at the concert and after-party. You're as key to Mayfair as the board members. And, by the way, I've made sure your seats are just as good as theirs."

Jennifer looked at me. "Anything else?"

"Not much. The Royal Suite will be mine tomorrow at three, normal check-in time. I'll see you all there Wednesday evening. It's also a safe place for your valuables or essentials during Thursday and Friday events. Thank you, thank you, thank you." As my team departed Bill approached with an unreadable expression.

"Warehouse question?" I asked.

"No, Emma. Frankly, since you still haven't mentioned it, I'm wondering when the hell you plan to inform us."

I frowned. "I've overlooked something? I haven't reviewed the faxes yet if that's what you mean."

He swore like a rapper, tugged me back to the table, shuffled papers and slapped them down. "Julian's moving us to Zurich."

Chapter Twenty-Four

"No, no. Julian's consolidating his fragrance interests into Imperial. Yes, he'll merge the separate entities under a corporate umbrella and yes, core headquarters are in Zurich. But he'd be crazy not to keep a major fragrance base in North America. You know that. North America's the toughest territory, smallest profit margin. Julian's in total agreement. Leaving makes as much sense as running his sports interests from Switzerland," I skimmed his sports division stat sheets. Bill studied me. "You really don't know, do you?"

"State-side people are key. He knows that as well as you."

"I also know I've got teenagers and a wife with teaching tenure. A transatlantic transfer is not in the cards. Neither is job hunting at fifty-two. Have I mentioned upcoming college tuitions? And Abdul's older than I am..." He glanced at his watch.

"How much time can you give me?"

We grabbed lunch from the lobby sandwich shop, then pored over fragrance merger and Zurich real estate expenditures. *Imperial relocation* had its own section. Bahnhofstrasse corporate headquarters would reconfigure and expand to encompass the branch. Line items included *COP—current oils production, Long Island, NY; Mayfair Fragrance/New York City; Nudes-Elixir, organic skin care and fragrance/California.*

No more Madison Avenue office. "He's never said a word about shutting down New York," was all I could manage. "Emma, corporates never included this in board meeting number crunching or projections. If it's honestly news to you—"

"Bill! It's either a brand-new decision, which these financials dispute or Julian's kept it from me."

"I believe you. Forgive me." He gathered the income and expenditure sheets. I pulled the sports category over, soon speechless at the depth of Julian's corporate involvement, from *NBA: Dallas Bulls,* to *Baseball: Buffalo Nickels; Class-A Advanced;* to *Bat & Glove, Ltd.*

Bat & Glove, Ltd. Julian Petrenko owned Paul Jacoby's scouting business? "Bill, I'm positive some of this was included by mistake. Not meant to leave headquarters or at least not meant for my eyes. Somebody's head will be on the chopping block when Julian finds out."

"You'll bring it up?"

"You're bloody hell, bugger all, damn right. I just have to figure out when."

He loosened my arms from the death grip across my own ribs.

Instead of clearheaded preparation for Wednesday's staff extravaganza, Thursday's press conference, pre-concert meet and greet, and Friday's board meeting, I closed Monday tangled in confusion, suspicion and doubt. Shoving my hands through my hair while staring at my desk photos of Ethan-in-uniform and Muriel Beausoleil accomplished nothing. I called Darlene and laid out my situation. "Before you reply," I added, "attorney-client privilege lets me give you information and explain my creepy feeling about Carmine?"

"As your attorney, I strongly suggest you remove your toe from uncharted *creepy feeling* waters. Plus a client's communication isn't privileged if she intends to cover up a crime or fraud."

"I'm not covering up anything. Isgro is. Or, more probably, Julian is." I forced myself to stay on the Carmine track.

"Emma, this could be a colossal waste of your money and my time but I'll stick *my* toe in for you. Nevertheless, you've got better and safer things to do than turn over rocks looking for more dirt on Carmine and his idiot gangsters."

Bouncing my angst and suspicion off my attorney rather than my photographer loosened my knots. After the board meeting and members' departures, for sure my stress level would plummet. Without a doubt Julian would suggest a review of the week's success before he flew home Saturday morning. I could yank the celebratory evening from the Swiss spa.

My concerns required calm demeanour and complete sobriety. My file snooping and Thomas's duplicated photos put me on shaky ground. I had no intention of betraying Wilma's indiscretion, but no qualms sharing spread sheet information. My WTF punch list grew.

Zurich Move: Facts and timeline. Who goes? When?

Kinetic counterfeiting: Knowledge? Involvement?

Relationship with Carmine: Truth!

Ethan's Jacoby offer: Misha; Julian/Bat & Glove. Truth!

If nothing else I'd see Ethan at the concert and Friday marked the end of our no-contact agreement. The light from an empty weekend shone at the end of my boulder strewn, Launch Week tunnel. Here to there seemed an eternity.

An overdue Central Park run under bright May skies kick started Tuesday. Thomas texted as I crossed Fifth Avenue. *U ready?* I tapped back: *All ok. Clear headed & ready to launch.* Darlene called. "Anything not in the public domain regarding Kinetic and Imperial, and especially possible Petrenko connections will take digging. Carmine has seven months left in the Danbury FCI. He'll likely be released by New Year's."

"Let that old acquaintance be forgot," I muttered.

"Take it to heart, Toots," she replied.

At three o'clock I launched myself over to the Waldorf

Astoria, unpacked and set up Command Central with Jennifer and Dustin. Their enthusiasm for my Royal Suite and upcoming events kept us focused. Constantly ringing cell phones underscored this was not the time to embroil them in anything but the tasks at hand. We finished over supper served in the suite's renowned dining room, soon to be transformed for our celebration.

Wednesday evening kicked into high gear as my New York team mingled in my suite. Andrew Case arrived from Chicago and chatted playlist with Dustin. Thomas and I went over last-minute photo suggestions until impromptu jazz suddenly wailed from the living room piano. Atticus sat on the bench; head cocked toward the keys. Surprise enough, but Julian, impeccably business casual, stood at the lid prop tapping his foot. Like a scene from a cheesy thriller, he turned and we locked glances. "Julian! I had no idea you'd be able to stop by."

"Just a pop-in on my way to dinner with a few of the board members. I've no intention of interrupting. Looks to be a superb night. With all firm and in place for tomorrow, I hope you'll enjoy yourself." Something flickered in his studied blue-eyed stare. *He knows* erased everything else in my head. My files snooping? Thomas's? *He knows, and he knows I know.* At that moment Amanda Denton pounced into the foyer and bounded over.

"I'm here! Flew in with Atticus but needed a nap." I introduced her to Julian and she offered her hand.

"Lovely to finally meet you. I'm coordinating *Mesmerise* placement for the release. I'm here to pay close attention to tomorrow's controlled chaos."

His expression returned to normal. "Emma's assured me we're to come out alive."

"A good thing. By the way, congratulations to you both on the Windmill purchase." She turned to me. "Maureen McDaniel knows I work for Mayfair and gave me the details personally Monday morning. She did say nothing's public as of yet. I only mention it since here we are face-to-face. When you fold Windmill into Imperial, I'd welcome the chance to talk strategy and my place in your plans."

I turned to Julian for his correction. His expression shifted as it had at the piano, as it had in Zurich when I laid out my Ethan accusations. "We've all manner of business opportunities up for discussion, but it's prudent to wait until Launch Week's put to bed."

"Absolutely. That was my thirty second pitch. I look forward to the right time and place to continue." Amanda thanked us then headed for Atticus still playing the piano. Julian avoided my stare by checking his international everything watch. "I've much to explain, of course, though we can agree this is neither the time nor the place."

"Yes we can but Maureen McDaniel is Gregory's wife so I'll assume Amanda's information is accurate."

He paused. "Yes."

"I'll see you out."

"No need."

Like hell. I accompanied him anyway, past imbibing team members and camera-laden Thomas giving no indication he was listening. If he had recorded my snooping, he knew my discoveries gave me leverage. I opened the foyer door. "Julian, I was so clear about the pitfalls of this purchase. Windmill's entire P&L is exaggerated. You'll have McDaniel-the-amateur at your heels. My question's not why you changed your mind but why behind my back?"

"If you've a mind to jump right in, I give you my word. Friday when we've cleared the decks we'll use the evening to walk through current developments step by step."

I bit my tongue to keep from spewing, "Shutting down our New York headquarters as well?"

He left. Dinner was served. As we ate, I tossed out tidbits about the Duchess of Windsor's dinner for Estee Lauder and compared those queens of high style and fragrance to the UK-Connection. It brought laughs from my crew and kept me focused. CFO, Sam Garten, raised his glass. "To our very own Duchess of Mayfair and this royal evening."

Over the "hear, hears," I gave everyone a one-thousand-dollar American Express gift card, plus a smaller one for *Find Your Soul* candle shop. My enthusiasm was real. I concluded by asking Bill to stand. Dustin and Sebastian Ballantine, our Director of International Business, set down a package. "In appreciation for all your overnights in the office." Bill tore away the wrapping and pulled a large bottle of Belvedere Vodka from inside the coiled LL Bean sleeping bag.

Atticus clinked his glass. "Dessert will be served in the salon. Life's a cabaret, old chums." We assembled, the play mix rebooted and he introduced two female impersonators. The drag queens knocked Whitney Houston and Diana Ross songs out of the park. As Thomas packed up his cameras, the evening settled into camaraderie that closed my throat.

This group, this family of professionals, had cleaned corporate house, turned Mayfair around and put us on the fragrance map. More change was in the air. I owed every one of them honest information I didn't have, honest answers to where we were headed. Julian owed them.

The stress of separating my personal issues from professional refused to let up. By midnight I was pacing my now deserted suite. Anxiety blindsided me. Imagined Julian arguments swam in my head. I struggled to remember who of my crew knew what. Bill unearthed the Zurich move. Amanda knew of the Windmill turnabout, Thomas, the photo files. I was blurry over how much of his scouting job and Misha info Ethan had admitted to me, versus how much I'd thrown at him. Should I confide in Jennifer?

The dreaded flush heated my cheeks, oozed into my scalp, then drained into a cold sweat. "I can count on Thomas to be at the press event well in advance. Hotel staff will clean and clear while I'm with Julian." I grabbed someone's half-empty glass sitting on the dining room sideboard and threw back watered-down scotch not giving a thought to screaming teenaged hoards, press briefings, escape routes, or the Madison Square Garden frenzy awaiting me.

The following morning looping mental images of Julian's photos, detailed files on our private lives and Misha Baskin as some sort of hired marriage assassin nearly obliterated the murky details of my professional situation. By then I'd made it to Julian's thirty-third floor Cole Porter Suite, read the commemorative plague and knocked.

271

He opened the door, all charm and enthusiasm while gesturing to the dining room. Alistair called hello while he circled the mahogany table and laid out board meeting agenda folders. Would I like a tour; Of course the piano was not the composer's; Frank Sinatra also used the suite as a residence. I was in no mood for Julian's to-the-manner-born routine and it must have showed. He took both my hands.

"Bollocks, Emma. Amanda Denton's charming and no doubt qualified, but you've not been informed only because I wanted to ensure your week was clear of the very distractions such as Windmill." We crossed to the sitting area. "Earlier in the week I alerted your team that I've scheduled our Versteckte Hügel getaway for Sunday. They heartily approved my whisking you away for a well-deserved retreat to celebrate your achievement. Zurich, then on to St. Moritz where we can lay out future plans in a far more relaxed atmosphere. I'd planned to surprise you this afternoon."

Bloody hell! "Weekends are my own."

"I alerted Ethan, as well. He's keen on the idea."

"Julian! Why this meddling in my marriage?"

"A few spa days to rejuvenate?" He scoffed; I fumed. "More than spa days. Since you've brought up Ethan, perhaps you'll explain why my housekeeper's Las Vegas room number is on Paul Jacoby's business card? When I mentioned this Jacoby issue in Zurich, I assumed that number was Ethan's room." I explained the faxed sports sheets. "Now I learn you own the California baseball scout's company and besides setting up Ethan in Las Vegas, it's obvious somehow, some way, you're behind Misha's concert tickets."

"This must wait."

"No, this must be explained now or I walk."

"Hysteria's not necessary." I stood. He followed. "Emma, I admire Ethan. I enjoy his company and recognise his abilities. He captivated you, the biggest achievement of his life. I admit I crossed the line, but I recognise your frustration and the constraints of your crumbling marriage. Your talents are diminished, perhaps wasted, on a man like Ethan. If you've a mind to discuss it, the three of us can chat tonight."

"Your manipulations—" I chose my words. "—disappoint me. Even more serious, they're distractions. I have an obligation to my staff, to Mayfair, to you, Julian. I need today and tomorrow free of anything but business at hand. I'll see you in the lobby as planned, but it's best if I leave now."

Once back in my suite, I punched out Ethan's number which, per usual, went to voicemail. I let it kick in. "Ethan, don't come to the concert tonight. It's what you wanted anyway. Stay away. Julian's manipulating you. Us. He admitted he owns Jacoby and somehow Misha. You've got to believe me. Tonight in the concert box is my only chance to get the facts out of him. He's got you by the balls! I'm with the bastard for the rest of the day so don't call me back. I'll make excuses. Stay home. Promise me. It's my only time alone with him, my only chance to get the truth. I'll call you after the concert."

In the Town Car an hour later, as the Petrenko security detail drove along Fifty-first Street and around the corner onto Fifth Avenue, I morphed into Miss Congeniality. Julian and I reviewed his press conference talking points while inching through NYPD crowd control, NYPD barriers as far back as Rockefeller Plaza, paparazzi as far back as the barriers, swirling helicopters, and hordes of school-skipping teenagers. Across the avenue mid-day parishioners dodged UK-C fans filling the steps of St. Patrick's Cathedral for a glimpse of their heroes. UK Connection, *Mesmerise* and Mayfair had indeed arrived.

Julian cupped my elbow as we entered the high-rise. "The screaming!"

"Imagine the pitch when the boys arrived."

Five flights up we entered loft space fit for an album release listening party. As promised, Dustin's design had everyone where they needed to be. I greeted him, Axel, Taylor, and their music industry bigwigs, then waved at Thomas. The band members entered, all smiles and positive vibes. Julian propped himself on a stool, as relaxed and charismatic as the boys.

Once again the five were prepared, witty, and sincere. "I speak for me mates," Ennis said. "We put our hearts into creating *Mesmerise* for our fans. We hope they love it."

This time Jasper leaned in. "We know they will."

Perfection reined despite my internal chaos. As the event shifted to the press rotations, Julian's security detail wedged us out through the external chaos. On the street bogus reporters shouted their bogus publication credentials and fans yelled over each other, all for inside scoop. We pressed into the car. It would have been quicker to jog back to the hotel.

I changed into my private-box-concert-appropriate cashmere sweater over designer jeans, while obsessively checking my phone. Ethan's silence relieved me. I reminded myself, as irritating and frustrating as his phone habits were, he'd never missed a message.

Jennifer was due to meet the board members in the lobby but I needed a confidante. I thought twice, and tapped out her number. The minute she answered I laid out a condensed version of the Ethan situation, Julian's surveillance of us, and my opportunity to dig for information alone with him in the VIP box. "I need facts, facts, facts."

"What the hell is he up to? I probably should tell you he's planning to surprise you this afternoon with plans—"

"To whisk me away to some damned Swiss spa. He told me. I need to talk it out here Friday night before he flies out, not hop his plane and have him blindside me halfway across the planet."

Twenty minutes later I hit the lobby where Julian waved me over to arriving board members and poker-faced Jennifer, their guide for the whole evening. I fabricated an Ethan student emergency that would keep him in New Jersey. From there I hustled Julian out the back door via hotel security for the wild ride down Park, along Twenty-seventh, up Sixth, over Thirty-third and down Seventh Avenue to the Garden. The pandemonium of gathered spectators, arriving fans and VIP ticket holders filled my ears. Once inside the Meet and Greet area I hugged each of the boys. As I explained about Ethan, guilt, laced with emotions too complicated to name, had me swiping at tears.

"Blimey, Mrs Baseball!" Sean patted my shoulder. "He'll miss our genius tonight but you tell him we'll trade tickets to one of his games for another concert."

We took advantage of the photo ops and once the event wound down, Julian and I left for the corporate box. Even with security credentials around my neck, we moved at a crawl and arrived to my team schmoozing with our esteemed buyers, press core and board members over drinks and finger food.

Jennifer and I double checked the after-party guest list and floor seat assignments and I leaned in. "I'll be civil but short with Julian. He has a shitload to answer for and I need to make clear what I want, what needs discussion. I need about thirty minutes, hopefully before the boys are on. If the concert blasts any of our VIPs out of their comfort zones, then they're welcome to move up here with him." She handed me two extra tickets, "I'll use these and sit-down front."

When the schmoozing wound down and the assembled group left for their seats, I joined Julian at the Plexiglas box front partition and watched fans fill one hundred and eighty degrees of seats. "Prime viewing. No better way for your investors to experience their first American rock concert," I said. "They know they can move up here if it's too hard on their eardrums. Either way, it's been perfection so far. They'll be primed for tomorrow morning."

"Spot on, per usual. Now's the time to enjoy yourself. I've you favourite merlot right here."

We stayed at the edge of box watching bright beams of light bounce off thousands screaming their approval before anything even started. Had I ever been that girl in the throes of innocence, transported by music with my whole life ahead of me?

Julian filled out glasses. "It's been a long week. I realise to your way of thinking I've a bit to apologise for but everything's in order."

I let that hang for a moment. "Far from everything. We'll enjoy the concert but tomorrow night I expect honesty. I'm sorry Ethan's not here but it's a chance to clear the air. Too many clouds hang over events, Julian. Too many actions affect my private life and my professional ability."

"You're not to think my Windmill decision's had anything to do with your competence. Contrary to Amanda's source, I only bought controlling interest of fifty-two percent. McDaniel keeps the remaining forty-eight. We've signed an extensive confidentiality clause regarding my status as silent partner. No public knowledge regarding my involvement."

"Except for his wife's Pilates partners."

"Mrs McDaniel understands she was mistaken and the deal did not go through. She'll explain as much to Amanda and you'll confirm." He paused, clearly letting the implication sink in.

"Why silent partner? You're done with Kinetic; do you need a new dumping ground? Is Imperial dealing in noncompliant ingredients? Counterfeiting?"

"Emma, you're a brilliant woman who knows my *modus operandi*. Pragmatic decisions require study and consideration."

"Such as deliberate materials shortages to hike prices? I want to believe Windmill's overstated financials are only tweaks to interest investors, but this rabbit hole's too deep for preconcert discussion. Tomorrow night you'll need to convince me with stats."

"I'd expect nothing less," he said. "I've been watching you for some time." His smile oozed satisfaction.

"That needs explanation."

"1998, within months of Kinetic contracting with Imperial as a supplier, Carmine Isgro sought me ought personally. He'd taken a bit of a shine to me. I encouraged it. Quite the bloke. He made clear he was serious about the fragrance industry and in line to inherit his uncle's business. The sooner the better, as far as he was concerned. I naturally considered Imperial's # potential with him."

"Schmoozing."

"Bloody hell. Thinking it harmless, I put up with his Yank braggadocio. I undercut my management's advice and made foolish decisions providing our oils. Found myself with contracts set in stone. I badly underestimated the bastard's cunning. He resorted to veiled threats regarding my involvement in schemes far wider than I'd imagined."

He expected social rejection so I took Machiavelli's advice and kept my enemy close, right down to an NBA Texas weekend and excruciating Priory Bay golf outing. Extricating Imperial and surveillance were crucial, yet planting inside Kinetic would have been foolhardy and perhaps dangerous. "I've a closer association with Marsha Johnson than I've led you to believe. Over dinner one night she complained about the pressure to address the company's financial shifts. Platinum forced her hand and she'd had to let you go. With reluctance. She said you're quick on your feet and as savvy as she thinks she is. I remembered you from the *Charade* launch and brought myself up to date."

"You didn't contact me until Ciao!Beauty collapsed."

"Indeed, but you'll recall the night at the St. Regis? The Perfume Society of America's, *Winners Table* Hall of Fame event."

"What about it?"

"I arranged to have Nikos Christopoulos seated at your table, and was delighted to spot the two of you in the King Cole Bar afterward. I couldn't hear a word but, as hoped, it was clear you were making a pitch to him. From there a trusted member of my executive team convinced Nikolas Christopoulos the young, savvy consultant who'd masterminded his Nordstrom presentation should be brought on board permanently and quickly before Chanel or Prada spirited her away."

"Julian!"

"A nudge, Emma, that's all, and one of the best business decisions of my career. Keeping tabs on you has proven a complete pleasure. During Cannes' luxury trade show, I was delighted to see you work your magic with the Christopoulos directors, each as taken with you as I was. ...all their encouragement to visit Milan... Your skills impress me to this day and back then they proved invaluable. I was able to bring the ugly Carmine Isgro chapter to a close as rapidly as possible."

"You?"

"I was rarely in the states, or active in Mayfair management so he targeted Wilma Nash with sudden and transparent interest in Mayfair. His behaviour forced me to install boardroom surveillance. Nikos's mistake was naïveté. Bringing his nephew into Ciao!Beauty with exceptional responsibility doomed them. Carmine envisioned Imperial as some sort of bottomless resource. His hints of blackmail forced my hand. To raise your alarm I needed the obvious so I arranged documents at the copy machine, and bogus backpack deliveries among the real ones."

"My God, Julian! You set me up to give the FBI a witness who had no relationship with Imperial."

He shrugged a *yes*. "I freed you from a potentially catastrophic situation."

"Which you'd placed me in." No doubt the surveillance shot of me at Carmine's desk preceded others as I pulled off the radiator cover. Reality knocked the breath out of me.

"You're an amazing asset on every level."

"I'm horrified."

He waved it off. "There's nothing about your career I don't know. Folding Mayfair and Windmill into Imperial, and Imperial into Robo-Technik opens your perfect next opportunity."

"And you expect to relocate my New York team to Zurich by January. Another agenda item you've neglected to mention to anyone in my office."

"Certainly not. You've convinced me it's imperative to maintain a physical presence in North America. No, they'll remain as indispensable as always right here. It's you who's proven qualified to oversee our consolidated fragrance venture from corporate headquarters. We were to discuss this opportunity in St. Moritz. I've a file all prepared. Covers everything from our corporate objectives to travel requirements. It lays out complete relocation information regarding your Bahnhofstrasse office and a lakeside residence in Enge—"

"You're moving me to Zurich."

"I promise details tomorrow night with less uproar."

The lilt had left his voice; outrage entered mine. "The uproar has nothing to do with this concert. You must also have an *Ethan* file. You've mastermind his new job, new location, a separate life. My god, you've thought of everything."

He shrugged. "Emma, you combine instinct with an acute understanding of the fragrance industry, a composite of everything desirable in business. You must know from Day One you've been critical to my developing this niche." I waited.

"I confess your interview on Priory Bay was a bit of a test."

"For me, as well."

"Professionally you offered extraordinary insight. Socially you moved among royalty with grace. On a personal level, suffice to say, the evening you spent with me in Oksana's pearls altered our lives. You've proven to understand me as few others have."

I let that sink in. "I take enormous pride in my work. I'm grateful you recognise my effort, but I'm not a chess piece you can slide all over the Petrenko empire game board."

"Bollocks. We've chewed on enough for this evening."

"One more question. When you offered me Priory Bay for the getaway and sent me for your watch, why not arrange for me to pick it up from security at the desk?"

"No harm done from a nudge into my dressing room. Let's lay our cards on the table, shall we?" He turned from the commotion of arriving fans and smiled at me. "Chemistry between us is obvious. I weighed the intimacy factor. Frankly I'd have offered my suite had it not been full of tradesmen."

"There's been times when chemistry's been powerful. We made a strong team because of it."

"With your marriage little more than a signature on a legal document. Ethan can never give you the life you deserve."

"Ethan's none of your business. Tracking us is an outrage."

"For your protection."

"My protection in case your manoeuvres go haywire. You've manipulated our relationship like it's some failing perfume contract." Arguing was pointless. I'd never win; I'd morph into my ranting Missouri self I'd worked so hard to abandon. "Julian, you're a smart man who gets what he wants. I'm flattered you needed me to make it happen. In terms you can understand, I've proven myself a good investment. However, you've moved from mergers and acquisitions to a hostile takeover. I don't need you or Ethan for my success. I took responsibility for my future a long time ago."

I swear the fog lifted. As if I'd summoned a spokesperson into my head, I offered my hand. "These fifteen minutes have convinced me it's time to step aside."

"Don't be daft. I promised St. Moritz. Go. Take whatever time you need. Take Ethan, if need be."

"Julian, we're done. You're a man with a lot to keep secret. I can't in good conscience be part of it, and I can't address your board knowing what I do."

"This is insanity."

"You know it's not. Jennifer and Bill are already in charge of the concert follow-up tonight You're as prepared as I am for tomorrow's board meeting. I give you my word everything you need will be in your suite tonight." I didn't dare blink.

"Christ, Emma. You cannot bloody well walk out on our contract – or me – without consequences."

"You've forced this decision. You stand to make over twenty million dollars on the *Mesmerise* licensing deal and Imperial's racking up massive profit with development derived from it. I brought you the UK Connection contract; I put the entire project together, right down to where we're standing. I assembled the executives who transformed your company. I walk but my team will keep Mayfair running without a hiccup. If you'd rather dismantle it, they'll serve as interim support."

Out beyond us strobe lights blinked and microphones squealed. "Despite how you feel about severance or compensation for me, if it comes to separation for my team, no one knows better than you what a small world fragrance is. I expect financial generosity and sterling recommendations for them. It would be foolish not to agree."

"Foolish I am not," he said over screaming fans tripling the decibel level.

"No, you're not. I trust you to do the right thing by them and by me. No threats; no rants. I swear resigning never crossed my mind until your explanations these past fifteen minutes convinced me. You've crossed the line and invaded every aspect of my professional and personal life. I've known you as a man of your word but you've destroyed my trust."

For the first time since that blustery spring interview he looked vulnerable. "Bollocks. Emma, give yourself and Mayfair twenty-four hours."

I shook his hand. "All right, fair enough. But Julian, You do not want me speaking to your directors tomorrow."

Chapter Twenty-Five

Willpower propelled me out of the corporate box and along the winding hallways of Madison Square Garden. I fought tears and muttered obscenities as the concert burst into action. Electric guitar mania from the front band became the soundtrack of our ending credits.

I exited through the main doors and side stepped two girls breaking up their homemade posters, dead ringers for Genevieve and me in middle school. "No tickets?" I asked.

"As if," the younger one said.

"We were jerks to think they'd go in the front doors."

"They would have if it hadn't been so crazy out here. I happen to know the boys love their fans."

"You know them?"

"I do. George, Jasper and Tommy are English. Cian's Welsh and Ennis, Irish."

"Oh my gosh. Sweet."

I took off my credential lanyard and slung it over the older girl, then rummaged through my satchel for my tickets. "No way, no way!" she screamed.

"This is a scam," her sister added.

"No scam and the longer we talk, the more you'll miss." I walked them inside. "*Jennifer Rocket*. Remember the name. She's the organiser at your seats. Tell her Emma will explain."

"What if somebody stops us? This can't be for real."

"Cross my heart. Totally, totally for real." I placed the tickets in her small hand and pressed both girls toward the thundering music and screaming. "Get going!"

After my short text to Jennifer with promise of voicemail details, I hustled into the blazing lights of Pennsylvania Plaza, pausing this time to call my husband. "Ethan! You've got to call me. Julian's set you up. Me, too. Total Manipulation. I need you. I need to explain this craziness in person. Call me!"

I hit Herald Square and my Memory Mile: Macy's, Lord and

Taylor, Saks Fifth Avenue, Bergdorf Goodman… *What the fuck have I done* rattled through my head all the way to the Waldorf. What the fuck had Julian been doing?

Within twenty minutes of reaching the hotel, I'd handed my board meeting file plus speaking notes to the concierge for immediate delivery to Julian's suite. Whether Alistair intercepted didn't phase me. As I emptied my Royal Suite closet, Thomas called. "Jennifer updated me as I finished the preconcert shoot," he said, "You are one hell of a tough cookie."

"Repeat that in a week when this sinks in. Julian and I stared each other down. He only mentioned surveillance of his old board room and infiltrating Ciao!Beauty to keep tabs on Carmine. Rifling his files stays between you and me. Even if he knows, it creates the perfect impasse. Either way, tomorrow please show up for your board members shoot as if you expect me."

"As if you know zip. I've put you in enough jeopardy already." I thanked him with racing heart and closed throat. Next I left Jennifer voicemail details, the promise to talk over the weekend, and to expect me first thing Monday morning to clean out my office and address the team. Sometime after ten I checked out of the Waldorf and into my apartment, snapping on lamps as if it could brighten the dark places in my head. When that didn't work I shot Ethan another call.

It rang twice. "What the fuck, Emma, give it a rest. Ethan forgot his phone."

"Darby?" I stared at my Nokia before putting it back at my ear. "Where is he? What are you doing out here?"

"I'm not out there; Ethan's here, staying with me but I've been at work. Barely seen him. Him and Maxine went to dinner after the wake."

"What wake?"

"The wake before the graveside thing for his old man."

"Darby!"

"He said no way you'd make it."

I dressed for the funeral as Julian would be speaking to his board members, arranged for my doorman to return of my first edition Jane Austen, and left for LaGuardia.

Three hours LGA to STL plus car rental and drive put me in Brucknerfield Saturday afternoon, unavoidably delayed for the *graveside thing.* Not by much but I hadn't been included, plus I was sporting the charcoal Chanel dress Ethan called my 'Jackie O plus sexy' outfit. I drove past Gerty's on Thirty, cold sweats pulsating like their ever-blinking *Vacancy* sign, thinking back to Ethan leaving for Australia with me, his pregnant obligation convinced we could survive.

A fashionably late grand entrance was not appropriate for the town butcher's small, graveside funeral. A mile beyond the motel I veered into the BHS parking lot. Girls in BHS tracksuits rumbled off in their yellow bus. I got out of the car like the ghost of my high school self-sprinting the cinder track. *That Old Rugged Cross* drifted from under the funeral awning where a robed figure, no doubt Maxine, lead Ethan and his siblings. I climbed the bleachers up to seat twenty-four. Did his view of the football field yank him back to hard scrabble kids in desperate need of each other? My reverie evaporated as the most familiar figure I know jogged out of the landscaping and across the football field in the Hugo Boss suit I'd bought for the opera. At the edge of the cinder track he looked up; eyes shaded. I sat still, heart hammering. as he climbed the metal risers. "Well if it isn't Mrs. Robinson, You're in my seat." I slid into twenty-three.

"You had five boyfriends, a concert and board meeting—"

"I have a husband and marriage." I looked over his shoulder. "The service isn't over."

"I left. Maxine asked for a remembrance from both sets of us kids." He opened a piece of paper against the breeze. "All I could think of was Dad cramming us older three in with his new three in his decrepit, converted bread truck to take us for ice cream and singing *Old Country Church* at the top of his lungs. I had to that far back to find something decent to say." He looked at the funeral awning. "He and I made peace this week. Wherever he is, I hope it's with his friends in the old country church, but me digging around for kind words? Bullshit. I did what Maxine asked and I sat with everyone acting like they care. Hardly a one's ever been part of my life."

He crumpled the paper. "All these years whenever the bottom drops out? I never told you but I think, 'There's always Brucknerfield.' Always Brucknerfield? There's nothing here but emptiness. Maxine called me forward to speak but I stood up and caught sight of you climbing the bleachers. You're here just like the first time I saw you."

"We don't need reminders of beaten down childhoods. We were right to get out. You've got nothing here. But you have me."

"Do I? You've built one hell of a Beautyland career. I'm proud of you but the invisible husband in that shadow, chasing his half-assed dream's not an easy place to be."

"That's how you want it."

The wind spun the paper away. "*Wanted* it. I thought I had my own future. I can't compete any more. It's not your Platinum days, or the years with Ciao!Beauty, or even when the asshole took it over. This Julian thing's pushed me out. Nicole's not some other woman I'm shacking up with. She's the grandmother of two of my players. I'm no billionaire but I'm not stupid. Dinners at his club? Knick's night together? Even the Vegas weekends. I swear Julian dumps his perks on me to make it crystal clear I'm no competition. Hell, that's why I took the California job."

"It's worse than you think. He arranged your California job. He owns Jacoby's outfit. Julian's got you by the baseballs." I laughed. "Literally by the balls."

He turned away so fast I thought he'd slip through the riser spaces. I threw my arms around him but he stayed rigid. "Okay, pro ball hasn't worked out but trying brought you the real prize. You're great with kids. You work magic with the ones who need it the most. You've landed right where you belong."

I pressed into his suit jacket. "You're the only one who knows the girl who's still afraid you married her because you had to. You've been the only one since I ran track down there trying to get your attention and convince you. Julian knows only the persona I invented for the world to see. Ethan, no one can take your place. I quit last night."

It wasn't exactly bone crushing, but he relaxed and hugged me. "You really quit?"

"Julian keeps ongoing files on both of us," I said into his shirt. "He's stalked around our rocky marriage, found the cracks, even made up the Misha concert prize to throw you together in Vegas, He set you up for the California move and finalised plans to move me to Switzerland headquarters."

He put me at arm's length. "Jesus!"

"He's dipped into unethical fragrance production. And his personal background's mostly smoke and mirrors. I have no self-respect without my integrity. I'll move into Nicole's boarding house or Neil's San Francisco guest room to prove there's no future without you."

"You really quit."

"I did and I've dropped through the Beautyland trapdoor back to where we started."

"The odds were against us when we married. We knew it. This week on his death bed my old man said, 'whatever happens you and Emma will make it, you always have the talent for survival.'"

"At another gargantuan detour. We can talk about survival here on seat twenty-four or maybe we should discuss it after we communicate the way we do best. There's that *vacancy* sign blinking about a mile back."

"I've got Domino's Pizza coupons in the dash."

That's when I got the feeling, we'd figure out which route to follow. He put his hands on my face. "You were and always will be on my mind."

The End